TENDERLOIN

OTHER BOOKS BY SAMUEL HOPKINS ADAMS

Revelry

The Harvey Girls

Canal Town

A. Woollcott: His Life and His World

Banner by the Wayside

Sunrise to Sunset

Grandfather Stories

TENDERLOIN

Samuel Hopkins Adams

RANDOM HOUSE
New York

TENDERLOIN

This glowing, flowering city of warm hopes and high ideals, peopled and conducted by the finest type of American manhood, pure in soul, vigorous in mind, lofty in purpose, unselfish in their civic spirit and broad patriotism, inspired by the spirit of righteousness, progressing from good to better down the generations—who can look upon its splendors, its beauty, its riches, its churches crowded with Godly worshipers, its abounding charities, its towering buildings, its noble parks, without echoing the proud boast which has come echoing down the ages from that mighty metropolis of the past: "Civis Romanus sum"? For we, too, are citizens of no mean city.

From the sermon of the Reverend Brockholst Farr, D.D., upon assuming the pastorate of the Old Stone Presbyterian Church of New York City, September 16, 1887.

1

Wisps of smoke from the bell-funneled locomotives of the New York Central Railroad drifted into the busy waiting room at Forty-second Street and Vanderbilt Avenue. The vault of the lofty room rang with the appeal of hawkers crying cough lozenges, shoeshines, squirt-guns, guidebooks to the city, balloons, bright-hued oleographs, chicken, ham and tongue sandwiches, Franklin Square paperbacks, roasted chestnuts, and the latest murder. Outside, less articulate voices quavered in the bright January sunlight, where the overworked draft-animals protested their forced labor, for in the early 1890's the Central still snaked its freight cars by mule power from the terminal across Forty-second Street into the mouth of the waiting tunnel. At intervals a whistle shrieked and a stentorian gateman announced:

"Train for All-b'ny. All-b'ny train. All aboar-r-r-rd!"

Above the concerted clamor, there rose from time to time a bravura call, precise and persuasive, promoting the vendor's wares:

"Here you are, folks! Ridley's Broken Candy. Fresh *and* fresh. Only a dime, a dime, a dime."

The salesman, an alert and rakish youth, was Thomas Howatt, late of Skunk's Misery, Madison County, New York State. One shoulder beneath his limp denim coat sagged from the weight of a large knapsack. His right hand waved rhythmically a pale blue and white cornucopia as his voice soared briefly in a clear tenor sales-lyric:

"Ridley's bro-o-o-o" (high A of an amazingly pure and ringing quality) "-ken can-dee."

Noon was slack time between trains. The candy butcher weaved his way in and out among the people. He was about to ease down the burden from his shoulder when his eye fell upon a smartly dressed and athletic figure crossing the room. A young fellow, there to meet his girl, the merchant surmised. What more appropriate greeting than a gift of well-assorted sweets in their delicate-hued wrapping? He advanced upon his quarry. A look of surprised recognition overspread his face. He paused, grinned, and went into his formula, confident and solicitous:

"Ridley's Broken. All fresh."

The new arrival made a detour.

"No candies? No Ridley's?" The voice was mildly incredulous. Its owner had fallen into step with the prospect. "Only a dime, a dime, a di—"

"Don't want any."

There was a swift pass of hands, like a conjurer's. A small paper-back volume materialized.

"*Joe Kerr's Jests, Jingles, and Jottings.* Only a quarter. Ten laughs to a page. You'll split yourself."

"I don't want to split myself," the young man replied wearily.

The other's manner changed from the professional to the personal. "Look," he said. "Howatt's the name. Tommy Howatt. Mean anything to you?"

"Howatt? Howatt? No, I can't say it does."

"Didn't figure it would. I was a townie in Clinton and carried water for the Hamilton team you played right guard on. Cleaned up Syracuse and Colgate that fall. Only Union licked you. You were a fast man for a linesman. Dan Adriance. Handsome Dan, they called you. Right?"

The young man nodded. "I'm meeting a train," he said.

"Number Five? Twenty minutes late."

"What a hell of a way to run a railroad!"

"Come and sit down," Howatt suggested. "Trade won't pick up any till Five is in."

"How did you land in New York?" Adriance asked. He was not specially interested, but Howatt at once interpreted the question as an invitation to autobiography.

"Never knew my old man, did you?" he began.

"No."

"He was a gospel-shouter. A soul-snatcher. Street corners. I used to sing for the collection. It was a hell of a life. It wore Ma out and she died and I ran away."

"To Clinton?"

Tommy nodded. "*And* way-stations. I got chucked off a train there. Went to work in Chet Parmalee's poolroom. Clean-up boy. After midnight."

He outlined a career of petty adventurousness, privation, and hunger. Casually and inexplicably he had contrived to pick up an education of sorts. At fifteen he left New York State on an unpaid-for high-wheel bicycle, in search of adventure. The listener gathered that his departure was not wholly voluntary. He hop-picked and cranberry-bogged through the East, harvested in the prairie states, and made

4

his way to California, where he became in turn ranch-boy, cook's helper in a lumber camp, odd-jobber at circuses and fairs, and pick-up musician at country dances. He could play banjo, guitar, or piano with equal facility. Occasionally he sang at revivals or picnics.

A short and unsuccessful spell as a printer's devil on a Cheyenne newspaper inspired him with the burning ambition of his life: to become a star reporter on New York's Park Row. Five years after his western trek, he was in the metropolis, a patient and dogged applicant at editorial gateways. Memory stirred in his hearer's mind.

"Richfield Springs," he said.

The youth grinned. "Sure. The summer you were there on Mrs. Goldthwaite's four-in-hand. I peddled berries. Howatt's special stemberries."

"And got into a little trouble, didn't you?"

"That goddam botanist bastard," Tommy said without heat. "What did he have to go sticking in his snoot for, telling my customers that my stemberries were nothing but ordinary blackcaps with a special name at a special price?"

"You didn't stop to argue the point, as I recall."

"No. I had a few dollars in the kick, and I always did like wheeling. Look! Did you ever take a header from one of those five-foot machines?"

Adriance shook his head. "How did you get into anything as respectable as candy butchering?"

"Look! I gotta eat, don't I?"

"Can you, on this job?"

"Better than a dollar, net, so far today," the butcher replied complacently. "It isn't what I want, though. Look, Mr. Adriance; I know about you. You're a Park Row crack."

"I'm a newspaperman, if that's what you mean."

"Could you get me a newspaper job?"

"I shouldn't think so. What makes you think you're qualified?"

"Look! I'm a hustler. All I need is a chance."

"Ever done any writing?"

"A little. Smarties for the funny papers. Poetry, too. Wanta see some of it?"

"God forbid!"

"Okay. You don't have to if you don't want to. Just keep Tommy Howatt in mind if you hear of anything."

"Better forget it," the newspaperman advised.

Howatt shook his head doggedly. "I've tried every city desk in town. *Sun, World, Times, Star, Tribune, Press,* evening papers, too. I even tried Brooklyn. Got the old ranikaboo everywhere. They don't know what they're missing," he concluded with conviction.

Adriance was mildly amused. "You don't think too badly of yourself, do you!" he said.

"All I ask is a start. Just a little luck. This is the town for me. There's nothing like it. I'd rather be a Bowery bum than Mayor of St. Louis. One of these days I'll have New York eatin' out of my hand. They can't keep a good man down."

A wild, metallic shriek vibrated the air. Adriance said, "Good luck, Howatt. See you again some time."

He joined the crowd which surged forward to overrun the platform and join the incoming passengers. All salesman again, Tommy Howatt found a vantage spot near the exit. He resumed his patter. At the same time he kept an eye out for Dan Adriance's friends, for he was a youth of active curiosity. Now Adriance was greeting a girl in a floppy, frivolous hat which, at that angle, concealed most of her face. Back of her walked a tall, gaunt man in black clerics beside a slim woman of middle age.

A young fellow back of Tommy said to a companion, "Know who the glum-looking parson is?"

"No," the other replied.

"That's the Reverend Brockholst Farr of the Old Stone Church. Hellfire Farr."

Immediately interested, for he was an avid reader of current news, Tommy craned his neck for a better view of the celebrity. "Glum-looking" was the word of the bystander who had identified him. Tommy, a judge of faces in his own opinion, did not concur. It was an extraordinary face: large, bony, rather ugly by esthetic standards. It had a look of patience and endurance that might have been grim but for the tolerance and humor of the broad-set, twinkling eyes and the firm but sensitive mouth. As for the square-built figure shambling toward him, it was later indelibly pictured to him by a Meredithian phrase in the mouth of the fashionable Mrs. Steevens Parke: "a fortuitous cohesion of relaxed angles."

The group moved forward. Mechanically Tommy gave voice: "Ridley's Broken, ladies and gents. Here they are. Fresh *and* fresh. Only a dime, a dime, a di— Oh, *gee!*"

The girl lifted her face and Tommy had a full view of it. His heart gave an unprecedented jerk. He heard a voice, gay and young to match the face:

"I've bought him, Dan. I've got the horse. He's a darling."

Adriance answered something, which the listener did not catch, then turned to the older woman, whom he addressed as Mrs. Crosbie. Tommy made a mental note of the name.

Dr. Farr said, "It's a good enough cob, but she paid too much."

6

"I always do," the girl said in her enchanting voice. "I can't live forever in New York with nothing to ride."

"We've lived here only two months," the middle-aged woman pointed out. (Tommy assumed that she was the girl's mother.) "You could have waited until spring. Where will you ride in dead of winter?"

"Central Park, of course." (Tommy made another mental note.) "Don't you think Jerry is up to bridle-path standards?"

"You'll stampede them," Adriance assured her.

The clergyman and Mrs. Crosbie crossed the room, leaving the girl with the reporter. The young pair strolled over to a bench, chatting. Tommy trailed after them and hovered hopefully, gathering his forces. After all, she was only a girl, and he was a man of experience with the sex. Not in the class with this one, maybe. But women were pretty much off the same piece of goods. The thing was to make a start, and the obvious start was by way of trade. He sidled up and struck into his line:

"Ridley's Broken, miss. Fresh *and* fresh. Only a dime, a dime, a dime."

The beauty's eyes flicked past him. Tommy perceived himself to be invisible. His voice lost something of its customary assurance:

"Just as good as Huyler's. And only a dime, a dime, a dime."

Adriance half turned. "Skin out, will you?" he muttered.

"A fella's gotta living to make, Mr. Adriance," Tommy protested with artful pathos.

It worked. The radiant being became conscious of him. "Don't be so *mean,* Dan," she protested. "Maybe he's hungry. Here! I'll take one," she added, addressing the dazzled huckster. "I'll take *two.*" She smiled angelically at him and fumbled at her bag for a quarter.

"Thank you, miss," Tommy said, making change with tremulous fingers. "They're fresh *and* fresh."

"That'll be all," Adriance said firmly.

Tommy tipped his cap in jaunty farewell. "Okay, okay. See you in the morgue."

Hitching his load into place, he withdrew, but only to make a wide circle and station himself at the Vanderbilt Avenue exit where he could observe their departure.

"He seems to know you," Laurie Crosbie remarked to her escort.

"Yes. He was a townie when I was in college."

"What did he mean about the morgue?"

"Just being funny. Trying to attract notice. You've made a conquest."

She laughed. At the sound, people stopped and turned and stared. Some laughed in sympathy. A majestically homely old woman, tall as

7

a policeman and straight as a ramrod, said to her young male companion in a voice that carried like a French horn, "Who is that exquisite creature?"

"Haven't the faintest," the foppishly dressed young man murmured regretfully.

"Find out, then, dammit!" the old lady commanded. She added, peering, "She looks too lovely to be quite a lady."

"What an awful old person!" the girl said. "Emeralds at this time of day!"

"Let's get out of here," Adriance suggested. On the sidewalk, he added, "Another conquest, Laurie. An important one, too. Mrs. Steevens Parke. Four e's, if you know your way about in the top circles."

"I don't. And I don't believe that I want to, if she is part of them."

"Grandma Parke is the one to show you, if she had a mind to it. She pretty well runs Society in this town; she and a couple of sister hags. Stand by," he warned in a lower tone. "Something's up."

The foppish young man approached Adriance, lifting his hat. "May I present myself?" he said pleasantly. "I'm Stannard Barto."

"How do you do, Mr. Barto?" Adriance said noncommittally. He made no move to present the newcomer, whose lifted brows suggested expectancy, to the girl.

After a moment's pause, Barto said, "My aunt, Mrs. Steevens Parke, thinks that she has met this young lady somewhere."

Laurie smiled vaguely and shook her head. Adriance said, "I'm afraid Mrs. Parke is deceived by a chance resemblance."

Barto looked incredulous. That any young woman should ignore an opportunity to profit by the acquaintanceship of the powerful Grandma Parke, was hard to believe. "If Miss—Miss uh—uh—if she is living in New York—" he began.

"She isn't. My cousin and I are just passing through on our way to the West," Adriance cut in courteously but definitely.

The emissary got the point. "If you come back, I hope you will let my aunt know," he said, saluted again, and left them.

"What a liar you are, Dan!" Laurie Crosbie said admiringly.

"Defending your privacy. Your mother says that you want to live quietly. Being taken up by Grandma Parke isn't exactly the gateway to a secluded life."

She wrinkled her nose at him. "The protective cousin. You take to the role quite naturally."

"It was wished on me, remember," he returned with a grin.

"What shall we do now? Are you too busy to take me shopping?" (He shook his head.) "Dr. Farr will escort Mother home. Let's go down to Twenty-third Street."

8

From his coign in the doorway, Tommy Howatt, unobserved, watched them board a southbound Madison Avenue car. His brain hummed with conjecture. What was the bond between Handsome Dan Adriance and the radiant goddess? They were at least friends. Tommy was all the more convinced of the expediency of cultivating the reporter. Sooner or later he might work an introduction. And Dr. Farr? Presumably he was on pastoral terms with the Crosbie family. Something might be done there. The romantic notion of joining the church entered his mind. He dismissed it. No need to go so far as that until other measures had been explored.

This much he cherished in his mind with a glow of satisfaction: Miss Crosbie was a fellow New Yorker. It lent a new glamour to the city of his choice.

New York of the early 1890's, goal of Thomas Howatt's designs and ambitions, was a city of crime and gaiety. Its million and a half inhabitants traveled in horsecars, hansom cabs, or private victorias. They breathed the stench of littered streets, fortified by the soft-coal-and-cinder belch from the clatter-banging elevated trains. They paid uncomplaining tribute to a political overlord, who, holding no office, ruled the city by a loose tyranny of extortion and blackmail through the agency of Tammany Hall and the organized corruption of the Police Department, selling dispensations to law-breakers who ranged from the highest to the lowest, from the powerful presidents of railway and shipping lines down to the dope-joint proprietors of Mott Street.

On the upper levels the city paraded its wealth ostentatiously. On the lower, which often overlapped the upper, it gambled and whored blithely. Wall Street men drank Manhattan cocktails. The Tenderloin drank champagne when it caught a Willing Willie from Chicago or a sunshine-spreader from St. Louis. The Bowery drank mixed ale at the bars of McGurk's Suicide Hall and of Steve Brodie, who might or might not have jumped from Brooklyn Bridge. Young girls raved over the hyacinthine masculine pulchritude of Kyrle Bellew. Clubmen adored the seductive Marie Tempest of the Casino and the unimpeachably virtuous Georgia Cayvan of the Lyceum.

Lovely, happy Lillian Russell, that prince-of-good-fellows-in-skirts, rode a bejeweled bicycle through Central Park, with legs no longer displayed to her theatregoing adorers because they had grown too plump for tights. Chauncey M. Depew made humorous after-dinner speeches, waving a graceful hand upon which he wore a $2.00 nickel ring guaranteed to prevent rheumatism. From a bench in Madison Square a white-clad millionaire-philosopher dispensed shrewd criticism and sagacious commentary upon public affairs to disillusioned but respectful reporters. What George Francis Train had to say of public events was usually wise and always pungent.

Two young godlings of Newspaper Row, Arthur Brisbane and Richard Harding Davis, outglamoured the stage idols. A soberer journalist, the beloved "Jake" Riis, told the public about the reeking, airless and lightless, dumbbell tenements of the deep East Side. Everyone read *How the Other Half Lives,* but nothing much was done about it because those overcrowded ant-heaps paid fat returns to some of the most distinguished families on Manhattan Island. Rich folk lunched at Delmonico's, and those inured to economy, at the Dennett five-cent chain, where the coffee was just as good as Delmonico's and the pie better. Bars offered gargantuan free lunches.

Ward McAllister was acting as Cerberus at the gates of the Four Hundred, to which he had given its sobriquet and which Mrs. Steevens Parke ruled with an unbridled tongue. Rates were as high as five dollars a day at the fashionable Fifth Avenue Hotel and as low as five cents a night at Dirty Dick's flophouse on Hester Street, where typhus fever once wiped out half the temporary populace. Haircut, shampoo, and shave cost half a dollar at the standard barber shops. The Black Cat, on South Fifth Avenue, shattered a tradition by raising its table-d'hôte-with-wine price to fifty cents. A quarter tip marked the giver a millionaire or a sucker. The mansions of the mighty lined Fifth Avenue from Washington Square up; the city reservoir, presenting to the eye the massive, blank stone walls of a fortification, dispensed city water from the corner of Forty-second Street; and over the checkered scene the lovely Saint-Gaudens statue of Diana poised for flight at the top of Madison Square Garden, which was then authentically at Madison Square.

The intelligentsia sharpened their minds on the *North American Review* and the *Atlantic,* and discussed William Dean Howells, *Life,* and that shocking new portent, young Rudyard Kipling; while their teen-aged daughters wallowed in the virtuous slop dispensed by Laura Jean Libbey and E. P. Roe. Social lights read (and pretended not to read) *Town Topics,* the profitable scandal-and-blackmail sheet of Colonel William D'Alton Mann.

Saloons kept open, morning, noon, night, and Sundays. Professional faro and roulette games were conducted behind uncurtained windows at street-level in the West Thirties. Two-dollar harlots paraded Sixth and Seventh Avenues. Peep shows flourished in Fourteenth Street. Pestilential tenements and profitable brothels paid their ground rentals to fashionable churches.

New York was a wide-open city and capitalized upon its tolerance. That's the way people wanted it, Richard K. Fox pointed out in his *Police Gazette,* and if they wanted it that way, why shouldn't they have it?

The Reverend Brockholst Farr, D.D., who had changed his views since his initial sermon, differed. He called it Hell Centre.

Thomas Howatt, fiercely loyal New Yorker, considered Mr. Fox right and Dr. Farr wrong.

2

As a journalistic prospect, the *Police Gazette* had not entered into Tommy Howatt's calculations. He read it from pink cover to pink cover in the rear rooms (ladies' entrance) of the saloons which he patronized not so much for the drinks as for the free lunch which they liberally provided. He looked up to it as the arbiter of the world of sports. But, professionally considered, it was a cut above him, together with *Scribner's, Harper's,* and the *Century.*

His high regard was not misplaced.

The *Police Gazette* was, indeed, a national institution. Built up from obscurity by the genius for journalistic specialization of its editor-owner, Richard K. Fox, it flourished on its unique repute. It originated the newspaper prize contest and sponsored important athletic events.

No barber shop was complete without it. It represented literature to the barroom, the brothel, and the political club. Libraries deprecated it; Y.M.C.A.'s banned it. For the juvenile offspring of a respectable household to be discovered with it meant a painful correction at the hands of shocked parents. Simeon Ford, the leading wit of the day, dubbed it: "The paper that everybody reads and nobody takes." Its devotees called it the *Pinky,* from the hue of the paper on which it was printed. Proprietor Fox, who had a high sense of professional dignity, resented this as a cheapening of his product. He objected still more indignantly to its popular sobriquet, the *Barber-Shop Bible.*

At $4.00 a year it attained a circulation of 400,000, and its line of spicy articles, leggy pictures, and sexual advertisements that would have made a West Third Street cruiser blush, had put a million dollars in its till.

The editorial output emanated weekly from a brick building which rose, bright and neat, amidst the grubby tenements flanking Brooklyn Bridge on the south. On the top story Mr. Fox had his private sanctum. The rest of the floor was given over to a spacious, clean staff-room with several alcoves. Here the changeful force toiled intermittently in an atmosphere of cheerful inebriety. For, in a time of keen competition when the dailies tolerated no drunkenness in working hours, Mr. Fox ran his business on milder standards.

The dean of his staff, the ever-reliable Deacon Waldo, was an authentic official in a Jersey City Baptist Church and got drunk only on legal holidays. The Deacon was a silvery and dandified little man, a connoisseur of the risqué. In his role as head copyreader, he could often be heard vocally relishing some specially spicy item, his throat palpitating like a happy frog's:

"Whuck-whuck-whuck! Oh, my! Naughty-naughty! Whuck-whuck-whuck-wah!"

Often it happened that the regular crew of half a dozen would be depleted and the paper would find itself short of copy at the week-end. Mr. Fox would then summon the Deacon.

"Deacon, where's Enders?" Enders was the sports specialist.

"Search me, Boss."

"Bill Strong?" This was the scandals expert.

"At Andy Horn's. Said he'd show up after dinner."

"Think he will?"

"No."

"Well—Spunk Wood?" Wood was a news-rover and a good one when sober.

"His old grandmother's taken bad again."

"Either of the art men here?"

"Yep. Terhune's asleep in the back room."

"Wake him up."

"I can't."

"Better go out and round up some talent."

Thereupon the veteran would lift his coat from the peg, brush it carefully, comb out his silvery whiskers, equip himself with his Dunlap derby and malacca stick, for he was always mindful of his reputation as a dude, and sally forth on Newspaper Row to hunt his prey. From bar to bar he passed: from Andy Horn's to the Times Café; from Perry's back room to Katie's sawdusted floor; and even as far slumwise as Paresis Hall, until he had collected three or four journalistic derelicts who were still sufficiently sober, or could be sufficiently sobered, for the work in hand. It was not the top talent of Park Row, although some of it may have been at one time, but it served the *Gazette's* purposes well and cheaply.

To his captives the Deacon administered a secret preparation unofficially known as "the *P.G.* potent gut-scour," led them to the office, and, as it were, chained them to the galleys: i.e., the long, littered table of the workroom. Off this, smaller rooms offered couches, a bath, and a plenitude of viands, reinforced at need. Each man was provided with pen, ink, and stationery, a pile of assorted dailies with sensational or

13

potentially sensational articles red-penciled for rewriting, and a list of suggestions typed on Mr. Fox's office calligraph, the one and only machine in the place. The irrefrangible rule was: No Leave. The doors were kept locked against egress. A former contributor who had lowered himself from a rear window, under the impression that he was being pursued by a spider, was never hired again.

A pint of whiskey per man was supplied, with the understanding that it must last out the stint; there would be no more. On Monday morning ten dollars would be given to each survivor.

The product was unique in American journalism. Printed on its distinctively tinted paper, the *Gazette* specialized in the Four S's: Sin, Sex, Sensation, and Sport. It leaned heavily upon illustration, the art style being its own. The covers, line-drawn by the two staff artists (newspaper photography was still in its infancy), rotated in subject.

Leggy ladies, preferably in skirt-lifting action; example: church picnic invaded by snake.

Pneumatic-bosomed star of theatre or music hall, décolleté essential; example: Lottie Gilson, the Little Magnet.

Prize-fight champion or challenger; example: almost any pugilist of note except John L. Sullivan, who had incurred Mr. Fox's displeasure by an injurious reference to the *Gazette's* diamond-studded championship belt as "Dick Fox's dog collar."

Titillating crime; example: murder in a brothel, or discovery of adulterous wife by avenging husband.

Any sort of sensational church happening; example: clergyman denouncing choir-singer for misconduct with sexton.

Sometimes Mr. Fox himself would take a hand with the headlines; always the impress of his journalistic individuality was upon them:

UNADULTERATED DEVILTRY
PEEKING PEDAGOGUES
GIRLIE, GET YOUR GARTER
SPELLED DOWN AND LOST HER VIRTUE
SENATORIAL SATYRS: WASHINGTON UNVEILED
WHAT WAS HE DOING UNDER THE BED?
MARY, MARY: NOT SO CONTRARY!

Though the captions were often coy, the text of the more alluring aspects of human misbehavior was infused with a spirit of high moral reprehension. Scandals were exposed and rebuked. The secret archives of the *P.G.* were reputed to have an unbelievable and explosive content. Mr. Fox had been heard to observe that if he printed half he knew about New York, the outgoing railroad trains would bulge with fugitive respectabilities.

What little original news appeared in the Fox weekly was brought in by tipsters: broken-down newspapermen as unreliable as they were disreputable, dealing in rumors, gossip, and once in a while a bit of available scandal, for which they would whiningly demand five or ten dollars and gratefully accept two. But the great bulk of the magazine was made up from hundreds of exchange publications, which poured in by every mail to be sifted at the long table of the editorial room for items suitable to the *P.G.'s* clientele. These were scissored out and altered to the provocative style which the *Gazette* had made its own.

On a Friday evening Mr. Fox, blue pencil in hand, was cautiously expunging the libel from an article about a Philadelphia society beauty and a chimney sweep, when Deacon Waldo appeared in the doorway. Mr. Fox's eyes peered upward from the copy.

"Sullivan's just been knocked out."

"*What?* How? John L.?"

"John L., himself. The champ."

"What happened? Who did it? Fetch the man here," the editor clamored.

"Can't do it, Boss."

"Why not? What's the matter with you?"

"Man's in the jug. Oak Street Station."

"Well, dad-rat it!" shouted Mr. Fox, who, as a good Presbyterian, eschewed profanity except upon extreme provocation. "Chase downstairs and get him out. I'll telephone Mulberry Street" (the generic term for Police Headquarters, which stood in that slum). "What a story! Hustle your old bones, Deacon!"

Andy Horn's highly respectable saloon at the entrance to Brooklyn Bridge had tided many a hopeful neophyte of Park Row through thin days. In volume and variety there was not the equal of its free-lunch counter in the city. For the price of a beer, the discriminating patron might make his choice of beef both roast and corned, ham on the knuckle, pork-and-beans, three kinds of sausage, two kinds of cheese, white bread, rye bread, pumpernickel and pretzels, olives rank and vinegary, dill pickles, pig's knuckles, potato salad, and cole slaw. How Andy could do it and make a profit was an unsolved problem in contemporary economics.

That richly garnished counter sustained Tommy Howatt while job-seeking among the newspaper offices.

On the evening of his great adventure, Tommy stood at Andy's bar. His nickel, the open sesame to the gastronomic profusion across the room, slid over the mahogany. As he was reaching for the tall, frothy schooner, the swinging door back of him swished violently.

An enormously thick man, with beetling eyebrows and a black

15

handle-bar mustache, lurched in, followed by a group of obsequious henchmen. He cocked his silk hat, advanced upon the counter, threw out his barrel chest and bellowed:

"I can lick any son-of-a-bitch in this room. Yours truly, John L. Sullivan."

An awed silence fell, followed by a feeble cheer. John L. scowled about him.

"I can lick any *three* sons-a-bitches in this room. Yours truly, John L. Sullivan."

The satellites contributed their bit. "Sure, you can, John." "That's telling 'em!" "Show 'em your muscles."

The giant stripped off his Prince Albert coat, rolled up his sleeves, and flexed his mighty biceps.

An undersized and ragged bootblack edged forward. "Shine 'em up, mister?" he said reverently.

"Yes." The champion extended his foot, and as the urchin bent over, lifted him with a mighty kick that sent him sprawling against the bar.

The boy scrabbled away on all fours, groaning. The champion roared with laughter.

A dozen drinkers quietly withdrew from the bar. With John L. on the rampage, it was no place for peaceable men. Tommy Howatt, too unfamiliar with sporting standards to know the etiquette of submission, kept his place. The man of brawn addressed him.

"Hey, punk."

Tommy looked about.

"Whatcha drinkin'?"

"Beer," answered Tommy shortly.

"No, you ain't."

The mighty-muscled arm swept the schooner from the bar, smearing the mahogany with suds. Seizing the youth by the neck, the pugilist bent him over and rubbed his nose in the spilth.

"Attaboy, John!" his gleeful claque applauded. "That'll learn him."

Relinquishing his grip on the struggling captive, John L. turned to wave an airy acknowledgment to his admirers. He did not see Tommy dive across the bar, catch up a handy bung starter, and vault back.

"Look out, Jawn!" a follower shrieked.

The warning came too late. Tommy, with heart and mind given over to murder, was set. The mallet swung with deadly accuracy. Down went the champion of the world, wriggled once upon the floor, and was at peace.

The next instant, his assailant was buried in a wave of outraged citizenry. He might have been trampled to death then and there had not a patrolman, roused from sleep in the rear room, clubbed his way through the riot. Tommy, sorely mauled, was haled to the station house, a block away, trailed by a loudly execrating crowd. A hard-faced desk sergeant took the culprit's pedigree, shaking his own head in wonderment.

"A nothin' from nowhere an' he done this to Jawn L.!" he marveled.

"Is he dead?" Tommy asked, feeling of a loosened tooth.

"No," somebody answered. "He's comin' out of it."

"Hell!" the battered youth growled vengefully.

"Tough guy, huh?" the desk man commented. "Felonious assault. You'd oughta get ten years for this."

Consternation swept the newspaper offices when the news was brought in. John L. Sullivan knocked out by an unknown kid in a barroom brawl. What a story! But—

There were grave consultations over editorial desks. This was, indeed, a hot potato. The prestige of a great American institution was at stake. The prize-ring was the prop of the manly art of self-defense, a character builder for the emulation of American youth. As world's champion heavyweight, John L. Sullivan was its chief exponent and the idol of all two-fisted, red-blooded, right-thinking citizens. The legend was that nothing but dynamite could prevail against him. To expose his temporary frailty would be a blow to the public morale. A champion should be sacrosanct. Besides, it might affect gate receipts. Lay off!

Not a newspaper printed a word of it.

While the prisoner was patching himself up as best he might in the cell, Deacon Waldo was in consultation with the sergeant. The latter was prophesying a dire fate for the unknown assailant when a message from Mulberry Street made him change his tune. Evidently the attempted murderer had a pull. R. K. Fox had intervened on his behalf. He was promptly released in the custody of the Deacon.

Deacon Waldo conducted his ward to the editorial sanctum and presented him to Mr. Fox.

"Tell me about it," the editor invited genially.

Tommy obliged.

"With a bung starter, eh?" Mr. Fox pounded his knee in an ecstasy of appreciation. "I'll have to write this story, myself."

"How much stir-time will I get?" Tommy asked. "The sarge said a tenner."

"Don't worry. Leave it to me. Where did you hit him?"

"Under the jaw."

"Wham!" the editor gurgled. "Socko and kerflop. I'd have given a hundred dollars for a ringside seat. Call my diamond championship belt a dog collar, will he! The undefeated John L.! You ought to get a medal."

"Yeah; but what'll the judge say?"

"Oh, that! Can you see that big dummox's manager let him come into court and be questioned about getting knocked cold by a kid? No, sir! All they'll want is to forget it. The judge will maybe fine you ten dollars. You don't have to worry about that, either. I'll take care of it."

"Gee! Thank you kindly, Mr. Fox."

"What's your job, young man?"

"Candy butcher. Ridley's Broken."

"Not much for an up-and-comer."

"I'd like to get on a newspaper."

"Had any experience?"

"Not much. But I'm a hustler if I could get a chance."

"Lean over."

Suspicious but docile, Tommy obeyed. Mr. Fox rose and slowly circled him, muttering in an undertone dimly audible words of incomprehensible import, "Perceptiveness . . . M-m-m-m . . . Self-esteem, prominent . . . Secretiveness, ah-h-h . . . Constructiveness, well developed." Then, sharply, "Are you familiar with the works of Dr. Orson Fowler?"

"No, sir."

"The mightiest scientific intellect of our time. Phrenology! I have no use for anyone whose cranial contours do not measure up to Fowlerian standards. Yours do. You may leave your name and address with Deacon Waldo. . . . Under the jaw, eh? The Great Jawn L.! Oh, cricketty-splits! Good day, young man."

The sagacious Mr. Fox was right about the court proceedings. Nobody appeared to press the charge of felonious assault against the accused T. Howatt. Having reduced the case to one of simple assault, the judge fined the accused ten dollars and remitted the fine.

The *Police Gazette* had a resounding beat on the John L. Sullivan story, of which it bragged inordinately and intermittently for a year.

Thomas Howatt was added to the staff at a satisfactory wage of ten dollars a week.

3

For nearly two months before the encounter at the Grand Central Depot, Laurie Crosbie and her mother had been residents of New York City. They had been foisted upon a dubious Dan Adriance by his cantankerous Great-Aunt Martha, a confirmed globe-trotter, rich and sporadically generous. Her instructions to her grand-nephew, per letter enclosing a gratifyingly liberal check, were that he was to "be nice to my two friends," ask no ill-bred questions, and, insofar as his duties permitted, act as their escort about a city with which they wished to familiarize themselves, at least in its outer aspects. Furthermore, the letter forewarned him not to make a fool of himself by falling in love with Laurie Crosbie, which admonition he interpreted as meaning that the writer expected (and probably wished) him to do that very thing.

Shortly after their arrival, he had called on the Crosbies at their home in the Valdevia, one of the new and elegant railroad-flat structures on Madison Avenue: two apartments to a floor, divided by a dark and narrow hallway and extending, front to rear, in a single file of rooms like a string of passenger cars. The Valdevia boasted an elevator and a hallman. The caller estimated that the rentals must run as high as seventy-five dollars a month. Plainly, the Crosbies were people of means.

Lifted to the second floor, Dan Adriance was admitted to the apartment by a neat colored maid and escorted to the front room. There he moved cautiously amidst teeming rarities: bronzes, ormolu knickknacks, an eighteenth-century etui, a *doré* jewel chest, a richly framed painted fan of unimaginable delicacy, a cabinet crowded with dainty ivories and glowing jade, ecclesiastical silver unmatched in any local collection; precariously perched on its pedestal a Gérôme marble; on the walls, a lovely, hazy Corot, a fine Eastman Johnson, two Troyons and a softly smiling Greuze; on the floor a large oriental silk carpet. One whole end of the room was given up to a pale rosewood Knabe grand piano.

Laurie Crosbie entered and came to him with outstretched hand. "Aren't you good to come so soon!" she said.

He responded with a polite commonplace about its being a privilege, adding a compliment upon the profusion of art. "I'm almost afraid to turn around," he said.

"Old Curiosity Shop, isn't it?" she said.

"Something on that order," Dan admitted.

"One of these days I'll have a place for all this."

"Are you renting the Metropolitan Museum of Art?"

She laughed. "We're planning to build a house on Riverside Drive. That's going to be the nice part of town, so Uncle Harry says."

The trend of wealth and fashion at that time was predicted to be toward the Upper West Side. "Uncle Harry knows his real estate," the young man said.

"He's not really an uncle. Just an old family friend. He looks after my—our money. His name is Harrison M. Perley. Perhaps you've heard of him."

In the course of business the reporter had run across the Honorable Mr. Perley. He was a millionaire contractor and a quiet power in Tammany Hall. Also, he was a trustee of the Old Stone Presbyterian Church. Dan said that he had met him while reporting one of Dr. Farr's sermons.

"I think Dr. Farr is wonderful," she said, with shining eyes. "We've joined his church, Mother and I. I suppose you know everything about New York," she added.

"Not quite everything," he said modestly.

"But all about the places to go to and the things to see, and all that."

"It depends upon what you're after."

Laurie's achievements in familiarizing herself with New York, it developed, consisted of the usual rounds of museums and art galleries, opera and theatre, and church receptions. She had ridden in the park on a hired mount from Durland's. She had played chess with the automaton at the Eden Musée. She had attended an Author's Reading at the Music Hall on West Fifty-seventh Street, and had admired with her own eyes and heard with her own ears Richard Watson Gilder, George W. Cable, and Mark Twain. She had tooled it down Fifth Avenue atop a private four-in-hand. Allen Hardwick, a member of Dr. Farr's congregation, had escorted her to watch the live whale disporting itself in the Hudson. Life in New York was fun. Didn't Mr. Adriance think so? Mr. Adriance agreed.

"Here's my mother," Laurie said. He rose.

The woman who entered was thin to gauntness. She carried herself with grace and with that ineradicable poise possessed by women who have had beauty. The caller guessed her to be nearing sixty, which was an overestimate by ten years. Her eyes, deep-set, were like her daughter's, but they were restless. She had none of the girl's happy tranquillity. At first he thought she was ill or had been ill. But she did not move like an invalid. He got an impression of watchfulness, even of wariness.

"We expect to live quite privately, my daughter and I," she said in a faded voice.

Adriance reflected that a girl with Laurie Crosbie's looks was likely to find her privacy assailed if not invaded, but did not think it necessary to say so. As he rose to go, mother and daughter exchanged a look.

Mrs. Crosbie spoke. "We are celebrating Laurie's birthday next Sunday, Mr. Adriance. Will you come to dinner?"

"Yes," the girl said complacently. "I'll be eighteen."

"Good Lord!" said the guest.

"Did you think I was older?" Laurie said, pleased. "It's the new way I do my hair. I told you, Mother."

He accepted the invitation with alacrity.

It was on that Sunday evening that his friendship with Laurie Crosbie began. The only other guest was Harrison M. Perley. Mrs. Perley, Adriance learned, was a confirmed invalid who never went anywhere. After the elaborate dinner Mrs. Crosbie and Mr. Perley addressed themselves to a consideration of plans for the projected house on Riverside Drive, leaving the art-cluttered drawing room to the young people.

Laurie leaned back on a chaise longue, her hands clasped behind her sleek head. "It's fun to be rich," she said meditatively.

"I've always understood it to have advantages," the young man agreed.

"I want to ask you something. Will you think me silly?"

"If I do, I'll conceal my scorn."

She looked at him doubtfully. "Well, do you believe—you do believe, don't you, that a boy—I mean a man and a girl can get to be real friends without—without any foolishness?"

"Such as falling in love, you mean?"

"Yes."

"I seem to have read about it somewhere in a book."

"Are you making fun of me?"

"No. Are *you* warning *me?*"

"Warning . . . ?"

"Not to fall in love with you."

"I had no such idea," she said indignantly.

21

"Still, I suppose it has happened in your life."

"I couldn't help it."

"I can well believe that! You liked it, didn't you?"

"No. I hated it."

"Oh, come now, Miss Crosbie!"

"I don't want anybody to fall in love with me," she said with soft vehemence. "I've never yet seen the boy I wanted to kiss. Let alone anything else," she concluded pensively.

It was cruel to laugh, but her naïveté was too much for Adriance. She flushed an offended red. "You needn't be horrid," she sniffed.

He apologized hastily.

"I want—I hoped—I thought we might get to be dear and devoted friends."

The simplicity, the primness, the prettiness of the old-fashioned phrase touched him. "I'd like that," he said.

"Would you truly?" She opened up a course of questioning, with, he soon began to suspect, an ulterior purpose. First, she wished to know about newspaper work. Did Mr. Adriance like it? Wasn't it terribly exhausting? Weren't reporters very poorly paid? Didn't he have a play or a novel or something in mind? She had been told that all good newspapermen had. Hadn't he ever thought of some easier employment that would give opportunity for other work? Presently the preposterous truth began to dawn upon him.

This chit of a girl was exploring the possibilities of employing him. Hence her intimations of wealth. Hence her solicitude for his supposedly starveling employment as a reporter and her ill-concealed design of rescuing him from his wretched lot. But in what capacity? Was this some unholy machination set in motion by that old vixen of a Great-Aunt Martha?

"Let's get this straight, Miss Crosbie," he said. "Are you looking for a dear and devoted friend, or a hired hand?"

"That isn't a bit a nice way to put it," she complained.

"Put it any way you like; you're trying to offer me a job, aren't you?"

"No. That is—well, being a reporter and knowing all about things, I thought you might take Mother and me around."

"Guide to the city, with speaking trumpet?"

"Don't girls—people, I mean—in New York have private secretaries?"

"They also have tame cats."

"Oh, dear! Now you're angry. I don't see why."

Dan relented. After all, this was hardly more than a child. "It's all right," he assured her. "I'll be glad to show you what I can. But not for pay."

She brightened at once. "I know I'm going to love New York. I want to see it all. I want to go to Chinatown and the Bowery and Central Park and Coney Island. And I want to climb the Statue of Liberty and eat at an East Side restaurant, and see Hell's Kitchen, and ride in an electric horseless carriage, and walk across Brooklyn Bridge, and fish off the Battery, and go wheeling on the bicycle path and everything. Have you got a bicycle?"

"Not here."

"I have. If you were my secretary, I could get you one and we could do a century together."

"Would you buy me a saddle horse for Central Park and a top hat for the opera, too?"

"You needn't make fun of me. It wouldn't be so very hard, being my private secretary."

"I can see that with one eye. What would the other duties be?"

"Oh, just to be around and keep me from doing foolish things and take me places and let me talk to you about myself and tell you all my troubles."

"I'll look around and see if I can't find some paragon who would qualify."

"You needn't bother. I don't want just anyone."

"The implication is flattering," he said, "but I'm afraid I couldn't come up to requirements."

"Anyway, I think it would be nice and convenient to have you for a cousin."

"All right," Dan agreed. "We're cousins, on the explicit understanding that you're not to buy me any diamond scarf pins and I'm not to fall in love with you. Right?"

"Don't be a tease," she said with dignity.

All that Laurie Crosbie asked of the world—this Dan Adriance was to learn as their acquaintanceship ripened—was that it should unquestioningly oblige her wishes and purposes, these being, in her opinion, eminently moderate and reasonable. Thus far in life she had pretty much had her own way. Logically she should have developed into a spoiled little tyrant. She was nothing of the kind. A naturally sunny disposition had saved her from the arrogance of overcherished youth. On the rare occasions when she had been thwarted by hard facts or incomprehensible people, she accepted the injustice with surprise and disappointment, but without rancor or pettishness, readily recovering from the shock in the serene belief that everything would come out all right for her in the end. It generally did.

At first acquaintance, what most struck Dan was a lovely and joyous serenity, a sweet confidence that the fates are kind, the world good, and gods and humans well disposed toward Miss Laura Frances Crosbie. She exhaled femininity as a flower exhales fragrance; she was all woman, yet there was about her an unconscious elusiveness, a hovering withdrawal. The pursuant male, Dan guessed, might well find himself balked by impalpable barriers.

For the rest, she was gay, confident, trustful, with a quick and apprehensive mind, a sound and unworldly education from the convents of two European capitals, and a vitality apparently immune from the ills that flesh is heir to. Of the past she seldom spoke. If she had formed friendships, they had seemingly waned. She and her mother appeared to be quite sufficient to each other. Dan Adriance guessed that, emotionally, she was an unawakened child. Sometimes he wondered whether perhaps that side of her personality might not be lacking.

By the time of the episode in the Grand Central, Dan had become Laurie's regular escort, but his interest in her was as impersonal as she, herself, could have wished.

More than a year before the Crosbies came within his orbit, he had had a passionate encounter without sequel. Though the partner of his experience had passed from his ken as abruptly as she had entered it, the memory still filled all his emotional horizons.

4

Back in the 1880's, when the verb *graft* was rogue's jargon for *work,* a metropolitan police captain, promoted from the thin pickings of a downtown district to the fleshpots of the Nineteenth Precinct, enriched local topography with a new term.

"I've been living on rump steak long enough. Now I'll have some tenderloin," said that thug in uniform, "Slogger" Williams.

Thenceforth the district of theatres and brothels, of lordly hotels and half-dollar bed-houses, of the Metropolitan Opera House and the Haymarket Dance Hall, of Delmonico's on Fifth Avenue and Clark's on Sixth, of Ward McAllister, social boss, and Big Bill Nelson, political boss, of Pete the Pimp and the Reverend Brockholst Farr, of Cockeyed Connie, the streetwalker, and Mrs. Steevens Parke, of the St. Nicholas Club which admitted hardly anybody and the Tenderloin Club which took in everybody, of the Old Stone Church and the House of Nations, became known as the Tenderloin. Within its boundaries, Fourteenth Street on the south to Forty-second Street on the north, Fourth Avenue on the east and the North River on the west, the name was accepted and adopted. It was the area of froth and glitter; of night life, and lawlessness. According to the point of view, it was the very essence of New York, or its enduring shame. Public opinion fostered it. It was the gay and glowing light that flowed from the portals of a wide-open town. People liked it that way. It was good for business.

The focus of Tenderloin night life was Clark's restaurant. The most notorious and the best of the Sixth Avenue eating places, it knew no law but its own profits and the convenience of its patrons. While one customer remained to be served, its door stood open. Besides good food and drink, it purveyed feminine charm in its marketable form. The *Police Gazette* dubbed it "New York's Sex Exchange." Its clientele were ten- and twenty-dollar girls, half price to newspapermen, a concession which Selah Merrill Clarke, the acid-tongued cynic of the *Sun's* night desk, characterized as "commercial courtesy to an allied profession."

Clark's was well conducted. Drawing rich and regular graft from it, the police maintained a watchful guardianship over its interests. It had its own standards. Drunkenness in the noisy or disorderly degree was reprehended. Patrons were not robbed or rolled or overcharged. Open soliciting was frowned upon. The raddled "hookers," "cruisers," and "hatchets" of the dim-lit side streets, while not barred if they had the price, were ostracized by the superior sisterhood and, finding the competition above their caliber, seldom paid a second visit to the resort.

The regulars had their own rooms, usually within a few blocks. About midnight they would start to come in, singly, in couples or triples, or with the temporary lovers whom they had already picked up, to have a drink or supper before bedding down. The place was clean, the service friendly, and the prices not exorbitant. One got a good T-bone steak for half a dollar; whiskey sours were fifteen cents. The tables, set at right angles to the wall, and holding eight customers each—twelve if the place was overcrowded—suggested a school refectory. Cutlery, china, and linen were coarse and serviceable. At the rear were a few small stands for singles or couples. Active ceiling fans formed whorls in the smoky canopy that represented a note of license: the female patrons were allowed the public use of cigarettes, an indulgence which would have been visited with instant expulsion at any standard eating place.

Although Clark's was strictly for business, there was about it a saving grace of festivity.

On this February midnight Dan Adriance, just back from an upstate assignment, was seated at a small table. He had come to Clark's not because of interest in the restaurant's main article of traffic, but to satisfy the less imperious appetite of the stomach.

Oscar, the scarred and shambling dean of the waiters, came over. "Haven't seen you around in quite a while, Mr. Adriance," he said in his quiet gutturals. "The kidneys is fine this evening."

"All right," the reporter said. "Give me some with French fries and a mug of beer."

"Expecting a lady?"

"No."

"There's Miss Nita over there," the waiter said suggestively.

The girl, one of the most popular of the "double eagles" ($20.00 habituées), was seated several tables away, and, for a surprise, manless. As the young man turned, she smiled and nodded, which was permissible under the Clark code. To have joined him without invitation would have been a solecism. He raised his glass. Nita came over. He rose, drew out a chair, and put the usual question.

"Whiskey sour, thank you," she answered.

26

Oscar brought it.

"Here's how." Adriance lifted his beer.

"Here's Hummel," she responded in the current Broadway smartiness. Howe and Hummel were New York's leading shyster lawyers, enormously prosperous in their practice of fixes, blackmail, and extortion.

"Waiting for Chicago?" Adriance said.

The bearer of this *nom de nuit* was one of Nita's regulars. A robust, fiftyish, free-spending Illinois sewer-pipe manufacturer, with a trick of phrase-making, he once described her as "five cents' worth of girl with a million dollars' worth of eyes." She was small, trim, rounded, and swarthy, with straight, lank black hair which had given rise to the legend that she was of Indian ancestry. Actually she was the seventh daughter of a respectable Italian grocer in Mount Vernon. No one would have called her pretty, but she was clean and fresh and sparkling, and, at twenty-two, had preserved both the contours and the gaiety of girlhood.

"Waiting," she said. "But not for Chicago."

"A new friend?"

"Haven't you heard? Tommy Howatt."

"Howatt?" the newspaperman repeated. "Why, I know him."

"Everybody knows Tommy," the girl said.

"Do they? How come?"

"Wait till you hear him do his turn," she said with a pretty air of proprietorship.

"And now he's keeping his toothbrush in your tumbler," Adriance interpreted, "He *is* in luck."

"You ought to know, Dan," she said demurely.

"Have you ditched the sewer-pipe king for him?"

"Of course not. I've got my living to make."

"And the lucky Mr. Howatt's?"

"Don't get any funny ideas," she replied quickly. "Tommy buys his own groceries."

"Well, if he comes in before I leave, don't tell him I'm here. He'll be bracing me for a job again."

Nita tossed her sleek head. "Don't worry. He's got a job."

"Where?"

"The *Pinky*."

"The *Police Gazette?*" Adriance said in surprise. "Probably I'll be seeing him in the office then."

"What! You haven't left the *Star,* Dan?"

"No, indeed. But I'm taking on a little one-day-a-week trick for the *P.G.* on the side. Got a desk there. Any more news to give me?"

"Yes; the Tenderloin's got a new pantata."

27

"No!" the newspaperman exclaimed. "What's happened to Police Captain Lonergan?"

"Gone to the sticks. He raided the wrong house."

"A top cop ought to know his business better than that," Adriance commented. "Who's the new man?"

"Bernie Schmidt from the Upper West Side. Let's shift our drinks to the big table until your order comes, if you want to get an earful from the girls. They're all steamed up over it."

Several of the regulars, seated at a large table, pressed together to make room for the newcomers. One of these, a ten-dollar girl known as Jersey Jenny, appealed to the reporter: "You must know something about this Schmidt, Mr. Adriance."

"Not much," he answered. "He's supposed to be one of the Super's special pets."

"That's how he gets into the easy money," Annabel, a languid blonde, remarked. Superintendent Byrnes, the head of the Police Department, was noted for placing his favorites.

"Will he hike the ante on us?" Gwendolyn, a plump redhead, anxiously inquired of the table at large.

"Fox-face Willie Frye told me the old five-and-ten-dollar rates would hold," the experienced Nita announced. Frye was a fly-cop, a confidential plain-clothes man who acted as collector of tribute from the half-world.

"Willie Frye is a bastard and I hear this new pantata is another," Annabel said in her refined voice.

"They're all alike," Long Distance Lou declared. "All after the old mazuma." Lou was distinguished by having a telephone of her own, which, she claimed, paid for itself over and over, citing professional claims upon her services from as far afield as Milwaukee and Charleston, South Carolina.

"Yep," Jerry confirmed. "Christmas is a-comin'. The captain's stocking is hangin' up. Brace yourselves, girlies. You gotta dig." She was a homely little bunch of mischief with a figure to lure St. Anthony.

"Nobody minds kicking in with a ten-spot for the Police Fund once in a while," Gwendolyn asserted. "It's these extra holdups that make me sick. Twenty for a welcome-to-our-district when the new pantata comes. Then, first you know, it's his birthday and another twenty will be appreciated. Or there's a christening in his family or some cop is getting married or buried, and along comes Willie Frye with his hand out. It's enough to sour a girl on the business."

"Nobody has to stick that don't want to," a late-comer said. "Look at Sue. She's graduated."

They made room for the plump, tightly jacketed form, greeting

28

the wearer as "Ollie" and "Sophomore," the latter title in deference to her status as a product of Wellesley, which she had left in her second year after being discovered in bed with the handsome young assistant professor of mathematics.

"What's about Sue?" someone asked.

"Her steady-boy's wife died and she's moved out to Cleveland."

There was a sigh of envy. "She'd oughta bank money on that," somebody commented, and another voice said, "Yeah. But think of having to nuzzle up to that harelip, even if he does own a horsebook."

"He's a bum," Lou declared. "Remember last fall when he gave us that sure thing at the Gut?"

"McGinnity. The Iron Horse. In the second. Seven-to-one and he ran last, the louse. Cost me a ten-spot."

The sisterhood, all of whom were inveterate bettors on the Guttenberg races across the Hudson River on the Jersey Heights, were in the midst of a discussion of the past season's equine disappointments, when two men entered the restaurant, strode down the center, and headed toward a private room at the rear. A hush settled upon the chatterers. The burly leader of the pair was the new police captain, Bernard Schmidt. His companion, lean, sinewy, and watchful, paused to greet Adriance by name.

"Hello, Frye," the reporter responded with a curt nod, and returned to his own table.

When next he glanced upward from his dinner toward the group he had quitted, Nita was standing and waving a hand. Her face was alight.

"Hi-hi, Tommy!" she called.

Tommy Howatt made his way to her, rubbing his hands together.

"Br-rr-rr!" he chattered. "It's cold enough outside to freeze the brass off a bald monkey."

"Now, *Mister* Tommy!" the veteran Oscar expostulated, for this was a bit beyond the standard of the proprieties as interpreted in Clark's. Nevertheless he chuckled as he shoved a chair for the young man in between Nita and Lou. Obviously Tommy was a privileged character.

There was a stir of femininity throughout the assemblage. The occupants of the long table focused their attention upon the new arrival. Some came from other tables, committing the solecism of temporarily abandoning their disgruntled escorts. It was a small ovation. Nor was it confined to the girls. Several of the male customers called out:

"Hi, champ!"

"How's the knockout boy?"

"Where's your diamond-studded belt, Tommy?"

"Who you going to take on next? Slavin?"

Jersey Jenny had left the table, at which Tommy was now seated close to Nita, to go to the ladies' room. Coming back she stopped beside Adriance.

"What do you think of our Tommy?"

"What's all this champ stuff?" the reporter asked in turn.

"Where have *you* been that you haven't heard? He knocked out John L. Sullivan; that's all."

"I'll pick up the details when I get back to Park Row, I expect," the reporter said. "He seems to be a hit with the girls."

Jerry nodded. "He makes us laugh. Wait till you hear his act. He's literary, too. One night he'll recite a pome, and next week you'll see it in *Puck* or *Leslie's.*"

Adriance took another look at the clown-laureate of this female world. The object of his scrutiny was soapy-clean. His suit was new and dreadful, and his cherubic countenance glowed with self-appreciation. Someone pushed him up on the bench-seat. He spread wide his arms and declaimed:

> *"Miss Dora White*
> *Will now recite*
> *'Red Ravens Shall Not Split Tonight.' "*

Squeals of glee greeted this reference to the popular cathartic, Red Raven Splits.

Tommy slipped his arm around Nita and raised her to her feet. "Introducing Miss Unda Ware of the Schurz family," he announced.

Shouts of acclaim.

"Have a drink, Tommy," someone called.

He made a flat-palmed gesture of negation. "Licks that touch lipper shall never touch mine." Tommy was, indeed, a card.

"What's your latest, Tommy?" blonde Annabel inquired.

He affected a look of modesty. "Oh, it ain't much."

"Come on!" "Let's have it." "Quiet there." "Tommy's going to spout."

The virtuoso struck an attitude. "A little tribute," he said, "to the swellest gal in the Tenderloin. Entitled 'Naughty Nita.' "

"Oh, you Indian Princess!" shouted the diminutive manager of a string of mixed-ale fighters. The little harlot bridled happily.

Tommy launched upon a panegyric that would never have made the *Police Gazette*.

The final stanza brought wild yelps of appreciation from the poet's admirers:

> *"She will charm you; she will warm you.*
> *Her caresses cannot harm you.*
> *But, oh, Nita!*
> *In your tighty little nightie*
> *You're a sinful little skinful."*

They were still clamoring their applause when a banjo materialized from somewhere and was thrust into the performer's hands. He plink-plunked it knowingly. Somebody shouted, " 'Woodpecker'!" The crowd took it up.

"Okay, folks," Tommy said. "All in on the beat."

He struck into an ancient and not-too-ribald upstate song which Adriance had not heard since college:

> *"Stuck my head in a woodpecker's hole,*
> *Mister Woodpecker said, 'God damn your soul!' "*

The whole assemblage came in with enormous gusto, hammering the table tops with fist, spoon, or stein on the downbeat:

> *"Take it OUT! Take it OUT! Take it OUT!*
> *Dixie Land."*

"Not bad!" the leader approved. " 'Annie Rooney.' "

He led them into the musical waltz rhythm and after that into "Comrades" and "Love Me Little: Love Me Long" and "Farewell Forever." The whole assemblage was in it now. They sang whether they knew how or not, responsive to the magnetism of the leadership. An olive-grower from the Ojai Valley, who was romantically clinging to Long Distance Lou's hand, shouted, "Can that crap. Give us something like Mother used to sing."

"Shall I?" The songster swung his head around, collecting impressions. Was his audience ripe for sentiment? "All right," he decided. "We strive to please. Ladies and gentlemen, 'The Picture That Was Turned Towards the Wall.' "

Warning cries of "Ssshh! Ssshh!" sounded. Tommy swept the strings softly and launched into Charles Graham's lachrymose ditty:

> *"There's a name that's never spo-kun.*
> *There's a heart that's almost brok-kun.*
> *There's a pick-shure that is turned towards*
> *the wall."*

The last swell of the music died away in a silence broken by the soft catching of breaths. Nita was sobbing freely and enjoyably. A

31

race-track tout near her laid his head between his outspread arms and shook the table with his emotion. From Jersey Jenny's eyes, fixed upon the singer's face, tears streamed. The prize-fight manager kept muttering, "My God! My *God!*" A popcorn-ball maker from Trenton, trying by a mighty effort to control his voice sufficiently to buy champagne, broke down and was led from the room by the weeping Annabel. Oscar, the tough waiter, was murmuring, "Ach! Ach! Ach!"

The virtuoso laid his instrument gently upon the table, waved a benign hand in acknowledgment of the applause, and swaggered over to where Dan Adriance was sitting.

"Hello, Mr. Adriance."

"Hello, Howatt." No invitation to sit down was extended.

"Look, Mr. Adriance! Howja like it?"

"Quite a performance. Does the management pay you for it?"

"Nah-h-h. Art for art's sake." The other grinned.

"You certainly brought down the house."

"Whores are easy weepers," was Tommy's comment.

"Minnesinger to the Soiled Sisterhood," Adriance said, disgusted at the other's callousness.

"Don't think much of it as music, huh?" the other said without rancor.

Adriance began to feel a little ashamed of himself. "I wonder if you know what you've got in that voice of yours," he said. "It ought not to be wasted here."

"Look," Tommy said. "I'm doing all right. I can sing a bird out of a bush or a gal into a bed. Any time."

Adriance paid his bill and rose. "I'm on my way," he said.

"Wait a minute," the other protested. "I got something I want to ask you."

"Go ahead."

"That young lady who was with you in the deepo. What's be-come of her?"

"Abroad," Adriance answered shortly.

"Oh! That's why I haven't seen her riding in the Park."

"How would you see her riding in the Park?"

"I been kinda hanging around the bridle path, odd mornings. There might be an accident."

The preposterous romanticism implied in the suggestion moved Adriance to sardonic amusement. "Hanging around," he repeated. "Hoping for a runaway so that you could rush to the rescue, I suppose."

"Well," said Tommy, unabashed, "you never can tell."

"I'll tell her that she has a knight-errant on guard."

Tommy caught it up quickly. "She's back, then." He added, thoughtfully, "I wonder, does she like music."

"That's no business of yours, you young cub," Adriance said in exasperation. "You stick to Nita."

"Nita's all right. This is different."

The reporter rose and reached for his hat.

"What's your sweat?" said Tommy.

"It's home-time."

"Look! I could walk along a ways."

"Well, the sidewalks are free."

"Meaning you don't want my company."

"It might be taken that way."

"You needn't be such a stinker," Tommy said, hurt.

Adriance, who was a kindly enough person at heart, sat down again. "All right," he said. "What's on your mind?"

"Look, Mr. Adriance! I'm not going to pester you any more about a job. I got a job."

"Yes, I heard about that."

"Well, look," the younger man continued. "You're a big space man and I'm a lousy *Pinky* scrub. It wouldn't hurt you any to give me a few pointers now and then."

Adriance reflected: Oh, hell! I'm stuck with this queer duck, anyway. Might as well be decent about it. Something in the young fellow's indomitable cheerfulness and perseverance appealed to him. He said, "I'm likely to be in and out of the *Gazette* office, myself. We'll have a talk there one of these days."

"Gee! That's slick," Tommy returned enthusiastically. "Thanks, Mr. Adriance. So long. See you in the morgue." He flipped his fingers in the air and returned to Nita.

In the secluded back room of Clark's the new police captain was drinking champagne on the house. No cop who knew his way about ever paid for a drink in the Tenderloin; certainly not a lordly pantata. Across from Captain Schmidt sat Willie Frye, he of the foxy face and subdued smile.

Willie was a typical police henchman. He knew the district like the back of his light-fingered hand. The chance son of a bachelor ex-mayor and a Coney Island side-show beauty, he had absorbed an education from the streets of New York. At twenty he was a fairly skilled "dip," but quit after a six-month term in the pen, and adopted the less risky occupation of con man. Having accidentally discovered his paternity, he appealed to his aging father, who still retained sufficient political pull to land him on the police force. His wide familiarity with the underworld plus an obsequious attitude toward his superiors brought him a moderate success in the Department as business agent and money collector for the head of the precinct. Captain Bernie Schmidt found him indispensable.

"Easy does it, Boss," he was saying to his superior.

"I been here a month," the captain said discontentedly. "How much longer I got to wait?"

"The girls'll come through all right," his underling assured him. "I'm working on it now. But we don't want to make it too heavy."

Bernie Schmidt's little pig-eyes glittered.

"I need the money. Do you know what the shift here cost me?"

"Fourteen thou', I understand."

"Fifteen, by God! I had to borrow to pay it."

Willie Frye cited the encouraging instance of Schmidt's predecessor, who had managed by rigid economy over a four-year period to save $65,000 out of a yearly salary of $2,200.

"Yeah," the new pantata complained. "But there's so much damn divvy. Gotta pay off everybody from the Commissioners down. Hell! It's a crime what they do to you downtown."

The fly-cop opened up his private directory and shoved it across the table. It was a small, leather-bound, and extremely secret book containing a list of the precinct's joints and opposite each, the sum collectible. The captain studied it.

"What about the Bower?" he asked. "Only down for one-fifty a month. Hell, that ain't half enough for the business Etta Holmes is doin'."

"Etta's been to a lot of expense fixing up the place."

"Well, Flo Durant's then. I hear they rolled a sucker for fifteen hundred there the other night."

"Only about a thou'. I got our cut right here in my kick."

"That's business," the captain approved, carefully counting the roll of bills handed to him. "I don't see Georgiana Hastings. Her place looks rich."

Willie stared at his superior in astonished consternation. "Jesus, Cap! Don't you know about Georgiana?"

"No."

"Lay off, for Chrissake! She ain't paid a dollar of protection since she opened."

"What!" the scandalized captain said. "Runnin' a joint in this precinct and don't pay? How come?"

The other leaned forward and shot a whispered name from the corner of his mouth.

Schmidt grunted. "Any more of these fireside pussies in the Nineteenth?" he asked.

"Here's the hands-off page. It ain't too long."

34

Schmidt ran his eye down the list and checked at a name. "Harrison M. Perley," he said. "What's his setup?"

"Nothin' in our line. Quiet little flat over at the Valdevia. Couple dames, call themselves Crosbie."

Schmidt leaned forward. "What's that? Crosbie?"

"Yes. Know anything about 'em, Boss?"

The captain hesitated. "I had a letter from a friend of mine in San Francisco. He didn't say anything about Perley."

"We don't want any trouble with Harrison M. Perley, Boss," the fly-cop advised. "He's solid with the Hall."

Schmidt nodded. The other passed on to happier things.

"I got a roundsman workin' on the streets; the cruisers are comin' through fine."

"How much?"

"Five apiece."

"Couldn't you jack 'em up to ten?"

"Have a heart, Cap. Trade ain't too lively these days. A lota those hatchets don't get more than two dollars a throw. We don't wanta tax 'em outa the precinct. Besides," he added, "since this Reverend Farr has been squawkin' to Headquarters they've had to watch their step."

"Farr? The Old Stone Church preacher? What's his trouble?"

"He thinks New York ought to be run like a Sunday school. No drinks, no gamblin', no women, no nothin'."

The pantata was properly indignant. "Preachin's what he's paid for, ain't it? Let him mind his own goddam business."

"He can't do much, I guess," the subordinate said comfortably. "Those anti-vice people are all alike. They make a lota noise and then forget it."

"Jesus! How I hate reformers, the snoopin' sons-a-bitches! Tell 'em to fetch another bottle of this stuff."

The quart of champagne was brought and sampled. Under its genial influence, Captain Schmidt announced himself, with interpolated thumps on the table with a beefy fist: "I'm captain of this precinct and I'm going to run it like I want to, and no goddam pulpit-pounder is goin' to tell me how."

"That's the talk, Boss!" said Fox-face Willie Frye.

The Old Stone Church was a landmark. It was not blatantly fashionable, being far too stable and solid to rely upon such superficiality. Its congregation comprised much of historic New York's wealth, power, and prestige. In its Calvinistically uncomfortable pews sat much of old-time New York: Deys, Turnures, Mauries, Tailers, Grosvenors, Verplancks, Ainsleys, Woolseys, Gilliats, Vreelands, DeKays, Cuttings, Goodwins, Edies, Wilders, and their connections, to whom the Astors were suspect as being too showy and the Vanderbilts negligible as being too new. The Honorable Thomas Cassius Corbin, State Republican leader, was a faithful attendant.

The Old Stone was a stronghold of conservatism: religious, ethical and social. It had stood, generation after generation, with unshaken stability, for the fine old Presbyterian standards: eternal damnation, foreordination, perdition of unbaptized infants, predestined salvation for the Presbyterian few, and original sin. By preference and practice it was isolated from the secular life of the community; more than isolated, it was encysted. Sunday after Sunday it was a refuge of peace and dogma to its parishioners. All for creed and the world well lost.

For forty years a sweet-souled divine, the Reverend Eliphalet McColl Bronson, had automatically accepted the church's soul-satisfying inhumanities. Then, out of a clear sky, fell the bolt that wrecked his career. His three-month-old grandchild died unbaptized, and by all the tenets of Presbyterianism, went to hell.

Through sleepless nights Dr. Bronson pondered in bitter travail over the immutable law. On Sunday morning he stood in his pulpit and put to his astounded congregation a question which had the potentialities of a bombshell.

"How," he asked in gentle appeal, "can I who preach an all-merciful God believe that He would condemn to eternal torture the soul of an infant whose only sin it was to die before being baptized?"

Some ascribed the outbreak to a temporary derangement of grief;

others, to senility. That it was heresy, none could deny. The Reverend Dr. Bronson's usefulness to the church was ended. Casting about for a successor, the trustees came upon the Reverend Brockholst Farr, D.D., then winning repute in Rochester, New York. Dr. Farr's theology was irreproachable; his antecedents a guaranty of reliability.

Graduated in 1855 from that rugged stronghold of Presbyterianism, Hamilton College, he had completed his religious education first at mildly conservative Auburn Theological Seminary, and finally at stern and rockbound Princeton. He was known for piety, austerity, and eloquence. The Old Stone Church called him with confidence.

Brockholst Farr, a childless widower, had lived and preached there five years before he discovered what manner of city it was in which he had so long dwelt, unseeing: eyeless in Gaza. He was then a gaunt and learned product of orthodoxy, with dogma in his blood, steel in his backbone, and love and pity in his heart. By derivation he was Scotch on one side and New World Dutch on the other. When a D.D. is appended to this blend of racial inflexibility, Satan had better watch his step. For the rest, Dr. Farr was possessed of a selfless courage, and had the rudiments of civic sensibility.

These might never have developed but for his acquaintance with Dan Adriance, whose uncle had been a classmate. The reporter took him on a superficial trip through the Tenderloin, to Hell's Kitchen and Five Points, and into some of the less habitable parts of the East Side. Adriance did not show him too much and told him very little, on the theory that it would only trouble his mind, and there was nothing to be done about it anyway.

What he saw did trouble Dr. Farr's mind. He wrote a letter to the newspapers, which was received with politely cynical amusement and duly printed. Dr. Farr had discovered Sin upon the streets of New York. It shocked him. His thesis was that the nocturnal representatives of Babylon should be banished from all public places. Let the police, who were presumptively ignorant of what was going on, arrest and jail these scarlet women, and all would be well. In his innocent mind it was as simple as that. He had no conception whatever of the political and commercial ramifications of vice.

Dr. Farr preached a sermon which caused misgivings on the part of his congregation. He gave a brief résumé of what he had seen under the tutelage of the *Star* reporter. New York, he set forth with sorrow, was not wholly the temple of radiance and virtue that he had, in his innocent and ignorant early days, believed. It was in danger of lapsing into disorder, immorality, and contempt for law. This should be the concern of every good citizen.

His Elders did not approve. They were further upset when he joined the Anti-Vice Society, which had been feebly protesting against metropolitan conditions for years. Nothing formal was done about Dr. Farr's developing radicalism, as Harrison M. Perley called it. Mr. Perley, who was the clergyman's old and valued friend, took him mildly to task.

"Let the politicians run the city, Dominie. The church has no business in politics. They don't meddle with us. Let's not meddle with them."

Sound and reasonable advice. In time Dr. Farr might have followed it, but for one of those minor mishaps which befall the most correctly reared youth, in this case, Stacey Hardwick.

The Hardwick family had, for six generations, worshipped at the Old Stone Church. When they moved to Brooklyn Heights, they still maintained their membership. They were father, mother, and two sons, ten years apart. Both boys were handsome, athletic, and popular. Allen, though only twenty-nine years old, held an important position of secondary rank in an insurance company, and was the youngest elder on Dr. Farr's Board. Stacey was in the highest scholarship group at Amherst and played on the football team.

The brothers sat in Dr. Farr's study. Allen's face was seamed with anxiety. The younger brother, flaccid in his chair, stared at the floor. Allen Hardwick said, "Dr. Farr, we need advice."

"That is my function and my privilege," the clergyman answered. "How can I help you?"

Stacey Hardwick muttered, "Nobody can help me."

"That's foolish," his brother said sharply.

"All right; I'm a fool," the boy said.

"So have most of us been at one time or another in life," Dr. Farr said briskly. "Is this a matter of money?"

"No, sir. Worse."

"Are you involved with a woman?"

"Yes, sir."

"And you've gotten her into trouble?"

"I'm the one that's in trouble."

Dr. Farr's tone was carefully matter-of-fact. "Is it the evil disease?"

"I've got it. I might as well kill myself."

"That is wicked nonsense," the clergyman said calmly. "How long ago was this?"

"Three weeks last Sunday. I was on my way to church."

The clergyman winced. "What have you done about it?"

"He hasn't done anything," Allen answered for him. "We had to keep it secret. It would just about kill Father. You know how bad his heart is, sir."

"You did right to come to me." The pastor went to his desk, where he sat down and wrote a brief message which he handed to Stacey. "This is a note to a physician. He is a wise and experienced man. Do not try to conceal anything from him."

"No, sir," said the boy miserably.

"Do you wish to tell me how it happened?"

Stacey appealed mutely to his brother. Allen said to the clergyman, "Did you ever hear of Georgiana Hastings, sir?"

"No."

"She keeps a fast house around the corner on Thirty-second Street."

"A house of prostitution? Within a block of this church?" the clergyman said in a tone of outrage.

"Yes, sir."

"Well? Go on."

Stacey Hardwick took up the story. "The girl spoke to me. She was young—and I guess I didn't know what she was. I swear to God, Dr. Farr," the boy said hysterically, "I didn't know what I was in for until—until it was too late."

"Did you know anything of this place before, Allen?" Dr. Farr asked the older Hardwick.

"Everybody knows about Georgiana Hastings."

"Except myself. Do you include the police authorities?"

"Of course."

"Then why do they not take action?"

"What can they do? Georgiana is the best-protected madam in the city."

"Protected by whom?"

"Principally by a Supreme Court judge, I believe. There is also a Tammany bigbug in the picture. The police are powerless, even if they wanted to act."

"We shall see about that. Give me the number." He noted it down.

Dismissing his callers, the Reverend Dr. Farr put on his well-brushed silk hat, took up his gold-headed cane, and set out for the West Thirtieth Street Police Station.

His approach was noted by the vigilant fly-cop, Willie Frye, who was taking his comfort in the captain's private room. Rushing out to the desk, he gave orders to hold up the visitor until a reception could be prepared for him. He then interrupted a poker game in the back room at the auspicious moment when Captain Schmidt had just called three sevens with three tens. The pantata quit the game resentfully.

"What's the old geezer want?" he demanded.

Willie Frye, who was supposed to know everything that went on in the precinct and did, in fact, know most of it, had heard that one of Dr. Farr's young fellows had got burnt at the Hastings house. Dr. Farr's visit, he surmised, might be due to this.

"I'd oughta give the old bastard a sock in the puss," the indignant pantata declared. "What do I have to see him for?"

"Now, Boss!" the fly-cop deprecated. "You gotta handle them church people with gloves. Treat 'em polite and give 'em the old run-around. It's a cinch," and he set himself to instruct his chief.

The Reverend Dr. Brockholst Farr was ushered into the captain's room, greeted courteously, and introduced to Plain-clothes Detective Frye. He stated his case. The two policemen looked at each other in surprise.

"Hastings? Hastings? Did you ever hear of the woman, Detective Frye?"

"No, sir."

"I'm kinda new to the precinct, Reverend," the captain explained to his visitor. "Lemme call in a couple of old-timers."

Sergeant Rooney and Patrolman Callahan, who had the West Thirty-second Street beat, were summoned.

"Do either of you men know anything of a disorderly house at this address?" Captain Schmidt asked, handing them Dr. Farr's penciled notation.

"No, sir," the sergeant said wonderingly.

"In this precinct?" the patrolman said incredulously.

"That number is in the precinct, ain't it? What's more, it's your beat."

The policeman shook his head. "Must be some mistake, Captain. Couldn't be anything like that going on and me not know it." (He was a canny young officer and afterward rose high in the Department.)

Willie Frye turned to the visitor. "Could it be, sir, that the young man had been drinking and got the address wrong?"

"It could not," Dr. Farr said.

"Sometimes places like that run awful quiet, Reverend," Captain Schmidt said, after some thought. He took a step forward and shook a monitory finger at the two men in uniform.

"I don't allow nothing like that in *my* precinct," he said. "Get that, you men?"

"Yes, sir," said Sergeant Rooney.

"Yes, sir," Patrolman Callahan echoed.

"I'll hold you responsible. What was that name again, Reverend? Hastings: Georgiana Hastings. Make a note of that, you two. If there's any funny business going on there or anywhere else, I want it stopped, and quick. Thank you for bringing it to our attention, Reverend. Drop in again any time. Always glad to have the help of the clergy."

Dr. Farr thanked him and withdrew. The four policemen burst into uproarious, knee-slapping laughter.

"Kee-ryst!" the sergeant said. "Can you beat that?"

"I like to bust a gut to keep from haw-hawin' in the old geezer's face," Willie Frye gurgled.

"Dearie-me!" Captain Schmidt tittered. "We mustn't have any naughty doin's in the good ole Tenderloin Precinct."

"Just the same," the fly-cop said thoughtfully, "I'll tip off Georgiana to be more careful about having her girls inspected."

"Yes," the captain confirmed. "We don't want some of our leading citizens coming down with the old ral."

"Are you gonna put Georgiana wise to his Nibs?" the sergeant asked Willie Frye.

"Naw," the plain-clothes man answered scornfully. "Why worry her? What can he do? Georgie'll be carryin' on at the old stand when his Whiskers is preachin' to the crows in a cornfield."

Dr. Farr returned to his study, innocently satisfied with the outcome of his errand.

6

Tommy Howatt had pictured journalistic life to himself as a series of dazzling adventures. His first month in the office on Oak Street disillusioned him. The routine was dull, with a monotony which caused him to reflect wistfully upon his abandoned career in the lively depot. That had, at least, a measure of variety. His employment on Mr. Richard K. Fox's paper had not.

Day after day the tyro hung about, listening heedfully to the great man's frequent instructions to his staff.

"This piece won't do, Deacon. It's limp. Sex it up, man; sex it up." . . . "Enders, you can't give *Sunday School Times* treatment to a lover under the bridal bed." . . . "That illustration's got no character. Put some legs into it, Harris." . . . Or it might be that the article beneath the editorial scalpel erred in the opposite direction. Then it would be: "Do you want to bring Anthony Comstock down here to Oak Street, Wood?" Or, "Can't you boys ever learn the rules? No goddams in my *Gazette,* no matter who says 'em."

Although a man of original mentality, Mr. Fox was not so narrow-minded as to abstain from adapting a sound idea wherever he might find it. A competitor in the weekly field was profitably marketing fifty-cent paperback excerpts under the generic heading: "Pickings from *Puck.*" Each separate volume was composed of homogeneous selections from the magazine: *Hayseed Hits, Best Girl, Funny Baby, The Great American Boarding House, Just Dog,* and the like. They sold well. Why, then, the enterprising Mr. Fox asked himself, should not items from his own publication find an equally profitable market under some such general heading as *"Gazette* Gleanings"? He directed Deacon Waldo to select a staff member for the task of scissoring out a sample lot of items. The Deacon picked his newest subordinate.

"Here's your chance to show the stuff that's in you, young fellow," he said.

"What do I do?" Tommy asked, staring in dismay at several capacious envelopes, labeled: "Sins of Society," "Beauty Unadorned,"

"Playful Parsons," "Girlies and Garters," and "Tricks of the Tenderloin."

Old Reliable pointed to a shelf. "There's the duplicate bound volumes. Here's a pair of shears. Go through the last ten years and cut out anything that's got plenty of zzzzing to it. Fetch the clippings to me and I'll go over 'em and see if you've got the makings of a *P.G.* man in you."

It was not a fair test, Tommy thought. Certainly it was an uninspiring one. Equally lacking in stimulus were the Foxian precepts, framed and hung upon the wall facing him.

BE BRIEF. BE TRUTHFUL. MAKE IT SNAPPY.

GOOD IS NOT GOOD ENOUGH. BEST IS NONE TOO GOOD.

ACCURACY, TERSENESS, ACCURACY.
(Cribbed from the newsroom of the *World*.)

IF YOU CAN'T TELL IT IN THREE STICKS, TRY TWO.

THE "POLICE GAZETTE" IS FOR PEOPLE.

GOT AN IDEA? TELL IT TO THE BOSS.

All day long, six days a week, the new employe clipped and pasted. In his spare hours he tried his hand at composition. He had been drearily plugging away for a fortnight when Dan Adriance, coming from the boss's office to get a drink at the cooler, stopped for a word with him.

"How goes it, young fella?"

"Lousy," was the morose answer.

"What's wrong?"

"Look what they got me doing."

"It's a start, isn't it?"

"Look, Mr. Adriance; I wanta write."

"Well, what's stopping you?"

"The Deacon won't take a thing I hand in."

"Maybe you haven't got onto the *P.G.* style yet."

"I've sold some stuff outside. I wish you'd look at some of it."

"All right. Got it with you?"

Tommy brought out from his breast pocket a sheaf of clippings, which he anxiously submitted to the other. They were typical examples of the conventional humor which found a ready if not very profitable market in the standard weeklies.

43

A First Class Fellow—A Freshman. (*"Judge,"* Tommy commented. "Half a dollar.")

Troubled Waters—A Flood of Tears. ("Got seventy-five cents for that. *Puck.*")

A Double Life—The Siamese Twins. (*"Leslie's,* and they only paid me a lousy quarter.")

He hopefully drew attention to a quatrain which had fetched two dollars. (*Judge* again.)

> *Mary had a little lamb,*
> *And a piece of apple pie.*
> *She got a check for fifty cents,*
> *Which she considered high.*

"How's that strike you?" he asked anxiously.

"Not too bad. Hardly *P.G.* stuff, though."

"No, I don't suppose it is. Here's one I hoped they'd take. But they didn't."

He handed over a slip of paper for the other's consideration. Dan read:

> *I would not take my luck to wed,*
> *I'd warrant her a faithless mate,*
> *Ready to quit my board and bed,*
> *And cuckold me with old man Fate.*
> *So I will smile and turn away,*
> *And I will laugh and have my right.*
> *And I will live from day to day,*
> *And I will love from night to night.*

"Is that your own?" the reporter asked in surprise.

"I got a two-spot for it. *Mademoiselle New York.*"

"I asked you whether you wrote it yourself."

Tommy scratched a freckle on his nose. "I kinda adapted it, as you might say."

"From what?"

"I forget the fella's name. A book of poems I found."

"Where?"

With no sign of abashment he revealed that he had been spending his spare hours among the old-book stalls of lower Fourth Avenue, free-reading. "You'd be surprised what you can pick up there sometimes," he remarked.

"For adaptation, eh?"

"I change a word here and a word there," Tommy explained. "It's all safe stuff. Copyright played out."

"Did you ever hear of such a thing as plagiarism?"

"What's that?"

"Stealing the other fellow's stuff, in plain English."

"Crap! Nobody's hurt, is there? Most of these fellas are dead, anyway. So, what's the harm?"

"You might get caught at it."

He grinned. "Well, I have," he said.

It was that sophisticated weekly, *Life,* then edited by the four M's: Mitchell, Martin, Miller, and Metcalf, who had been too smart for the ingenious borrower. From them his offerings came back with curt marginal notes: "Diluted Lyly." "Bowdlerized Swinburne." "No improvement on the original Lang," and the like.

"I'm working on one that I didn't get from anywhere, though," he said. "It's a kind of a—well, I guess you'd call it an ode."

"To what?"

"The title is 'To Laurie,' if you wanta know," the poet said. "I heard you call her that. Look! Don't she ever ride in the Park?"

This query being received in stony silence, Tommy reverted to a former theme.

"Look, Mr. Adriance. You got education. You got culture. You know what a guy oughta read to improve himself. Couldn't you kinda learn me—teach me, I mean. Hell! I can't even talk right. One evening a week, say. Look! I'll pay you as soon as I'm in the money."

Another who wanted to pay him money, Dan Adriance reflected sardonically. Laurie Crosbie and now Tommy Howatt.

"I'm not running an infant class for cub writers," he said.

Tommy sighed. "Well, couldn't I just come around for a talk once in a while?"

The mixture of humility and effrontery amused and disarmed the older man.

"Why, yes, if you want to," he said.

He had misgivings that he was letting himself in for something.

Tommy was not through yet. He had adopted Adriance as his model, and he was resolved to make a careful study of him.

"Look," he continued. "I'd like to read some of your stuff. Find out how you do it. Haven't you got some, laying around?"

"No," Adriance answered. He had another thought. A few weeks earlier Mr. Fox had assigned to him a private desk just outside the main office. The desk had a lock. The *Star* did not permit its reporters locked desks. On getting the *Gazette* job, Adriance had transferred his small scrapbook, in which he kept a few of his pet articles, to his new quarters; also some of his private matters. "Come to think of it, I have got a few things here," he said.

He released the padlock, took out a folder and handed it to his admirer, with the directions: "Put it back and snap the lock when you're through."

Tommy read the Adriance pieces with absorbed attention, making notes and copying passages. It was after midnight when he finished his studies, closed the folder and bore it back to the desk, lifting the slant top to replace it.

A number of loose papers were scattered about. Tommy examined them. Nothing of interest. Two letters in fashionable blue envelopes promised more. Daniel Adriance's name was written on the envelope, in a bold finishing-school handwriting. An undecipherable monogram ornamented the flap.

"Class," Tommy murmured appreciatively. A quick survey showed him that he was safe from observation, the only person in sight being the clean-up man at the far end of the room. He took his discovery to his place at the long table, removed the letters from the envelopes, and spread them out for study. They were undated, but the postmarks showed the precedence.

The first was couched in terms of raillery which Tommy thought inappropriate if not actually unseemly. Who was this girl, to be making game of the Newspaper Row crack! There was a jocular reference to an unidentified A.D.: "Please don't shoot him; I may have use for him later." There was no signature at the bottom more legible than what looked like an R but might have been a K or even an N. No address, either. At any rate, Tommy figured with relief, the writer was not Laurie Crosbie.

The second letter, postmarked eight months after the first, was a mere scrawl of a note.

> Dan: I'm afraid. You and I have come too near—well, finality. What an awful fool I'd be, ever to see you again. And yet— Oh, darling!

This time the signature was plainly a K.

Dopey way to write a letter, Tommy thought. He carefully restored the documents to their place. He was pleased with his find. It was his theory that you couldn't know too much about the folks you had to deal with. You never could tell when inside information might come in handy. Who was it that said, "Knowledge is power"?

Tommy agreed with him.

7

One fact became painfully obvious to Tommy Howatt: Dan Adriance had no intention of introducing him to the laughing goddess of the Grand Central Depot. In vain had he thrown out what he regarded as tactful hints; they were ignored. Vanity suggested that he was being balked of his wishes because Dan wanted no rival in the field. Yet Tommy had several times seen him in the company of the girl, and Dan's attitude toward her appeared to be companionable rather than lover-like.

Tommy simply could not understand it. How mortal man could be in close association with a girl like Laurie Crosbie and not fall in love with her— Then he remembered those fashionably scrawled notes in Dan's ravished desk. He had made a mental note of the postmarks. The earliest one was September, a year and a half ago.

Yes, that might explain Dan's immunity to the charms of Laurie Crosbie. A previous attachment and a powerful one, since it had lasted all this time. He recalled amused references by some of the girls at Clark's to Handsome Dan's strangely virtuous attitude since more than a year. The *Star* reporter still frequented the restaurant and continued to be on friendly terms with several of the sisterhood to the extent of buying the drinks, but that was all. Shrewd Tommy judged that this access of chastity might be the influence of the unknown K.

Seeking clues, he ran over the letters in his mind. There was little in either of them to satisfy his avid curiosity. Who was this A.D., he wondered, and why should Dan want to shoot him? Above all, who was K?

The mysterious A.D. of the violated letter was Acton Daggett, man-about-town, big-game hunter, bachelor and eccentric, one of whose diversions was making safaris to unexplored parts of Africa. Late in that distant August, word had reached the office of the *Morning Star* that he had returned from a prolonged trip, with sensational photographs of a pigmy tribe whose males exhibited a peculiar and picturesque inversion of lower abdominal physique. Ramsey Kelly, the city editor, telephoned to the Daggett house and was told that he might send a reporter up. This surprised him; Daggett was notorious for his dislike of newspapers and newspapermen. Kelly gave Adriance the assignment. The reporter was not pleased. "Even if it's true," he objected, "how am I going to write it for a supposedly respectable daily?"

Kelly played a desk-top rataplan with his knobbed fingers, one of his less endearing habits. "That's your problem," he said. "Don't take your eyes off him, though. He's sudden."

"Trying to scare me, Mr. Kelly?"

The editor grinned. "Remember that chorus girl at the yacht party that he tossed into the East River last year? Crazy as a bedbug, if you ask me."

The ground floor of Daggett's Madison Avenue house was opened to Adriance by a bland butler. He withdrew as his master came forward. Daggett was a thick-framed man of forty, with a tanned, handsome, and rather peevish face. With a grunt which was more of an acknowledgment of the visitor's presence than a greeting, he led the way the length of the house, dropped back of Adriance, motioning for him to open a rear door, and with no warning whatsoever, sent him sprawling into the areaway below.

"God damn all you reporters!" he snarled and locked the door.

Adriance's football training saved him. He landed with all muscles relaxed, angry and unhurt. He was in a jail-yard. Back of him were the locked door and iron-guarded windows. On three sides of the grass plot where he found himself, rose an unscalable eight-foot fence topped with barbed wire. There was a small door in it, bolted on the far side. He threw his two hundred pounds of weight against it. It did not budge.

Two courses were open. He could sit down and await developments. Or he could lift a disconsolate voice like a hound and bay the shade-drawn rear windows of the adjacent houses on Fifty-third Street, a procedure which would certainly be humiliating and probably unprofitable. That type of house would be closed for the summer while the family was at Newport or Richfield Springs.

While he was considering the situation, one of the rear-window shades went up, revealing a poised and extremely attractive presentation of a young woman whom, after a moment's hesitancy, he recognized.

Miss Kathleen Tennant was a luxury item. Although not yet twenty-one she was already a figure in metropolitan life. Graduated from Farmington and fashionably burnished by a year in Europe, she had become the youngest member of the ultra-smart Comedy Club and had appeared with success in minor parts. By virtue of a distant relationship with Mrs. Steevens Parke, she was one of a small coterie of girls privileged to address that formidable dowager as "Aunt Agatha." She had a charming speaking voice, impeccable manners when she so chose, an allure deeper-rooted in personality than any mere beauty, and an avid, adventurous, and intrepid spirit.

Now she sat, framed in the open window and looking down at the imprisoned young man with a smile. The smile was not kindly; it was amused.

Dan did not like it. He called up to her: "Good afternoon. Could you let me out?"

Her answer amazed him. "I suppose I could. But you'd get away."

He took a moment to digest that, and then said, "Yes, that's the idea."

"I really don't see why I should trouble."

So she was trying to get a rise out of him, was she? All right; if she was going to take that tone—

"I might go so far as to buy you a drink," he offered.

"Not inducement enough."

"Well, have you got a telephone?"

"Not a public one."

"What would be your terms for calling up my newspaper, the *Star,* and letting them know—"

"Oh! You're a reporter. Have you been interviewing Acton Daggett? He doesn't like reporters."

"That's why I'm here."

"Tell me more," she mocked.

"Let me out and I'll tell you the story of my life."

She yawned. "I suppose I might as well." She vanished. A door slammed. Another door opened. He could not hear her footsteps on the grass, and the high fence shut her from his sight. The bar which closed the fence panel on her side was lifted, and Dan Adriance stepped out of one captivity into another.

"I'm Kathleen Tennant," the girl said. "How do you do, Mr. Reporter?"

"My name is Adriance," he said.

"I know. I knew you at once, though you don't know me."

"But I do. I've seen your photograph in the Fifth Avenue show windows."

"Is that all? You don't remember nearly trampling me to death?"

"Certainly not. What's all this?"

"Oh, years ago. At the Lenox Tennis. You were one of the cracks and I a small and adoring brat. I didn't mean to get in your way when you went back for that lob. It hurt my feelings when you cursed me."

"Did I? I'll apologize. Though you'd no business inside the lines, you know."

"Oh, I always break the rules," she said composedly.

"I'm beginning to remember now. I was so rattled for fear I'd hurt you, that I lost the match."

"Served you right," she replied vindictively. "You picked me up and dusted me off as if I were a doll. It made me so mad I tried to kick you, and you laughed and kissed me and dropped me over the side net."

"And you've been holding it against me ever since?"

"I'm not accustomed to being kissed and forgotten."

"I can well believe that," he murmured.

"So now you're a reporter," she commented.

He did not quite like her tone. "Yes. Did you never see one of the strange creatures before?"

"Not so near at hand. But I don't mind. I have low tastes. My family wouldn't approve of my entertaining you, unchaperoned, though."

He said politely, "Thank you for the rescue, and good day, Miss Tennant."

She said in an altered voice, "Have I annoyed you? I didn't mean — That's not true; I did mean to. I'm in a vile temper today. New York in summer rasps my soul. Do sit down." She motioned him to a lawn chair near a cast-iron stand. "We'll have a drink, shall we?"

A maid appeared, brought a bottle, glasses, a bowl of ice, and a siphon.

"Would you like me to telephone?" she asked.

"No. I'll go back to the office. First, I've got something to say to Mr. Acton Daggett."

She regarded him intently. "That's not a nice expression on your face."

"Have you ever been thrown out of a back door?"

"No. I'm not a reporter. Don't trample me under again," she added with a chuckle. "I won't tease you any more. And don't hit Acton. He's quite capable of shooting you."

"A friend of yours, perhaps?"

"He's my some-kind-of-a-cousin, for one thing. Besides, he wants to marry me."

"Does he? Well, America is the land of boundless ambitions."

"I don't know why I told you that," she said reflectively. "Though it's common property. *Town Topics* had it."

"I thought it wasn't quite respectable for a young girl to be in *Town Topics*."

"It isn't. It's a sort of loss of maidenly status. Does that shock you?"

"Terribly," he said with a smile. It did, rather.

"Aunt Agatha says I'm damaged goods because my name gets into the papers and that I'm practically an old maid at twenty and that I'll be lucky to get Acton Daggett."

"Your Aunt Agatha must be a sweet soul."

"My Aunt Agatha is an old hellion. She's Mrs. Steevens Parke. You must have heard of her."

"I reported one of her charity bazaars once. By the way, I think I will call up my office if I may."

When he returned, another pair of drinks was waiting.

"Do you have to go back?" the girl asked.

"Not to the office. I have to cover a minor political meeting on Thirty-fourth Street."

They sipped their drinks. "I haven't a thing to do this evening," she murmured after a silence.

He smiled. "Would you like to be an assistant reporter?"

"I think it might be fun."

"You've got a job."

"What do I have to do?"

"Put on your hat and come out to dinner with me."

"Can you afford it? I've got an expensive appetite."

"The Fifth Avenue? Or Delmonico's?"

"Oh, no!" she said. "Take me to one of those places where good reporters go when they're hungry."

"The Park Avenue, then," he decided. "Hurry up and we'll get a place on the balcony."

They did. He suggested a Lone Tree.

"What's that?" she asked.

"A cocktail."

"I never heard of any cocktails except Manhattan and whiskey."

"In Boston they call it the Lone Tree, after Mr. Lithgow Devens' place. He invented it."

"Let's try it." She looked at him with interest as he gave instructions to the head bartender: one part of French vermouth to three parts of gin. It was the cachet of her set always to be up with the newest thing. She was learning something and was appreciative and a little impressed.

She drank the unfamiliar mixture slowly and with an air of connoisseurship. "I want another," she said.

After that they had clams, an excellent T-bone steak with specialty potatoes, and asparagus and a bottle of 1889 Beaune. The girl was apparently alcohol-proof. She showed no signs of being affected, unless it were in the relaxation of her talk.

Over the coffee (she declined brandy, "No, I always know when I've had enough") she said, "What a fascinating place! More like

Saratoga than New York." She looked out over the courtyard below, with its ornamental trees in tubs and its two flashing fountains.

"It was built by A. T. Stewart as a home for fallen women," he said.

"What a temptation!" She laughed. "What happened? Didn't they like it? How foolish! Is it quite respectable now?"

"Oh, eminently so."

"I'm not too sure. There's a lingering enchantment in the air. Don't you feel it?"

"Too much," he said.

"As if one were isolated from the world. Or two," she amended. "Just for tonight. A page torn out of the calendar. Episode without aftermath.

> *We twain once well asunder,*
> *What will the mad gods do?*
> *For hate, with me, I wonder,*
> *And what, for love, with you.*

Do you like Swinburne?"

"Not that poem for this occasion."

"Let's not be solemn," she said.

Dan did a poor job on the meeting. With the warm sense of the girl's nearness, it was hard for him to keep his mind on the proceedings. As they walked back at eleven o'clock, Kathie remarked ingenuously that reporting wasn't as exciting as she had supposed.

"It's been a pretty exciting evening for me," he said.

"I've loved it," she said primly. "Thank you for everything."

She had the basement key, with which she unlocked the grille door. She went down one of the steps into the dark well, with its band of light from an intrusive street lamp, and turned to face him. There was mischief and mirth in her eyes, and in the bird-poise of her body the conscious and potent adduction of sex.

"You know, Dan, I never really got over you," she said. "It was your brutality, I suppose. The overmastering male."

She reached up and put her arms around his neck. Her lips rose to his, clung, then opened to his kiss. Her eyes were heavy-lidded. Her body quivered against him.

"Foolish," she said. "You'd better go."

"Not yet . . . Must I, Kathie?"

For a long, sweet moment he thought she would say, "No." Her voice was low but steady as she said soberly, sadly, "Don't get up any futile hopes, Dan."

"When shall I see you again?"

"I—don't—know."

"Tomorrow?"

"Tomorrow I shall be going back to Richfield."

"Next week?"

"I shan't be back next week. Nor for lots of weeks."

"Do you think you're going to put me out of your life—now?"

"I ought to. But I can't. Not yet. I'll write. But you'd much better forget me." She opened her arms to him again. "Once more, darling."

He took away with him into the night an inexpungeable memory: a woman-creature hardly more than a girl, slight and supple and as sweetly put together as a leopard, bearing herself with the grace of self-confident physical vigor. Those public photographs, from which he had first recognized her, did her scant justice, so far did beauty in her fall short of the unsubdued flame of her charm and vitality. Her face was a little irregular in outline; the greenish-gray eyes broad-set and grave; the full, faintly shaded lips suggestive of passion, above a chin firm enough to deny it full sway. But Kathleen Tennant was quite definitely a luxury item. Not for him, his good sense told him.

Yet— Forget her? After those kisses? His dreams would not let him.

It was a month before her letter came. They met again and again, through the fall, into the winter, into the spring, always clandestinely, which he hated and resented. Never did she give him hope of permanency in their fitful relationship. Always it was the same sad prophecy: they would get over it, both of them. He would forget her. He must.

Then, in the spring, came the desperate little note of farewell. She would not see him again. This was the end.

Dan accepted it because he must. He did not believe it.

Kathleen Tennant was the reason why he was immune to the beauty of Laurie Crosbie. Or of any other woman.

8

Whenever he could promote a couple of afternoon hours away from the office, Tommy Howatt sped uptown to occupy a bench beside the Central Park bridle path. In the grip of his romantic obsession he felt it in his bones that, soon or later, Laurie's mount, for all that it was an unpromisingly sedate creature, would be obliging enough to turn skittish and give him opportunity of a gallant rescue.

Fate worked out a pattern quite different from his hopes. Still afraid to risk a direct approach to his lady, he had been a patient bench-warmer for some weeks when, on a balmy March afternoon, the unforeseen befell. A small boy rode a pony along the bridle path, attended by a bored groom on a roan. Attracted by a flirtatious nursemaid, the groom dropped back. A vagrant breeze whisked the page of a newspaper between the forefeet of the pony. The pony shied, did a dance step, and bolted, with its small rider clinging to its neck.

Laurie Crosbie, cantering a few rods in the rear, spurred her mount to a lope. She quickly overtook and reined in the pony, which was only having a little fun, anyway. Tommy had leaped from his seat and darted down the path, but before he could reach the spot, the alarmed groom and a policeman had closed in and it was all over. No opening for a hero there.

To the enterprising, opportunity presents more than one facet. Balked of his dramatic hope, Tommy perceived another way of winning the lady's favor. He would glorify her in appropriate prose through the medium of the *Police Gazette*. To this end he interviewed the groom, he interviewed the small boy, he interviewed the policeman, he interviewed the bystanders, and, having been lucky enough to find out her address, he hastened to the Valdevia Apartments to interview Laurie. The doorman blocked him off.

That evening an agitated voice called Adriance at the *Star* office.

"Dan? Oh, Dan! It's Laurie. Are you very busy? Can you come up right away?"

"I guess so. Anything wrong?"

"Oh, yes! Dan, have you ever heard of the *Police Gazette?*"

"I have also seen the Statue of Liberty."

"Will you take me there?"

"The boats don't run this late."

"Oh, don't joke, Dan. This is serious. I'm so afraid the *Police Gazette* is going to write something about me!"

"Hello! What have you been up to?"

"Nothing," she explained. "One of those awful reporters wanted to fight Adolph because he wouldn't let him up to see me. Oh, Dan! I just know he's going to write something about me. And you know how Mother is about newspapers."

Dan did know and had speculated about Mrs. Crosbie's sensitivity to public print.

"I shouldn't call the *P.G.* precisely a newspaper," he said. "It isn't likely that your mother would see it."

"She might. Anyway, I'd *hate* to be in it. Can't you do something?"

Dan sighed. "All right. I'll be up in an hour."

At the apartment he admitted that he had a pull with Mr. Richard K. Fox. "I got him out of what looked like a bad libel suit," he explained. "It saved him a lot of money. He's a grateful sort of bird, and gave me a one-day-a-week advisory job. It's a sinecure, of course. I even have a desk there."

"Then you'll take me to see him," Laurie said.

"Why, if you really want to. Shall I get a hack?"

"No, let's take a streetcar. I love 'em. So jouncy. And the horses look so wise and metropolitan." Riding in a public conveyance still represented adventure to her unsated mind.

"You know," the reporter said, as they settled down in the Broadway rattletrap, "this is a fool's errand."

"I don't see why."

"Besides being immoral."

"Pooh! What's immoral about it?"

"Trying to suppress news. That's practically criminal for a newspaperman."

"I'm not a newspaperman," she said composedly. "And I don't want to be news."

"Then you'd better get another face."

"You needn't be cross about my face. I can't help it. You said Mr. Fox—is that his name?—was a particular friend of yours and would do anything you asked him." This was one of those generous feminine exaggerations to which Laurie was prone. "Besides, I'll pay," she added.

"Pay whom?"

"That paper."

"Bribery and corruption, eh? Well, don't try it on, this time. The *Pinky* may have its faults, but you can't bribe it."

"Would that be bribery, asking them to keep something out that nobody wants in?"

The horse-bells jangled to a stop, and Dan was spared the chore of attempting to explain the ethics of publication to an unreceptive mind. They had made City Hall Park in twenty-five minutes, which was fast time from Thirty-first Street. The clock above the lovely façade of the City Hall marked 5:40. Benches were occupied by a few early-settling bums, hopeful of snatches of sleep between the rounds of the cop. Only Dan's explanation that they were open-air addicts prevented his companion's design of giving to each a dollar for a hotel room. He pointed out Newspaper Row; the lordly dome of the new *World* Building; the squat and rickety tenement in which was housed the *Sun,* most expert, most waspish, and most cynical of American dailies; the tarnished red-brick Victorianism of the *Tribune;* and the dull gray angularity of the *Times.* His own paper, the *Star,* was around the corner of Beekman Street.

At the entrance to Oak Street, Laurie stopped and gazed down the cavernous slope, between the massive palisade of the Brooklyn Bridge approach on one side and the darkened buildings on the other.

"Is this a slum?" she asked with lively expectancy.

"Don't let your sense of romance run away with you, my child," Dan answered.

He guided her in at the entrance of the *Police Gazette* and up the stairs. Their nostrils were refreshed by the characteristic pressroom odor: the smell of live paste, which is acrid and stimulant, and of printer's ink, which is that of fermenting molasses.

Laurie wiggled her nose. "I like it," she said.

The door of the inner sanctum, which bore the owner's name on a brass plate, was half ajar. The reporter knocked and entered.

The great man sat in his office chair with his feet on the desk. His silk hat was on his head. His coat, with the expensive name of Cavanaugh on the label, swung from a hanger. His teeth were firmly clenched on a fragrant cigar. His face was florid, cheery, and handsome. He was reading a proof, from which he detached one hand to wave the caller to a chair.

"Hello, Dan," he said. "What fetches you here? This isn't your day. Glad to see you, anyway."

"I've brought you a caller," the reporter said. "Come in, Laurie. Miss Crosbie, this is Mr. Richard K. Fox."

"How do you do, Mr. Fox?" the girl said demurely as the editor rose and stared.

"Great Jehoshaphat!" said Mr. Fox and sat down again.

56

The room which the newcomer scanned with interest was of an elegance foreign to her experience. Everything that was not mahogany seemed to be gold. The vast desk glowed with the precious metal in every appointment. Three walls were covered with pictures of race horses in action and pugilists about to go into action. The fourth wall was devoted to personalities: close-crowded photographs of celebrities, male and female, sporting and theatrical, flourishingly autographed "Yours truly," "With love," "To a good pal." A gold desk frame supported an editorial theorem:

When it Comes to
Truthful and Perfect
Delineation the
POLICE GAZETTE
Corrals the Clam, as it Were

Fronting the desk was a massive chair, inlaid with ten- and twenty-dollar gold pieces, the gift, as a plaque specified, of Mr. Fox's "sincere admirer, Silver-Dollar Smith." A small safe, elegantly inlaid in red, white and blue, stood in a corner.

Mr. Fox toyed with a jeweled paper cutter. He eyed the girl with undisguised admiration, which was not offensive because it was, somehow, impersonal.

"What a cover!" he said. Laurie looked puzzled. "Haven't got an artist that's up to it though. Might get A. B. Wenzell. Or Charles Dana Gibson."

"Mr. Fox," Dan explained to his companion, "thinks your picture would look pretty on the front of his magazine."

"Oh, no! Mr. Fox!" Laurie appealed. "You wouldn't do that!"

("Like a very young angel asking God for a special favor," the editor said afterward.)

"Miss Crosbie doesn't like publicity, Mr. Fox," Dan said.

"Please, Mr. Fox, don't put my name in your paper," she appealed.

"And I thought young Howatt was faking her description," the editor went on, as if he had not heard. "He didn't tell the half of it."

"May I see the story?" Dan asked.

"Rule here," Mr. Fox said. "However, in this case . . ." He glanced at the girl's anxious face and handed over a proof from the desk.

The episode was made to order for the *Pinky*. Daring young equestrienne, beautiful, mysterious, in desperate rescue of scion of wealth (the runaway-with urchin, it developed, was a great-grandson of Mrs. Steevens Parke) on the fashionable bridle path. Four of the *Gazette's* own sensation-stirring elements were compressed in the event: beauty, mystery (injected by the egregious Tommy), adventurous courage (which was far from the fact), and Society with a capital S. The article was a-glitter with adjectives: "thrilling," "heroic," "beauteous," "queenly," "fashionable," "romantic," and the like. It was awful.

"The lad can write," Mr. Fox approved. "What d'you think, Dan?"

Dan thought it was an admirable example of the *Pinky* at its worst and most slushsome, but this was not the time to say so. "Hot stuff!" he said.

The proprietor turned to Laurie, tapping the proof with a well-manicured finger. "Not many young ladies would object to being called the most beautiful girl in New York," he observed.

"I'm not. And I don't want to be in the paper, please."

"Why not?"

She hesitated. "I don't know. I just don't like it."

"That's a poor reason for killing a good story."

"Mr. Fox, that story will be just as good with the name and address left out," Dan lied. "Let me rewrite it, stressing the mystery and leaving it a mystery."

"What's your interest in this, Dan?" the editor asked. "Though perhaps I could guess," he added with a smiling glance at Laurie.

"Miss Crosbie is my cousin."

"I see. Well, if you make a point of it—"

"I do."

"Very well. It's a deal. When can I have copy?"

"It will be on your desk in the morning."

"Oh, thank you, Mr. Fox," the girl said fervently.

"You go over and sit in that chair and make yourself comfortable," he said kindly. "Look these over while Dan, here, and I have a little talk." He handed her some copies of the weekly, then pulled in to his desk and drew some notes from a cubbyhole.

"You're a Hamilton College man, aren't you, Dan?"

"Yes," Dan answered.

"All you Hamilton fellows seem to know one another. Did you ever run across the Reverend Farr of the Old Stone Church on Madison Avenue?"

"Oh, yes! Classmate of an uncle of mine."

"Know him pretty well?"

"I ought to. He got me my job on the *Star*. He's about the finest character I know."

"Hm! Has he ever talked to you about this crusade of his?"

"Yes."

"I think he's crazy."

"Then you're one hundred percent wrong," the other said flatly.

"That's your opinion, is it? Well, he's been down to Police Headquarters. Wants 'em to close all the houses. Practically threatened he'd get up in his pulpit and blow the lid off if something wasn't done. What does he think New York City is—a Dorcas sewing circle? What's the matter with the old galoot, anyway?" the great man demanded angrily. "Trying to stir up some publicity for himself?"

"No. You don't know him if you think that."

The editor frowned. "Somebody ought to warn him that he's headed for trouble, bad trouble, if he doesn't look out."

"That would never stop him."

"Then he's a fool. New York's a wide-open town. It always has been and it's going to stay that way. That's the way people want it. It's good for business. Farr will find himself up against the police. Nobody can buck the police. They run the town and they run it the way folks want it run."

"Haven't I read pieces in the *Pinky*—in the *Gazette*—denouncing sin and vice in New York?"

"That's different. Those articles really stir up trade, bring the yokels to town with money burning in their pockets. It's sound journalism. But it's nothing for the pulpit to mix into. I'm a good Presbyterian, myself, and I don't like to see the church involved."

Dan smiled. "Why don't you have a talk with Dr. Farr?"

"Would it do any good?"

"Not the slightest, I should think. Once he starts on a course that he thinks is right, Hell itself can't stop him."

"What started him on it, anyway?" Mr. Fox asked discontentedly.

Dan glanced at Laurie, absorbed in the pink pages, and lowered his voice discreetly. "From what I hear, he doesn't like a whorehouse doing business openly just around the corner from his Sunday school. Would you, in his place?"

"Around the corner, eh? That'll be Georgiana Hastings, I suppose. She runs a high-class place. There's never any trouble there. Why should anybody want to make trouble for her?" He raised his voice in sudden annoyance. "Even money the police run your Dr. Brockholst Farr out of his pulpit before it's all over."

"No takers," Dan said.

Laurie looked up from her reading. "I go to Dr. Farr's church," she said.

"Do you?" Mr. Fox said. "I shouldn't want a daughter of mine to. What do you think of my *Gazette?*"

"I don't know," she said. "It seems so—so kind of excited."

"You mean exciting," the owner said, gratified.

"No, I don't. I mean excited. As if whoever wrote the articles was awfully stirred up about it."

"That's good," he said. "I want 'em to be. Want to see the cub who wrote the glory-story about you?"

Laurie's expressive face indicated distaste. "No, I don't believe I do."

"He's quite a celebrity now. He's the lad that socked John L. Sullivan."

"Who is John L. Sullivan?"

"Oh, my God!" Mr. Fox said, for once startled into profanity.

"Heavyweight champion of the world," Dan explained. "Don't you read the papers?"

"Not very much."

"I'll put you on the *Gazette's* free list," the proprietor promised.

Laurie said sweetly, "Thank you so much for everything, Mr. Fox."

"Don't mention it," the genial editor returned. "Keep an eye on that young cousin of yours, Dan," he advised as he ushered them out, "or Chuck Connors will be selling her the Brooklyn Bridge. Never heard of John L. Sullivan! Whee-oo!"

Bitter was Tommy's disappointment when he read the substitute article in the next week's issue. He sought out the writer.

"Look, Mr. Adriance! What was the matter with my story?"

"Mr. Fox wanted it handled differently."

"I thought I made a dandy job of it," Tommy said sadly. "I'll bet Miss Crosbie'd have been crazy over it." An idea struck him. "Look! I'm going to get my copy back and send it to her."

"Don't."

"Why not?"

"She'd laugh herself to death."

"Laugh! What'd she laugh for? It ain't funny."

The time had come, Dan Adriance decided, to put this young fellow straight about himself. "It's blather and blubber," he said.

Tommy withstood the shock like a man. After a thoughtful pause he said, "You mean I don't know how to write, huh?"

Dan tried to put it mildly. "You don't know what not to write."

"How'm I going to learn?"

"Don't ask me."

"I *am* askin' you."

"Oh, well! Go to the Public Library and read."

"What'll I read?"

The contemporary newspapers were full of literary advice to seekers for self-improvement. Dan referred the inquirer to several lists.

Tommy sighed. "Jeez! If only I coulda had a college education. Lookit all I gotta learn."

"A lot of good newspapermen have started from scratch," Dan encouraged him.

"Well, anyhow, I got idears," Tommy encouraged himself.

Skillfully depersonalized by Dan Adriance's expert pen, the episode of the bridle path, as set forth in the *Gazette,* was innocuous enough. It had a sequel for Laurie.

The next time she rode in Central Park, and many times thereafter, she had for volunteer escort the adoring small boy of her unheroic rescue. From many light-hearted conversations, saddle to saddle, she learned that his name was Robin Ely and his age, nine years, and that arithmetic was the tragedy of his young life. Otherwise, his lines had been laid in pleasant places. Although he said little about it, his companion gathered that he was the happy and unspoiled child of wealth and privilege. Further than that he told little of his environment, and Laurie was constitutionally incurious.

Not having read the proofs of Tommy Howatt's rejected article for the *P.G.,* she was not aware of Robin's connection with the imposing Mrs. Steevens Parke. Had she known, it would have made no particular impression upon her.

In composing his bridle-path panegyric, Tommy had a double purpose. First, he hoped to appeal to the vanity of his hitherto unreachable inamorata. Second, he counted on his effort to convince the Deacon and Mr. Fox that he was worthy of better things than the dreary job of compiling stale sensations. Both expectations having failed, Tommy's ingenuity sought another channel.

Although Dan Adriance was a meager and grudging source of information about the Crosbies, Tommy's persistent questioning had elicited a few pertinent facts, one of which was that Laurie had a strong penchant for music. Here was a hopeful indication.

Music filled the air of New York in those days. Small, untuneful German bands blared brassy disharmonies from the sidewalks, the musicians gazing hopefully upward at windows whence coins might be cast by the benevolent. The Salvation Army challenged Satan with drum and trumpet on chosen corners.

Laurie Crosbie, having a pitiful heart for all those less fortunate than her happy self, kept a store of silver at hand for dispensation to the minstrels, sacred and profane. Perched in her favorite window seat on a mild April evening, she spoke across the room to Dan Adriance: "Here they come. Such forlorn little people. Nobody pays any attention to them."

A preliminary flourish on brass sounded from below. Through the open window came the syncopated batt-and-jinkjink of the tambourine, the spat-and-twang of an ill-played banjo, and the quaver of pleading voices:

> *"Jesus loves me, this I know,*
> *For the Bible tells me so."*

The music ended with a bump of the drum and a bleat of the horn. The captain, a spindly fellow with a flaxen wisp of beard, testified passionately to the Lord's intense personal interest in him, the speaker. He proclaimed himself saved and bespoke a like blessing for all his hearers. More of the same followed, each fervent soul taking his or her turn in the revelation of glory. Traffic flowed past, unheeding.

From her window, Laurie saw a glaringly dressed youth approach the captain. After a colloquy the banjo was handed to the newcomer. He carefully retuned it, and ran a scale on the G-string. Even that simple exercise bespoke the expert. He struck a single chord and nodded. The captain announced to an imaginary crowd:

"Our brother in Christ will oblige with a sacred solo entitled 'The Poor Wayfaring Man of Grief.' "

"This is going to be *awful*," the girl said to her companion.

She made as if to cover her ears with her hands, but changed her mind abruptly as the opening notes reached her. The volunteer was singing as quietly as if he were repeating gentle thoughts to himself:

> *"A poor wayfaring man of grief*
> *Has often passed me on my way,*
> *Who begged so humbly for relief,*
> *That I could never say him nay.*
> *I had no power to ask his name,*
> *Whither he went or whence he came,*
> *But there was something in his eye*
> *That won my love, I knew not why."*

The strain was as simple and touching as the words. All the pathos and passion and pleading, all the loving kindness, the grievous acceptance, the grandeur and the humility of the Man of Sorrows spoke through the music. Even the abrupt pizzicato of the banjo-gut was purified to harp tones. It was infinitely tender; movingly human.

Windows were thrown open. Faces appeared and gaped in amazement. Hacks drew to the curb and stopped. The circle around the uniformed group swelled magically. Laurie Crosbie's nervous fingers closed and opened and closed again. A long, shuddering sigh parted her lips.

"Oh, Dan!" she breathed.

At the first sound of the music Dan had jerked galvanically from his chair and crossed the room to stare out the window.

"Great God!" he said, and began to laugh.

"Hush! Oh, hush!" the girl begged.

The voice took up the second stanza:

> *"I spied him where a fountain burst*
> *Forth from the rock. His strength was gone;*
> *The heedless waters mocked his thirst,*
> *He saw them, heard them hurrying on.*

I ran and raised the sufferer up,
Thrice from the stream he drained my cup,
Dipped and returned it running o'er,
I drank—and never thirsted more."

"Dan, I think I'm going to cry," the girl whispered.

A spell of silence was upon the crowd. The Salvationers lifted voices of praise. "Bless the Lord!" "Praised be His name!" "Let the Light shine." A man in opera cloak and silk hat jumped from a hansom, pushed through the ranks and thrust a bill into the tambourine. Others followed. Coins were tossed from near-by windows.

Plink-plink-plink-plunk, sounded the string. A hush fell again. The singer sang:

"Once when my scanty meal was spread,
He entered. Not a word he spake,
Tho' perishing for want of bread.
I gave him all; he blessed and brake,
He ate and gave me part again.
Mine was an angel's portion then,
And as I fed with eager haste,
The crust was manna to my taste."

Someone started hand-clapping. He was quelled. The deep rumor that filled the air was a more profound testimony. The singer stayed it with hand uplifted. Now the measure was slower, more solemn, with overtones of triumph and reverence:

"Then in a moment, to my view,
The stranger started from disguise,
The token in his hands I knew,
My Saviour stood before my eyes.
He spoke and my poor name he named,
'Of me thou hast not been ashamed,
These deeds shall thy memorial be,
Fear not, thou didst them unto me.'"

As the last clear note died away, the performer lifted his eyes to the girl in the window seat, and lowered them again. Laurie clutched at her companion's arm.

"Dan! Who is he? I've seen him before somewhere. Haven't I?"

"Yes. You bought candy from him. Ridley's Broken."

"Did I? How extraordinary! Is he in the Salvation Army?"

"Well, no. Not precisely." Dan looked amused.

"Then what is he doing with that banjo?"

"Serenading you, if you must know."

"What nonsense!"

"Not nonsense at all. This whole performance was staged for your benefit."

"Mine? How could he know—?"

"He asked me once what kind of music you liked, and I incautiously told him that you liked all kinds."

"It's an angelic voice. Do you suppose he'd come up if we asked him?"

"He'd jump at the chance. But are you sure you want him here, Laurie?"

"Oh, yes! Why not?"

"He isn't exactly your type, you know."

"What do I care! There must be something wonderful about anyone who can sing like that."

"It was a great performance," Dan admitted. "All right. I'll get him." He left.

Outside the Salvationists were vociferously proclaiming:

> *"I am saved (Boom!) saved,*
> *By the blood (Boom!) blood,*
> *I am saved by the blood of the (Boom-boom!) Lamb."*

The emissary crossed the avenue to the spot where the tambourinist was staring raptly at a little heap of bills and the others were crowding around Tommy with thanks and congratulations. Tommy broke away.

"Hello, Mr. Adriance," he said.

"Quite a stunt, Tommy," the reporter said. "Miss Crosbie wants to see you. Will you come up?"

"Wants to see me, huh? I thought the old voice would turn the trick."

Dan could have kicked him for his complacency. "Get a move on," he said.

They went up in the elevator, Tommy nervously patting and smoothing his coat. Laurie was seated in an armchair as they entered. She smiled at the stranger.

"Thank you for your song," she said.

"Oh, that's all right, ma'am," he replied airily.

"It's a lovely song. Where did you get it?"

"I had an old hen of an aunt used to sing it to me."

She regarded him with some disappointment. Tommy at close quarters lacked the seraphic quality of his music. The girl saw a rather commonplace youth of medium height, medium plumpness, medium coloring, medium everything. His face was chubby and fresh, his expression cheerful with a touch of impudence. He had rather large grayish eyes, and rather thick brownish hair. There was a general effect of good humor, self-confidence, and resilience, complicated in the present instance by a new bashfulness and uncertainty. He smiled vaguely and his face took on a cherubic quality.

Rather like a nice baby—Laurie thought. "Do you sing often with the Salvation Army?" she asked. "Do sit down, Mr. Howatt."

"No, ma'am, not often," he answered, distrustfully testing a spidery gilt chair before confiding himself to it.

"But you do know other sacred music?"

"Sac— Oh, hymns. Yes, ma'am. Quite a few."

"I wonder if you would do something for me sometime?"

"Look, lady! There's nothing in the world I wouldn't break my neck to do for you," he replied with such fervor that she was momentarily disconcerted.

"It's only to sing to my Sunday-school class."

"Surest thing you know. Where is it?"

"The Old Stone Church on the next block."

"That's Hellfire Farr's layout, ain't it?"

"I've never heard Dr. Brockholst Farr called that," she said in rebuke. "He is the best and dearest man I have ever known," she added with emphasis.

"Yes, ma'am," Tommy agreed in hasty apology. "I got nothing against him. The girls at Clark's call him that because—" He mumbled himself into embarrassed silence. This was no place to mention his habitual associations.

"When can you come?"

"Any time you say."

She pondered.

"Next Sunday?"

"Huh? Well—uh—yes; I guess so."

A doubt assailed him. "Look, miss, do I have to join the church?"

Her laughter rippled. "No. You needn't go that far."

"I don't reckon they'd let me in, anyhow, ma'am."

"I'm sure you could sing your way into heaven," she said gaily. "And don't call me 'ma'am.' I'm not your old-maid aunt."

"No, ma'—lady."

"Oh, dear!" said Laurie, but she looked at him with kindly eyes.

Tommy rose and brushed off imaginary dust from the knees of his trousers. "Well, I guess I'd better be on my way," he said with a praiseworthy effort at social ease. "Good night, ma'am."

"Good night, *sir,*" Laurie said, and laughed again.

"Oh, hell!" Tommy said, but he managed to repress it until he got into the hall, whither Dan accompanied him. Outside, he recovered his customary aplomb. "How'd I do?" he asked his companion. "Pretty slick, huh?"

"You damn hypocrite!" Dan said.

"Aw, cheese it!" Tommy protested.

"Faking that religious stuff."

"Look! That's no fake. I feel pious as all hell when I'm singing it."

"You've done the street stunt before, I'll bet."

"The Salvation Army turn? Sure."

"Where?"

"Oh, out through the West. Ten percent of the tambourine money."

"Did you get a rake-off tonight?"

"Not a dime! I didn't ask for any."

"Because you won't out of Miss Crosbie's Sunday-school class," Dan said, with intent to be disagreeable.

Tommy's face took on a rapt expression. "Look!" he said. "I'd do anything just to have a chance to see her."

"Are you imagining that you're in love with Laurie Crosbie?" Laurie Crosbie's pretended cousin demanded severely.

The question disconcerted Tommy. "In love," he repeated. "Yeah; I've read about that."

"And that's all you know about it, I suppose."

"I always thought it was hogwash."

"What about those moony poems of yours, then?"

The maligned poet grinned. "I get paid for 'em, don't I?"

"My advice to you is to quit your damnfoolishness right here and now."

"Never quit in my life," Tommy averred.

"Are you really going to show up at her Sunday-school class?"

"Surest thing you know."

"Don't get absent-minded and sing 'em some of your Tenderloin ditties."

"Look, Mr. Adriance," said Tommy, aggrieved. "I guess you don't have to tell me to respect a real lady." He waved his hand and walked downstairs with dignity.

Back with Laurie, Dan said, "You've taken on a contract, my child."

There was a suspicious quiver at the corner of her lips as she said, "You wouldn't care to come Sunday and hear the performance, I suppose?"

"No, thank you. You can tell me all about it later."

On Monday he dropped in at the apartment to get the report. "Well. Did your sweet singer appear?"

"Of course. Did you think for a moment that he wouldn't?"

"It wouldn't have surprised me to hear that he'd got stage fright and backed out."

"Poor dear!" she chuckled. "He *was* pretty scared! But he sang like an angel. The children loved it."

"Is it to be a regular Sunday feature?"

"Now you're being disagreeable, Dan. No, it isn't. I didn't have the heart to ask him. But I'm going to suggest that Dr. Farr invite him to the Sunday-school picnic."

"After which I suppose he'll join the church and be a little pink-winged angel."

"Dan, I don't think you're fair to the poor boy," she said pathetically. "He's never had a chance in life."

"Is that the line he's carrying now?"

She ignored this. "I believe down deep, he's good."

"Or that you can make him so. The unruly passion of the good woman to reform the bad man."

She repeated her fond delusion. "Nobody who is bad could sing as he does." Her face became thoughtful. "Dan, what is it in his singing that stirs one so—well, so uncomfortably?"

Dan knew well enough what it was. Unlike the run of tenors, Tommy's voice, for all its tenderness of appeal, was essentially, provocatively male. (Dan remembered Tommy's boast: "I can sing a bird out of a bush or a girl into a bed.") This quality, however, could hardly be explained to Laurie Crosbie. Dan's reply was vague.

"It would be fun if you'd bring him up here again sometime soon," the girl resumed. "I think he's too shy to ask if he may come."

It was on Dan's tongue to tell her of the potentially "good" Tommy's way of life in the Tenderloin; of Clark's and Nita and the fabled "woodpecker." That would put an end to her innocent illusions. He could not bring himself to it. Men did not give away their fellows in such matters.

Tommy received the unexpected invitation with a mixture of exultation and apprehension. He must have time, he told Dan, to ready up. When he appeared at Dan's apartment on the fateful evening, he was fearfully and wonderfully dressed for the occasion. Item: coat and waistcoat of an unhealthy steel-blue from the Six Little Tailors ("Fifth Avenue Style; Park Place Prices"). Item: Plymouth Rock Pants of a richly striped brown ("Latest Patterns, $3.00"). Item: Douglas's Three Dollar Shoes of the congress gaiter type, whose wrinkled elastic sides did not sufficiently conceal ten-cent white socks. Item: a lamentably jaunty tan derby with a faked Dunlap label pasted in the crown. Item: a cross-barred shirt in light blue with white rounded-corner Tynonga cuffs buttoned on. Item: the new Ubique E. & W. collar (pronounced by its devotees to rhyme with *unique*) a size too small, and snugged close beneath it a prismatic made-up ascot tie secured by a diamond pin worth a thousand dollars if it was worth a cent and had been genuine. Item: a tight pair of yellowish glacé gloves. Altogether Tommy was a striking spectacle. Dan maliciously foresaw the effect upon Laurie.

As the pair got off the Fourth Avenue car, Tommy stopped short on the sidewalk.

"Well?" Dan said impatiently. "What's up now?"

"Look!" Tommy said in hollow tones. "How does a fellow get started in this game?"

"Just say 'Good evening, Miss Crosbie,' and for God's sake don't call her ma'am."

"Okay," he said. "But—but what'll I *talk* to her about?"

"Oh, Shakespeare and the musical glasses," Dan said, with no intent to be helpful.

"That's Oliver Goldsmith, ain't it—isn't it?"

"Yes," Dan answered in surprise. "Don't tell me you've been reading *The Deserted Village!*"

"We-el, not exactly. I bought me a *Bartlett's Familiar Quotations,* second hand."

(Carefully "adapted" excerpts from which, Dan foresaw, would presently crop out in the pages of *Puck, Judge,* and *Leslie's.*)

"Be careful not to pick the too-familiar ones," he advised.

"Huh? Oh! I getcha, Steve. Look, Mr. Adriance! You'll be right there to help me out, wontcha?"

"Where would you think I'd be? On the fire escape?"

"Well, look; you do the talking, willya, and I'll wait for an opening."

Laurie was at her loveliest, smiling and demure, as she gave Tommy her hand. He took it limply, murmured a "How-d'you-do," bit off the terminal "ma'am," and lowered himself with extreme caution into a delicate and receptive armchair. The girl's eyes widened in momentary surprise as she took in the painful details of the visitor's costume. Mrs. Crosbie came in. Tommy was presented. He rose, mumbled a "Pleased-to-meetcha, ma'am," and sat down again. Fifteen minutes later, when Mrs. Crosbie excused herself, he was still clinging to the arms of his chair as if they were the gunwales of a storm-tossed skiff, while Dan and Laurie chatted. Tommy's face was set in a cast of intense concentration. Later he confessed to Dan that he was conning over various openings from *Polite Conversation for All Occasions,* which he had been studying in anticipation of this call.

Laurie had been telling Dan of the plans for the Sunday-school picnic, when Tommy sat up stiffly in his chair and addressed her with determination.

"Look, Miss Crosbie! Are you familiar with the works of Mr. Henry W. Longfellow?"

"Why, yes," said the girl. "I've read some of them."

"Which are your favorite selections?"

Thus put to it, Laurie named the two which came first to mind. " 'The Psalm of Life' and 'The Skeleton in Armor,' I guess."

"I can recite them both," Tommy said. "I took a school prize once in rhetoric. 'Horatius at the Bridge.' "

"Everybody recites 'Horatius at the Bridge,' " Dan interpolated.

Tommy, now in charge of the conversation, was not to be diverted.

"Doubtless," he said, still addressing the girl, "you are conversant with the literature of Mr. Rogers Kipling."

"Who? Oh, Rudyard Kipling. I think he's wonderful."

"And Thomas Nelson Page? His novels are considered by competent critics to be instructive and meritorious and to maintain a high moral tone."

"I'm afraid I haven't read enough of them—"

"Look! Do you prefer prose or poetry, Miss Crosbie?"

"Why, I hardly know," poor Laurie answered.

It was high time for the rescue squad. Dan said, "Mr. Howatt is something of a literary figure himself."

Tommy made hoarse, deprecating noises. "Aw, cheese it, Mr. Adriance," he muttered. He looked apprehensively at the girl, but she had taken no cognizance of Dan's remark.

"Perhaps you would sing for us," she said.

"I gotta cold."

The conversation languished. Tommy undertook to restore it to the subjects on which he had so carefully prepared himself.

"Look, Miss Crosbie," he began. "Are you familiar with the works of—?"

He broke off with a wounded look as Laurie began to laugh. "Oh, no!" she protested. "I'm not up to Chautauqua standards. I'm a very commonplace sort of person, Mr. Howatt."

Tommy rejected this feebly, and fell into an unhappy silence. He took no part in the personal talk that proceeded with enviable ease between the other two. Indeed, there was no place for him in it. He reflected bitterly upon the two dollars squandered on the *Polite Conversation* book. When Dan Adriance rose, Tommy got up with relief.

Outside, he said gloomily, "I guess I was just a goddam flop."

"Why didn't you sing when she asked you?" Dan inquired.

A crafty look came into the grayish-green eyes. "I couldn't think of anything to sing," he lied.

He could have thought of twenty suitable songs. And he fully intended to sing for Laurie Crosbie, at his own time and choice. That would be when they were alone together.

Life, in Laurie Crosbie's opinion, was good. Being rich was grand. The source of the riches gave her little concern. Somewhere down in the Southern Tier at a town called Empery, so she was informed, bubbled and gushed an oil well left to her by the father she had never known. Its unfailing current flowed straight into the vaults of the Corn Exchange Bank, where, by some beneficent financial alchemy, it was transmuted into a stream of dollars.

For Laurie the bank was a place of enchantment, the grizzled cashier who attended her wants a genie of infinite potentialities, summonable by the mere rubbing of a pen against a check.

"Good morning, Mr. Blauvelt. How much money have I got today?"

A confidential murmur from the amiably smiling cashier.

"Oh, my! All that! Isn't oil wonderful!"

Mr. Blauvelt agreed that oil *was* wonderful.

"Then I can draw out a lot?"

Miss Crosbie was informed that her account was in a healthy condition and could withstand quite a strain.

"A thousand dollars?"

"Certainly."

"*Ten* thousand dollars?"

"Yes."

"Well, I don't want it. I just like to know that it's there if I do need it. Let me have fifteen dollars, please, sir."

She was not always so moderate. One morning, with Adriance in attendance, she cashed a check for five hundred dollars. Dan protested.

"That's too much money to carry around with you."

"Oh, it won't last long," was the airy reply.

"What are you going to do with it?"

"Spend it. Buy you a gold watch."

"No, you're not."

"Why aren't I? It's my money, isn't it? And your birthday's coming. You're awfully old, aren't you, Dan? Just think! You'll be thirty before you know it. And you told me, yourself, it didn't keep time." Laurie's mode of conversation was frequently skipful.

"The watch is all right."

"You needn't be so stand-offish. I'll buy it for that funny Tommy Howatt, then. I'll bet he'd take it."

"That's a safe bet."

"You don't really like him, do you, Dan?"

"I like him well enough. But—"

"But you wouldn't approve of my giving him a watch. All right." She dismissed the subject with a queenly wave of the hand. "Just the same, I'm going to give you a birthday present that you can't turn down. Wait and see."

"I'll keep an eye out. You haven't seen him since that evening, have you?"

"No. When are you going to bring him again?"

"Why this consuming interest? Have you fallen for his sartorial splendors?"

"Don't make fun of the poor thing, Dan. He's never had much chance, has he? I surely would like to hear him sing again."

Apprised of the good news, Tommy was elated. "Look, Dan. Put me wise about the layout, will you?"

"What do you want to know?"

"A lot of things. Where does Harrison M. Perley come in? Uncle Harry! Uncle, my pratt! How does he come to be her uncle?"

"He's her guardian. How do you know she calls him 'Uncle Harry'?"

"I heard her at the Sunday school. Besides, he's in and out at the apartment all the time."

"Yes? And where do you get so much information?"

"When I wrote the *P.G.* story that you and R.K. bitched up, I interviewed the Valdevia doorman. He opened up like a paper bag, but not till after I'd slipped him two bucks. I had to live on Andy Horn's free lunch the rest of the week."

"You make me sick, Tommy. Of all the low-down, sneaking tricks! Bribing servants for information that you have no right to!"

"Well, you never tell me anything," retorted the justly aggrieved Tommy. "The old woman, now. What about her?"

"Do you mean Mrs. Crosbie?"

"Sure, I mean Mrs. Crosbie. Where does all the dough come from?"

"Oil," Dan said shortly. "Down around Olean. Now, how about minding your own business for a change?"

"Oh, all right! Only I think there's something fishy somewhere. When do we get to go?"

Tommy suffered three days of impatience before Dan notified him that Laurie was expecting them that afternoon. He had been preparing himself.

"Look, Dan," he began. "I guess I was off on the wrong foot before, thinkin' she was literary. How about art? My conversation book has got a slick chapter on art."

"Forget that damned book," Dan advised. "You'll do better on your own."

A smiling Laurie greeted them. Tommy did do better this time. His handshake was still flabby, but he made a gallant attempt to abstain from saying "ma'am," and he lowered himself into his chair more trustfully than on his previous call. As Mrs. Crosbie came in, something was said about Dr. Farr and the Old Stone Church.

"Farr?" Tommy put in. "The Doc and I are like that." He hooked his middle finger over his forefinger.

"Really?" Laurie looked interested.

"I been interviewin' him on this clean-up campaign of his. He don't know yet what he's lettin' himself in for. I gave him some pointers that curled his whiskers. What that bird don't know about New York! He ast me to keep him up to date. Well, if I can't, who can?" Tommy's chest protruded.

"Is that the political reform movement?" the girl asked.

"Yep. Crazy in the head, if you ask me."

"I don't believe it's crazy a bit," Laurie said stoutly. "I've sent Dr. Farr a check."

Mrs. Crosbie said, "Five hundred dollars. Mr. Perley does not approve."

"Uncle Harry generally disapproves of the way I spend my money." Laurie laughed. "But I wish I could find out more about it. Dr. Farr is so reticent."

Dan, reflecting that the nature of the Farr investigations was hardly a subject for a young girl's ears, broke in with a suggestion that Tommy sing something.

"Oh, yes!" Laurie seconded. "Please do, Mr. Howatt."

"Well, all right." Tommy rose. "What'll it be?"

"The song you sang for the Salvation Army," Mrs. Crosbie suggested.

"Oh, no!" Laurie interposed quickly.

"What's wrong with that?" Tommy asked, discountenanced. "Didn't you like it?"

"I loved it. It made me cry."

"I pretty near cry, myself, while I'm singin' it."

"But I don't feel like crying."

"Okay. I'll sing you a little thing of my own," he said, with his air of showmanship. "Words and music by T. Howatt."

He seated himself at the piano. The words were commonplace and the music a crass theft from the Gilbert and Sullivan operetta, *Iolanthe*. Laurie's lack of appreciation was expressed in perfunctory words. Tommy rotated the stool to face her.

"Didn't think much of it, huh?"

"Not very much."

Tommy glanced around. Mrs. Crosbie and Dan were bent over plans for the projected house on Riverside Drive. In a lowered and cleverly saddened tone, Tommy said, "I don't expect you think much of me, either, Miss Laurie."

Her laughter was a bit forced. "What kind of an answer do you expect to that, Mr. Howatt?" she asked with a touch of annoyance.

Instead of replying, he turned back to the keyboard, touched it gently, and sang under his breath the first stanza of "How Can I Leave Thee?" then looked at her across his shoulder.

All the annoyance had passed from her face. "Don't stop," she breathed.

He changed from English to the lovely, simple German of the original:

> *"Blau is das Blümlein,*
> *Das heisst Vergissmichnicht."*

At the end of the song, the singer had the art—or artifice—to rise and leave the piano. Laurie, breathing tremulously, spoke her uneven and effortful thanks.

Her mother was looking at her now with a little frown. Mrs. Crosbie spoke: "That was charming, Mr. Howatt. Where did you pick up German?"

"Workin' in hashhouses in the Northwest," he answered readily.

Dan filled in with, "Give us something else, Tommy." He, too, was covertly eying the girl.

"Some other time."

Laurie caught it like a cue. "Oh, yes!" she said. "You must come back. Mustn't he, Mother?"

"Yes," said Mrs. Crosbie nervously and without warmth.

"Sure," said Tommy.

His satisfaction was dimmed when the girl turned to Adriance. "You must bring him, Dan."

Dan nodded. Shortly after, the callers took their leave.

The next visit was of the nature of a one-man concert. Tommy sang until his repertoire of respectable numbers was exhausted. Dan and Mrs. Crosbie applauded at appropriate intervals. Laurie sat quiet, with that rapt, dimmed look which the others had noted before. She spoke hardly a dozen words to the musician.

On the occasion of the next call, he had better luck. While fumbling for some introductory chords, he found himself left alone in the room with Laurie. He plunged.

"Let's make a deal," he said.

"A deal?"

"Yes. Look, Miss Crosbie. I'm an ignorant sort of fella."

"Ignorant? Of what? I don't think I know what you mean," Laurie said, taken quite aback.

"Sure, you do. I don't know anything about the things that you and your mother and Dan Adriance and folks of that kind are—well, you know—are kinda born with."

"Why, Mr. Howatt—"

"Look," he interrupted, "I want you should learn me."

"*Teach* me," she said, mechanically falling into the role.

"That's it!" he cried, delighted. "That's the ticket. That's what I mean."

"But why me?"

"Who else have I got?" he asked simply.

"It's flattering." She smiled. "But I don't exactly see myself as a schoolmarm. What's my end of your 'deal'? What do I get out of it?"

"Why—well—I kinda thought— Look, Miss Crosbie; you like music."

"I love it. Are you offering to give me singing lessons?"

"No. But I thought if you'd sorta help me out with the way I talk and the way I act and all that, I'd be glad to sing for you any time. I'll pip up my old stuff and I'll catch up with the new songs. All I ask is that you lemme come here and talk with you and you jump me when I go wrong. I got a long ways to go. I know that. But I'm on my way, and I'm goin' to get there. Only, I need help at the start."

Laurie smiled upon him like a seraph. "Of course, I'll be glad to help you," she said. He glowed visibly with satisfaction. "So will Mother," she added, which considerably diminished the glow.

Notwithstanding his crudities, Tommy's knack of ingratiation was considerable on any social level. Within a month of the evening when he sang to and for Laurie, he had become almost as much of a familiar in the Crosbie household as was Dan Adriance. Thanks to Laurie's easy kindliness, he was gradually relieved of his early gaucherie and would sit amidst the luxurious clutter of the front room talking about himself, his work, his plans, his ambitions, with never-flagging ardor. If he was the only caller, the evening would end with him on the rotary piano stool, Laurie listening, rapt and lost in the music, and Mrs. Crosbie a dim but watchful chaperone.

Dan Adriance observed developments with interest and curiosity. One day he commented casually to Laurie: "Young Mr. Howatt seems to be making hay here."

"Mother loves to hear him sing," she said demurely.

"And you love to hear him call you ma'am, I suppose."

"Oh, Tommy's coming along. Give him time."

"Is he 'Tommy' now?"

She considered him thoughtfully. "Are you being cousinly, Dan?" she inquired. "You don't approve?"

"Would it make any difference whether I do or not?"

"Dr. Farr thinks that there's a lot of good in Tommy," she said.

If Tommy was not "coming along" too rapidly, it was no fault of Laurie's. Every very feminine woman has a touch of the joyous bully in her make-up. Laurie took to exercising that penchant upon her pupil. When a woman thus assumes an attitude of proprietorship, she accords to the man the privileges of a vassal. Tommy played his part well. He was a quick and receptive learner. He assured her that self-improvement was the main desire of his soul, and that the Crosbie household was the one refining influence he had ever known in his rough-and-ready life.

Laurie bullied and badgered him, and he loved it. She jeered him about his clothes. She made him discard the mock diamond pin from his tie and the fake ruby ring from his finger. She rigorously banned his congress gaiters and his pseudo-Dunlap derby. ("And don't be smarty and call it a tile.") Nobody, she informed him, went to Nicoll the Twelve Dollar Tailor, nor were Levy's Dollar Delight shirts the habitual wear of gilded youth. She made out a list of the proper shops. Tommy, adoring and submissive, plunged into debt.

No detail escaped her critical observation.

"Tommy" (sniff-sniff!), "you've got something on your hair."

"Yeah. Barry's Tricopherous. Pretty tony, huh?"

"That's a horrid word."

"Well, classy then."

"That's worse. And" (sniff-sniff!) "it smells awful."

"Look, Laurie. Mr. Ward McAllister uses it. The ads say so."

"I don't care what the ads say. You're not Ward McAllister. Go and wash it off."

"But, look, Laurie—"

"*Do* stop that silly 'Look! Look! Look!'" She mischievously mimicked his upstate nasality.

77

"Oh, *rats!*" from the pestered youth, which only got him a lofty reprimand:

"I don't like cheap slang."

All this friendly persecution, instead of adding to his self-consciousness, built Tommy up in his own esteem. His goddess was taking a personal interest in him. When other callers were present, he was still something of an awkward bumpkin. But when he was alone with Laurie and her mother, he was his natural and often picturesque self, and would sit, relaxed and happy, holding forth on his favorite topic. His two hostesses became well informed upon that fascinating subject, Mr. Thomas Howatt, his life, his career, his opinions, his ambitions, and his prospects on the *Police Gazette*.

These latter, they gathered, were disappointing. The young employe was not, it appeared, valued at his true worth by his superiors. They were unreceptive to the new ideas issuing from his fertile mind. He even hinted darkly that, unless there was a change of official attitude, he might be impelled to seek other employment and leave the *P.G.* flat. All this was a cover for his fear of losing his job.

He was still maintaining the bluff for Dan Adriance's benefit as the pair of them walked up Fifth Avenue on a bright May afternoon to call at the Valdevia and take Laurie Crosbie out for the latest thing in drug-store refection, the newly invented vanilla ice-cream soda.

As they came to Madison Square, Tommy broke off his complaints to say, "What's that swell candy place, Dan? Named after a duck."

"You mean Maillard's?" Adriance surmised after some thought.

"That's it. Mallard's. Is that about the classiest joint in town?"

"Well, that or Huyler's."

"Let's stop there."

Dan nodded. He stood outside while the other went in to make his purchase. When Tommy returned he had a daintily wrapped box under his arm.

"Jeez!" he exclaimed. "Two smackers for this and I bet it's no tastier than Ridley's Broken."

"What's all the free-spending for?" his companion inquired.

"Little celebration. Tell you later."

Tommy presented his costly sweets with a bow straight from *Etiquette for All Occasions*.

"Thank you, Tommy," Laurie said. "I love Maillard's. But what's it all about? It isn't my birthday or anything."

"I've struck it," Tommy announced with a lordly gesture.

"A big story?" the girl said indulgently.

"No. Money. Real mazuma. I'm going to let Dan, here, in on it."

"Another stemberry deal?" Dan asked.

"Nah! That was chicken feed. This is Wall-Street-size stuff." He paused, then said impressively, "Fellow I know has invented a chemical wash for postage stamps."

"Where is the money in that?" the girl said.

"Don't you see? Wash the cancellation off, put a dab of stickum on the back, and sell 'em for new."

"At two cents apiece? It wouldn't be worth the work."

"You don't know what you're talking about," he cried, forgetting his manners in his enthusiasm. "Newspaper stamps run as high as five dollars. Soak 'em off, clean 'em up and sell 'em for four."

Laurie looked doubtful. "It doesn't sound honest to me."

"About as honest as shoplifting," Dan put in. "It'll land you and your friend in the federal penitentiary, Tommy."

"Not a chance!" Tommy protested. "I've seen the washed stamps. You can't tell 'em from new with a microscope."

"That doesn't make it right, Tommy," the girl said.

"Right?" he repeated. "What's wrong about it? Nobody's gettin' hurt, are they?"

"Now you're getting excited and dropping your g's again," she reminded him.

"Can you blame me?" He brandished his arms in a nervous, characteristic, and forbidden gesture.

"Don't shoot your cuffs," said his relentless preceptress.

Tommy controlled his voice to the calmness of a suppressed croak. "Look, Laurie! Can't you see it ain't any more' dishonest than—"

"Isn't," she interrupted composedly.

"Huh?"

"Isn't. Not ain't," she said with sweet inexorableness.

"Oh, my *gosh!* Look, Laurie—"

"Aren't you ever going to stop using that idiotic 'Look'?"

"Oh, NUTS!" Tommy shouted.

The word was a bombshell. It carried with it in those days of verbal innocence, all the force and shock of its worst modern four-letter congeners.

Tommy's lower jaw dropped. His eyes glazed. He began to pant forth broken and apologetic incoherences. The girl rose and performed a queenly stalk out of the room. A door slammed down the hallway.

Dan bent a stern look upon his companion. "What's the matter with you?" he demanded. "Gone crazy?"

79

"I didn't mean it," the culprit gasped.

"You've cooked your goose this time."

Tommy stared at him, glassy-eyed. "That ain't—aren't—isn't, goddammit!—the half of it. I think I'm in Dutch at the office, too."

"Sorry to hear it, Tommy," said Dan, to whose ears a rumor had already come.

"It don't matter. Nothing matters now, only Laurie. She'll never speak to me again. Be a pal, Dan, and see if you can't get me out of it. Tell her I only meant rats, and the other slipped out between my teeth. Oh, geez! What a bum I made of myself!" He seized his hat and stumbled out.

After a time, Laurie came cautiously forth. "Has he gone?" she asked Dan.

"He's gone," the reporter assured her. "He left a message. All he meant was rats."

"I don't care what he meant. He's a vulgar, low-minded *creature*. I never want to see him again. Never!"

It struck Dan that she really meant it. Just as well, too—he thought. Tommy Howatt was no suitable house pet for any well-brought-up young girl. And there would be plenty of masculine attention to divert her mind from him.

The Valdevia apartment was on its way to becoming a popular resort for several of the town's gilded youth. Of the attendants who might be ranked as overt suitors there were three first-rank contestants: two cousins, Laurence Ranney and Piet Van Dorp, and Allen Hardwick. The cousins were of the social elite, rich, well born, and with much to offer. Ranney was a bit of a gay dog. He had something of a stage-door reputation, and was supposed to have been the lover of a famous chorus-girl beauty. His attitude toward Laurie was correctness, itself, and he had asked permission to bring his mother and sister to call. Van Dorp was of a solider type. He was a grandson of the "Dunderhead" Van Rensselaer, whose error of stupidity was supposed to have elected John Quincy Adams President of the United States. Piet inherited much of the stolidity of his Dutch ancestry, and with it the doggedness, integrity, and steadfastness of the breed.

Allen Hardwick seemed to be Mrs. Crosbie's favorite candidate. He was an attractive chap, with his stalwart frame, his rugged handsome face, and his friendly manner. There was in him a quiet gaiety, an inherent strength, an instinctive gentleness and courtesy. Laurie, from the moment Dr. Farr had introduced them, had accepted him as her devoted slave. He was quiet, intent, and purposeful in his devotion. He, too, was a good match; already successful, beginning to be prominent in civic affairs, popular with older people: a little too much on the zealous side, perhaps, for joyous Laurie. That she liked and respected him was obvious; but there was no present evidence of anything more definite.

Within the privilege of his assumed relationship, Dan Adriance would rally the girl on her conquests.

"Well, Laurie, who's ahead this week in the race for your young affections?"

"There's no race, Dan. Don't be silly."

"In sporting circles they say it is no contest when one horse is so far out ahead that the others are nowhere. Who is it? Van Dorp?"

"I don't want to marry Piet."

"He'd make a good husband."

"He's so Dutch. And so dumb."

"Allen Hardwick, then?"

She chuckled. "I could never live up to him. He'd want me to be too good."

"Larry Ranney?"

"He'd want me to be too bad," she said with unexpected shrewdness.

"I can't canvass the whole court of your Majesty. Is there some modest, yet aspiring, violet lurking in the background?"

"No, there isn't! Why are you and Mother so anxious to marry me off? Aren't I all right as I am?"

To all outward appearances, Miss Crosbie was very much all right as she was.

It was only natural that Mrs. Crosbie should be concerned for her daughter's future. But Dan was surprised when she broke through her habitual reserve to bring up the subject. Since the episode of the *Police Gazette* and Dan's good offices in preserving Laurie's anonymity, her reserve had been greatly modified. She was disproportionately grateful to the reporter.

"I hate that sort of thing, Dan," she said on the occasion when she first used his given name.

"Why?" he asked.

"Young girls ought to keep out of print."

"It's going to be hard to keep anyone with Laurie's beauty under cover, Mrs. Crosbie."

She looked at him earnestly. "Do you think she's so beautiful?"

"Of course. Everybody does."

"I want her to marry. I want to see her safely and happily settled. For a long time I hoped—I thought you might be getting fond of her, Dan." She gazed at him anxiously.

"Mrs. Crosbie," Dan said. "Laurie is a lovely child. I am a grown man. Nobody could be more devoted to her. But she no more thinks of me in any sentimental light than if I were an oyster."

"I'm afraid that is true. That is what troubles me. She never has shown any interest in any man. She treats them all as if they were— well, oysters."

"Give her time," Dan said easily. "She's hardly grown up yet. She'll fall in love one of these days."

"I'm so afraid she won't, Dan," the mother said. "I think there's something left out of her make-up; something she knows nothing about and perhaps never will know. She has an instinctive revulsion against the approach of a suitor. You must have noticed it."

Dan recalled his first real talk with Laurie and her shamed and shocked reaction when he laughed at her for her ingenuous disclaimer of "anything else" but a kiss.

"I thought she might have had some terrifying experience in her childhood," he said.

"No, there was never anything of that sort," Mrs. Crosbie assured him.

"You're not really worrying about her, are you, Mrs. Crosbie?" Dan asked.

She did not answer directly. "I wonder what you think about us," she murmured.

He said, "I'm not a very curious person. Not about my friends."

"No," she said. "No, you're not. That is good. I like that. You could be a good friend, Dan, at need."

"I hope so," he replied.

"There may be need."

"I hope not," Dan said.

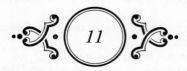

Whatever Tommy's faults as a *Police Gazette* staff member, lack of assiduity was not one of them. Modeling himself professionally upon the admired Dan Adriance, he had spared no pains to fit himself into the pattern of an all-around newspaperman, as he conceived it.

Dan was not wholly pleased at having acquired so insistent and worshipful an acolyte. His self-appointed pupil would drop in, uninvited and unannounced, at the Washington Square apartment, or call the *Star* office to suggest dinner at Katie's or some forty-cent-with-wine table d'hôte on Second Avenue, or say that he had an afternoon off and could he go along with the crack reporter and watch him at his work? Dan came to feel a reluctant liking for him, despite his callow push and brashness, his cocky self-assurance.

Also, the older, more experienced newspaperman was able to profit professionally by Tommy's surprising knowledge of the city's dirty political underlinen. In a few months the *Pinky* man had delved deeper into the seamy side of metropolitan politics than had the *Star* reporter in his whole term of service. The Tenderloin was an academy for him who would learn.

The Public Library on Lafayette Street soon accepted T. Howatt as a regular. There he specialized on how-to literature. He became an avid student of such instructional books as promised to make him a sparkling conversationalist, a practitioner of the most elegant etiquette, a publishable writer, a bottomless well of learning, and a master of any foreign tongue in six weeks of conscientious application. Not only would all this endeavor metamorphose him into a gentleman and a scholar: it would also, he innocently believed, advance him in his chosen calling.

The dreary routine of selecting items for Mr. Fox's paperback compendia had occupied him exclusively for the first few weeks of his employment. Then he began to get an occasional minor assignment or a small rewrite job. Here he was aided by Deacon Waldo, who had early taken a kindly interest in the tyro and edited his copy with a paternal eye. As Tommy's style developed, it assumed forms which were sometimes more picturesque than appropriate. Reporting a minor prize fight, he wrote:

In the fifth round Marko roused himself to action, became very sluggish, and hammered his opponent all over the squared circle.

Poising his editorial pencil above this, the Deacon summoned the writer to the copy desk.

"Tommy, what do you mean by sluggish?"

"Why—why—you know, Deacon. He slugged the other guy."

"You'd better get a thesaurus."

"What's that?"

"A kind of dictionary. It'll teach you about words."

Tommy devoted $3.50 of his hard-earned salary to the acquisition of Mr. Roget's valuable book. It was a lot of money, but if Old Reliable said so, it must be worth the price.

Another effort brought him to the attention of R. K. Fox himself. It was a rewrite job, pat to the *P.G.* formula; a church elder in a New Jersey town, caught *in flagrante delicto* with a fellow elder's wife. After inserting some sprightly touches, Tommy wound up with what he considered a happily appropriate moral reflection:

Well for Elder Mullins had he taken counsel of the Sage's wise warning: "The posture is ridiculous, the pleasure momentary, and the results lamentable."

Somehow the story got past the Deacon's watchful eye and into the proof, in which form it reached R. K. Fox's desk. Tommy was summoned to the sanctum.

"Howatt, did you write this?"

"Yes, sir."

"Do you read the magazine?"

"From cover to cover."

"Have you ever seen anything like this in it?"

"Well," said the young man modestly, "I thought it was pretty good, myself."

"Then you're a blasted fool," shouted the editor, hammering the offending print before him. "We don't allow such dirt in the *P.G.*"

"Why, Mr. Fox," his employe expostulated, "that's Benjamin Franklin."

"I don't care if it's Dwight L. Moody. D'you want to bring Anthony Comstock down here, stopping the presses? This is a decent

84

paper. None of your Ben Franklin tripe. He was an old rip, anyway. Now, get out!"

Two weeks later the offender redeemed himself by a two-stick piece of his own composition, beginning:

The night train from Washington rumbled into the Pennsylvania Station, drawing the fine new sleeping cars, Insomnia and St. Vitus.

It brought an almost tearful assistant general passenger agent of the Pennsylvania into Mr. Fox's office, where he was diplomatically soothed and presently persuaded to sign a contract for a year's advertising, on the tacit understanding that nothing further detrimental to the railroad's interests would appear in the pink columns. As a producer of revenue, Tommy was warmly commended and had his salary raised. At twelve dollars a week he was on his way.

Still he was not relieved of the drudgery of scissoring and pasting. To relieve the monotony, the unwilling bibliographer fell to a study of back numbers of competing publications. He was not lacking in the journalistic instinct. His investigations developed the heretical notion that the *Pinky* was not as good as it might be. Shrewd questions directed to the circulation and advertising departments hardened his suspicion into conviction. He awaited his opportunity.

It came through Deacon Waldo. Observing with sympathetic interest the neophyte's industry, which often kept him at work after regular hours, Old Reliable asked him, "What are you sweating over, son?"

Tommy raised reddened and print-strained eyes. "Trying to find out what's wrong with the paper."

"There's nothing wrong with the paper."

"The hell there ain't!"

"Tell it to R.K."

"Would he listen?"

"Sure, he'd listen." The Deacon pointed to the framed wall sign. "You'd better have your facts, though, if you don't want to get fired."

"Let him fire me. I'm not getting anywhere with these goddam clippings."

"You're getting your pay. More money than you're worth, at that."

"To hell with the money!"

This was bravado. Nevertheless Tommy had been reckoning up his assets. His salary took care of his necessities, with a little to spare. What he made on the side from his jokelets and verselets was velvet. He had nearly seventy-five dollars in the sock: a respectable reserve fund.

He waited his opportunity and presented himself at the editorial sanctum, with the latest bound volume of the *P.G.* under his arm.

"Ah. Our young giant-killer," the owner greeted him genially. "How goes the job?"

"Not so good, Mr. Fox."

"Why? What's wrong?"

"I came here to learn the newspaper business, and what do I get? A pair of scissors and a paste pot, to make up a lot of books that'll never sell."

(The prophecy was sound. The first and second issues languished on the newsstands; the third died in the printer's hands.)

"Why won't they sell?" the progenitor of the scheme demanded.

"They're full of the same old stuff."

"It's *Gazette* stuff. The *Gazette* sells."

"Not as much as it ought to," Tommy said, and added with deliberation, "Not as much as it used to."

Touched on the raw, for circulation had been slumping, Mr. Fox turned sardonic. "And what's your diagnosis, Dr. Whatever-your-name-is?"

Here's where I get the boot—thought Tommy. "The paper's dull," he said.

The swivel chair creaked with the convulsion of its occupant's burly body. "Dull?" he exclaimed. "The *P.G.* is dull?"

"Yes, sir. Same old stuff over and over. Folks are beginning to get sick of it."

"One hundred thousand barber shops take it." Mr. Fox was exaggerating generously. Why should he be on the defensive, anyway, with this young squirt?

"Yeah!" the young squirt retorted. "The *Barber-Shop Bible*. That's what they call it."

"Let 'em! A hundred thousand subscribers is a pretty good start."

"Start, huh? One of these days it'll be a finish," Tommy prophesied. "Who else takes it? Did you see about that lawyer examining a man for jury duty in that murder case?" He quoted:

"QUESTION: Do you read the *Police Gazette?*
ANSWER: No, I shave myself."

"I don't think that's so doggone funny," Mr. Fox snapped.

"There's a point there, though. Where does he shave himself, Boss?"

"On the face, I suppose."

"In his home," Tommy corrected. "Why don't we go after home circulation? There's more homes in this country ten times over than there are barber shops and barrooms and whorehouses put together."

"We're not putting out a home paper. The *P.G.* is for men."

"There's a lot of women in the world, too," the cub suggested.

"The *P.G.* is full of woman-stuff."

"Woman-stuff for men. Not woman-stuff for women. What does a woman care for other women's legs?"

"Don't get flip with me, young fellow," the sensitive owner warned. "We have to have something to make the drummers cackle. Legs are as close to the real thing as we dare to come, with Anthony Comstock poking his long nose into everybody's business. What's the matter with legs anyway? God made women with 'em, didn't He?"

"One pair of legs is all right," Tommy conceded. "But legs on the first page and legs on the last page and legs in between— Look, Boss, what are we running? The Centipede Special? Every time another cover comes up with a chippy's bare knees peeking out of her panties, I wanta puke!"

"Puke outside," Mr. Fox growled, pointing to the door.

Judging that he was on the skids now, the critic lost all caution. "If you like to lose circulation, it's all right by me. And look at our advertising. Look what we're missing there."

"What d'you mean, missing? We cover our field."

"Yeah! The For Men Only field. Don't you figure that women are buyers, too? What do we carry? Cheap sport goods, gambling gimcracks, marked cards, and crooked dice. How to beat the races. Hair restorers. Cheesy advice books. Clap cures. Lost manhood. We don't touch the home-woman field, and it's rich."

"Who does?"

"The Elmira *Telegram*. The Utica *Globe*." Tommy cited the two chief competitors of the *Gazette* in its chosen field.

Mr. Fox turned red. "You've been reading those stink-sheets?"

"I've been studying 'em."

"Then you'd better look for a job on one of 'em. Good day to you."

Outside, Tommy ran into Deacon Waldo.

"How'd it go, Tommy?"

"I think I'm fired."

"Oh, deary-dear! What did you do?"

"Told him the truth about his stinkin' old mag."

"Shouldn't have done it. He's a grand man, R.K., but he can't stand to hear anything against his *P.G.*"

"I didn't have a chance to spring my notes on him," Tommy said ruefully, taking some sheets from his pocket. "Sat up till midnight working on 'em, too."

A cunning gleam came into the gentle old face. "Show," the Deacon said, extending his hand.

Tommy handed him the copy. He glanced through it. "Mmm," he murmured. "No— Mmmm. Might— Mmm. Don't think so— Hmm-ha! Naughty-naughty—! Mmm. Can't tell."

"I suppose *you* think it's no good, huh?" said the belligerent Tommy.

"I'll tell you," Old Reliable said with an air of candor and help-fulness, "you got R.K.'s dander up. If you turn this in to him now, he'll chuck it into the spittoon. I know him. You leave it with me, and when he cools off, I'll see he gives it a reading. Stay away from the office till the chief cools down. Say a couple of weeks."

It was at the beginning of this period of uncertainty that Tommy uttered the disastrous monosyllable which rendered him outcaste at the Crosbie home. From there he returned to his hall bedroom and spent some days pouring out his soul in woeful measures with a double purpose. If not effective in melting the heart of his lady, some of them might at least prove marketable. He was going to need the money, too, now that he was shut off from the stamp-wash deal by Laurie's interdict. Laurie! What would she care if he went to jail! What did he care, himself, for that matter! All was lost by that one haphazard word. Nevertheless he bought a fresh pad and continued his pursuit of the muse.

About this same time Laurie asked her friend and counselor, "Dan, do you know any poets?"

"Superficially. Tennyson, Browning, Austin Dob—"

"I mean, personally?"

"Yes. I know E. S. Martin and Clinton Scollard."

"Somebody's been writing love-poetry to me."

"I don't believe it's either of them. They're respectable married men."

"These poems are *very* respectable. The postman brings me one a day. Hand printed. Unsigned. *Who* do you suppose it could be?"

"Hm," said Dan. "Probably that well-known lyric poet, Anony-mous."

"You aren't much of a help, are you!"

"Give me time. I've got a clue."

When Tommy next appeared at Dan's Washington Square apart-ment, he opened the conversation with his usual wistful query: "Has she said anything about me?"

"Hasn't mentioned your name."

"Look, Dan. How about my writing her a letter? Respectful as hell, of course."

"I doubt if she would read it."

"I doubt it, myself," Tommy said lugubriously.

"You've been sending her poems, haven't you?"

"Yes, and that's all it got me."

"Perhaps the style is over her head."

"You're a sympathetic guy, I don't think! Some of 'em are pretty swell, if I do say it, myself. I don't suppose you'd—huh?"

"All right." Dan was resigned. "I'll take a look."

The lovelorn poet produced a specimen of his latest wares. Dan read:

> *This is the end of all things kind and good.*
> *This is the last of striving and desire.*

"Echoes of Algernon!" he commented and continued his reading.

> *Had you been kinder, had you understood,*
> *I'd not be standing by a dying fire,*
> *Warming my heart at memory's last glow,*
> *Before I, too, into the darkness go.*

"Pathetic touch," the reader observed. "When does it come off?"

"When does what come off?"

"Your suicide?"

"Oh, nu—rats!" returned Tommy, who was training himself in abstention. "It's only poetry."

Dan continued:

> *For one base word, to ban me from your face,*
> *It was not like your graciousness and grace.*

"Coventry Patmore, too," he remarked and quoted the original:

> *"It was not like your great and gracious ways."*

"You can't claim that's plagiarism," Tommy defended himself. "Look how I changed it."

"Not for the better, I'd say."

"You think it's n.g.?"

"I wouldn't go that far. Try it on *Leslie's*."

"I'm going to. How do I know she reads *Leslie's?*"

"You don't."

Tommy's gloom was dispelled in some measure by developments at the *P.G.* office. The two weeks suggested by the Deacon had passed, and two days on top of that, when he was recalled from exile. This is what had taken place.

After Deacon Waldo's conference with Tommy, the veteran put in some overtime at the office, painfully finger-picking at the lone calligraph. The result was delivered on Mr. Fox's desk. It was a fairly skillful digest of Tommy's notes, and was headed "Suggestions for Enlargement" (which the prudent Deacon considered more tactful than Tommy's original "Improvement") "of the *Police Gazette,* by Gabriel N. Waldo."

The stolen suggestions were ingenious if not all practicable.

Confessions of a Streetwalker. First of a series to be followed by Ditto of Madam, Shirt-card Gambler, Snow Peddler, etc. (Mr. Fox nodded thoughtfully.)

How to Win at Policy, with a weekly list of the successful "gigs." (Might be all right, the proprietor thought.)

The City's Heroes: Brave Deeds of Police and Firemen. (Good. It would make useful friends for the magazine.)

Go after the woman circulation with a sentimental novel by the popular Miss Laura Jean Libbey, who is ready to write one to order for two hundred dollars. Suggested subjects: beautiful young pupil who makes up to the handsome principal and imperils her virtue. See P.G. for last July 5th. (Mr. Fox's handsome face took on an expression of frowning dubiety.)

Serial: Day Book of a Pimp. (Mr. Fox shook his head violently. Some words were rigidly barred from the *Gazette's* pages.)

Further suggestions to come if these were approved.

Mr. Fox was a shrewd judge of character. In thirty years of faithful service, Deacon Waldo had never been known to exhibit a gleam of originality. How account for this sudden proliferation of ingenuity? After thinking it over, the editor called up Miss Laura Jean Libbey, one of the few novelists in town prosperous enough to have a private telephone, and introduced himself.

Had a representative of the *Police Gazette* called upon her recently?

A genteelly languid voice answered yes.

Was he an old gentleman with white whiskers?

The voice, surprised now, said certainly not: he was a very young, pleasant-mannered youth in remarkable clothes.

"Blast my guts if I didn't know it!" Mr. Fox so far forgot himself as to say into the mouthpiece.

The voice said, "I *beg* your pardon, sir-r-r!"

"I beg yours," the editor said hastily and hung up.

The Deacon was put upon the editorial carpet. He broke down and wept under the inquisition.

"I thought it might get me a raise of five dollars a week," he quavered. "My granddaughter is getting married next month."

"You can have it, you old fool," the tender-hearted Mr. Fox said. "But don't try any more funny tricks."

The old man chirked up. "I thought it wouldn't do any harm, since the young fellow is fired anyway."

"He isn't fired; he's hired," the editor said. "At fifteen a week. Get him back here."

12

Job security restored Tommy's self-confidence, which had been shaken by Laurie's rejection of him. If only he could get a hearing, he was sure that he could break down her obduracy. How to reach her? That was the difficulty over which he pored.

No help could be expected from Dan Adriance. The *Star* man had made that clear. Casting about for some other go-between, Tommy thought of Dr. Brockholst Farr. Though hopelessly wrong-headed in his social theories, from Tommy's viewpoint, the pastor of the Old Stone Church was an essentially kind and fair-minded human being who would give a fella a boost in a good cause. Once he understood how harshly Tommy had been punished for a chance word, the clergyman would doubtless be sympathetic and could probably be enlisted in an effort to right the injustice. Anyhow, it was worth a try.

The maid at the parsonage took in the name of Mr. Thomas Howatt of the *Police Gazette* and returned with the message that he was to come to the study. The clergyman welcomed him pleasantly. Tommy gazed about him at what seemed to him an infinitude of books.

"Gosh! D'you read 'em all?" he asked.

"Most of them," the Doctor replied.

"I'm a sucker for culture, myself, but I couldn't get through that lot, not in a hundred years. I s'pose that's where you get your sermons."

"Those sermons of which the *Police Gazette* disapproves?" Dr. Farr smiled. "Are you preparing a new attack?"

"Nix, Doc, nix," Tommy assured him. "It isn't *P.G.* business this time."

"A personal call? That is pleasant. When are you going to sing for us again, Mr. Howatt?"

"That's just it. She hasn't asked me."

"She?" Dr. Farr's heavy brows went up.

"Miss Crosbie. And I'm scared she'll never ask me again."

"Indeed? Why so?"

"There's been a sort of a ruckus."

"Ruckus? A misunderstanding?"

"I guess I got fresh. I said the wrong word. I didn't mean to. It just slipped out."

In his unworldly way the clergyman was something of a romantic. He had come to feel for Laurie Crosbie the affection he might have given a daughter, and the idea of this poor, ambitious, self-improving young journalist humbly devoting himself to the rich and beautiful girl so far above him, stirred sentimental sympathies.

"Miss Crosbie, I am sure, is not one to resent permanently a little unintentional crudity," he said kindly. "Perhaps I could effect a composition."

"Gee, Doc! That'd be swell of you. Look! She comes here to see you sometimes, don't she?"

"Oh, yes; quite frequently. On church business."

"Well, look! Would you put me wise? So as I could kinda drop in while she was here?"

"Would that be quite straightforward?"

"Oh, hell! I s'pose not," said Tommy, depressed, and hastened to apologize. "Excuse *me,* Doc. That was a slip."

"I can well understand Miss Crosbie's resentment," the clergyman said coldly.

"I know." The young man's face expressed self-abasement. "I'm just a bum. But I'm trying to learn. She was helping me. Now it's all spoilt."

Dr. Farr was touched. "Do you wish me to intervene for you?"

"Yes . . . Well, I dunno. I got another idear. You know, Doc, that time I sang for her class, she said something about a Sunday-school picnic."

With an effort of memory Dr. Farr said, "Yes. She mentioned it to me at the time. As she did not bring it up again, it slipped my mind. You were to sing, were you not?"

"Yeah. That's it," Tommy confirmed.

"I am sure the children would enjoy hearing you again."

"You mean you're givin' me an invite?" Tommy asked, sacrificing a terminal *g* in his eagerness.

"I see no reason why I should not. It is to be next Saturday."

"Gee, Doc! That's swell of you. Only a few more days to wait. Holy—" He caught himself and repeated, "That's swell of you."

"You can profitably employ the interval in practicing control of your tongue," Dr. Farr suggested.

"Yes, sir. Just one more thing, Doc. She don't have to know I'm coming, does she?"

"Why should she not?"

"She might put the kibosh on it."

"If by that extraordinary expression you mean that you fear objection on Miss Crosbie's part, I think you have no cause for apprehension."

"Just the same, I'd sooner she didn't know, Reverend."

"Very well. I will stretch a point and say nothing."

Thanking him, Tommy reached for his hat, and, as he did so, brushed against a frail inlaid stand, which rocked under the impact. Two delicately carved ivory checkers fell to the floor and rolled. He replaced them, remarking upon their evident costliness.

"I'd be almost scared to play with 'em," he said.

"Are you a player, then?" his host inquired.

"Oh, I play now and then," Tommy answered with a casualness intended to deceive.

"It so happens that I have an hour of leisure. Would you care to try a game?"

"Don't care if I do," said Tommy. He set the board swiftly.

"Your movements suggest familiarity," the clergyman commented.

"Look, Reverend. When you're playin' as high as two bits a game, you gotta know your moves. I wouldn't wonder but what you're pretty hot yourself," he added patronizingly.

"Hot? Why, no; I feel no discomfort— Oh, I see! Well, I have so few opportunities of playing nowadays that I fear I have become rusty. In the words of the poet, 'non sum qualis eram.' "

"Come again, Boss."

"I beg your pardon. Should I be more intelligible if I adopted the vernacular and adverted to the words of a humbler poet, 'The old gray mare, she ain't what she used to be'?"

Tommy squinted at him suspiciously. "I getcha. You want odds, huh?"

"Why, no. If you will dispense with the stakes and make due allowance for an amateur, the equitable arrangement, I think, would be for us to start even, with a view to subsequent adjustments."

"Anything you say, Doc."

Dr. Farr hitched his chair into place, then regarded his opposite benignly. "It is a small matter," he said, "and I should be most reluctant to injure your feelings or to impair the growth of a developing friendship. So, I hope that you will accept my suggestion with understanding."

"Shoot, Doc," said Tommy, puzzled.

"A case in point. Your familiarity of address is flattering and doubtless well meant. But only my Elders call me Doc."

"Huh?" Tommy said, startled. "Your Eld—" He caught a quizzical gleam behind the spectacles. "Keno! I getcha." He laughed strainedly. "Okay, Parson."

"No, not Parson. Still less, Reverend. Dr. Farr, if you please. Or, if that be too formal, Dominie. Is that clear? Good! Take the first move."

"Yes, sir, Dominie," Tommy said.

The first game consumed seven minutes; the second, a little more than five. At the close of the fourth the guest arose. His face wore a slightly dazed expression.

"Look!" he said. "I guess I better go back to shootin' craps."

"You play very well, Mr. Howatt," the victor said, "but perhaps without due consideration."

("The old son-of-a-bitch!" Tommy said reverently, recounting the episode over a schooner of Andy Horn's lager that evening. "He ought to be a side-show automaton. I never had a look-in.")

Tommy made his farewells. At the door he stopped, fiddling with his hat.

"Doc-tor Farr."

"Yes?"

"You've been pretty swell to me."

"Not at all. I have enjoyed our association."

"If there's anything I can ever do for you, I'd go to—I'd break my neck to do it."

"I'll bear it gratefully in mind, Mr. Howatt."

"And, look! Couldn't you cut out that 'mister' business?"

"Why, yes, Thomas," the clergyman said with his disarming smile. "Come in when you feel inclined. I'll give you your revenge."

"I'll do that little thing," Tommy replied with fervor.

Every June the Old Stone Church, following an ancient tradition, held an all-day Sunday-school picnic. The festival was conducted under the aegis of an internal organization called the Little Crumbs of Comfort, which gave to the poor, the sick, and the needy. This year the place was the riverside estate of the Herrendens, old members of the congregation, on the west side of the Hudson below Haverstraw. A special two-car train was provided by the West Shore Railroad. Allen Hardwick was Grand Marshal for the occasion.

Laurie Crosbie's aggregation of eight-to-ten-year-olds reported at the Weehawken Ferry, short one member who had the mumps. This mischance put them out of competition for Hundred Percent Attendance, though their teacher still cherished hopes for the Neatest Appearance prize and perhaps for Best Behaved Class. Allen Hardwick had undertaken to help preserve order among them, insofar as his general duties would permit.

Laurie had another escort for the day in the person of Dan Adriance, who had come along on special invitation of his old friends, the Herrendens. He aided in herding her contingent aboard the ferryboat, then went forward to get a breath of air. On the open deck he was hailed by a cautious voice:

"Ss-ss-ss-sst! Dan!"

The door of a broom closet opened slightly. Tommy Howatt's head protruded. Dan crossed the deck. "What are you up to, my brash young lad?"

Tommy grinned. "I'm a Little Crumb."

"The hell you are! What's the game?"

"Just a song at twilight. I'm the songbird. It's a surprise."

"Does Dr. Farr know?"

"He's in on it. Here's my props." He exhibited an accordion with a color picture of Tony Pastor on the panel. Over his shoulder there hung by a strap one of those new contraptions, a Kodak camera. Dan identified it with interest.

"Going to take some pictures?" he asked.

"If I get a chance. Look, Dan, where is she?"

"Laurie Crosbie? Inside, talking with Allen Hardwick."

"That mealy-mouthed bastard!"

"Mind your words. Allen's no bastard."

"A holy-boly," Tommy sneered. "One of the Purity Boys. Betcha he never got a jag on or touched a woman in his life."

"Which makes him a bastard in your book."

"Look, Dan. Do you think she really likes him?"

"What business is that of yours?"

"Well, I don't see what the hell any girl could see in that sissy."

"That sissy is the crack middleweight of the Crescent Athletic Club. So maybe you'd be wise to keep your ideas between your teeth."

"Ah-h-h-h! I ain't afraid of him." Which, Dan thought, was probably if imprudently true.

By skillful maneuvering Tommy managed to get on the rear platform of the special, unnoticed, and, at the end of the ride, to make his way to the appointed place by a circuitous route.

The broad, sloping lawn of the Herrenden property was surmounted by a gracious Gothic mansion to which the new arrival straightway repaired to report to Dr. Farr. There he lunched in seclusion while, outside, the Little Crumbs festally gorged themselves upon frankfurters, oyster patties, chicken salad, charlotte russe, strawberry shortcake, three kinds of ice cream and four of pie, all liquidated with lemonade, cold cambric tea, sarsaparilla, and orange pop.

When the refuse was cleared away, Dr. Farr, advancing to the front of the pillared porch, opened the formal exercises with a prayer. An Address of Welcome by Trustee Harrison M. Perley was followed by the official song of the Crumbs, composed by the church organist and sung by the entire assemblage:

> *". . . From happy Christian homes it comes,*
> *The message of the Little Crumbs . . ."*

Crumblet Davies, aged ten, performed a tin-pipe solo with credit.

Junior Crumb Randall Van Patten delivered a Biblical passage with fervent piety.

Crumblet Alicia Merritt recited "The Wreck of the Hesperus" to generous applause.

Two Crumblets of opposite sex obliged with a humorous dialogue between a cat and a mouse. (Prolonged laughter.)

There were further recitations, patriotic and scriptural. The Comfort Fife and Drum Corps roused the echoes in a finale which evoked tumultuous enthusiasm. Distribution of prizes by the Grand Marshal brought to an end the regular program. Laurie's class got one for Best Behavior, which she accepted with the correct blush of modest gratification. Dr. Farr then announced as a special feature a sacred musical number by Mr. Thomas Howatt, whom many of them had heard before.

Laurie Crosbie, seated on a bench between Dan Adriance and Allen Hardwick, gave one little gasp and was very still.

The musician stepped through a French window and came forward, a performer's set smile on his lips. He shook out his instrument, squeezed a few experimental chords from its inner recesses, and began. His selection was a simple old ballad about the Garden of Eden:

> *"A very, oh, a very long time ago*
> *When God first made the flowers,*
> *There was but one man and one woman, you know,*
> *In this beautiful world of ours."*

He sang it as a child might have done, without art or emphasis, his face gentle, absorbed, strangely peaceful; his voice so just, so right in every pure intonation that the words took on meaning and beauty beyond their purport. It was as fine a bit of virtuosity as his Salvation Army performance—and as much of a stunt.

His small listeners were entranced. They edged forward as if mesmerized, taking possession of the steps, pressing close upon the veranda with avid, uplifted faces. When the last couplet died away,

> *"And God came down at the close of the day*
> *And talked with Adam and Eve,"*

clamor rose.

"Sing it over!" "Do it again!" "More!" "More!" "More!"

97

Tommy smiled like a cherub on a cloud. "You want to hear it again?" he asked cunningly.

"Yes!" "Yes!" "More!"

"Then you must sing it with me. Come on."

He lifted again the lovely, clear tenor. Laurie, in her seat below, closed her eyes. Here and there among the small fry a timid pipe was raised. Some of the older voices joined in for encouragement. Tommy coaxed, cajoled, beguiled.

"Never mind the words. Sing! Everybody sing!"

The swelling chorus seemed to inspire the leader. His eyes uplifted in pious rapture (What a faker!—thought Dan Adriance), he carried them all with him on the wings of the music. Dan felt the girl next to him shiver. Then Allen Hardwick spoke to her from the other side.

"Oh, yes," she said with a catch of the breath. "I'll be glad to."

She stood up, and for the briefest of moments Tommy sang straight to her. Then she was gone across the open space to help Allen organize the games: prisoner's base, blind man's buff, still-pond-no-moving, pom-pom-pullaway.

Dan joined those who were moving forward to thank and congratulate the singer. His own felicitations, when he got Tommy aside, were ambiguous.

"Good going! A little different from Clark's, eh?"

"The hell with Clark's!"

"You wouldn't oblige with 'Naughty Nita'?"

"What's eatin' you?" Tommy demanded angrily. He was ranging the place with anxious eyes. "Where'd she go?"

"Over yonder with Hardwick."

The profane response to this was cut short by Dan's raising a hand. "Listen to what's going on inside."

In the small front room Dr. Farr and his senior Elder had seated themselves. Weighty matters were under discussion, every word being clearly audible to the two young men outside. Brother Perley was protesting:

"No, no! I don't say that, Dominie."

"You imply it."

"This is a metropolis. Those places are—well, an unpleasant necessity. The best the police can do is to see that they are run in a decent and orderly manner."

"Decent!" Dr. Farr said bitterly.

"Oh, well, you know what I mean."

"I fear that I do, Brother Perley. I greatly fear that I do. When citizens of your position condone vice and lewdness, the outlook is black, indeed."

The trustee defended himself vigorously. "I don't condone it. I merely take a practical view. There's nothing effective to be done; those things exist. Let well enough alone. Don't involve the church in it."

"You say there is nothing to be done. I will confute you from my own experience. One of these hellholes has been closed following my individual protest."

"Which one?"

"The Hastings brothel."

Tommy nudged Dan. "Will you listen to that! Where in hell does the Doc get his info?"

"Where do you get yours, if it comes to that?"

"Look! Was I in there last night and had a drink on the house, or wasn't I?"

"Tell it to Dr. Farr," Dan suggested.

"What? That I was sporting around in a cathouse?"

"Not necessarily. Tell him you know the place is still open." He raised his voice. "Dr. Farr, Howatt has something he thinks you ought to know."

"I'll be glad to hear it," the Doctor said pleasantly. "Come in."

The pair entered and were cordially invited to partake of lemonade from an icily sweating silver pitcher on a stand. The clergyman looked inquiringly at Dan.

"We couldn't help but overhear, sir," the reporter said. "About Georgiana Hastings."

"Ah, yes. Now closed, as I was telling Brother Perley."

"Closed!" Tommy broke in. "Closed like Central Park. What galoot ever put that over on you?"

"Howatt is an expert on the Tenderloin, sir," Dan explained.

"So I am informed," Dr. Farr said, with a look that made Tommy uncomfortable. "And you wish me to understand, Thomas, that the Hastings place is still open?"

"Wide as a hornpout's mouth."

The clergyman looked stubbornly unconvinced. "After our talk at the parsonage, I paid a second call on Police Captain Schmidt. He assured me—"

"Yeah," Tommy interrupted. "I know what he assured you. I was in the station house next day. They were still laughin' their heads off. Doc, they made a ringtailed monkey outa you."

"Mind your manners, young man," Mr. Perley interposed in sharp admonition.

Tommy turned upon him. "You know dam' well that Georgiana Hastings never quit business for a night."

"How should I know?" Mr. Perley was annoyed.

"You got Tenderloin property, haven't you?"

"Leaseholds only. And I don't know how you are so familiar with my business," the contractor snapped.

"There isn't so much that the *P.G.* isn't wise to," Tommy informed him smugly.

"Brother Perley," the minister said gravely, "one of our finest young men contracted a foul disease there."

Mr. Perley was shocked. "That's impossible," he cried. "An accident, anyway. The Hastings girls are inspected. The police must have been negligent."

"Then you are aware that the police are involved," Dr. Farr charged.

"Only as a health measure," the other said uneasily. Consulting his watch, he announced that he must leave.

The clergyman rose and sighed. "I shall have to look into this further," he said.

There was still a good hour left before preparations for departure must begin. One traditional feature remained.

"Who's for the river?" Dr. Farr called out.

The Hudson, even in June, was a test for the hardy. A dozen virile souls, including Allen Hardwick, had brought bathing suits, and now followed their pastor into a room in the mansion set aside for them.

"Stinkin' show-off!" Tommy muttered to Dan, as Allen's stalwart form appeared, followed by Dr. Farr. "Jeez! Look at the Doc!" The clergyman, broad, gaunt, and rangy, was an extraordinary spectacle in his trunks and neck-high top-garment. "What a build for a tackle! I gotta get that." Unslinging his Kodak, he contrived to draw Dr. Farr aside while the rest of the bathing contingent went on.

"Know what that is, Dominie?" he asked, patting the box.

"Certainly. A Kodak. You press the button. But not in my direction. Point it elsewhere, if you please."

"What's the matter? Gun-shy?" Tommy chuckled, proceeding with his preparations.

"I have a natural prejudice against perpetuating the image of a physiognomy such as mine," Dr. Farr replied with a disarming grin. "Call it Mohammedan superstition, if you will. No photograph of me has been taken since my college days."

"Then it's time there was," Tommy declared.

He set himself to argument and plea. He descanted upon his regard and respect for the pastor. He wished to have the likeness of him as a keepsake, a memento, to carry about with him, a mascot. He hinted that it would act as a talisman to avert him from sinful ways. Dr. Farr was touched. He weakened.

"But you must keep it quite private," he said; adding shamefacedly, "My foolish parishioners have long harassed me to sit to the professional photographers. Having refused them, how shall I appear if I accede to your request?"

"Aw, a Kodak isn't the same thing," Tommy argued. "It don't amount to anything. Besides, nobody but me will ever see it, if you say so. I'll keep it under cover like it was a phony hundred-dollar bill."

"Very well. Upon that stipulation. I put you on honor, Thomas."

Dan Adriance having gone outside to speak to a friend, Tommy was left a free field for his operations. They were soon over, the subject loped off to the river, and the satisfied amateur rejoined his fellow reporter on the veranda.

"Am I coming up in the world! The Doc wants I should go to dinner at his sister's," he bragged to Dan.

"Congratulations. When's it coming off?"

"It ain't. I ducked."

"That wasn't too polite."

"Look, Dan. I'd be too scared to eat. Why, I don't even know which knife to load my potatoes onto."

"You'll have to learn sometime."

"Yeah? Those etiquette books don't tell you what you need to know," he said gloomily. He brightened up. "Anyway, mine didn't cost me anything."

"No? How's that?"

"Review copy. For the *Pinky*."

"The *P.G.* doesn't review books."

"I know that. But the sucker in the bookshop didn't. Got an ad out of him, too."

Dan stared at him with a sort of admiration. "You'll go far, young fellow, if you don't get sidetracked into Sing Sing."

"Not me. I stand in with the Right People."

A bugle sounded. "Twenty minutes to train time," a voice of authority announced.

The swimmers splashed to shore and rushed for their clothes. Tommy said to Dan, "Time to pack up the old squeeze-box."

Inside the small room where he had left his accordion, he noticed the pitcher of lemonade still a quarter full. Pouring out a glass, he sat down to enjoy it at ease. As he was drinking, he heard voices below the veranda, a man's and a girl's. He moved to the window for a look, stepped back, picked up his instrument and drew out a long chord, then sang in a half-voice:

> *"There is a lady, fair and kind.*
> *No other face so pleased my mind."*

He stopped. From below the girl's voice said breathlessly, "Oh, please!"

> *"I did but see her passing by,*
> *Yet will I love her till I die . . ."*

Footsteps mounted and advanced. Laurie Crosbie stood, staring at him with mazed eyes. He sang:

> *"Cupid is wingèd and doth range*
> *Hither and yon, his fancies change.*
> *But, change the earth or change the sky,*
> *Still will I love her till I die."*

She said, "Oh, Tommy!"

He said, "Who was with you?"

"Allen Hardwick."

"What became of him?"

"I sent him away."

"Why?"

"I don't know."

"I do." Without lifting his hands, he bent forward and kissed her softly on the mouth. She stood, quivering. "I'm coming to see you to-morrow."

"No. You mustn't." All that was virginal in her stood instinctively on defense.

"You wouldn't let me in?"

"Oh, Tommy! Please!"

"Are you scared of me, Laurie? You needn't to be."

He bit off an oath. Footsteps were approaching from the far end of the veranda. Allen Hardwick's handsome face appeared in the doorway.

"Oh, there you are, Laurie. I couldn't find any handkerchief. Hello, Howatt. Quite a treat you gave the kids."

Tommy said abruptly, "So long," tucked his instrument beneath his arm, and left. For him the day was over.

He called at the Valdevia the next afternoon. Laurie was "not at home." That was what he had feared. Lurking in an areaway opposite the apartment house, he saw Allen Hardwick admitted a few minutes later. He wrote to Laurie. She did not reply. He composed a melancholy and reproachful poem. No response.

Forced separation from his lady-love stimulated the pace of the Howatt Pegasus. Over the next few weeks Tommy poured out his poetic soul, with the aid of assiduous research among the Fourth Avenue bookstalls, in rhymed sentiments of the loftiest yearning. If his goddess would not accept these offerings in direct tribute, she might by happy chance catch sight of and recognize them in print.

Leslie's, Harper's, Puck, Judge, the *Evening Post* and the *Sun* were successfully bombarded. Tommy's lacerated heart brought him in more than fifty dollars in that grievous period of his banishment.

The Kodak picture of Dr. Farr came out, clear, strong, and a vivid likeness. Pride of workmanship led him to exhibit it to Dan Adriance.

"Don't give me away, though," he said. "The old boy's touchy about havin' his mug taken."

Dan nodded. "We all have our kinks," he said.

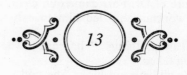

13

Having achieved a measure of economic stability, Tommy now felt the stirrings of social ambition. He aspired to join the Tenderloin Club, then at the zenith of its brief but spirited existence. To his innocence, membership appeared as a patent of the Higher Bohemianism.

The Tenderloin Club was rather easier of entry than Brooklyn Bridge. Practically the only requisite for membership was a ten-dollar bill. Nonresident candidates joined by sending in name, address, and check. A witty mayor of Brooklyn gave after-dinner thanks for election to "the most inclusive club in the United States." The roster comprised a wide representation of the sporting world: jockeys, fighters, six-day-bicycle racers, tipsters, promoters, bookmakers and hangers-on of ring and track; a sprinkling of high-class and well-behaved crooks; newspapermen ranging from Park Row stars down to the humble twelve-dollar-a-week hacks of the "flimsies" (local news agencies serving the dailies, so called because their reports were issued on yellow tissue paper manifolded with a stylus); daring spirits from the Calumet and Union Clubs, to whom anything west of Fifth Avenue was terra incognita; and a comprehensive selection of high police officials and local politicians.

Nothing short of recorded criminality was cause for rejection, and not always that. Legend of the organization preserved a dialogue between the secretary and a minor politician who had proposed a candidate.

SECRETARY—Hey, Mike, who is this Bibbs Baker you put up?
POLITICIAN—Oh, he's just a fella.
SECRETARY—What's his business?
POLITICIAN—Nothing much, right now.
SECRETARY—What's his address?
POLITICIAN—Sing Sing.
SECRETARY—Oh, come, now, Mike! We can't take a con.
POLITICIAN—Don't I know that? His time's up next week.
SECRETARY—Okay. Tell him to mail the ten.

(Makes an entry on his calendar and they go down to the bar for a drink.)

The organization was shabbily but comfortably housed in two con-joined red-brick buildings on West Thirty-second Street, which had formerly been medium-priced brothels but had succumbed to compe-tition, there being three other institutions of the kind in the block. Near the corner, at street level, were a roulette stand (crooked), a faro joint (reputed to be straight), a policy room which had the reputation of paying off its winning gigs on the nose, and a horse-book which had welshed twice in one year but still ran under powerful protection. Within a stone's throw across-roof to Sixth Avenue, stood all-night Clark's and the celebrated Haymarket, where one could take the girl of his nocturnal choice to dance at fifty cents a session, ladies free. A more favorable site for the club could not well be conceived.

In broaching the subject of his ambition to Dan Adriance, Tommy exhibited one of his rare moods of diffidence.

"Look, Dan! You a member of the Tenderloin?"

"Yes."

"How does a fella get to be?"

"Like any other club."

"Hell! What do I know about clubs?"

"Well, you ask some friend to put up your name and someone else to second you, and there you are," the reporter explained.

"Look, Dan! Do you think I'd have a chance?"

"Of getting in? Are you serious?" (Adriance, of course, could not know that Richard K. Fox, who was a bit of a practical joker, had represented the Tenderloin to his young employe as being an organi-zation of careful selection and high exclusiveness.)

"Sure, I'm serious."

"Would you like me to put you up?"

"Gee! Would you? That's swell!"

By the simple method of posting the name of Thomas Howatt on the bulletin board with Deacon Waldo as seconder, the nomination was effected. Within the week and upon the payment of the fee, Tommy became a member in full standing.

To celebrate, his sponsor took him there for dinner. Tommy's first wide-eyed thrill came to him in the entrance hallway, where he stopped, enthralled, before Archie Gunn's famous mural, afterward denounced by Dr. Brockholst Farr, as "a color print for the Book of Lust." It was a life-size oil depicting a violently scarlet Satan casting dice for her virtue with the nudest female short of the Metropolitan Museum of Art, who brandished a beading glass of champagne; both were seated in the cusp of a new moon.

"Oh, momma!" the new member ejaculated. "I guess that's art!"

An open rear door gave a view of the back yard, where an eighteen-foot boxing ring was a permanent summer fixture. Lively contests were held, distinguished professionals going on for four rounds, both members and outsiders. For the coming Saturday there was a match scheduled between the leading contender for the championship and the best lightweight amateur in New York and perhaps in the nation, scion of a distinguished local family.

At dinner the initiate was politely appreciative of the club special: an excellent small steak with fixings, at twenty cents. Pie, coffee, and beer brought the total for two up to seventy cents, cash. There were no checks at the Tenderloin. Everything was paid for as served. That particular organization could hardly have survived on any less assured basis. The fiscal responsibility of the members was variable.

The pair took their beer up to the third floor to see what was going on. Before the half-open door of the small writing room, the tyro halted, staring.

"Who's that at the desk?" he half whispered.

Dan peered in. "Ned Townsend of the *Sun*," he said.

"Edward W. Townsend," Tommy breathed reverently. "Geez! I thought it was! What's he writing?"

"How should I know? One of his Chimmie Fadden stories probably." These were the dialect sketches which had taken New York by storm.

"Oh, gee!" Tommy said. "Oh, *gee!* D'you think I could speak to him?"

"No," Dan said. "Against the rules. No talking in the workroom."

They went up to the card parlor, where a group of top-flight Newspaper Row workers were playing table-stakes poker: Jersey Chamberlain of the *Sun;* Hart Lyman of the *World;* Rudolph Block, the later "Bruno Lessing" of the Hearst magazines; Willy Willis, Steve Mather, Jesse Lynch Williams, Eugene Walter, not yet known as a playwright, and the toweringly handsome David Graham Phillips, just starting his prolific career as a novelist. Tommy greeted each name with exclamatory respect.

"Look!" he muttered. "D'you spose I'll ever get to *speak* to those fellas?"

Dan assured him that there was not a swelled head among the lot. The initiate was mistrustful.

"They look kinda snooty. I'd never have the nerve to brace 'em."

He did an injustice to his nerve. Within a short time he was on easy terms with his fellow members. Police captains greeted him as "Tommy." Big Bill Nelson, Tammany District Leader and the undisputed boss of the Tenderloin, spoke affably to him. Some of the most distinguished dive-keepers in town invited him to the bar. Partly it was the trailed clouds of glory from the champion-felling bung starter that commended him. Eventually, however, it was his voice which won for him his singular prestige.

A music-loving gambler, operating by grace of political pull, had inaugurated a prize contest for the best police precinct quartet. With only a month to go before the test, the Tenderloin Station's first tenor went sour with a bad throat. Several substitutes were tried out in the upper room of the Tenderloin Club where they held rehearsals. None met the requirements. Two candidates had been dismissed on the evening when Tommy, with several others, was listening outside. Willie Frye, the first bass and leader, was heard profanely bewailing a lost evening which they could ill afford at this late date.

Whatever modesty attached to Tommy's journalistic capacity (and this was soon eliminated) did not extend to his music. He stepped to the door.

"Look!" he said confidently. "Want somebody to fill in?"

"Who the hell is this little pisswink?" the second bass, a brutal-faced roundsman named Lambert, demanded of his companions.

Somebody volunteered: "He's the guy that flattened John L."

"That's all to the good," said Gilligan, the second tenor, "but it don't make him no canary."

"Gimme a show," Tommy said airily.

"How about sight readin'?" the leader asked.

"Not too good," Tommy admitted.

"Then get the hell outa here before I fan you out with my night stick," Lambert growled.

"*Wait* a minute," Willie Frye said urgently, waving the second bass down. "You say you can't read good?" he inquired of the volunteer.

"No, but I got a quick ear."

"You been listenin' in?"

"Yes."

"Pick your tune."

" 'Soldier's Farewell.' 'When the Corn Is Waving.' 'Sweet Molly-O!' I don't care," Tommy said.

Frye gave the pitch for "When the Corn Is Waving." Hardly drawing breath he led on into "How Can I Leave Thee?" Then into the more intricate "Lovely Night." Here Tommy stumbled a little.

"That'll do," said Willie Frye. "Thanks."

As the door closed behind the candidate, the three men looked at one another and used police language.

"Christ!" Lambert growled.

"Jesus!" Gilligan confirmed.

"Goddam!" said Frye.

"Didja hear how he faked them modulations when he didn't quite know his way?" Lambert said.

"We gotta have him," Gilligan declared.

"Yeah? How?" Lambert demanded.

"Leave it to me," said Willie Frye.

The very next day Frye telephoned Tommy to meet him at the club. The plain-clothes man came to the point at once.

"Want to join the force, kid?"

Tommy goggled. "Who? Me?"

"Sure. You. We need you in our business."

"How could I be a cop?"

"Easy."

"And quit my job on the *P.G.?*"

"You wouldn't hafta."

A chilling thought struck Tommy. "Look, Willie! Where'd I get the two hundred?" Two hundred dollars was the sum required (unofficially and privately, of course) from every entrant into the force.

"Ah, who astcha for any dough?" Willie Frye growled.

Still dubious, Tommy asked, "What do I do?"

"Sing, for Chrissake!"

"Is that all?"

"Well, if you want your pay, you'll have to come and get it. Reserve doorman—that's your job. Eighty-five a month and pickin's. Okay?"

"I—I guess so."

"Atsaboy! Rehearsals every evening now. And see to it you don't catch cold and croak out like that son-of-a-bitch Bamberg did. You're better'n he ever figured to be, at that."

Willie Frye went to Big Bill Nelson, the district boss, who, himself, had a pretty ear for music and took a local pride in the precinct. After listening to a rehearsal, Boss Nelson approached a friend of his on the Board of Police Commissioners. As a personal favor, he said, work this young punk in. He was forgoing his own cut of the usual fee. That's how good he considered the young fellow. The appointment went through at the next meeting. Tommy was a cop.

Results justified the move. The quartet took the thousand-dollar chief prize and placed third in the impromptu. The new captain, Bernie Schmidt, was so pleased that he cut Tommy in on the Guttenberg race-track book, which was minor graft, but steady. To the close of his service the reserve doorman enjoyed a reliable extra income of fifteen dollars a week while the horses were running at "the Gut," with no more trouble than making the rounds like any other police collector.

It was too good to last. Mr. Richard K. Fox chanced to attend a concert where the Police Prize Quartet sang, and recognized with astonishment the junior member of his staff, in full uniform for the occasion, dispensing a melodious first tenor. Tommy was called on the carpet in the morning.

"Are you working for me or for Superintendent Blunt?" the proprietor demanded.

"Look, Boss. It don't take any of my office time."

"That isn't the point, my boy. You're either a cop or a reporter. You quit the force or you quit the *Gazette*. Make up your mind."

Tommy's choice was not difficult. Being a policeman was fine and dandy. But journalism came first. The reserve doorman of the Nineteenth Precinct officially resigned. Officially his resignation was accepted. By now, however, he was a bosom pal of Willie Frye, knew every cop in the precinct by his first name, and was a familiar of the station house. He still sang with the quartet in practice. Quietly he was still cut in on the minor pickings, an occasional five- or ten-spot. In his heart he was one of the force. The system had grappled Tommy to its soul with hoops of steel.

Meantime he was assiduously endeavoring to best Dr. Farr at checkers. Often, after the game, he would linger to discuss local developments with his host. On one of the clergyman's rare days of slipshod play—Tommy almost won the second game—the guest said, "Got something on your mind, champ?"

Dr. Farr smiled indulgently at the epithet. "Yes, Thomas, I have."

"Anything I can help with?"

"It may very well be. You are acquainted with Mrs. Georgiana Hastings, I believe."

"Well—sure. Professionally. Every newspaperman knows Georgiana."

"I have had a letter from her."

"From Georgiana? Look, Dominie, what would a whore—a sporting lady be writing to a minister about?"

"She apologized courteously for the accident—so she termed it—sustained by one of the younger members of my flock and pledged herself that there would be no repetition. She does not cater to the Sunday-school trade, she assures me; hers is a high-class, respectable establishment, and she asks only to be let alone."

"What could be fairer?" said Tommy.

Dr. Farr frowned. "Don't you see that she confidently purposes to continue her evil trade?"

"Why, sure! What's to prevent? She's the best-protected madam in New York City."

"By whom?"

"Oh, let's not get gay with names. You'd be surprised."

"I *am* surprised," the Doctor said grimly. "I have forwarded the letter to the Police Captain Schmidt."

"That'll give him a laugh."

Dr. Farr flushed. "I fail to see anything humorous in it. How well do you know Captain Schmidt?"

"He's a member of my club," Tommy answered with pride.

"He impressed me as a well-meaning man."

"Oh, I guess he means all right. Takes it with both hands, like all of 'em."

"Takes what?"

"The dibs. The dollars. Mazuma. Spondulix. Cash."

"Are you speaking of bribery, Thomas?"

"If you want to use mean words. Ask Georgiana."

"Do you wish me to understand that police officials accept money from these women?"

Tommy regarded him with pity. "Look, mister! Don't you ever get anywheres west of Broadway?"

"Not often, I fear, Thomas. Do you think I should?"

"It might wise you up to a few things. Look, now! D'you want the low-down? The inside info? The straight tip? I'm the lad can give it to you."

"I should appreciate it, Thomas."

Tommy pondered. "I'm not giving away anything that everybody don't know from the Battery to Central Park. And I wouldn't be telling you this if you could do any damage with it. But it's time you knew what you're up against. I don't want to see a square-shooter like you get in wrong."

"Thank you, Thomas," the clergyman returned gravely. "I, too, have come to feel a genuine esteem for you."

"Okay. Here's the setup. We'll begin at the top. There's the Commissioners, the Board. They get theirs from appointments."

"Could you be a little more specific?"

"Sure. Every fat job on the force is paid for in cash. An inspector has to come through with twenty thousand. It costs a captain ten to fifteen. The Board of Commissioners split the loot amongst 'em. It's not all velvet, though. Don't think that. They have to pay their percentage to the Hall."

"Tammany Hall?"

"Keno. City Hall, too. But that's the same thing."

"Thomas," the Doctor said sternly, "these are grave charges. Are you sure of your facts?"

"Why, everybody knows it. Take Captain Schmidt, now. What do you reckon he had to pay for being shifted to the Nineteenth—the Tenderloin?"

"I have not the faintest idea."

"Fifteen thousand nice, round rollers. And where's he going to get it back?"

Dr. Farr made a gesture of ignorance.

"Why, from the madams. Every madam in the precinct comes through with so much, monthly. Everyone but Georgiana Hastings. Yep! Willie Frye, the fly-cop, comes up the steps on the tenth of the month. That's collection day in the Tenderloin. Rings the bell just like any other customer. Ushered into the parlor. 'Sit down, Willie.' That's the madam. 'Have a little drink?' 'Don't care if I do, Hattie or Carrie or Isabel.' whoever it is. Plunk! That's the cork out of a bottle of fizz that would cost a St. Louis man a ten-spot. Maybe a girl comes in. They kill the bottle. All very nice and friendly. The madam slips Willie Frye an envelope. He don't even trouble to look inside. Shoves it into his pocket. 'Good night, Hattie.' 'Good night, Willie. My respects to the pantata.' So everything's sweet and lovely till next payday rolls around."

"How much is in the envelope?" asked Dr. Farr in accents of hushed fascination.

Tommy enjoyed the sensation he was producing. "Depends on location and how much business the house is doing, and whether the place is on the level or a panel-joint."

"I must ask you to explain that term, Thomas."

"Panel? Trick walls. The wall slips aside while the customer is asleep in bed, and the operator rolls him."

"Would that not be likely to awaken him?"

"Huh? Oh! I getcha." Tommy laughed indulgently. "Goes through his clothes and pinches his roll. Rolls him. See?"

Dr. Farr nodded. He was acquiring enlightenment at a dizzying rate.

"Panel-joints pay an extra divvy on the take," his instructor proceeded. "Then, when the sucker shows up next day at the station house with a beef, the cop on duty fans his pants out into the street. He never gets as far as Jefferson Market Court, and it wouldn't do him any good if he did."

"And the other establishments operate on a stated tariff?"

"That's it. Five hundred a month for the classy places like Hattie Baker's and the French Madam's. As low as two hundred for some of the joints over Seventh Avenue way. Then, of course, there's the hookers."

Dr. Farr's eyebrows were elevated again.

"Hookers. Cruisers. Streetwalkers. You know. Take me home for a two-spot."

"And do those poor creatures have to pay blood-money to the police?" the clergyman asked.

"Oh, a five now and then to the cop on the beat isn't going to bust 'em," Tommy said airily.

"Then this corruption extends down to the very policeman who patrols in front of my door?" the shocked clergyman asked. "Surely there must be some honest men on the force."

"Well, maybe," the expositor conceded. "But it don't get 'em anywhere."

"I can hardly believe it," the minister said despondently.

"Come on! Be reasonable. A cop's got to live. Do you know how much he gets? A lousy twelve hundred dollars a year. And it costs him two hundred to get on the force. It isn't the cops who are hard on the cruisers. It's their own ponces."

"Again I must plead ignorance, Thomas. What is a ponce?"

"A runner. The girl's business-getter. Well, I guess you'd call him a pimp."

"A name for which the pained'st fined in hell
Would not in reputation change,"

the Doctor murmured.

"Well, I wouldn't want to be in that line, myself," Tommy admitted. "But those birds have got their use, too."

"Yes? And what is their function in this dark coil of vice?"

"Every so often a cop makes a pinch. For the record. See?"

"A pinch? An arrest?"

"That's it. Soliciting. Maybe the girl is on the wrong corner. Out of her district. Up comes the cop. 'Come along, Annie. We're on our way to the station house.' The sergeant at the desk books her. 'Can I send word to my friend?' 'Why, sure, Annie. Bill, get her a messenger.' The messenger costs her two dollars. The ponce quits his pinochle game and arranges for bail so his girl won't have to spend the night in jail. One of Big Bill Nelson's boys furnishes the bail. That costs Annie a ten-spot."

"Who is Big Bill Nelson?"

"You don't know your own district leader?" Tommy was aghast. "Big Bill's the Tammany boss of the precinct. He's got the bail-bond privilege for the whole Tenderloin. And you never heard of him?"

"Apparently there is much that I have not heard of," the clergyman said grimly. "Proceed, Thomas."

"Next morning, the gal comes up in Jefferson Market. 'What's the charge?' That's the judge. 'Soliciting in a public place,' the cop says. Or maybe dee and dee if they want to make it hard."

"Dee and dee?"

"Drunk and disorderly. But usually it's just plain soliciting. The judge gets the high-sign from the cop. That means that it's one of Big Bill's bails. 'Ten dollars or thirty days.' Her ponce comes up with the ten. That night she's out there doing business again. 'Can I show you a good time, dearie?' "

"And if the unfortunate girl does not submit to Mr. Nelson's extortion, I suppose—"

"Sixty days," Tommy said promptly. "But they all know better than to try that. It's worth a cool fifteen thousand a year to Big Bill."

"And our courts of justice are party to it?"

"Sure! A judge has got to live, same as anyone else."

"Thomas," the clergyman said, "you will forgive me, but I find this impossible of credence."

"You don't believe me?"

"It cannot be as bad as you make out."

"That's what *you* think. You ought to talk to the boss."

"Big Bill Nelson?"

"No, no! My boss, Richard K. Fox of the *P.G.* You know, the *Police Gazette.*"

"I have not the pleasure of the gentleman's acquaintance," the clergyman said, "though I have read excerpts embodying his opinion of me."

Tommy felt a little uneasy. "That stuff about your crusade, you mean. That was all in the way of business. You couldn't expect the *Pinky* to back you up."

"Perhaps not. But I could expect more respect for the cloth."

"That's all right. R.K.'s got just as much respect for a parson as the next fella. But, the way he looks at it, you're off your beat. Would you talk to him if I can get him up here?"

"Why, yes. I should be pleased to."

The visitor went to the telephone and presently returned with the message that Mr. Fox would stop on his way uptown, in an hour.

Tommy made the introduction in his best book form. He had a feeling that the two men ought to like each other, both being straight-shooters.

"Look, Boss," he said. "I've been telling Dr. Farr," and he proceeded to repeat the exegesis which had so shocked the clergyman. "He don't believe me," he ended.

Dr. Farr looked inquiringly at his caller.

"This young man," the editor-proprietor of the *Police Gazette* said, laying a kindly hand on Tommy's shoulder, "sometimes talks through his hat. But it's probably true, what he told you."

"Then this city is Sodom and Gomorrah," the clergyman said hoarsely.

"Oh, no!" the other deprecated. "But it's a big city, a metropolis. You can't run a metropolis on Sunday-school lines. How long have you lived in this district, Dr. Farr? Must be eight years or so."

"Nearly that."

"Long enough to know something about it. What would you say was its principal business?"

The clergyman took it into consideration. "Why, amusements, I should think. Or perhaps the hotel business."

"You were right the first time: amusements. And what would you say is the principal form of amusement?"

"Theatre."

"Wrong. Women."

"Surely you are not serious," the clergyman protested.

"Surely I am. Kill off the woman-trade and this district would be as dead as Jersey City. What keeps the out-of-towners coming? Women. What's the bait for the visiting businessman? Women. What keeps the bright lights burning and the green money circulating? Women. After seven P.M. they're the chief industry, and anybody who doesn't realize it must go around with his eyes shut. The city's politics are figured out back of the red lights. The important madams sit in on the unofficial conferences. Why, the present mayor was practically nominated at an all-night blowout in Georgiana Hastings' place. This is Whoretown, Dr. Farr, begging your pardon."

"The monstrous regiment of women," Dr. Farr murmured.

"That's John Knox, isn't it?"

"Yes. I am no John Knox, God knows. But I am a citizen of New York. Do you expect me to hold my peace amidst this orgy of vice?"

"Oh, come now, Dr. Farr. This—er—woman business, you and I may not like it, but it's a part of metropolitan life. People that come here—business people and such—expect it. They want it that way. A wide-open town is good for trade. Anybody who tries to interfere is wasting his time and is hunting trouble for himself into the bargain."

"Are you trying to warn me off, Mr. Fox?" the clergyman asked more mildly.

"No— Why, yes. I suppose I am. Let's put it this way. You

can't go into this without involving your church. You would find yourself up against politics right at the start. Politics is a dirty business. Prostitution is—political."

"You are opening my eyes, Mr. Fox."

"Then close 'em again. As a good Presbyterian, I appeal to you. Don't mix your church in that muck."

"Mr. Fox, any church that ignores such conditions is shirking its duty. If all the churches would but unite against this infamy—"

"All the churches!" the editor interrupted. "Dr. Farr, I'm going to tell you something you probably don't know. The swellest church in New York City draws rentals from a lot of whorehouse property."

"I don't believe it," Dr. Farr said, shocked out of his habitual courtesy.

The editor shrugged. "Come down to Varick Street with me some day and I'll show you sample places."

"I beg your pardon for contradicting you, Mr. Fox. What other churches do, however, is no concern of mine."

"What do you propose to do, then?"

"Spur or shame the police to uphold the law."

"See here, Dr. Farr," the other said kindly. "Nobody can buck the police in this town. They run it."

"Then you agree with Howatt that they condone professional vice?"

"Condone it! Why, man, they live on it."

"So he told me. Since you confirm it, I am bound to believe it. And no pulpit has ever lifted a voice against it?"

"Oh, yes! The Reverend DeWitt Talmage preached a series of rip-snorting sermons on New York vice years ago. And what happened? Nothing. Reverend Madison Peters took a swing at it. Same result."

"I must pray over this." Dr. Farr spoke with head bent.

The *Gazette* man continued. "I think you should understand, Dr. Farr, that this is a pretty nearly universal condition. It has ramifications everywhere; in your own church, for a bet."

The clergyman looked up sharply. "Will you be more specific?"

"No. Just reflect before you go too far that all kinds of interests are tied up with the system: churches, banks, railroads, real estate, politicians, everybody."

"The city administration, too?"

"Up to their fat necks. Everybody knows that."

The pastor looked at him curiously. "You are the owner of a medium which, I assume, has influence. Have you done nothing about this?"

"Oh, we take a crack at vice every now and then. But I'm not a reformer. Reformers aren't popular in this town. They hurt business."

"Then the course that you advocate is that we should stand with hands folded while our youth are corrupted."

"I don't say that. I only say it'll do you no good to tackle the system. You can't save the soul of a city. It hasn't got a soul."

"The citizens have souls."

"Its citizens are human beings. You can't change human nature, Dominie."

For the first time in their acquaintanceship, Tommy saw Dr. Farr lose his temper. Dark blood rose to his temples. He doubled a powerful fist and brought it down on the desk top with a thump that set pens, pencils, and paperweights to rolling. Wrath rumbled in his voice.

"Of all the damnable heresies ever propounded, that is the wickedest, the most destructive, the most nullifying. Not change human nature? In the name of Almighty God, what purpose has religion other than to change it for the better and to lift the soul of man above the animal! If it be true, indeed, that human nature is fixed and unchangeable, then all creeds are aimless, all faiths empty, and Christ, Socrates, Confucius, and the glorious host of saints and martyrs have lived in vain. Deliver us from such blasphemy!"

"Steady, Dominie," Tommy muttered, startled.

Dr. Farr drew both hands down over his contorted face, and became once more the courteous host. "I have to ask your pardon, Mr. Fox, for my lapse of self-control," he said in low tones. "Believe me, sir, I have nothing in my heart but gratitude toward you for your kindness in coming here."

"That's all right, Dr. Farr," the editor returned lamely. He, too, was shaken by the clergyman's vehemence. "Any time I can be of help— Want a lift, Tommy?"

"No, thank you, Boss. I'm staying on for a minute."

Mr. Fox left.

Tommy hesitated, then said, "You're not going to lay off, then, Dominie."

"No, Thomas."

Tommy sighed. "I didn't figure you would. Well, I meant it kindly."

The gaunt face warmed. "You have never meant otherwise by me, I am sure."

"That's a safe bet, Dominie. How about a little game?"

"No, my boy. I am not in the spirit. But come again soon."

The visitor left, shaking an ominous head. He could see nothing but ructions impending.

So impressed was Dr. Farr with R. K. Fox's viewpoint that he made use of it in a manner which did not earn that astute editor's approval. He took the historic John Knox diatribe for his text and preached a sermon on The Monstrous Regiment of Women, which would have greatly astonished the ancient Scots divine, his "regiment" having reference to something quite different. The Farr denunciation was a tissue of resounding generalities which, while true, would have been more effective had they been less vague. However, they served to inflame still further prejudices on both sides. The *Sun* denounced them as a baseless libel upon the fair name of the city.

14

Not all the glory of being a full-fledged clubman could compensate Tommy for his continued exclusion from the enchanted precincts of the Valdevia. His poetic output suffered. It became so suffused with gloom as to be unmarketable. He now visualized and apostrophized Laurie Crosbie as a distant star. An unforeseen event lifted her to still loftier heights in his fancy. A formidable old lady was responsible.

As the ancient Romans used the phrase, *"Planco Consule,"* New York Society after the nineties looked back and said in fond remembrance, "In the days of Grandma Parke." Mrs. Steevens Parke, born a Van Cortlandt before the family dropped the final t, was the ruler and the terror of the upper crust. The widow of a millionaire railroad pirate, when financial piracy was not only respectable but laudable (if successful), she was, at the time of her first encounter with Laurie Crosbie, a withered beldame of eighty who drank her liquor straight, expressed her opinions without curb, and looked more like Punch than like Judy. She was massive and gaunt, with a parchment face, large, intelligent gray eyes, a predatory nose, and an upper forejaw whose two surviving teeth would have done credit to a diamondback rattlesnake. In her youth she had been a famous amateur contralto; her speaking voice still retained an extraordinary richness and softness of timbre until something roused her hair-trigger temper.

That irreverent weekly, *Town Topics,* which claimed to be the organ of Society, and actually did exercise a potent influence through its system of spy-news and informed scandal plus blackmail and intimidation, dubbed her "Goddess Almighty." Her factotum was Ward McAllister, that preposterous and eventually pathetic figure who created a caste in one inspired utterance: "There are but four hundred people in New York who know which fork to use."

Hence the Four Hundred.

The inventor of the honored phrase has come down in history as the arch-flunky of an age of triumphant snobbishness. He was more.

His pomposity was redeemed by his devotion to a lofty and fanatic ideal. It was his mission to guard the sacred portals of Society (with a capital S) against the intrusion of hoi polloi.

"There is no side entrance to Society," said Mr. Ward McAllister, and, as self-appointed Cerberus, did his devoted best to prove it.

Grandma Parke was wont to say, "Ward is a blithering ass. Everybody knows that. Couldn't even make a strike in the Gold Rush of Forty-nine. But what should we do without him?"

Invitations to the one large party per year, with a list rigorously supervised by Mr. McAllister, in the stately and stuffy Parke mansion at Seventeenth Street and Fifth Avenue, were prized above rubies. Every year Mrs. Parke swore that she was sick to death of the half-wits, drink-cadgers, and raddled trollops who pretended to be Somebodies and ought to be in the Home for the Feeble-minded; and, so help her God! this would be her last entertainment. It never was.

And in this year of grace and of Dr. Brockholst Farr's ill-advised prowlings ("Whatever drove poor Brock out of his mind? Must have been addled," was Grandma Parke's comment) she gave not one party, but two. The second was forced upon her by the fact that Christopher Columbus discovered America. Even the Four Hundred knew that. Nobody gave it much thought until announcement was made that a lineal descendant of the discoverer, and a duke into the bargain, was en route for the continent upon which his distinguished forebear had set neither foot nor eye. There would be parades, and official welcomes, Keys of the City, brass bands and receptions.

That was not enough. Society must do something special about it. It was foreordained that it should be a Mrs. Steevens Parke soiree. The Duke, a courteous and ugly little man, wept tears of exhaustion when informed that an extra function had been added to his routine. It could not be helped. Grandma Parke's invitations were tantamount to royal commands.

The date was set for Thursday, July twenty-seventh. Society, which would come back from Newport, Saratoga, and Watch Hill for the event, hung breathless over the crisis of who was to be invited, who excluded. A week before the fatal date, Laurie Crosbie, who had been mysteriously occupied for several days, called up Dan Adriance at the *Star* office.

"Hello! Dan? . . . Hello! Hello. Is that you? . . . Yes, it's Laurie. . . . Dan—I've made a mash."

"You shock me. Such language!"

"Never mind my language. Aren't you going to ask me who?"

"I'll guess. Here goes. Anthony Comstock. President Cleveland. George Francis Train. Steve Brodie. Stanford White. Richard Harding Davis. Kyrle Bellew. Bishop Potter. Diamond Jim Brady—"

"Oh, do stop it! I hate you. Aren't you curious a bit?"

"Professionally, yes."

"Well, listen. The Duke."

"Say it again."

"The Duke of Caldara."

"That old rip!"

"He isn't an old rip. He's an old sweetie."

"Mm-mm! See here, Laurie, nice young girls don't take up with casual dukes."

"I didn't take up with him. And you needn't mm-mm about it either."

"What *is* all this?"

"I'll tell you though you don't deserve it. I've been sitting to him."

"Sitting to him? For God's sake, Laurie, make sense."

"Well, I *have*. He's an artist and he has been painting me, and he's a friend of Mr. Ward McAllister, and Mr. McAllister is going to call on me and don't ask me why because I don't know, and I want you to come up late this afternoon to help me out and it's something about Mrs. Steevens Parke and—"

"Hold it!" Dan said. "Take your weight off the wire before it breaks. Will five o'clock be all right?"

"Make it four-thirty."

"All right. Have the details ready."

The Duke of Caldara! And Laurie! It sounded crazy. Seeking advance information, the reporter bethought him of an acquaintance in the State Department who was acting as diplomatic cicerone to the distinguished visitor. Over a drink at the Hoffman House bar, he explained his position to young Mr. Bevier and put his question: "What's the ducal game?"

"No game. All quite correct."

"Nonsense!" Dan said with some heat. "Itinerant dukes don't pick up young girls like that."

The diplomat grinned. "His Grace does. All in the sacred name of art."

"Yes, Miss Crosbie said something about his painting her. How did they meet?"

"She was sitting in a window box when the official parade went by. His Grace caught sight of her and nearly fell out of the four-horse barouche. Nothing would do but that he must paint her. So he asked me to take his sister to call on her and offer a respectful request. No girl would say no to that. Your beautiful cousin was very nice about it. Charles Dana Gibson turned over his studio, with Mrs. William Dean Howells as chaperone. That ought to relieve your mind of any doubts. You know the Howells' reputation for correctness."

"Then his ducal Nibs is really an artist?"

"You should see his work. It's awful, even for a duke."

"And you think that's all there is to it?" Dan asked doubtfully.

Bevier smiled. "There's no vice in the old boy. Anyway, it's notorious that he's been impotent for years."

"Where does Ward McAllister figure?"

"Society's watchdog is pricking up his ears, I suppose. Our Ward must have a finger in every social pie, you know."

Dan did know. Every reporter in New York knew Mr. McAllister as a reliable source for news of the Four Hundred.

On the stroke of five, the impressed doorman of the Valdevia announced Mr. Ward McAllister. At Laurie's instance, Dan received him alone. The pudgy and dandified little man was in full afternoon rig, with a flower in the buttonhole of his frock coat. It struck Dan that his gravity of demeanor did not quite cover an inner agitation.

The caller regarded the young man doubtfully. "I had hoped to have the honor of meeting Mrs. Crosbie," he began with a slight and gentlemanly upward inflection.

"Mrs. Crosbie is not well," Dan said. "Miss Crosbie will be right in."

The visitor looked about him at the *objets d'art* with surprise and appreciation. He knew. "Sound taste," he murmured. He adjusted his glasses the better to observe Dan. "I believe I have seen you before," he remarked.

"You have," Dan said. "I'm Adriance of the *Star*."

"Ah, yes. How d'ya do! Always glad to meet the press. You are here—er—professionally?"

"No," Dan said. "To meet you." He added the convenient lie: "I am Miss Crosbie's nearest male relative."

Mr. McAllister blinked. "Quite so," he said. "Then you can tell me about her."

"What do you want to know?"

"Who is she?" he said bluntly, and with equal bluntness and some added emphasis the young man replied, "My cousin."

Mr. Ward McAllister may have been all that is ridiculous in his self-appointed role; he was, nevertheless, a gentleman. "I beg your pardon, Mr. Adriance," he said gravely. He spread his beautifully kept hands in a gesture at once appealing and explanatory. "I find myself in a difficult position."

"I don't see why."

"The Duke of Caldara's sister, the Countess, has requested Mrs. Steevens Parke to send a card to your cousin for the Parke soiree to be held after his Grace's return from an official visit to Washington."

"Well?"

Mr. McAllister's agitation became more apparent. "Mrs. Parke does not even know Miss Crosbie."

"And you are here on an errand of inspection?"

"That is one way of putting it," the emissary admitted. "You see, Mr.—er—Adriance, this is the great social event of the season. The list of invitees has been most rigorously censored."

"By you?"

"Mrs. Parke has done me the honor to consult me."

"And you are dubious about Miss Crosbie's qualifications. Is that it?"

The caller flushed painfully. "That is hardly a fair assumption," he said. "Consider my responsibility to Society."

"Where did you leave your other two heads?" Dan asked. It was an inexcusable rudeness to an older man, but he was nettled. Rather to his surprise the visitor got the allusion and acknowledged it with a rueful grin.

"Somebody must man the portals," he said. "Where would Society be if every Tom, Dick, and Harry had entree?"

"Which of the three would you identify her as?" Dan asked quickly and low, for he heard Laurie's footsteps.

The pudgy little man bowed over the hand which she held out to him. She bore his scrutiny with a smiling gravity.

"I do not wonder at the Duke's desire to paint you, mademoiselle. May one old enough to be your grandfather take the liberty of saying that you are very beautiful?"

"Thank you," Laurie said.

The caller pattered along with conversational trivialities until Dan broke in with malice prepense: "Mr. McAllister has come to see whether you qualify."

"My dear young man!" he protested.

"For what?" Laurie asked.

The social arbiter plunged. Indeed, Dan had pushed him so far that he had no choice. "Your name has been put on the list for Mrs. Steevens Parke's Grand Soiree."

"Yes," Laurie said. "A card came in the morning's mail."

"Already?" he said, aghast.

She studied his face with interest developing into enlightenment. "Don't be worried, Mr. McAllister," she said gently. "I am regretting."

For him it was the ideal solution. Yet his face betrayed an involuntary consternation. "Declining Mrs. Steevens Parke's invitation?" he exclaimed in scandalized accents.

"Yes. I don't know her."

"Everybody knows Mrs. Parke!"

"Oh, I've heard her name, of course. It's very kind of her to ask me, but I shouldn't find anyone there whom I know. It would be stupid."

The social arbiter was stunned. "Stupid?" The premier event of the season stupid! He recovered himself and his sense of courtesy. "While I must accept your decision," he said and rose, "Mrs. Parke will be sorry indeed not to have the company of so charming a young lady."

Thereupon he bowed himself out. That awkward dilemma was conveniently resolved; so he thought with gratification. An hour later a dozen of the fashionable Maréchal Niel roses, with the McAllister card attached, were delivered at the Crosbie apartment.

From Laurie, the social bear-leader went direct to Mrs. Parke. "The situation is saved," he told her. "The young lady declines."

"What's this! Nobody declines my invitations," the grande dame barked.

"I've no doubt it cost her some heart-burnings. Nevertheless everything has turned out for the best," he assured her. "Once open our doors to these incognitae, and what becomes of Society?"

"Nonsense. What's the matter with the girl?"

"Nobody knows who she is."

"What of it?" (Mr. McAllister shuddered at the heresy.) "Anything wrong with her morals?"

"Not that I know of."

"Manners?"

"Simple and charming," he reluctantly admitted.

"Well, then! Is she vulgar? Loud? Illiterate? Humpbacked? Cross-eyed? Knock-kneed?"

To each question he responded by a negative. "She is very beautiful," he said. "So is Lillian Russell. You would not include her in your list of guests, I assume."

"My dear man, I include whom I damned well choose at my functions." (She gave it the Spanish pronunciation.) "And you may mind your own damned business."

The badgered visitor was stirred to protest. "It *is* my business to protect Society from persons without grandfathers."

"Grandfathers!" She let out a derisive "Ho-ho!" wagging a be-ringed and bony forefinger at him. "Steevens' grandfather smuggled Canadian goods into Oswego River. One of yours, I daresay, peddled tinware on country shun-pikes. A little further back the dear Duke's forebears rustled cattle on the Calabrian hills. Don't talk to me about grandfathers! *I've* got 'em! Great-grandfathers, too. But ninety-nine percent of our million-dollar families started behind the counter or the plough or a tandem of horses in the early days of the Erie Canal. This young lady is coming to my soiree or I'll know the reason why not!"

Dan was still at the apartment when the dowager called on the telephone. Laurie relayed the message to him in a whisper.

"She says she's a very old woman and will I waive formality and bring Mother to see her tomorrow. She's *sweet.*"

"Not by common report," Dan said.

"What shall I tell her?"

"Yes, of course."

A moment later she said into the transmitter-box, "Mother goes out very little, Mrs. Parke. May I bring my cousin with me?"

That is how Dan made entry into a house barred to newspapermen. Mrs. Parke received them informally. She was alone.

"You are kind to come, my dear," she said in her deep and still beautiful voice. "And this young man?"

Laurie presented him.

The gray eyes in the withered face twinkled. "I have seen him before. I have seen you both before."

"Yes," the girl said. "At the Grand Central Depot."

"He lied to my nephew, Stannard Barto," the old lady said affably. "I wonder why."

"It was a misunderstanding," Dan began.

"You said that you and your cousin were only passing through town," she continued without rancor. "You"—to the girl—"did not wish to meet me. I wonder why."

"Oh, Mrs. Parke! It really wasn't that."

"And now you won't come to my soiree. I wonder why."

Laurie flushed painfully.

"Has it anything to do with that ass of a Ward McAllister?" she continued. As the girl still made no reply, her interrogator added, "He can always be relied upon to act in the most impeccably bad taste."

Laurie laughed.

"Don't you *want* to come?"

"I appreciate your kindness very much, Mrs. Parke," the girl said. "But I'd be an entire stranger. I'd be out of my element."

"Fiddle-de-dee! You wouldn't be out of your element anywhere. Would you feel better about it if I invited this young man?"

"Dan? Oh, would you?"

"I'll send him a card tomorrow."

Outside they heard a door slam and a small-boyish voice, crying, "I won't! I won't! I want to tell it to my Granny."

"Don't let Robin come in for a minute, Nurse," Mrs. Parke called.

Dan very much wanted that card but had no desire to accept the invitation without making his position clear. "Do you know that I am a newspaperman, Mrs. Parke?" he asked.

She regarded him blandly. "Well, I suppose you could put that aside and be a gentleman for one evening."

Laurie's natural sweetness of disposition was not proof against a slur upon a friend. "Dan is *always* a gentleman," she asserted with emphasis.

Mrs. Parke snorted. "Don't bandy words with me, girl!"

The atmosphere had become electric. Laurie stood up. "Thank you very much, Mrs. Parke," she said quietly. "We shan't be able to come."

The famous Parke temper flamed. "You'll never have another chance. D'you know that there's many a young woman in town who'd give a year of her life or a night of her virtue for what you're throwing away?"

Laurie's nose angled into the air. "I think you're horrid," she said.

"I concur," Dan added.

Grandma Parke stretched out a tremulous hand, presumptively for something to hurl at their retiring heads—there were well-verified stories of her marksmanship when aroused—but retracted it as a roly-poly urchin rushed into the room. He caromed off Dan, bumped into Laurie, recoiled, and burst into an ecstatic yelp.

"It's my lady! My lady! Granny, it's my lady!"

"Come here at once, Robin. What do you mean?"

The child was dancing with excitement. "My lady! On the horse! In the Park!" He hurled himself forward and hugged Laurie's knees.

Mrs. Parke rose, grasped her gold-knobbed cane, and hobbled across the floor to confront Laurie.

"Was it you who saved my grandson?" she said.

"No," Laurie answered, looking and feeling uncomfortable. "There was no question of saving him. He was never in danger."

"That is not Robin's version. Will you forgive a bad-tempered old woman? And you, too?" she said to Dan.

"Come and see my new pony," Robin demanded.

It was a convenient relief from a difficult situation. "I'd love to," Laurie said.

"Take me, too," Dan suggested.

"Come on!" the boy shouted. They went out to the stables, Robin between the pair, holding to each by a hand. They came back to a hostess who looked as amiable as if no ill-natured word had ever passed her lips. They were both committed to the ducal blowout. To have refused now would have been too cruel a hurt to the remorseful old tyrant.

With only a few days' leeway, Laurie concentrated upon a toilette with all the ardor proper to a girl's first large party.

125

Mrs. Crosbie said to Dan, "Oh, dear! I didn't expect New York to be like this."

"Don't you want Laurie to have a good time, Mrs. Crosbie? What harm can it do?"

"Oh, I don't know. Her name will be in the papers—"

"It's in already. The society columns are printing advance lists of Grandma Parke's invited guests. Laurie is in today's."

"Is she really so eager to go?"

"What girl of her age wouldn't be?"

"I expect you're right. Very well; I shan't interfere."

Argus-eyed Tommy Howatt spotted the Crosbie name in the *Herald* and was properly awed. To his ingenuous mind publicity and social eminence were synonymous.

15

An assay of brains among Mr. Ward McAllister's Four Hundred would have panned out scanty metal. Society was largely mindless. Being stupid, it was dull and bored. Seeking refuge from its boredom, it went in for freaks. It was the era of monkey dinners, wedding receptions for Willoughby pugs, and twenty-five-thousand-dollar balls based upon this or that grotesquerie of fancy and supposedly historical costuming.

Mrs. Steevens Parke was neither stupid nor bored. She was too much the grande dame to truckle to the eccentricities and vulgarities of private entertainment. But she did follow the trend to the extent of seeking for something out of the usual for the titillation of Society's jaded palates. She found it through her nephew, Stannard Barto, who was a young man with a wide range of habitudes. Barto had first heard of and then heard a curiously effective and unconventional singer at Clark's. He reported to the old lady.

"Pooh!" she said. "I can get Plançon for a thousand dollars."

"So can anybody," the shrewd young man-about-town said. "This Howatt boy won't cost much."

"Never heard of him."

"Nobody has. That's the point."

"What does he sing?"

"Old songs. Weepers. Buckets full of tears."

"Sounds asinine. Why should I make my guests cry?"

"They'll love it. The Tenderloin girls go into spasms over him. Shall I bring him here for a tryout?"

The old lady yawned. "Oh, I suppose so. Let me see; when have I got time? Tell your songbird to be here Friday morning at ten o'clock sharp. But I'm not going to pay through the nose for someone that nobody ever heard of."

"I'll offer him fifty dollars and come up to seventy-five if I have to." Privately the enterprising Mr. Barto figured that the singer would grab at twenty-five dollars, in which case the balance would be his own well-earned fee as impresario.

Tommy was elated over the Barto proposition. He could not help but swagger a little as he crossed the *P.G.* office to tell Dan Adriance.

"Look, Dan! You know about Grandma Parke's big sworry for the Dook?"

"Everybody does."

"I'm liable to be there." He did not deem it necessary to say in what capacity.

"Are you? Maybe I'll see you."

"Huh? *You* going? For the *Star?* I thought she hadn't any use for reporters."

"Not for the *Star.*"

"Look, Dan. Do you *know* the old buzzard?"

"Slightly."

"But you get a bid to the show? A regular bid?" Tommy's superiority was rapidly deflating.

"Yes."

"Oh, nu—" Tommy checked himself. Since that unhappy evening at the Valdevia, the word had been on his index expurgatorius. "How come?" he asked.

"I went to call on the old lady with Miss Crosbie."

"Laurie? She'll be there, won't she? D'you think she'd snoot me if I asked her for a dance?"

"Didn't know you were a dancing man, Tommy."

"I can learn, can't I? Five easy lessons, three dollars. It's in the *Pinky.*"

"You're certainly coming on, my friend. 'To meet his Grace, the Duke of Caldara.' I don't know how you do it."

"To be on the square with you, Dan, it's a job. I'm going to rendah a few choice numbahs for the see-lect company."

"I see. How did you pick that up?"

"It ain't—isn't cinched yet. I'm going to have a tryout before the old hen. It's Stannard Barto's doing. Say, Dan, I hear the little snot is mugging up to Laurie. Has he been showing at the Valdevia lately?"

"Off and on."

"He's a shyster. Puts up a swell front with nothing to back it. Owes everybody in town. Know how he makes his living?"

"I supposed he was Mrs. Parke's heir."

"That old hellion! She hangs onto her dollars like a crab to a dead fish."

"What does he do, then?"

"He's a sneak-writer for *Town Topics.*"

This interested Dan. He had often wondered what kind of folk fed the scandal-sheet with its frequently authentic news. "How do you know, Tommy?" he asked.

The *P.G.* man flirted his hand in the air as he delivered his cryptic boast. "I got my lines."

"Town Topics, eh? It can't be much of a job," Dan reflected.

"I'd rather play the piano in a whorehouse, myself. He's got another hookup, too."

"What's that?"

"Ever hear of the Society Sleuths? They're Mr. Ward McAllister's smart boys."

"Go on. Open up. What do they do?"

"Well, I couldn't prove it, but there's a stink of blackmail in the air."

"You're telling me that Mr. Ward McAllister is a blackmailer?" Dan said incredulously.

"Nope. He's on the level. But he's got this little bunch of Society doods that he pays to collect information on anybody that wants to break in. McAllister uses the info to let 'em in or keep 'em out. How some of his smart little boys—and girls too—use it, I wouldn't be so sure."

"You think that Barto is one of them?"

"Surest thing you know. Being Grandma Parke's pet nephew gives him an inside track. Wish me luck with the old dame."

"When is your tryout?"

"Friday morning. I'll hand her an earful."

Prompt to the minute, Tommy presented himself. He was shown into the drawing room, at the end of which stood a grand piano of promising aspect. He went to it and struck a couple of chords, thrilling to its richness and resonance.

"Ooh—ah—ee—oh—oo!" he trilled, flexing his voice.

A rustling back of him brought him facing about. His hostess was advancing. She gleamed with jet and glistened with diamonds. Her black silk gown whispered as she came to a stop and fixed spectacles across her high-bridged nose.

"Very nice," she said.

Tommy rose. "Thanks," he said.

"Vaguely familiar, too. Never mind that for the present." She seated herself on a heavy old-fashioned sofa and consulted a tablet which she drew from a pocket of her voluminous gown. "Howatt," she said. "Thomas Howatt."

"Yes, ma'am. That's me."

"Business first. Can you come to me on the twenty-seventh?"

"Why not?"

"Don't ask me why not," she snapped. "What is your charge?"

"A hundred dollars."

Aroused by the enormousness of the sum, the old lady lapsed into that license of speech for which she was socially famous. "That's a hell of a lot of money," she said.

"I'm a hell of a good singer," Tommy assured her.

"Prove it."

He seated himself again and rippled over the keys. "Some box!" he murmured.

"Don't talk. Sing."

What was the pointer that Barto had given him? Oh, yes; that she fell for old-fashioned stuff. He cleared his throat and tried her out with "Caller Herrin'." She sat, immovable. He swung into "Annie Laurie" and followed up with "The Bonnie House of Airlie." Still no response. What the hell was the matter with the old, wooden image, anyway?—he asked himself indignantly. Something more sentimental might do the trick. He switched into five flats and put all that he had into Kjerulf's lovely *"Sehnsucht."* He thought that he heard a sigh back of him but couldn't be sure. A gay little German lilt popped into his head, and he sang that, half under his breath.

From the corner of his eye, he saw a ripple in the black sheen of silk over her knee. She was tapping out the time.

> *"Allemal kann man nicht lustig sein, lustig sein;*
> *Allemal hat man kein Geld.*
> *Allemal küss ich mein Mädelein, Mädelein,*
> *Weil es mir immer gefällt,"*

sang Tommy in his bad German, giving to the simple and sprightly little melody the full value of youth's gay defiance to fate.

The singer stood up. "That's the sample," he said.

"One hundred dollars?" Grandma Parke's charities were wide and generous, but she was notoriously well informed as to the value of a dollar in her personal dealings.

"One hundred dollars," he confirmed.

"Exorbitant." She regarded him with a lifted brow. "Surely I have heard that voice before."

"You might."

"Where?"

"At the Grand Central Deepo."

"The Grand Central?" She frowned. "Do you sing there?"

"No, ma'am. I sold Ridley's Fresh Broken."

Her face expressed puzzled astonishment. "Broken what?"

"Candy."

"You are a candy peddler?"

"Butcher, we call it."

130

"Butcher," she repeated with appreciation. "Is that your present occupation?"

"No, ma'am. I'm on the *Pinky*. The *P.G.*"

"Will you kindly endeavor to be intelligible?"

"The *Police Gazette.*"

"Is it a newspaper?"

"Mean to say you've never seen the *P.G.?* I'll send you a copy."

"Don't trouble yourself. We are considering your music. Where do you sing?"

"Where?" It was his turn to be puzzled. "Anywhere, I guess."

"In a church choir? In a concert hall? On the streets? Speak up, young man."

"Oh! At Clark's mostly."

"Never heard of it."

"Never heard of Clark's. Where have you lived all your life? You ought to drop in there some night after midnight when the crowd's getting good. It's on Sixth Avenue. Any cop can show you."

"I'll bear it in mind. I'd like one more sample from you. Do you know 'The Great Adventurer'?"

Tommy sang softly:

> *"You may tame the eagle*
> *To stoop to your fist.*
> *Or you may inveigle*
> *The phoenix of the East . . ."*

"That's it. No! Stay where you are."

For he had turned to sit on the piano stool again. Mrs. Parke hobbled over and seated herself. She arranged her skirts, felt for the pedals, and performed a little prelude of such virtuosity as brought a gulp of amazement from the hearer.

"Geez! What a harmonizer!"

She hammered imperatively upon one key. "Sing!" she barked.

Tommy sang. Rather poorly at first, for he was engrossed by the performance of his accompanist. He considered himself pretty slick on the ivories, but this—! Well though he knew the ancient words, he was having difficulty in following.

She stopped. "Do that again," she ordered. "It was slovenly."

He did better. When he reached the climactic stanza, he was in full command of his voice.

> *"You may esteem him*
> *A child, for his might."*

(Tommy's pure tenor had a note of wonder in it.)

> *"Or you may deem him*
> *A coward for his flight.*
> *But if once the message greet him"*

(There was triumph and challenge now.)

> *"That his true love doth stay,*
> *Though Death come forth to meet him,*
> *Love will find out the way."*

"Enough," Mrs. Parke said harshly. She hobbled back to her seat. "Young man, you have a devil in that throat of yours. Such a voice ought to be prohibited. It starts improper thrills in one's withered heartstrings. Of course, you are wholly ignorant of the first principles of singing."

"Oh, I dunno," Tommy defended himself and his art. "I may not be Jawn de Reszke, but I been doing all right."

"Because Belial, arch-fiend of lures and deceits, has set his charm on your voice, don't presume too much upon it. It would take years of drudgery for you to learn the art. And the effort might ruin what you have by nature— Never mind; I accept your terms. Be here at ten o'clock the evening of the twenty-seventh."

"What do you want me to sing?"

"What you choose."

"Is it soup-and-fish?"

"Certainly. Supper will be served to you in the small gallery."

"You don't get me, ma'am. Is it a case of swallowtail and boiled shirt?"

"Oh, that! It is of no consequence. You will be singing behind a screen of palms."

"I don't get to go to the party?" he asked, his jaw dropping.

"Certainly not. You are an employe, not a guest."

He reflected a moment and reached a determination. "Look," he said.

"At what?" said Mrs. Parke.

"Nothing. I didn't mean it that way. I'll make a deal with you."

"A deal? The candy butcher proposes to chaffer with me. State your terms."

"Fifty percent off, if I get an invite to the party."

"In the name of all earth's wonders," said Mrs. Steevens Parke, "why should you wish to come to my party?"

"I've never been out in Society," he said.

His naïveté touched and amused her. "So you cherish ambitions? And you think that my function might prove a springboard. You may well be right." She laughed. "Very well. Your honorarium shall not be reduced. Put on your—er—soup-and-fish. Trenchant expression! After your performance, you may present yourself to me. There is a condition, however."

"I'll sign, unsight unseen."

"You must come and sing for me privately some day."

"Will you play my accompaniments?"

"Yes."

"Lady!" he exclaimed with irrepressible enthusiasm. "What a team you and me would make!"

"Flattered, indeed," she cackled. "Good day to you, Mr. Butcher."

16

As it turned out, Mr. Thomas Howatt attended the Great Social Event of the Season and Mr. Daniel Adriance did not. A Pennsylvania mob inconsiderately chose that particular July day to lynch an innocent Negro, and the *Star* sent its best reporter to the spot. Dan was unable to get back to New York until the next afternoon.

Laurie went to the Parke dance with the Duke's sister as chaperone. That it was her first ball and a very grand occasion, indeed, did not in the least ruffle her composure. She had the happy gift of self-possession without vanity. She assumed, in this new and exciting environment, that people would "be nice" to her, because people always had been. Nor was she disillusioned.

She was the center of curiosity first, and then of attention. Everybody was asking everybody else: Who was the lovely young creature in the white-and-silver mermaid dress? That nobody seemed to know added the charm of mystery. The men crowded around for introductions. The women raised their brows and gossiped. A few daring souls ventured to question the formidable hostess and got themselves soundly snubbed.

"Who is she? My guest. Have you any further impertinent inquiries in mind?" which effectually ended that line of investigation. And the hostess summoned her young protégée to the dais on which she sat in lonely empery and held her there for fifteen minutes of talk, which was more than she accorded to any other guest except the Duke himself.

She must be *somebody*. Mr. Ward McAllister had danced with her. She had been warmly greeted by Dr. Brockholst Farr, who was present, looking austere and benign. The dear Duke, although not a dancing man, had paid special attention to her. Envious females expressed damaging surmises. The simplest inference, that of an affair between the young girl and the old nobleman, was untenable. Grandma Parke's social morality was rigid: she would never have countenanced such a relationship. But the beautiful incognita might well be a relative of the guest of honor on the wrong side of the blanket. That would account for her being chaperoned by the Duke's sister. Europeans are so queer about illegitimacy! Another guess placed the stranger as some unknown heiress whom Stannard Barto had picked up for his notorious financial needs and foisted upon Grandma Parke. Kathleen Tennant's theory was simpler and more charitable: that Mrs. Parke had run across the girl somewhere— Hearn's or Arnold-Constable's or Central Park or the Fifth Avenue Hotel—and taken a liking to her. "Aunt Agatha is always picking up strays in the street. Though," she added in an impulse of fairness, "nothing in the same class with the Crosbie."

There was an intermission for refreshments. Champagne circulated. Laurie tasted hers cautiously.

"Go ahead. It will do you good," Stannard Barto encouraged her, and on the other side of her, Piet Van Dorp said, "Grandma Parke has the best cellar in New York."

A voice from the musician's gallery announced in a monotone: "You will now be entertained by a Scotch ballad."

A ripple of chords sounded from an unseen piano. The voice of an invisible singer floated forth, clear and sweet and mournful.

"Who'll buy my caller herrin'?"

Two of Laurie's admirers, who were doing their best to entertain her with sprightly conversation, found, to their discomfiture, that she was paying no heed to them. Her attention was absorbed in the fringe of palms above.

"While ye were sleepin' on your pillows
Dreamt ye aught of our puir fellows,
Darklin' as they faced the billows,
A' to fill our woven willows?
Buy my caller herrin'!"

pleaded the voice.

"What's the matter, Miss Crosbie?" boomed Piet Van Dorp.

"Nothing. Do hush!"

"That fellow's a discovery of mine," Stannard Barto put in. "Picked him up in a Sixth Avenue eatery."

"Who'll buy my caller herrin'?
Oh, ye may ca' them vulgar farin'
Wives and mithers maist despairin'
Ca' them lives o' men,"

the voice soared out above the buzz of unheeding talk.

135

"Oh, how *can* they chatter!" the girl cried in an agony of resentment.

"I don't know that he's so wonderful," Van Dorp objected, expressing a view only too obviously shared by much of the assemblage. Tommy was not faring so well as with the more appreciative and perhaps more artistic Sixth Avenue audience.

One hearer listened with appreciation tempered by wrath. Mrs. Steevens Parke was not pleased with the reception accorded her singer. Before the final stanza, she lifted a clarion contralto:

"Will the chattering fools who would rather talk than listen, kindly leave the room?"

There was a titter of startled laughter followed by awed silence. The singer finished to well-bred applause which swelled to an encore. If Grandma Parke was going to take up this ballad-mongering nonentity, Society was ready to fall into line. The soloist, still invisible, followed with the lovely "Lady Franklin's Lament" for a love lost in the Arctic wastes:

> *"When swallows build and the leaves come forth*
> *My old love wakes and cries."*

As the hard-bitten old dame was unashamedly dabbing at her eyes, Dr. Farr came up to her.

"Unmistakable, that voice," he said. "Where did you discover my friend, Thomas Howatt?"

"Is that young ruffian a friend of yours?"

The clergyman smiled. "I might add that he is my political mentor."

"Then why doesn't he give you better advice?"

"On what point?"

"Involving your church in this vice mess."

"Oh, he does. That is to say, he advises me against it."

"And you pay no heed?"

"I did not know that you were interested in the subject, ma'am."

"All New York is talking about it."

"So much the better."

She shook her lorgnette at him. "I don't understand you, Brockholst Farr. You must have a streak of vulgarity in your make-up. Do you *like* seeing your name in the papers?"

With unruffled temper he replied, "The newspapers help me get my message to the public."

"They fill your church, I'm told. What's this about a hell-roaring tirade that you are supposed to be preparing? When is it?"

"The first Sunday in August."

"Admission by ticket only, I hear. In the best circus tradition."

"May I send you one, ma'am?"

"By all means, I'll give it to my butler. He has a taste for sensationalism."

"Oh, Aunt Agatha! Give it to me." Kathleen Tennant had stopped, a glass of champagne in her hand, her brilliant eyes eager.

"Since when have you taken up churchgoing, my child?" the aunt inquired.

"Oh, but this is going to be like a big first-night. Everyone I know is scheming and plotting to get in."

Dr. Farr's voice was crisp as he turned to the girl. "If you assume, Miss Tennant, that this is a performance gotten up for the amusement of the frivolous and shallow, you are in error." He stalked away.

"Oh, dear!" she said to her aunt. "I didn't mean to offend him. Shall I chase him up and apologize?"

"No. Leave ill enough alone. Go back to your dancing."

Summoning Stannard Barto, she bade him fetch the vocalist to her.

"Here?" said Barto, scandalized.

"Certainly, here. Why not?"

"I only thought—"

"Don't try to think. Do as you're told."

"Yes, Aunt."

Brought to the presence, Tommy bore himself with simplicity and confidence. His hostess presented him to a number of people who had nothing to say to him and to whom he had nothing to say. Presently she rescued him from the repetition of meaningless pleasantries.

"You have earned your pay. You don't have to suffer those fools gladly, in addition."

"Yes'm," he replied, puzzled, and added, "I didn't think I did too goo—too well."

"You've done better, I daresay."

"It's a tough bunch to sing to."

"Crackwits," she said. "You have a wandering eye tonight, young man."

"Uh?" Tommy said, recalled to himself. "Beg your pardon."

"Who is she?"

"Er—nobody. Just looking 'em over."

"Well, go and get something to eat and drink. It isn't in the contract, but you might give us another song."

"I'd sing all night if you'd play my accompaniments."

She smiled at the artful compliment. "Too bad I have other duties. I daresay we should be a hit. Come back and see me later."

Hardly had he left when Laurie Crosbie bade her partner guide her up to the dais. "Is there going to be more singing, Mrs. Parke?" she asked.

"If you'd been a minute quicker, you could have asked the performer, himself. Did you ever hear anything quite like it?"

"Yes, Mrs. Parke."

"Yes? How is that?"

"I've heard him sing before."

"Really! Perhaps you would like to hear him again."

The girl hesitated.

"Or, wouldn't you?" the old lady asked with a sharp look.

"Yes, I should."

"What would you like?"

"Oh, anything."

"You never heard him sing 'The Great Adventurer,' I suppose."

"No. I don't know it."

"I'll send word to him."

An impatient partner claimed Laurie and led her away into a set of lancers. After the set, as she was sitting out, the announcement was made of another song number. This time there was a respectful hush; nobody wished to risk Grandma Parke's ire. Thus, every word, every intonation of the ancient ballad came clear and resonant to the ears of one rapt listener:

> *"You may tame the eagle*
> *To stoop to your fist.*
> *Or you may inveigle*
> *The phoenix of the East.*
> *The tigress, you may move her*
> *To give over her prey,*
> *You shall ne'er move a lover,*
> *Love will find out the way."*

The passion and the triumph coursed in Laurie's veins long after the last note was over. As she danced mechanically, with her thoughts still ensnared by the inner echoes, she surrendered to chance. If they encountered, she and Tommy, before the night was over, she would accept it as an omen. She could not know that Tommy, watching from his gallery, was leaving nothing to chance.

How it was brought about she could not have told. A kind of hypnosis that possessed her as she was walking down the big hallway—she thought foggily. Or did he whisper to her as she was passing? She found herself dismissing her escort with some vague and crazy kind of excuse, and stepping into the side passage, and regarding Tommy with an eye suddenly grown critical, and saying, quite naturally, "Tommy, you must *not* wear a satin bow with a swallow-tail."

To Tommy's entranced hearing it was the music of the spheres.

"Oh, L-l-laurie!" he stammered.

"Yes, Tommy."

"Take me back," he blurted.

She looked at him silently.

"I haven't said it since. I'll never say it again."

She began to laugh. "D'you know what you're like? You're just like a small boy that's been caught in a mischief."

"That's what I feel like— Take me back, Laurie."

"You are back."

"When can I come?"

"Tomorrow."

"Tomorrow. That's today."

"Yes."

"I'm going out to walk the street all night."

No account of the function appeared in the daily papers, except at second hand. Let social climbers court cheap publicity. Secure upon her eminence, Grandma Parke would have none of it. But *Town Topics* published paragraphs of ecstatic laudation upon "the beauteous incognita," terminating in a comment upon "the marked attention manifested by that popular member of our *jeunesse dorée,* Stannard Barto." (The item, as it subsequently developed, was from the secret pen of Mr. Barto himself.)

Leslie's Popular Weekly came out with a half-page picture of "the bewitching Miss Crosbie, Society's latest pet," which, as a likeness, was one degree worse than the ducal portrait for which Laurie had sat. That *chef d'oeuvre* was presented by the Duke to the city as a memento of his visit. The city passed it on to the Metropolitan Museum of Art, which dutifully hung it until the day of the visiting noble's departure, when it was relegated to the cellar.

It is still there.

17

Laurie's cousinly birthday gift to Dan Adriance had been a telephone. She had picked a time when she knew that he would be out of town for a few days, to have it installed. Thus he had no chance to reject it, had he wished to. ("And you can just put that petty pride of yours in your pocket, Dan dear.")

Only the rich and important could boast of having such a luxury in their homes. Having no claim to either quality, Dan was appropriately surprised on his return to find one of the small oblong oaken boxes affixed to the wall of his front room, complete with circular mouthpiece fitted into the front, crankshaft on the side, and receiver on a long cord hanging in the metal fork. A polite note from the Bell Telephone Company stated that all charges were paid for a year in advance. In the course of time the name of Daniel Adriance appeared in the new issue of the thin but impressive Telephone Directory.

One morning, a few days after the party, the not-too-silvery tintinnabulation of the mechanism brought Dan out of his comfortable bed at the untimely hour of nine A.M. An indistinct, though unmistakably feminine, voice was fervently adjuring Central to ring again.

"Hello, Laurie," Dan said, trying to clear his head of fog.

"What now?" the voice said in desperation. "Who's Laurie? And where does she come in?"

"Good God!" Dan was no longer sleepy.

"Wrong number," the voice returned composedly. "Is it really you, Dan?"

"Kathleen!"

"At least I don't have to identify myself. That's very flattering. Dan, I want you to do something for me."

"Otherwise you never would have called."

"Don't be growsly." She used the current adjective from a popular play at the Lyceum. "Do you know Dr. Brockholst Farr?"

"Yes."

"Maybe you report his sermons."

"Sometimes."

"Will you take me?"

"No."

"Are you really so cross with me?"

"Do you expect me to like being dropped for a century or so and taken up only when you want something of me?"

Now—Dan thought, with a hard-beating heart—she will cut off and I shall have lost her. But the apparatus, still operative, sighed. Then:

"How petty of you! You could have called me, you know."

"You forbade me."

"What a silly reason! Didn't you want to see me?"

"That's beside the point."

She said irrelevantly. "You're very ka-tish, having a private telephone."

"Never mind the telephone."

"I do mind the telephone. It's all Dr. Alexander Graham Bell's fault, damn him!"

"Do you want to get my line cut off?"

("Profane or improper language in the use of the Bell Telephone Company's lines may result in cancellation of the offending subscriber's contract.")

She laughed. "Well, it is! I was looking for another number and your name popped up right into my eyes. Names ought not to do that, Dan. It isn't fair."

Something went wrong with the connection, an almost invariable occurrence. There was a frantic quality in Kathie's voice when it reached Dan again.

"Hello! Hello! *Dan!* What happened? Are you there?"

"Yes."

"Central did something to the line. I'll bet she's listening in."

"Central is far too much occupied with her own business to intrude upon private conversations," said a prim and ladylike voice.

"Oh?" Kathie returned with an upward inflection. "Dan, why don't you say something reassuring?"

"I don't think I'd better say what I want to, over the wire."

Her voice was suave and contented as she said, "You do want to see me, then."

"Yes."

"I'll own up, Dan. Dr. Farr was a subterfuge. There was your name, large as life—and all of a sudden I thought how silly it was for us to be so near and not see one another."

"Then you don't care anything about the ticket for the church."

"Oh, don't I though! I've bet Carola Cunningham a five-pound box of Huyler's that I could get to go."

"All right. I daresay I can fix it."

"Of course you can. What's your price?"

"I have tomorrow evening off. Come out to dinner with me?"

"Unchaperoned?"

"You did it before without any dire results."

"I'm not so sure of that. But all right. You can take me to one of your disreputable newspaper haunts. Come for me at six. Good-bye, Dan dear."

"Good-bye, Kathie."

Never was a longer wait than that one seemed to Dan. Kathleen greeted him as casually as if they had parted the week before. But her eyes, holding their soft and steady glance full upon him, as the Fourth Avenue car jolted them downtown, were warm and kind.

At the terminal he guided her into the dim cavern of Beekman Street. She tucked her arm beneath his and pressed it hard against her firm body.

"Where are you taking me, Dan?" she asked, and added happily, "Not that I care."

They turned the corner into William Street and entered Katie's, the simple and excellent restaurant in the heart of the Swamp, frequented by the leather trade for luncheon and by the more prosperous newspapermen from Park Row at dinner. A corner on the upper platform was vacant. From it they commanded a view of the long bar and the clustered tables below.

Ernst, the gruff, efficient German waiter, came up with the menu in purple handscript.

"What's specially good here?" the girl asked.

"Everything," Dan told her. "Don't think you're slumming."

"I don't," she assured him. "I think it's fascinating."

"Quaint is the uptown word," he said.

She made a face at him. "Do you think I'm so banal?"

"No. Cocktail?"

"Of course. Can they make a Lone Tree?"

"Yes. I've taught Ernst." He gave the order.

"Are you glad to see me, Dan?"

"Shall I tell you how glad?"

"Not here." She pushed the handwritten scroll across to him. "You choose." She drank her cocktail.

"Another?"

"Of course. School's out tonight."

He ordered one of Katie's specialties, grilled lamb chops with kartoffeln, followed by a green salad, apfelstrudel, a ripe cheese and coffee. After the cocktails, two tall seidels of Nicklausbrau, another specialty of the house, were placed beside them.

While the order was preparing, Kathie looked about her with interested eyes. Her interest was stirred by two youngish men at a corner table back of her, intent upon a chessboard. The one facing them lifted a bearded face and nodded to Dan.

"I didn't know that reporters wore whiskers," she whispered to Dan.

"The law against it was repealed last year," he replied gravely. "Besides, Hart Lyman isn't a reporter. He's credited with being the editorial brains of the *Trib*."

"And the other one? His beard looks new."

"That's Gene Wood. He's the best writer in the *World* city room. Does all the fancy stories."

A steady stream of diners followed, and were identified by Dan for his companion's benefit. "If a slug of dynamite were dropped in here," he said, "tomorrow's papers would be so thin you could see through them."

They sat in great contentment, reverting to the tall, flavorous, full-bodied services of Nicklausbrau, chatting happily of themselves. Customers came and went; nobody paid any heed to them. There was no hovering waiter to suggest that they had used up their time. This homely, comfortable little corner of the world was theirs for as long as they chose to enjoy its friendly seclusion.

It was nearly midnight when Kathie asked, "Dan, are you sober?"

"Reasonably."

"So am I. But not sober enough to be thinking of home. Let's go dancing."

"Where? There are no respectable places to dance."

"Do we have to be respectable tonight?"

"All right," he said. "I'll take you to the Haymarket."

"I've heard of it," she said. "But no one would ever take me there."

"I've got no business to."

"Why? Is it very dangerous?"

"No. Not dangerous at all."

"Is it very wicked?" she asked hopefully.

"Well, it's no church picnic."

"I'm supposed to be naturally fast," she said lightly. "Let's have one of those little things with gilt flakes floating around in it, and then go."

It was early for full tide in the Haymarket when they arrived, but there was a fair representation of the regulars, including a number from Clark's.

"Let's get a place where we can see everything," the girl whispered as they approached the box office. Dan led her beneath the double row of varicolored lights to a wall box which, while not too conspicuous, commanded a good view. Kathie's expression was avid. She wanted to know all about it. Were those girls seated in other boxes or parading on the floor really professionals? Could any man just go out and pick them up? Where did they live? How much did they charge? Did they *have* to go with any man that wanted them? Suppose some of them didn't catch a patron: would they go home alone? They all looked so—so easy and cheerful: did they really *like* the life?

"Morbid curiosity." Dan jeered at her. "They aren't so different from other people, except that most of 'em aren't too bright. Would you like to dance?"

"No. I want to find out things. Do you know any of those girls, Dan?"

"Some."

"Why don't they speak to you?"

"It wouldn't be good form, when I'm with you."

"Good form?" she repeated wonderingly.

"The Haymarket has its own code of etiquette."

"Well, there's someone who isn't bound by it."

One of the paper missiles which were a pastime of the place struck him on the shoulder. He turned. Tommy Howatt in a top-price box, his smart derby on the side of his head, his unlighted cigar forming a complementary angle, jerked his neck violently, signaling "Come on over," and waved a bottle as incentive. Dan gave him the savagest scowl he could command, though unhopeful that it would deter him.

"Who's the extraordinary little vulgarian?" Kathie asked, her eyes alight. Then: "Why, I do believe it's Aunt Agatha's hired songbird!"

"Right. Tommy Howatt. *Police Gazette.*"

"A friend of yours?"

"Yes. No."

"Don't commit yourself. That's a gay little person with him."

Nita, trim and piquant, was drinking champagne, at Tommy's expense so far as Dan could see, since they were alone in the box. He wondered at the prodigality. The solution came shortly. The orchestra leader announced:

"The Tenderloin's own Tommy has kindly consented to oblige us with a couple of vocal selections."

Of course! The box, with champagne trimmings, was payment by the management. The thought crossed Dan's mind that if his music was for general hire, Tommy might have done better.

Whisking his banjo from beneath the table, the musician opened up with one of his own ribald compositions, then announced: "The T. Howatt variation on the popular Mexican *cachucha*. All in on the beat." He led:

> *"She was riding down the pike*
> *On her bike*
> *With her Mike*
> *And her feet upon the handle bars."*
> (Choral antiphony) "HANDLEBARS."

The second stanza was quite unrelated:

> *"Oh, a lady on the river*
> *Got a sliver*
> *In her liver.*
> *Did it hurt her?"*
> (Choral antiphony) "YES, YOU BET IT DID. BET IT DID!"

and so on, into unlimited tooraloo-tooralooras. Then, after a pause for drink, and to muted strings, Tommy appealed to the ever-responsive sentimentality of whoredom with a tender rendition of "Robin Adair."

It was between two stanzas that Kathie murmured, "What a wicked voice!"

"Wicked?" Dan recalled what Laurie had said when first she heard Tommy sing.

"It makes you feel so—so thrilly," his companion said.

Dan was not pleased. Jealous already, he did not want Kathleen Tennant to feel "thrilly" about any other man, least of all Tommy Howatt.

She sensed his displeasure and smiled tolerantly. "Don't worry, Dan. He isn't my type. But I think he could do anything with most girls."

"So he thinks," Dan said.

"Do ask him and his little brunette over. She's cunning. Do you mind?"

"It's your party, my dear."

"It is. And you needn't be growsly about it."

Dan went over to deliver the invitation. Tommy was all for it, but Nita was dubious.

"What's the game?" she asked. "She isn't our kind. Is she your new girl, Dan?"

"No," he said. "Nothing of that sort. She's seeing the world."

They came over, Tommy carrying the bucket with the champagne in it. Nita, as the introductions were made, was prim and correct. Not so the flamboyant Tommy. After one searching look he said to Kathleen, "Off your beat, aren't you, sister?"

She looked to her escort for enlightenment. It was Tommy who afforded it.

"This is the evening session of the good, old he-and-she combination," he went on, "in case Dan, here, didn't tell you."

"Tommy!" said Nita, shocked. "Behave." She was being very much the lady.

Kathie said easily, "Dan said he would show me some of the wicked spots."

Tommy's grin was that of cynical superiority. *"This* wicked? Woopsy! This is the Second Baptist Church sewing bee. Looky, sister! Want to see something that is something?"

"Yes."

"Ever hear of the Slide?"

"Will you mind your own damn business, Tommy?" Dan put in angrily.

Kathie cut in, her quick curiosity aroused. "No. What is it? Will you take me there, Dan?"

"I will not."

Opposition stirred the spoiled child in Kathleen. She turned to Tommy. "Will *you* take me there?"

Tommy's recklessness had its limits. "Why—er—you see, you came with Dan and it wouldn't hardly be square for me to play Mr. Buttinsky."

Kathie's face became petulant. "I don't like being told where I can go and can't go."

"All right—all right, sister," Tommy soothed her. "Lots of time. The Slide isn't going out of business tomorrow. Here's my number."

A male voice from across the floor shouted, "Give us the boater, Tommy." Others joined in the demand. The singer nodded to the orchestra leader, who led his men into the pulsing waltz-rhythm of the "Eton Boating Song":

> *"Jolly boating weather*
> *With a hay-harvest breeze.*
> *Oars on the feather,*
> *Wind from the trees.*
> *Swing, swing together*
> *With your bodies between your knees."*

146

It was like a flow of fresh air through the foulness. Soon the listeners were swaying in their seats to the irresistible lift and surge of the measure. Imperishable youth sounded and challenged in the silver-clear tenor. With the final lines of the second stanza, the leader had them on their feet, abandoned to his mastery. Whore and pimp, wastrel and rounder, they lifted their spirits in the universal fellowship of song:

> *"Nothing in life shall sever*
> *The ties that unite us now."*

Tommy came back to the box, flushed and smug.

"You were wonderful, darling," Nita said.

"Got 'em, didn't I!"

"You've never had any training, have you, Mr. Howatt?" Kathleen asked.

"Nope. Never had time."

"Will you go to see a musician friend of mine if I give you his address?"

"I'm doing all right," he said a little sulkily. His eyes grew cunning. He was already pretty sure that this swell girl from uptown was the writer of the letters in Dan Adriance's pilfered desk. Now he saw a way to make sure. Taking a pencil from his waistcoat pocket, he handed it to Kathleen and pushed a menu across the table. "Would you write the address for me?" he requested.

She did so. One glance at the bold, fashionable writing satisfied him. Dan Adriance's girl! Here was something to have up the cuff.

He was pouring out the last round of drinks when Nita, who was facing the door, said in an amused voice, "Well, look at what got loose from the barnyard! Old Grampa Original Hayseed."

Two men were making their way along the row of tables on the far side of the floor. As Dan turned, they were settling into a second-row box and were only semi-visible in the dimness of the colored lights. The shorter of the pair seemed to Dan vaguely familiar. The other, a tall and whiskered individual, was clad in baggy, rustic clothes, and wore heavy, disfiguring glasses.

Dan's scrutiny was interrupted by a clutch upon his arm. Tommy said in his ear, "Do you see what I see?"

"I don't know," Dan said doubtfully. "That younger chap—"

"To hell with him. Pipe the country jay. Don't you get him?"

"No."

"It's Dr. Farr."

"You're off your base."

"Am I! Take another glim."

147

Dan did so and recognized not the tall man but his companion. "Maybe you're right. The other one is Allen Hardwick."

"Sure it is. The holy-boly. The little angel pal of the Reverend Brockholst Farr."

Craning her neck to see, Kathleen Tennant said, "I do believe it is Dr. Farr. What on earth would he be doing in a place like this?"

"Pickin' up evidence." Tommy chuckled. "Prob'ly for his sermon. 'West of Broadway—by One Who's Been There.' "

Kathleen said to Dan, "I'd just as lief he shouldn't see me. Aunt Agatha would not be pleased."

"Right. We'll get out."

As he was paying the bill, Kathleen turned to Tommy. "What was that place you spoke of?"

"The Slide."

"Will it be open?"

"Never heard of it closing this early."

"You'd like to go, wouldn't you?" she coaxed Nita.

"Why, I—I guess so if Dan—Mr. Adriance doesn't mind."

Adriance turned on Kathleen. "Okay. You win," he said in disgust. "I wish you well of it."

"The Slide"—owned by Frank Stephenson, a power in Tammany Hall—was a sinkhole of commercialized perversion, a port of call for the more depraved type of sensation seeker and the more adventurous type of traveling man with his mistress-for-a-night. When the Tenderloin went slumming, it visited the Slide.

A far-off rumbling from uptown gave warning to the quartet waiting outside the Haymarket.

"Run for it!" Tommy shouted, and they raced to the corner and up the elevated stairs, reaching the platform as the steamy, cinder-belching locomotive shook the structure with its approach. They got off at the Bleecker Street Station.

The Slide was almost in the shadow of the El, a basement dive with only two small wall lanterns at the front to indicate entertainment within. Descending three steps from the pavement, they entered through a discreetly frosted double door opening upon a long, murky room furnished with round oilcloth-topped tables. Dan had been there once before. Once was enough. Tommy, assuming an air of familiarity, remarked that it was pretty early to see much; the sightseers didn't start coming in until three o'clock or so. They got a table near the door. Two near-by tables were occupied; one by a furtive pair, conferring with heads close together, the other by three jovial drunks. At the rear were clustered the regulars, several of whom exhibited the bare shoulders of evening dress.

Kathie whispered in Dan's ear, "What queer-looking girls!"

Dan grunted.

A hulking, stupid-looking waiter with a cauliflower ear took Tommy's order for a pint bottle of rye. "With the cork in," he specified. "Don't ever get anything here that don't come in a sealed bottle," he added wisely, for the instruction of his less knowledgeable companions.

Nita spoke up. "Tommy, I don't like this place. I never liked it."

"Sister, here, wanted to see it," Tommy returned. "We can get the hell out after our drink."

Two dissipated-looking men entered with a handsome woman and took the adjoining table. One of them waved a greeting to the group in the rear. A monstrous bloat of a creature, in the lowest of evening gowns, rose and approached with a delicate flirt of pudgy fingers. The air was tainted with a reek of some gross perfume.

"Hello, folks," the apparition trilled.

"That's the famous Princess Toto," Tommy said.

Kathleen stared with starting eyes. She gripped Dan's arm. "Why —why—it's a *man!*" she gasped.

"If you don't care what you say." Tommy grinned.

Kathie got to her feet. "Take me out," she said in a thickened voice. "I'm going to be sick."

Dan got her into the open none too soon. After the first paroxysm was over, she sat on the top step, panting. She looked at him contritely.

"I'll know better next time," she said, and was racked again.

Nita came out to help. Tommy was still inside paying the bill.

"You go back, Nita," Dan said. "I'll take care of this." He hauled Kathie to her feet and set her down, none too gently.

"Oomph-a!" she gulped.

"Now that you've had your way," he said, "how do you like it?"

"Don't be horrid to me, Dan."

"Are you ready to go home?"

"Oughtn't we to say good night to the others?"

"They can take care of themselves."

She looked down her front with dismay. "Can't I get cleaned up somewhere?"

"You can come to my place."

"How far?"

"Only a few blocks."

"All right. I can walk now."

They climbed to his fourth-floor walk-up flat. Kathie looked around the large, bare front room. "How the other half lives," she murmured mischievously.

149

He got out a dressing gown, tossed it to her, and threw open the bathroom door. "Go in there and take off your waist," he said. "I'll clean it for you."

She obeyed without question, followed him into the kitchen and perched on the table while he went to work with soap and brush at the sink. "Not very romantic," she murmured.

He did not reply. For several minutes she sat silent, swinging her leg over the corner of the table. "Are you still cross with me?" she asked.

"Are you pleased with yourself?" he countered.

"You have the face of a medieval saint," she mused. "Ascetic. St. Augustine."

"Wrong saint," he said. "He was no ascetic."

"Wasn't he? Why?"

"Haven't you ever heard of his famous prayer?"

"No. What is it?"

" 'God give me chastity, but not yet awhile,' " he quoted.

She laughed. "You made it up, didn't you?"

"No. It's authentic." He shook out the garment and hung it to dry. "That's the best I can do," he said. "Give it an hour, and you'll be able to go home."

"Lucky I have my own key," she said. "A whole hour? What'll we do? Can you scramble eggs?"

"I can scramble an egg beyond human recognition. But I'm afraid there aren't any."

"Well, we can always pass the time in polite and polished conversation," she mocked.

Back in the front room she caught sight of Dan's new Edison phonograph. "Oh, you've got one of those!" she cried. "Play it."

He fixed the needle. It buzzed into a Maggie Cline song.

"Let's dance," she cried and slipped into his arms.

He drew her close. She pressed against him. There was no reservation in her embrace, nor in the fire of her kiss. At long last their lips sundered. "Oh, Dan!" she whispered.

"I love you," he said.

She shook her head. "Don't love me too much," she warned with a touch of sadness.

"It's too late to tell me that, darling."

She cocked a fist at the gramophone. "Shut off that damned thing," she said. "Look what it's got me into!" She looked about her, and laughed softly. "St. Augustine had something," she said.

He loosed her from his arms and threw open the door to the rear room.

Long, long afterwards as it seemed, she stirred against his breast, and murmured, "What time is it?"

"Must I look?"

"No, don't."

She said, after another long interval, "My things must be dry by now."

"I hope not," he said.

"I ought to hope that they are." She chuckled. "But, like St. Augustine again, 'not yet awhile.' "

It was gray dawn when they went down the stairs together. Her eyes had that smiling somnolence that told of sated nerves.

At her door Dan said, "When shall I see you again?"

"I don't know."

"Soon?"

"I don't know, Dan."

"Kathie, I love you. Do you love me?"

"I don't know, Dan. What is love?"

"Tonight was."

"Was it? I don't know. It was sweet and wonderful."

"Will you marry me?"

"No. Why should I? Because of tonight?"

"Partly."

"That's no reason. You're not my first lover."

"I know that."

"And it makes no difference?"

"Yes. It hurts. But it doesn't matter. I love you."

"You're a dear, Dan. But it's still no."

"I won't take it."

"I'm afraid you must," she said somberly.

"Unless you're secretly married already."

"No, I'm not."

"Then I shall keep on asking you. When shall I see you again?"

"At the Old Stone Church. Don't forget about that ticket."

"Damn the ticket. I mean, I'll get it. When am I to see you alone?" he persisted.

"How can I tell? I'll send you word. Good night, darling."

She kissed him gently and was gone.

18

Once more Tommy Howatt was breezily *persona grata* at the Valdevia. Between Laurie and himself the former half-playful relationship of teacher and pupil was restored, but the opportunity of tête-à-tête lessons was distressingly diminished. If he chanced to find Laurie alone, her mother always contrived to drop in on them.

"What ails the old hen, anyway?" he demanded. "Does she think I'm going to bite her gal?"

Dan had already noted the mother's watchfulness. She confided in him that she was worried.

"That's a normal, maternal condition, isn't it?" he returned lightly. She refused to meet his mood. "Laurie's not like other girls."

"That's a typical maternal view, too, I should think."

"Dan, I told you once that I was afraid Laurie had—well, a slant against men."

"Yes, I remember."

"I was wrong. Have you ever watched her when young Howatt is singing?"

"Not specially."

"Well, do. It's—it's uncanny, the effect he has on her. Like mesmerism. Maybe she is a one-man woman. And, oh, Dan! he isn't the right man. I did so hope that it would be Allen Hardwick."

"Has she turned Hardwick down?"

"I'm afraid so. He hasn't given up, though."

"I shouldn't expect him to give up easily."

"Then there's Stannard Barto."

"A bad bet, if you ask me."

"He's Mrs. Steevens Parke's favorite nephew, they say. What do you think of her, Dan?"

"Oh, there's no vice in the old gal."

"She's being wonderful to Laurie."

After the ducal ball, the old lady took up the young beauty with a fervor that bordered on devotion. She took her driving in the Park, asked her to luncheon, tea, and dinner, and would have made a constant companion of her, had not Laurie held off a little. She liked being made much of but not to the extent of being taken charge of. There was a streak of sturdy independence in her.

Most of the Parke counsel was shrewd and worldly, much of it cynical, some of it disconcerting. The old lady shocked Laurie by rallying her on her "blatant virginity."

"You're like one of those hundred-percent-pure advertisements," she jeered.

She did not approve of the girl's Sunday-school work with the Little Crumbs of Comfort Sewing Circle, which she derided as "knitting unwearables for untouchables." She was prodigal with aphorisms of her own composition. "Reputation is one thing that can't be preserved in alcohol." "Good form is ninety-nine percent don'ts." "Fashion is for those without taste; etiquette for those without breeding." "Virtue is a woman's most essential requisite, except, of course, reputation." "Remember always that you are part animal; try to live up to it." "If you must drink, drink in public; if you must smoke, smoke in private." "The way for a young girl to get on in Society is to cultivate the women; let the men cultivate you."

In pursuance of this latter policy, Mrs. Parke saw to it that her protégée met the inner circle of the debutantes and post-debutantes. The new beauty's adorers began to bring their sisters and their cousins, if not their aunts. Because Laurie was gay and simple and as good-mannered as she was sweet-natured and a pet of the formidable dowager, she was accepted without question. Soon the Valdevia apartment became something of a rendezvous for the younger set. There they gathered of an afternoon to drink tea or lemonade and munch little cakelets and large candies. No cocktails or highballs. Liquor was not for buds, except perhaps champagne at coming-out parties.

Thus Laurie came to know the kind of girls whose names appeared in the papers without any effort to put them there: the Gilliat sisters; the Mauries; Chessie Edie, the loveliest brunette of her year; Lily Devereux, whom all the painters solicited for her alluring figure; Flora and Fauna, the sparkling twin daughters of the famous Professor Sturdevant; Bess Whiting, the ingénue of the exclusive Comedy Club; the doll-like but daring Baby Kerr; and scores of others. She admitted all equally to her hospitality; none to her intimacy. This reserve enhanced rather than diminished her popularity.

Where the young charmers gathered, the men naturally followed. Half a dozen of them were regarded as more or less overt suitors of Laurie's, with Stannard Barto and Allen Hardwick in the lead, Van Dorp and Ranney having fallen behind, Dan Adriance something of a mystery, and Tommy Howatt very much in the background.

The girls were shy of Dan, since he was that rather fearsome creature, a reporter, and therefore presumptively, an outsider. Tommy was at first a bit shy of the girls—or, at least, distrustful—until several of them manifested an interest in him, as an unknown species.

To them the *Police Gazette* meant nothing; they had never so much as heard of it. But this strange young man's connection with so suggestively named an entity delightfully connoted crime and slums and a world of mystery. They plied him with questions and were fascinated by his revelations, which, indeed, were richly tinged with imaginative romanticism. When he let drop that he was a pal of Dr. Brockholst Farr, he became quite the center of attention. They were all subject to that burning curiosity, modified by caution, with which nice girls dallied with a topic by no means nice. Tommy enjoyed the sensation which he was occasioning, but he did wish that there was more chance of seeing Laurie alone.

The one point upon which the eager questioners found this queer and fascinatingly alarming specimen unresponsive was their hostess. However tactfully he was questioned, he took refuge in a stony silence.

Laurie's new friends were not alone in their curiosity. Mrs. Steevens Parke was also concerned and, as she would have maintained, with a better right than those chattering young chits. She telephoned Dan Adriance and asked him to tea. Dan went, wondering what now. He was not long left in uncertainty. Mrs. Parke's butler, after ushering him in, was instructed that his mistress was not at home to anyone else. The precaution struck Dan as a formidable prelude. The old lady opened up at once.

"Young man, I want to talk with you about the Crosbies."

"Why me?" Dan asked, instantly on the defensive.

"Because of the family tie. I have called on Mrs. Crosbie."

"That was kind of you."

"Not kindness at all. Curiosity. With a reason. It did me no good. I came away with a flea in my ear."

"You surprise me," Dan said politely.

"It surprised *me,*" the grande dame admitted. "Mrs. Crosbie begged to be excused. I am not accustomed to be turned away from obscure doors, with a polite social lie about a headache."

"Mrs. Crosbie is very subject to them," the visitor said diplomatically.

"Hmmmph!" She eyed him with suspicion. "You know my interest in Laurie Crosbie."

"Yes, Mrs. Parke."

"She has a brilliant social future, if she will let herself be guided."

"I am sure she could have no better guidance than yours, ma'am."

154

"Soft sawder! But you're right this time. Mr. Adriance, where does the Crosbie money come from?"

Dan was honestly astonished. "Surely you don't expect me to discuss their private affairs with you, Mrs. Parke."

"It was worth the trial." She chuckled. She leaned forward. "Young man, I am becoming foolishly fond of that girl."

"I'm sure it isn't foolish, ma'am."

"I have plans for her. I am prepared to take her back to Newport with me. I don't know whether you realize how much I can do for her. But only with her co-operation. Unless she is willing to go along, I cannot protect her against the gossip incident to—to certain associations. I may tell you that inquiries have been discreetly made as to Mrs. Crosbie's past. They are not reassuring."

"What is your source?"

"Never mind that. The point is, could Mrs. Crosbie be persuaded to leave the city for her daughter's good?"

Dan rose. "Not by me," he said. "And I have no intention of trying. Is that clear, Mrs. Parke?"

"Sit down. And keep your temper. I mean well by your lovely Laurie. And I have hopes that Mrs. Crosbie could be persuaded to see how advantageous it would be for her daughter if the girl were wholly isolated from the past. There is a brilliant marriage in prospect."

"To your nephew?" Dan was still standing.

"Stannard Barto will be my heir if he marries with my approval. And Laurie Crosbie is the girl whom I have chosen for him. You may have the item of the proposed marriage for your newspaper later. A scoop, I believe it is called."

"Only on the stage. On Park Row we say a beat."

"Stannard will join us at Newport. The announcement will be made there."

"I hope not, Mrs. Parke."

"You think it an unsuitable match?"

"Extremely so. For Miss Crosbie."

"Young man, are you trying to be rude?"

"No. Merely honest. Don't you think that you have said too much not to tell me more? What is this mysterious past of Mrs. Crosbie's?"

"Don't you know?"

"No. I'm wholly in the dark."

She pondered. "I don't like scandal, myself," she said at last. "But you're sure to find out, one day. Have you ever heard of the Calloway case in San Francisco?"

"No."

155

"Look it up." She rose and held out her hand, smiling. "You're an insolent young pup, but I rather like you. Don't think too hardly of the old shrew. Society is a cold-blooded proposition."

Deeply disturbed, Dan went at once to the Crosbies'. Laurie was reading a Richard Harding Davis story in *Scribner's*. Mrs. Crosbie was lying down. He asked the girl, "Are you going to visit Grandma Parke in Newport?"

"How did you know about that?" she said.

"She told me. I've just come from having tea with her."

"Oh, my! How social! You must be qualifying for the Patriarchs."

"Grandma's quite a girl. She's very fond of you."

"She's been sweet to me. Newport sounds rather fun. I've never been there. What do you think, Dan?"

"About your going there? I think no."

"Because of Stan Barto?"

"Yes."

"Mother doesn't like him, either."

"Aren't you riding in the Park today?"

"Yes, with Cecily Mannering. Why?"

"I want to talk to your mother."

"How mysterious! All right. If I'm not wanted I shall haughtily retire." She made a face at him. "I'll send Mother in. Good-bye."

Mrs. Crosbie looked as if she had not slept for nights. At the mention of Stannard Barto's name, she flinched. This was no time to be mealy-mouthed, Dan decided. He put it to her straight.

"Has Barto been threatening you?"

Her hand went to her heart. "How did you know?"

"Mrs. Crosbie, I want to help you and Laurie."

"Oh, Dan, if only you could! I'm so frightened!"

"I can't unless I know the facts."

Her hands clenched and unclenched. At length she spoke. "Yes, I've been wanting to tell somebody. It's more than I can carry alone."

"Blackmail?"

"I suppose you'd call it that. He wants to marry Laurie."

"I know that."

"He says that unless she marries him the whole story will come out in *Town Topics*. He says that marriage to him will stop it. There's something going to be printed very soon, and another, a terrible thing will come out later unless he stops it."

"Is it that Calloway case?"

"Yes," she said faintly. "You know about it, then."

"Very little. You'd better tell me."

Slowly and painfully she resurrected the twelve-year-old San Francisco scandal, the reputed murder in a high-class brothel, of the

156

mayor's brother, "Suds" Calloway. It was a sordid tale, never fully cleared up, of the nocturnal death of an elderly and lecherous millionaire; a story of vice and of suppression of facts by political influence, and of persecution of a too-vulnerable woman by officers of the law.

"Dan, I had no more to do with it than you. He wasn't killed. It was a stroke."

"But he did die in that house."

"Yes."

"And you were—" He groped for words to finish the ugly question.

"Yes. It was my place." Her voice was barely audible.

"How much does Barto know?"

"He claims to know everything."

"And Laurie?"

"Oh, nothing. Nothing!"

"Not your—your former occupation?"

"God, no!"

He stopped to think. Presently he said, "Anyone familiar with the circumstances would guess that you didn't get out of that San Francisco scrape with money enough to carry on your present scale of living."

"Her father's oil properties have been profitable."

"Mr. Crosbie's?"

"Yes."

"I understood that he was dead."

"So he is."

"As Laurie's guardian, shouldn't Mr. Perley be informed of this threat?"

"He knows about it."

"What is his advice?"

"To keep Stannard Barto on the string for a while. He's sure he can buy off Colonel Mann." (Dan thought it highly probable; the owner of *Town Topics* was always amenable to financial persuasions.) "But Barto could still tell Laurie. That would kill me." Mrs. Crosbie broke down and wept.

"We'll find some way to deal with him," Dan promised and left.

It occurred to him that Tommy Howatt might be useful in the crisis. He did not, however, propose to give away anything that the *P.G.* man did not already know. He found Tommy at the office and, feeling his way, asked if he had ever heard of the Calloway case.

Tommy gave him a startled look. "What do you know about it?"

"I'm asking you what you know."

"Plenty. It's in the files."

"You won't find the latest development in the files, though," the reporter said grimly.

"No? Spill it."

"Stannard Barto is using it to threaten Mrs. Crosbie because she doesn't want Laurie to marry him."

"I'll kill the son-of-a-bitch."

"That would be a neat solution. But it might get you into trouble."

Tommy became thoughtful. "Look, Dan. If I figure out a way to choke off this Barto bastard, it sure ought to boost me with Laurie. Huh?"

"Don't be a damned fool! Laurie mustn't know anything about this."

"You mean she isn't wise to it? Not any of it?"

"No. She's been away at school ever since she was a little girl. I doubt if she even remembers San Francisco."

"That's different." Tommy sighed for lost opportunity. "Oh, well! Tell Mrs. Crosbie not to worry about Barto."

"What have you got in mind for him?"

"A little private entertainment committee. That hombre is yellow, Dan. Before we're through with him he'll be hollerin', 'Po-leece, po-lyce, po-lousy!' for help all over the lot."

"I'll be listening," said Dan.

19

Every city editor in New York kept file on the Old Stone Church. Already established as news, the Reverend Dr. Brockholst Farr was potentially Sensation. It was the belief of Park Row that his sermon on the pre-announced text, "Her Feet Take Hold on Hell," was going to blow the lid off.

Notwithstanding the heat of the August Sunday, the church was packed for the occasion. Reporters filled one whole gallery: the top men of every New York and Brooklyn paper, with a considerable representation from outside. Thomas Howatt of the *Police Gazette* felt a thrill of pride at rubbing elbows with so distinguished a collection.

He gazed down wistfully upon the Crosbie pew, where Laurie sat between her mother and Allen Hardwick. A few seats away Harrison M. Perley leaned back, his face heavy with thought. The observer in the gallery thought that he looked worried. A charming face beneath an ultra-fashionable hat across from him caught Tommy's attention. Dan Adriance's girl—he thought. Wonder how she got here. Wonder if Dan's seen her. Dan's face was not visible from Tommy's seat.

The usual announcements, prayers, hymns hardly held the attention of the waiting congregation. They were intent upon their pastor, who sat in his high-backed ecclesiastical chair, his face taut. There was a restrained buzz when he spoke the bitter words of the text. Before he had spoken two minutes in his controlled, assured voice, his hearers were straining forward in their seats, hushed and tense, as the quick fire of accusal hammered in their ears.

"—the whore of Babylon whose handmaidens roam our streets, harpies of lust, seeking their prey. Shall I name their haunts for you? The brothels kept, under the protection of our police, by such queens of vice as Georgiana Hastings, Flo Durant of the Green Shutters, Etta Holmes of the Bower and Carrie Baker of the House of Nations? House of Damnations! Why do the police permit the hell-holes known as dance halls to flourish and flout the law: the Cremorne, the Alhambra, the Haymarket and others, where the devil-dance of harlotry is carried on under the stimulus of law-defying liquor?"

"The old boy does get around, don't he?" Pop Arnold of the *Press* murmured admiringly in Tommy's ear.

The calmly bitter denunciation went on:

"The network of prostitution is over our entire municipal structure. Through its meshes dribbles tribute to our courts, our law-enforcement officials, our highest office-holders. In its municipal life our city is thoroughly rotten. Every step that we attempt, looking to the moral betterment of this city, is taken against the pressure of the damnable pack of administrative bloodhounds that fatten on corruption. They are a lying, perjured, rum-soaked, libidinous lot. Every move to clean out this moral cesspool is fought by the Mayor and his whole gang of drunken and lecherous subordinates. Immunity for gambling, prostitution, and violation of the liquor láws is sold over the counter by the Police Department. Mayor, District Attorney and police are making New York a hotbed of vice and taking their profit of it."

"Whoa, *boy!*" Tommy warned, maintaining with difficulty his sotto voce.

The preacher went on: "Do you know what this district is called by the police? The Tenderloin. Easy meat! The police captain—he is an inspector now—who gave it that name was able on a salary of $2,200 a year, to buy a yacht and own his own house. Police officials, one after another, have grown rich in this Tenderloin. Upon what? Upon the loot of gamblers and the sweat of prostitution."

"He's got something there," Tommy muttered. "But what can he prove?"

Dr. Farr piled charge upon charge, denunciation upon denunciation, while a rapt and silent congregation listened in enjoyable shock. At the close, he paused and let his gaze wander somberly over the faces below him. Slowly and impressively he formulated for the first time the indictment which was to be the key theme of his campaign.

"Organized vice cannot exist without police complicity.

"Organized crime cannot exist without police connivance.

"Organized lawlessness cannot exist without police corruption."

Then came the direct challenge:

"An arrogant political boss named Tweed once defied the forces of law and decency in our great, rich, and cultivated city, with this challenge: 'What are you going to do about it?' I borrow his method.

"I ask the Mayor of New York, What are you going to do about it?

"I ask the Commissioners of Police, What are you going to do about it?

"I ask the District Attorney of the County, What are you going to do about it?

160

"I ask the Legislature at Albany, What are you going to do about it?

"Finally, I ask you, the people, What are *you* going to do about it?"

The church was buzzing as the pastor went from the rostrum to his study. The people did not leave as usual. They stood about in the aisles, in the lobby, on the steps, discussing the most sensational sermon ever preached from a New York pulpit. Harrison M. Perley hurried about, gathering his fellow trustees for an emergency meeting. Tommy saw Dan Adriance and two other reporters intercept him. He shook his head angrily. Tommy ran down the stairs and accosted the *Star* man.

"See that hombre over there?" He indicated a tall, spare fellow with thick glasses who was edging his way toward an exit.

"What about him? Who is he?"

"Ben McGloyne. His middle name might be Trouble."

"McGloyne? McGloyne? Ought I to know him?"

"Not necessarily. He's a quiet worker. Undercover man for District Attorney Delaney Marshall."

The *Star* man whistled softly. "I'd better have a crack at him."

Dan pushed through the buzzing crowd, but McGloyne had vanished. Turning back, the reporter came face to face with Kathleen Tennant. He promptly forgot about his quarry.

"Kathie!"

"Hello, Dan," she said softly.

"You got here all right."

"Thanks to you." She smiled. *"What* a show!"

He looked about him. Toward the front there was a secluded pew off a side aisle. "Come over here where we can talk," he said urgently.

She hesitated. "All right," she said.

When they were seated she asked, "Aren't you supposed to be at work?"

"It can wait."

"I noticed that beautiful Crosbie creature waving to you. Did you get her in, too?"

"No. She belongs here."

"Are you in love with her, Dan?"

"No."

"Why not? She's entrancing."

"I'm in love with you."

"Would you have been in love with her if you hadn't seen me first?"

"How can I tell? There's no room for anyone else."

161

"You're a satisfactory sort of person, Dan. But I still don't think we're good for each other."

"You haven't run any recent risk of contamination, at least," he returned. "Not so much as a word from you since—" He broke off.

"Yes—since," she laughed softly:

> *"How sad and mad and bad it was—*
> *But oh, how it was sweet!*

I've been trying to recover from you, since."

"I'm beyond recovery, myself."

"I didn't mean it to happen— That's a lie. I knew it would happen. But not so soon. St. Augustine again." She chuckled.

"Kathie, come back to me."

"Oh, Dan! It's so foolish."

"But you will?"

"I suppose so."

"When?"

"I don't know. Will you promise to behave?"

"No!"

This time she laughed aloud. "Within reason, I mean. There is such a thing as moderation."

"You shouldn't be so provocative."

She made a face at him. "You shouldn't be so stimulating— Friday evening? At the apartment?"

"Yes."

"Six o'clock." She touched his hand lightly. "Now go back to your work."

The Monday newspapers had a field day with Dr. Farr's sermon. It was front-page, first-column news. The *Times* treated the attack with cautious approval, as did the *Tribune*. The *Herald* was scornful, the *Sun* bitter, and the *Press* sensational. "Parson on the Rampage," the *Globe* headlined its report. The *World* demanded that the authorities answer the Farr charges.

Never before Dr. Farr's incumbency had the Old Stone Church figured in the news, except for conventional Monday morning reports. All this sensational publicity was a profound shock to the more conservative element. They felt that, unless the clerical accuser could substantiate his charges, both he and the Old Stone Church would be gravely compromised.

That was Tommy Howatt's opinion. He called at the parsonage to deliver it, a few days later.

"Look, Doctor. You stuck your neck out a mile."

162

"My sermon did not meet with your approval, Thomas?" the clergyman asked mildly.

"Oh, it was hot stuff all right. But it's liable to get you in Dutch."

The clergyman, who was becoming familiar with his young friend's phraseology, smiled wearily. "I am prepared for a certain measure of opposition among my parishioners."

"I wasn't thinking of that. It's Mulberry Street that's worrying me."

"You mean the police?"

"They've stirred up the Grand Jury."

"Excellent! I ask nothing better than an impartial inquiry."

"Impartial, hell!" Tommy was too disturbed to notice his slip. "It'll be packed against you."

The Doctor did not get it at once. "Against me? But I am not being investigated."

"Oh, is that so? Wait till they get you up there."

"I shall tell them the truth," Dr. Farr said firmly.

"Fat lot a good that'll do you. What can you prove?"

"All that I have charged is a matter of common knowledge."

"Common knowledge, huh? Look, Dominie. We newspaper guys got a good, old rule."

"I make no doubt that you have many, Thomas."

"One of 'em is: Don't write unless you got the facts in your pants pocket."

"The facts are glaring."

"Yeah? Well, look, they may glare one way to you and another way to a bunch of hand-picked jurors. You don't know what you're up against."

"The Hosts of Midian, if I understand you correctly."

"Don't know him. But I know Tammany. There'll be a hand-picked jury, and it'll be tough. There's the organization D. A.; he's tougher. His man was in church, taking it all down. They'll be on your neck for facts. And unless you can produce the facts, they'll ram it up —they'll ram it down your gullet, that you're talking through your hat."

"But you, yourself, have given me the facts. In this very study."

"Facts aren't necessarily evidence, Dominie. Suppose the Grand Jury holds you up for names, dates, and places; what do you know at first-hand except maybe a peek into the Haymarket and a front seat at the K. and B.'s?"

"I see. You advise, then, that I visit personally these dens of vice. Perhaps, indeed, I should."

"Huh?" Tommy was startled. "A minister in a cathouse? That *would* be something. Look, Doctor!" He spoke in rising excitement, then checked himself. "Never mind. Here's another point. Will the church folks back you up?"

"If they wish to retain me as their pastor, they will."

Tommy grinned. "I'd like to have a diagram of that underjaw of yours, Boss. Are the trustees doing anything about it?"

"There has been a preliminary meeting. No action."

"Hold 'em off if you can till we see what the D. A. has got up his sleeve."

Within a week the District Attorney had moved. Under his guidance the Grand Jury cited Dr. Farr before them and, as Tommy had foreseen, gave him a bad time. They invited him to present specific evidence. He could adduce nothing pertinent. He had publicly alleged bribery and corruption in the Police Department. Had he any proof? Only general knowledge.

That would not do. Had he seen money paid by brothel-keepers to police officers? No. Very well: he had referred to drunkenness and lechery in the City Hall group. Did he mean by that the municipal officials? He did. Was he prepared to specify which officials were drunkards? He was not. Could he name a lecher among the office holders? No.

Then he must realize that his charges laid him open to the penalty for criminal libel if not true?

He did.

Was he prepared to defend himself were such an accusation brought against him?

"By whom?" said the witness with such a force of quiet contempt that the questioner sat down.

It was the only point where the witness scored. For the rest, he fared ill.

Dr. Brockholst Farr emerged from the inquisition, pale, grim, and a wiser man than when he went in. The Grand Jury handed down a presentment denouncing the minister as a self-convicted scandal-monger, a reckless sensationalist, a libeler of upright officials, and a perpetrator of calumny against the fair repute of the great and law-abiding city of New York.

As soon as the news became public, Chairman Harrison M. Perley called an emergency meeting of the church body. The question before the meeting was whether the pastor could justify his sermon. If not, a powerful faction comprising the older and more conservative element believed that he should resign. This newspaper publicity, they held, was doing irreparable damage to the church. A younger faction, led by Allen Hardwick, supported both the crusader and the crusade.

"Everything that Dr. Farr charged, and more, is true," the youngest member of the Board declared hotly. "This city is being looted by a gang of thugs and grafters, and Dr. Farr is the only man with the courage to stand up and say so. The Mayor is a crook, the District Attorney is a tool, and the police are worst of all. If that gang wants a fight, I'm in favor of giving it to them."

"What do you propose, Brother Hardwick?" the chairman asked.

"A special committee to dig up the evidence."

"I should like to hear Dr. Farr on the subject," old Jared Duryea quavered.

The clergyman was summoned.

"Brothers," he said in his deep, quiet voice, "this church is my life to me. Rather than bring harm or trouble to it, I would cut off my right hand. I have wrestled in prayer with my problem. Conscience tells me that I owe a debt to my city as well as to my church; that the two claims upon me are indissolubly welded together. I cannot abandon what I see as my plain duty. Is it the wish of this body that I resign?"

"There is no such question before us," Chairman Perley disclaimed hastily. "For myself, while I deplore the political trend which our affairs are taking, I stand by my pastor."

Maitland Greig, one of the financial pillars of the church, rose. "You have made grave charges, Dr. Farr," he said. "Can you prove them?"

"With God's help I believe that I can, Brother Greig."

"Do you approve Brother Hardwick's suggestion of a special committee of investigation?"

"Unreservedly."

"How much time will you require to substantiate your charges? A month?"

Allen Hardwick was on his feet. "No, no. Not nearly enough."

They debated it back and forth and eventually compromised on three months. The committee was authorized, with Dr. Farr a member ex officio and Allen Hardwick the executive head, empowered to select three associates for the active work. Thereupon Mr. Greig contributed twenty-five hundred dollars for initial expenses.

One concession Dr. Farr was compelled reluctantly to make. He agreed to preach no more "politics" until the report was in.

The Grand Jury's denunciation had put Dr. Farr back on the front page again. This time not a single newspaper supported him unreservedly. The *Commercial Advertiser* expressed a general feeling which its competitors voiced in more decorous terms:

> The clerical gentleman tried to hitch his garbage cart to the Star of Bethlehem, missed his connection, and landed in the Slough of Despond.

Several editorials demanded that the pastor resign from a pulpit which he had disgraced. R. K. Fox was prepared to join the denunciatory chorus in his *Police Gazette*.

"Your parson friend has certainly fallen into the muck heap," he said to Tommy.

"What are we going to do about it, Boss?"

"Give him both barrels, upper case."

"We could do better."

By this time Mr. Fox had discovered that Tommy's journalistic ideas, if not always feasible, were at least worth attention.

"Shoot," he said.

"I put a flea in the Dominie's ear a while ago."

"Yes? What species?"

"Gave him the notion of making a personal round of the cathouses with me for guide," Tommy boasted. "It hit him right where he lives."

"What about it?"

"Sisterhood of Sin," said Tommy, making capital letters in the air with his forefinger.

"Nice title," the publisher approved. "Where does it fit in?"

"Dr. Farr's red-light experiences. Wow! What a series!"

"You mean get him to do it for the *Gazette?* You're crazy."

"Why am I crazy? You think he wouldn't do it? Betcha I can land him. Whaddaya say, Boss? Shall I try?"

Mr. Fox laughed. "Go right ahead. I'll give you a fifty-dollar bonus on the series, if you get it."

At the close of the Tuesday checkers game Tommy broached the subject. "Are you really going to make the rounds of the houses, Dominie?"

"Distasteful though it is, Thomas, I can see no other way of obtaining the necessary evidence. This is between us, my boy. You must not publish anything about it."

"But look, Dominie! How about doing the publishing, yourself? Instead of shootin' off your mouth out of turn—I mean preaching stuff you can't prove—how about a hot little series of articles for us? The *P.G.* would pay you top prices."

"Articles, Thomas? For the *Police Gazette?* Of what nature?"

"Personal experience stuff. What you see and hear while you're making the Tenderloin tour. That'd be a good subhead, too: Tenderloin Tour."

The Doctor was mildly amused. "But, you yourself have been chiding me for my reportorial shortcomings."

"Yeah. Well, you'd have to watch out for libel. Sock it to 'em, but make it general. No names. Names are dangerous."

"I see. And your publication would print such a series?"

"Like a mice! Why, Boss, we're just as much against sin as you are. From a different angle; that's all. I can show you pieces in the *Pinky* that rip hell out of sin."

This was true. The *Gazette's* frequent incursions into the field of exposure were highly moralistic in tone, while shrewdly harmless to established business. They lit up vice with the allure of the red light. "Write it so that it will fetch the yokels to town," was Mr. Fox's prescription. "Shock the blue noses and stimulate trade."

"Smite the devil in his home precincts?" the preacher answered his young friend. "But I know nothing of your—er—*Gazette.*"

Tommy whipped a copy out of his rear trousers pocket and spread it, in all its blatant pinkness, before the kind and spectacled eyes. The eyes grew wider as the clerical reader turned the pages. There was a quizzical gleam in them as they were raised to Tommy's face.

"You consider this a suitable medium for a minister of the gospel?" he asked.

"We've had 'em in it before." He did not mention the invariably scandalous correlation.

The other scanned the side columns and set his finger on an item. "What is this?" he said.

"Oh, that's just an ad," Tommy said carelessly.

"Big G. What does the G stand for?"

"It's a disease. I mean it's a cure for a disease."

"What kind of disease?" the other pressed.

"Oh, well—hell! A *disease,*" the harried representative cried. "You know."

"I fear I do. And this Dr. Grey and Old Dr. Grindle who promise a cure in three days. The same ailment?"

"Yeah, I guess so," Tommy replied unhappily.

" 'Don't Worry, Ladies,' " Dr. Farr read on. " 'Tansy Pills Will Fix Up Your Troubles.' What kind of troubles?"

"Oh, geez!" Tommy cried lamentably. "Those are only ads, Doc—sir. Whyntcha read about the way we showed up those night-running senators from Washington?"

"No, my boy," the clergyman said kindly. "I do not see myself as a contributor to Mr. Fox's publication. In any case, I shall be working with the committee and we are committed to secrecy in our operations."

Though he did not express them, Tommy had his cynical doubts as to any committee of amateur snoopers being able to conceal their activities from the professionals of the Tenderloin for very long.

20

Difficult days came for Tommy Howatt. He was suffering from divided loyalties. Though dropped from the official payroll, he was still indebted to the Police Department for certain benefits on the side, and regarded himself as bound in the *esprit de corps* of the organization: "Once a cop, always a cop." Professionally he held to the standards of the *Police Gazette;* he was grateful to Mr. R. K. Fox. More personal than either of these ties was the mutual friendship with Brockholst Farr, which inspired in him a blend of pride, reverence, and affection. He frequently bragged to Dan Adriance of his confidential relations with the minister.

"But you don't believe in what he's trying to do," the *Star* man objected.

"What's the diff? I can steer him right, can't I? The Doc and I are just like that." (Familiar gesture of finger looped over finger.)

"Are you trying to tell me that you're in with that committee of his?"

"Hell, no! Can you see me working with that Hardwick stiff? But the Doc knows where to come when he needs a straight tip."

"Guide, philosopher and friend, eh?"

"I don't say that he always takes my tips. Sometimes he just looks at me with that sideways smile of his and calls me an *advocatus diabolus* or something and jumps two men into my king-row."

As for the *P.G.,* Tommy had begged off from being obliged to write anything on the subject of the Old Stone Church and its pastor. "He's my friend, Boss," he said to R. K. Fox. "You gotta let me off."

"What have you and Dr. Farr got in common?" asked the amused and good-natured editor.

"Checkers," Tommy answered. "We play three mornings a week, before I come to work."

"Can you beat him?"

"Not so's you could notice it," Tommy said.

Nevertheless, he did not despair. He was learning; getting better every time they met, as he told himself. Obstinately he declined the odds offered by his opponent. His vanity would not accept so bald a handicap. He'd show up the Dominie yet!

"I know what I'd oughta do," Tommy would lament, eying the board. "And then, somehow or other I go and do something else, and it's always the wrong thing."

"An ancient complaint, Thomas. What said the penitent: *'Meliora video proboque; deteriora sequor.'* "

"I'll take your word for it, Dominie."

"Suppose we arrange for a formula of warning, then. When I judge you to be liable to a misplay, I might interpose, 'Would you not be well advised to reconsider?' and you could take further thought."

"Even with that, you'd probably lick me," his opponent said. "But let's try it."

It became a catch phrase between them.

Whether or not Tommy accepted the warning, he still could not manage to win. He did, however, achieve a couple of triumphant draws.

There came a day when Tommy's emotions overcame him. Several interruptions to their game had diverted Dr. Farr's attention. His play became careless. Tommy found himself in what looked to him like a commanding position. He pushed forward a man.

"Whaddaya think of that!" he crowed.

A familiar response fell with a chill upon his ear: "I think you would be well advised to reconsider."

Tommy studied the board for a moment and forgot himself. "Well, God damn!" he ejaculated in jovial disillusionment.

Dr. Farr rose. "The session is closed," he said.

"Out on Friend Ear, huh?" Tommy was striving to hide his chagrin under an assumption of jauntiness.

"You are guilty of a lamentable lack of sportsmanship," his opponent charged.

Tommy blinked. This was an unexpected angle. No rebuke for his profanity. Come to consider, it was worse than that. The clergyman, he perceived, was convicting him of being a bum sport. That hurt.

"It slipped out," he said.

"Good day to you, Thomas," his host replied. "You may return when you can command your tongue."

"Yes, sir." Tommy was meek. Then, with a sigh of relief, "Gee! I thought you were going to give me the bum's rush for good and all!"

Dr. Farr permitted himself a meager smile. "I do not propose to lose my expert adviser for a *lapsus linguae,* however gross."

Tommy stumbled out of the room. The door closed behind him. It opened again.

"Dominie."

"Yes, Thomas?"

"You don't know it, but I'd go to hell for you."

"I trust that may never be necessary, Thomas."

"I mean it, though," Tommy said.

For all his shortcomings, there was that in his reckless and rascally soul which paid instinctive tribute to the integrity lacking in himself.

Tommy was careful to explain to Dr. Farr that he personally deprecated the *P.G.'s* occasional slurs upon the Old Stone Church.

"I have not read them, Thomas," the object of them said.

"Don't you get the *Pinky* any more?"

"It comes, I believe. But I have no time to peruse it."

"There's where you're off beat, Dominie. You could learn a lot of things that you ought to know by reading the *P.G.*"

"For example?"

"Well, they're onto this new racket of yours."

"Racket?"

"Your gumshoe boys, making the rounds of the joints. They think we—they think nobody is onto them. That's a laugh!"

Strange happenings were, indeed, of frequent occurrence in the houses of the Tenderloin. At suspiciously short intervals "visiting firemen," as out-of-town patrons were known, made the rounds of the houses in festive bands. They purported to be from Chicago, Pittsburgh, Louisville, Indianapolis, Baltimore, and other alien sites. They were free spenders. They bought champagne. They willingly paid for "shows." But they exhibited one peculiarity: they were unanimously resistant to professional blandishments, whether ardent or subtle. They would not go upstairs with the girls. "Ground-floor Johnnies," was the Tenderloin's term for this species.

Such forbearances puzzled the practitioners of the oldest profession in the world. They were inclined to resent it, as reflecting upon their competence. Only a few of the insiders, like Etta Holmes, Georgiana Hastings, and the French Madam, who were on confidential terms with the police, knew that these exotic visitors were actually Dr. Farr's vice-sleuths on the prowl for evidence.

Captain Bernie Schmidt of the Nineteenth Precinct considered these operations as a personal insult. He so expressed himself to Tommy Howatt when, one evening, the *P.G.* man dropped in at the station house for a friendly call and found the captain in consultation with his confidential man.

Willie Frye took a cynical view of the visitations.

"The madams ain't givin' us the solid Muldoon on this thing," was his opinion.

"Why wouldn't they?" the pantata said.

"I dunno. Protectin' the customers, maybe."

170

"You don't think," Captain Schmidt began, when his factotum cut in with: "All them pious bastards are the same. They'll take it if it comes their way."

"Old Hellfire, too?" the captain asked eagerly. "Think we can get something on him?"

This was too much for Tommy. He glared at the speaker in scorn. "Of all the goddam fool notions! Woman-stuff and Dr. Farr! Don't make me laugh."

"I'm afraid he's right, Boss," Willie admitted. "I don't guess we could reely catch him in anything like that. There's nothing in his record. We cased it good."

"Oh, well, hell!" the captain spat out. "What can he do? Sermons! Who gives a goddam for sermons! It'll take more than old Farr to keep me awake nights."

Tommy had his own doubts as to the validity of the policeman's boast, but he said soothingly, "It probably won't come to much. So long, Cap."

He and Willie Frye left the station and went around to the Tenderloin Club for a drink.

"The boss is off his nut about Dr. Farr," the fly-cop said.

"Yeah. But maybe there's an idea there," the *P.G.* man replied thoughtfully. "The Doc is fireproof. But there might be something doing with some of his gang, for all they're so full of purity and reform and that crap."

"Amachoors."

"Sure. Suppose we could catch one of 'em with his pants down. Would that gum the game!"

"I thought you was pallin' in with the church crowd," Willie said curiously.

"Those Sunday-school sissies! They make me sick." Although there was no one within possible earshot, Tommy lowered his voice to a conspiratorial murmur. His friend listened intently, nodding his head from time to time. At the end, he had an objection.

"The girl'd hafta be a hooker or she wouldn't do it."

"There's plenty of hookers, Willie."

"Yeah; but where'll you find one smart enough? Hookers got no brains. If they had, they wouldn't be hookers."

"Nita," Tommy said.

"Ah, Nita!" the plain-clothes man repeated. "Never thought of her. She's smart, all right. But is she safe? Would she keep her trap shut?"

"She knows what would happen to her if she didn't. I'll guarantee Nita."

"Okay. You oughta know. She's your girl."

171

"Drink up, Willie. I gotta go. See you on a slab."

Tommy went back to the office. It was Dan Adriance's advisory day at the *P.G.* He was reading for possible libel a snappy scandal-story about an Albany politician caught transom-peeping, when Tommy approached and sat on a corner of the desk to wait.

After making some marginal notes on the proof, Dan looked up and promulgated a standard witticism: "Well, what's on your mind besides your hat, young fellow?"

"I hear there's a Farr crusade story in the proofs."

"It's killed. Vice is a dead issue."

"Until the Doc and his committee stir it up again."

"How long did the trustees give Dr. Farr to put up or shut up? Do you know?"

"Three months, but it's even money he springs it sooner." Tommy liked to pretend inside knowledge which he might or might not possess. "I'll give you a tip, Dan. It'll get 'em just nowhere."

"Hello! When did you round on your checker-playing pal?"

"Not me. Not in a thousand years! I think the Doc's got bugs in his wig on this whore thing. But he's on the level. That's more than you can say for some of the goo-goo sons-a-bitches he's got working on it. You know who I mean."

"Allen Hardwick?"

"He'd better watch his step. We're onto him like a ton of bricks."

"Who's 'we'?"

"He'll find out. I'll tell you this much, Dan. The Doc's gumshoes are working the cathouses, and Holy Hardwick is getting the kick of his life out of it. The girls are teaching him plenty he didn't know before."

"Are you trying to tell me that Allen Hardwick is a whoremaster?" Dan said in disgust. "You're crazy."

"Maybe I am and maybe I'm not. And maybe you don't know everything there is to know about it."

"I know Allen well enough to be sure he's straight. What have you got against him, anyway?"

"What's he got against the madams? They never did anything to him."

"His kid brother got burned in Georgiana Hastings' place. You know that."

"Ah, hell; what's that to beef about?" Tommy returned. He delivered himself of a Tenderloin apothegm. "A man ain't a man till he's had a dose."

"Speaking from experience, I suppose," Dan said contemptuously.

"Well, no," Tommy admitted. "I been lucky." Perceiving that he was making no hit with his friend along that line, he shifted to another topic. "I hear Hardwick has got the inside track with Mrs. C. Is that right?"

"I don't know."

"Does Laurie really like him?"

"Why don't you get some sense in your head and keep off the grass?" Dan said.

No use in trying to get anything out of him, Tommy decided.

As Dan Adriance had said, the Old Stone Church's vice-crusade was now dead, considered as news. By imposing their censorship upon the pastor, the trustees had gained a point: they had removed the church from the front page. Too good a newspaperman not to foresee that it would be back in the news one day, Dan Adriance was keeping an eye out for developments. He tackled Allen Hardwick, whom he found, one afternoon, talking with Mrs. Crosbie while waiting for Laurie to come in.

"When are we going to see some action by your committee, Allen?" he asked.

"Oh, we have plenty of time yet," the other replied.

"Will your report be made public?"

"In one form or another. Very likely as the basis for Dr. Farr's sermons."

"Give me plenty of advance notice, won't you?"

"Yes, indeed. We'll want all the publicity we can get."

"You know the police are onto your game, don't you, Allen?"

"Oh, sure! They trail us everywhere. That doesn't bother us."

"Well," said the reporter thoughtfully, "I don't doubt but that you can force the Police Department's hand. What good it will do is another matter. There'll be the usual raids and temporarily barred doors and police court fines for the inmates, and in a month the word will go around to open up, and everything will be going full blast again, just as everybody wants it."

"That's a pretty cynical view to take," Allen began, when Mrs. Crosbie broke in: "I agree with Dan. Why should you hound those poor girls?"

"We aren't hounding them, Mrs. Crosbie," Allen protested. "That isn't Dr. Farr's idea at all. We're after the corrupt politicians and police."

"It's persecution," she insisted. "What good can it do anybody?"

"Some of your fellow church members are likely to press that question, aren't they, Allen?" the reporter said. "How far do you think the Board will back Dr. Farr?"

"To the limit!" Allen said. "What else can they do?"

173

"Ask for his resignation."

"Not when they see the evidence we're piling up. We're not going off half-cocked this time, Dan."

"What's Harrison M. Perley's attitude? I understand that he's backing Dr. Farr."

"Mr. Perley has a deep personal regard for Dr. Farr," Mrs. Crosbie said. "You might call it devotion."

"That's the sort of feeling that the Doctor inspires," Allen said warmly.

"The more reason for him to be sure," Dan said. "If anything goes wrong—"

"It won't," Allen asserted. "The job will be done right this time."

"Batting around the Tenderloin night after night costs money," Dan observed. "Who's footing the bills?"

"Members of the congregation. Laurie sent Dr. Farr another check for five hundred."

"She did," Mrs. Crosbie confirmed. "In disregard of her father's expressed wishes. Only last week, right here in this room, he told her—" She stopped with a little gasp, pressing her knuckles to her bloodless lips. "Oh!" she breathed. "Oh!"

"Her father?" Allen repeated stupidly. "Laurie's father?"

And Dan added, "Mr. Crosbie? But I thought—"

Mrs. Crosbie stood up. "I didn't—" she began. "Don't let Lau—" She lurched forward in a dead faint.

Allen caught her and carried her to the sofa, while Dan ran for water. She came to with a groan, and stared at them pitifully. As well as they could, they reassured her; they had heard nothing, understood nothing, pledged themselves to forget everything that had been said. It would never go further. She could make her mind quite easy.

At the earliest moment compatible with courtesy, they left. It was better, they thought, not to wait for Laurie.

Outside, Allen began, "Did you have any suspicion of this, Dan?"

"No. But I should have had. All that money."

"I understood it came from oil property."

"So did I. Southwestern part of the state somewhere."

"She wouldn't need it, if only she would marry me."

"I wish to God she would, Allen. And the sooner, the better." Dan was thinking of Tommy Howatt.

"I wonder if there ever was any Mr. Crosbie," Allen mused.

"I ought to know, but I don't. My connection is on the other side, and distant, at that. Would it make any difference to you?"

"Good God, no!" Allen replied with such indignation that Dan was reassured.

After a pause, Dan said, "I suppose we're both thinking of the same man."

"Yes. No need to name names."

"Just forget it, eh?"

"Yes."

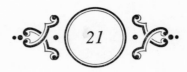

While the Old Stone Church's vice committee was quietly piling up evidence, while Tammany Hall was continuing to fatten on the easy money of protected crime and vice, while the Police Department, relieved of its earlier alarms, was enlarging and perfecting its system of graft upon the lawless and helpless, while R. K. Fox was banking increased profits on his enterprising weekly, while Dan Adriance was moping over Kathleen Tennant's neglect—she had gone on a round of visits from which had drifted back two postal cards and one brief note—while all this was going on, Tommy Howatt was having the time of his expanding life.

He was now a familiar of the Valdevia apartment. His only dissatisfaction was that so many others shared that privilege; he seldom had a chance to see Laurie alone.

"There's always somebody cluttering up the place," he complained. "Barto, or that Van Dorp dope, or Baby Kerr, or those giggling twins, or that da— or Hardwick. And if there's nobody else, it's sure to be Dan Adriance."

Laurie laughed. "Surely you're not jealous of Dan, Tommy."

"I'm jealous of everybody."

"But—Dan! That's too absurd."

His face brightened. "Well, maybe it is. He's got troubles of his own."

"It's Kathleen Tennant, isn't it?"

"Yes. How did you know? She's got him hog-tied."

"No wonder. She's so gay. So vivid. Oh, I do hope she's in love with him."

Tommy grinned. "There's symptoms," he said. "Though he's been looking sorta grumpy lately."

They were sitting in Laurie's drawing room that early September evening. For once she had no engagement, and there were no other callers. Mrs. Crosbie was, so her daughter assumed, in her own room, where she spent so much of her time. Tommy drew from his pocket a flat, frosted steel case from which he extracted an engraved card.

"Got something to show you," he said. "Pretty clas— pretty nifty, huh?"

Laurie scrutinized the exhibit.

Mr. Thomas duB. Howatt

HOTEL WINDSOR

"Very nice," she approved. "What's the du-capital-B for?"

"Short for Dubonnet."

The corners of her warm-lipped mouth quivered.

"I got it off a bottle at the Grand Union bar. All the birds in the society headlines have middle monickers. Anything wrong with it?"

"Never mind. Hotel Windsor," she read. The Windsor at Fifth Avenue and Forty-sixth Street was the latest thing in fashion and quiet elegance.

"Nothing like a Fifth Avenue address if you want to get anywhere," Tommy said complacently.

"Do you live there?" There was suspicion in her voice.

"Well, not exactly."

"Then what right have you to use that address?"

Tommy fidgeted. "I don't see as it hurts anybody," he protested.

"That it hurts anybody. It isn't honest."

"Well, I eat there sometimes." This was a slight overstatement. He had once had a sandwich at the bar and was shocked at being charged twenty cents for a Manhattan cocktail. "I could move there," he said hopefully.

"The Windsor? You can't afford it."

"I'm drawing down good money these days outside of what the *Pinky* pays me."

"Not the postage-stamp wash?"

"That went kerflump. Corky's in jail."

"You're lucky not to be there, yourself. I'm sure the Windsor is much more comfortable. But you oughtn't to splurge."

"Oh, they'd make me a rate." Tommy was constantly asking and frequently receiving discounts based upon his "connection with the press."

"Even so, they charge as high as six dollars a day, I understand."

"Yes, but look what you get for your money! Laurie, there's rooms at the Windsor with private bathroom attached. Would you believe it? Bathtub and—and everything," he continued lamely. "I'll bet they'd let me have one for twenty a week. Grandma Parke is all for it."

"You've been consulting her, have you?"

"She gives me a tip on things, now and then."

"You seem to have made quite an impression there."

"It's the old throttle." He tapped his throat. "We're a swell musical team. You ought to hear us."

"I'd like to. You can take me over there sometime."

"Any time," Tommy said enthusiastically. "Laurie, I've been making book on you."

"Am I a horse?" said Laurie, who was beginning to know something of the ways of Tommy's world.

"This is a scrapbook."

"Oh! Poetry?"

"No. Newspaper. You drew as much space last week as any girl in New York."

"No! Really? What fun! Not that it's very important."

"The hell it ain't—isn't!" Tommy cried.

"Mother doesn't like it."

"She's crazy in the head. You've landed, Laurie; landed with both feet. Know what Richard Harding Davis called you? The 'mirthful madonna.' Otho Cushing draws your picture every other week in *Life* as plain as a photo. And look at the society columns! 'Toast of the city's gilded youth.' 'Most courted heiress of the season.' 'Loveliest debutante of the year.' Geez!" (Laurie looked pained.) "I mean, hot stuff! They'll have to stretch the Four Hundred to Four Hundred and One."

"I'm not a debutante, though. I've never come out."

"You don't have to, with the success you got. Just watch out you don't gum it up."

"You do use the most awful expressions, Tommy. How could I 'gum it up'?"

"Oh, I dunno. Marry wrong. Like that Barto. Dr. Holy-Willie Hardwick."

"I'm not going to marry anybody. Talk about something else."

"All right. What'll we talk about?"

"Tell me why your horrid *Pinky* is so mean to Dr. Farr."

"You wouldn't understand the politics of it."

"Don't try to put me off," she admonished him. "You're not writing those things, are you?"

"Not me," Tommy said virtuously and truly.

"I'm glad of that. Dr. Farr is the best man I've ever known. I love him."

"Look," said Tommy.

"*No,*" said Laurie.

"Damn!" said Tommy.

178

"Don't be profane and vulgar," said Laurie.

"Well, what d'you expect? You told me once, yourself, that a fella couldn't learn manners out of a book. He had to associate with people. Doc Farr's sister, Mrs. Dennison, has been mighty kind about it. I've been there to dinner two-three times since you chucked me. But she ain't—all right, all right!—she *isn't* you."

"Oh, Tommy! I didn't chuck you. Not really."

"I don't know what you'd call it. This is the first chance I've had to see you alone since hell fro— since I don't know when."

She evaded that topic. "We were talking about Dr. Farr and your *P.G.*"

He sought for inoffensive terms. "When the Doc stirred up all this woman trouble, the *P.G.* was naturally ag'in him," he began.

"I don't see why 'naturally.' "

"He didn't know what he was talking about at first."

"He does now."

"He knows a lot more than's good for him," Tommy admitted.

"Your awful *Pinky* is pretending it isn't true; that the politicians are all honest. Isn't that it?"

"The Doc is playing politics himself. Only he don't know it."

"*Doesn't* know it. What doesn't he know?"

"That Tom Corbin is working him for a shiner."

"Do you mean that nice, quiet little Corbin man with the beard, who's a member of our church?"

"That nice, quiet little man is the Republican boss of New York City."

"What has that to do with Dr. Farr?"

"Do you want the low-down, straight from the Amen Corner?" Tommy asked importantly.

"The Amen Corner?"

"That's the place in the Fifth Avenue Hotel lobby where the top-notch Republicans sit around and figure out how to get the graft away from Tammany. The talk there is that Boss Corbin is laying low to see what kind of dirt Doc Farr and Hardwick and the snooper committee turn up. If it's pay dirt, Corbin will stir up the boys in Albany and get an upstate legislative committee down here to make an investigation in the holy name of reform and the hopes that it'll give 'em an issue against Tammany in the next election. Do you get it, Laurie?"

"No, I don't get it at all. Does Dr. Farr want the investigation?"

"What does the Doc know about politics? If there's an investigation, Tom Corbin will be running it; not Doc Farr. But there won't be any. Not a chance."

"Why not?"

"Too much against it."

"I don't believe any good people are against it."

"Oh, don't you! Ask Mr. Harrison M. Perley."

"You mean that Uncle Harry is against Dr. Farr?"

"No. But he's against this committee snoopin'. All the businessmen are. So is the City Hall. So are the police. So is Tammany. That's why the Doc is never going to get anywhere with this crazy reform business. They say he's got a working fund. I'd like to know who else besides Boss Corbin is putting up the dough."

"Would you? I am. Some of it."

"Well, lay off," he said earnestly.

"I'm not going to lay off. I'm going to give more. Any time he needs it."

"Does your mother—"

"No. Mother doesn't approve. I don't understand why."

"You don't understand anything," Tommy cried. "It's a dirty business and you hadn't ought to be in it at all."

"I don't see why you should worry over it," she retorted.

This, Tommy reflected, was getting them nowhere. He cast a glance toward the piano. "I got a couple of new numbers," he said insinuatingly.

"I like the old ones."

He brightened up and took possession of the piano stool. "What'll we start with?"

"Wait till I call Mother."

"Does she have to be here every time?" he protested.

"You know how she loves to hear you sing."

Tommy had his private doubts, but it did not matter. "This is the time she won't get the chance," he said.

Laurie stared at him.

"I saw her climbing into a hack, just as I was turning the corner."

"Wh-wh-why, she didn't say anything. Josephine may know. I'll ask her."

She went down the hall and knocked at the maid's door. A sleepy voice responded.

"Josephine, where did Mrs. Crosbie go?"

"I dunno, Miss Laurie. Mist' Perley telephoned. Reckon she went with him. Lef' word for you she'd be back around ten-thutty."

"Why didn't you tell me?"

"You was in your room, miss. Then Mr. Tommy came an' I kinda forgot about it."

Laurie returned to her caller. "Mother's gone out with Uncle Harry. Something about the new house, I guess. There's some kind of trouble with the carpenters."

Tommy rose and crossed the room to close the door. "So as not to wake Josephine up," he explained. He returned to the piano. "Come over and sit where I can see you," he invited.

After a moment's hesitation she drew a chair near. "Sing something funny," she said in an unnatural voice.

"Funny?"

"Yes. Like 'Maggie Cline.' 'T'row Him Down, McCluskey.' 'Down Went McGinty.' Something like that."

In a raucous, affected voice he caterwauled:

> *"Where did you get that hat?*
> *Where did you get that tile?*
> *Isn't it a dandy one*
> *And just the latest style?*
> *How'd you like to have one*
> *Just the same as that?*
> *When I go out*
> *The boys all shout,*
> *'Where did you get that hat?' "*

She pressed her hands to her ears. "Oh, Tommy, how awful!"

"Well, why don't you laugh? It's funny, ain't it?"

"Isn't," she said mechanically.

"Okay. Maybe this one will suit you better. Straight from the Imperial Music Hall. Joe Burke's latest. Through the nose.

> *"She was a nice girl, too.*
> *May God forgive the lie!*
> *She told me she would take me soon*
> *And show me the pictures in her room.*
> *She told me something else,*
> *That made my whiskers curl.*
> *Oh, I was a nice, soft touch*
> *For the rollicking Broadway girl."*

"It's horrid. Why are you teasing me?"

"Because you're so choosy tonight," he returned with a pretense of sulkiness. " 'Sing something funny.' Well, I don't feel funny. I feel like singing to you. And you don't want me to."

"Oh, I do! I do! But——"

"Don't tell me." He sang; it was an echo of rapture in her ears.

> *"There is a lady, fair and kind.*
> *No other face so pleased my mind.*
> *I did but see her passing by,*
> *Yet will I love her till I die . . ."*

181

"Do you remember, Laurie?"

"Oh, yes! On the veranda. At the picnic. Oh, Tommy!"

He smiled. His fingers brought forth from the piano stronger chords. "Listen," he murmured.

> *"Some think to lose him*
> *By keeping him confined.*
> *Some do suppose him—poor fools!—*
> *To be blind.*
> *But howsoe'er ye wall him,*
> *Do the best that ye may,*
> *Blind Love, if so ye call him,*
> *Still will find out the way."*

She was breathing deep and broken breaths. "What's the matter, Laurie?" he whispered. "What's the matter, darling?"

"I don't know. It does something to me."

Like a person mesmerized, she rose and slowly went to him. Her outstretched hand groped, touched his shoulder, rested there. He turned his head to press his cheek upon the straining fingers that crept around his neck. She gave a little moan as she felt his arms draw her, his kiss penetrate her defenses.

"Laurie," he whispered.

"Oh, Tommy! Oh, *no!*" His encroaching hand had slipped down between her breasts. She cried out in mingled terror and passion. With a rending effort she broke from him and ran down the hall to her own room, slamming and bolting the door after her. Tommy followed. Through the door he could hear her long, deep desperate sobs.

"I'm sorry, Laurie," he pleaded hoarsely. "Forgive me. I didn't mean to scare you."

She lay, trembling, afraid to answer. By and by he went away.

She pretended to be asleep when her mother came back. After a wan night, she rose late and called Dan Adriance at his apartment.

"Dan? Can you come up? It's important."

"All right. I'll be there in an hour."

"What's now, my child?" he asked as they sat together amidst the costly bric-a-brac. "Caught another duke?"

"Dan, I'm going to be married."

"Isn't this rather sudden? To whom, if it isn't a secret?"

"To Allen—I think."

Dan said gravely, "Do you love him, Laurie?"

"I trust him. He's so good. He's so gentle."

"That isn't what I asked you. Do you love him?"

"I—I—I—"

"See here, Laurie, how much has this to do with Tommy Howatt?"

"I hate him."

"You're quite sure of that?"

"I'm afraid of him, Dan. I'm afraid of myself when I'm with him. He makes me feel so—horrid. If you laugh at me, Dan, I'll never speak to you again."

"Because you feel that way about Tommy, you're going to marry Allen."

"Yes," she whispered

"Do you think that's fair?"

"I'd be a true wife to him."

"I can believe that, Laurie."

"You know Tommy. Tell me, Dan." She put it in one of her odd archaic phrases. "He isn't true, is he?"

"He's not for you, Laurie."

"Dan"—she averted her face from him—"is it true that he goes with women? Bad women?"

"Who told you that?"

"Mrs. Parke. She said that he was living with a—a girl. Stannard Barto told her. She laughed as if she thought it was funny. I didn't really believe it, but now— Is it true, Dan?"

"Tommy is not for you, Laurie," he repeated gravely.

"I've known all along in my heart that he isn't good. And he awakens everything that's bad in me. Oh, Dan! I never knew before that it was there. He makes me feel so—*female*. Is that a horrid thing for me to say?"

"Don't take it too hard, Laurie. After all, you are a woman."

"Y-y-y-yes. But I don't want to be. Not that way. Not so much. It—it frightens me."

"It wouldn't with Allen?"

"Allen is different," she said, and smiled.

Dan liked that smile. It reassured him. "You'd better tell Tommy and get that settled," he advised.

"Oh, Dan! You tell him for me. I don't want to see him again, ever."

"I seem to remember your saying that once before. This time I hope you mean it."

"I do. I do."

"All right. I'll pass the word along."

"Holy-boly put her up to it," was Tommy's sour comment, when Dan delivered the message.

"Allen? He doesn't know you're alive," said Dan contemptuously.

"He'll find out one of these days. Look, Dan; I'll take that direct from Laurie. I won't take it from anybody else this side of hell."

"You'll take it from me that she's engaged to Allen Hardwick, and you ought to be decent enough to play the game."

Herein Dan was upholding the eternal proprieties. According to the law and the prophets of the nineties, a betrothed young lady received no callers other than her fiancé and her relatives. So much Tommy did know, having read it in his *Book of Etiquette for All Occasions*. Now he gave Dan a black look.

"Goin' to marry the holy-boly, huh? Wanna bet?" he snarled, and turned his back on the news-bearer.

22

A third postal card, this one from Beaufort, South Carolina, as nonchalant as only that type of stationery can be, informed Dan Adriance that Kathleen Tennant had not wholly lost interest in him.

"Expect to be called up one of these days," it said.

A week thereafter the gay voice came to him over the telephone. "Dan? It's Kathie. Have you missed me?"

"Damnably."

"Want to take me to dinner tonight?"

"Equally damnably."

"I've got a better idea. Let's cook our own in the apartment. I was the best cook in school when I was at Farmington."

"All right. What shall I get?"

"Have you a pencil handy?" She dictated an extensive list. "And I'll bring a bottle of champagne to celebrate. I'll be there at six."

She was only a half hour late. He heard her footsteps on the stairs. Then she was in his arms, breathless. He lifted his face from hers.

"Kathie—again, will you marry me?"

"No, darling."

"Why not?"

"I don't want to."

"Don't you love me?"

"I love to be with you—like this."

"Isn't that the answer?"

"I don't know the answer. Perhaps there isn't any answer."

"Kathie, is there anyone else?"

"Not now. But there has been. I told you that."

"Yes, I know."

"And you still want to marry me?"

"More than I've ever wanted anything in my life."

"Oh, Dan!" she said. "Foolish Dan!" After a pause she asked, "Do you want to know who the man was?"

"No," he said.

"It's all over," she said. "He wanted to get a divorce and marry me."

"Well, if you were in love with him—"

"Who said I was in love with him?"

"If you weren't, why on earth—" he began helplessly.

"Love," she said fretfully. "It's such a vague word. Everyone attaches a different meaning to it. He was terribly attractive. Half the women in New York were crazy over him. I suppose that was the reason—partly. But I never would have married him."

"Why not? Or don't you know?"

"Yes, I know. He's an actor. A matinée idol. I'd never marry out of my own set. I couldn't."

"Is that the answer for me, too?" Dan asked. There was bitterness in his tone.

She touched his cheek with gentle fingers and answered, "Don't be hurt, Dan. I can't help it. Aren't we happy as we are?"

Kathie's cookery was impressive. After everything was cleaned up and put away, she showed her host a new and costly cigarette case with her initials jeweled on it.

"In your heart you think it's unwomanly to smoke, don't you, Dan?" she teased.

"I could never think of you as unwomanly," he said.

"Well, I shall be extra womanly tonight," she said softly. "I don't have to go home, Dan."

"That," he said, "is front-page, double-column good news in red letters."

"Keep it for the *Police Gazette*." She laughed. "By the way, I thought I saw your funny friend, Tommy What's-his-name, just now."

"Where?" he asked quickly.

"As I was crossing the Square."

"He didn't see you, did he?"

"I don't think so."

(Herein was her mistake. Not only had Tommy seen her, but he had surreptitiously marked her progress to the apartment house and up the steps. He then found a seat on a park bench, whence he observed Dan Adriance's front window light up. When, some minutes later, it blacked out, he went away satisfied.)

"I don't see what he would be doing around here," Dan said uneasily.

"There's no reason why he should be spying on us, is there?" his mistress asked.

"No."

186

"Probably it wasn't he at all; just my guilty conscience. Only, I don't feel guilty about us, darling. Not one bit."

It was a febrile and uncertain happiness for him. She was a capricious mistress to give or to withhold. Sometimes after they had dined together at Katie's or the Park Avenue or the Palm Garden she would say quietly, "I'm going back with you, darling," and they would be together for an hour or for the evening, or for the night. Again, he must take her home or to some engagement directly after dinner. He was too completely enslaved to complain or even to question.

Kathie was impatient of any constraint. One evening as they sat on the front-room couch looking up Fifth Avenue through Stanford White's lovely arch, she said below her breath, "This can't last forever, you know, Dan."

"Are you warning me, Kathie?"

She answered with a vague gesture, "We might get tired, you and I, dear."

"Not I!" he said vehemently.

Her hand stirred in his. "Shall I tell you my theory of all this?"

"I'm listening."

"Romantic love is moonshine and myth. But sometimes two people are mutually attuned. How shall I put it? Their timing is the same."

"You and I?"

"Yes. Don't you feel it?"

"I have from the first word you spoke to me, I think."

"I, too. Lust at first sight. Have I shocked you, Danny?"

"Yes. It's so much more than that for me."

"I love to have you think it is. But I doubt that essentially it is ever more, with anyone. Do you know what brought the climax with me? Those horrible painted creatures in that basement den. It was a revulsion from that. I felt a fierce craving for—for something to wash out that foul memory, for something sane, natural, normal. For you."

"You knew I was in love with you."

"Did I? I suppose I did, or I wouldn't have done what I did. I want you to be, Dan. But it's your risk. I've already warned you; don't love me too much, Dan."

"And I've already told you the warning comes too late."

"I'm glad. After all, I'm a woman. I shall be jealous and demanding and possessive and temperamental as hell."

"And I'll endure it all meekly, I suppose. And come back for more."

Across the dinner table at the Café Hungaria, far over on Houston Street, she said out of a clear sky, "Don't let your lovely Laurie get involved with Stan Barto."

"I don't think there's much danger of that," Dan said.

"He's a fortune-hunter and a bad egg. The best dancer in New York. She seemed quite pleased with his attention. He can be fascinating when he chooses."

"Have you found him fascinating?" Dan asked.

"For a while. He thought he was in love with me. Or pretended so. After I turned him down, he tried to blackmail me."

"About your actor?"

She nodded.

"What did you do?"

"I went to Acton Daggett. Acton threatened to kill him. Would have, too, I believe."

"Where does Daggett come in?" Dan asked jealously.

"After all, he's a sort of cousin. More my cousin, I daresay, than Laurie Crosbie is yours." She smiled.

"You have a mean, suspicious nature, my dear," was the best answer he could think up at the moment.

Her face became somber. "This will be our last night together for a while, darling."

"Why?"

"The family are coming back."

"You can't come to the apartment any more?"

"Oh, yes; for an evening sometimes. But I must be more careful. Tomorrow will be our last breakfast."

In the morning she was up first. She went to the makeshift kitchen, filled the kettle and set it on. Very domestic. Dan's heart swelled.

She came back, sat on the side of the bed, and looked down at him. "Have you been happy, Dan?"

"Unspeakably. Insanely."

"So have I," she sighed. He put his arms around her and drew her down. "No," she said. "Not yet. I've got something on my mind."

"Can't it wait?"

"No. Dan, suppose I became pregnant?"

"Kathie! You're not, are you?"

"I don't think so. I hope not. But I might get that way; we haven't been too careful, you know."

"Well," he said. "Fine by me."

"Why-why-why, you bum!" she stuttered wrathfully.

"Then you'd have to marry me."

"Don't think it!"

"Well, there are ways out. I could find a doctor who—"

"No. That I would *not* do. Don't ask me why. I don't know. But I just couldn't."

"What would you do, then?"

"Marry Acton Daggett."

"Kathie! You couldn't."

"Oh, yes, I could," she returned hardily. "He's got what I want in a husband. Money, position, everything. I've always figured that I'd marry him eventually."

"Without telling him about us?"

"Why should I tell him?"

"Oh, no reason! No reason at all. I merely thought he might be interested," Dan said sardonically.

"Oh, I owe him no odds," she returned coolly. "He tried to seduce me when I was sixteen and darn near succeeded. Since then he's been trying to marry me. So he has no kick coming."

"I think it would be a rotten deal, just the same."

"Oh, Dan! Be reasonable. Besides, a married woman has a lot more freedom than a girl. It needn't make any difference with us, darling."

"Don't be a fool!" he said violently. "Do you think I'm going to share you?"

"Aren't you assuming a good deal?" she retorted. "Share me? Do you own me? Or any part of me? Don't talk about sharing me."

"All right," he returned sullenly. "But understand this, Kathie; if you marry Daggett, I'm through."

She sighed elaborately. "Men! Men! Such stupid dolts. Why do women ever fall for them! . . . Oh, darling; let's forget it for now. Shan't we?"

They did.

In a few days Dan had a note in the bold, clear handwriting.

All is well, darling. Nothing to worry about. Please don't hate me if you get news that you don't like.

Two weeks later the mail brought him a clipping from the *Herald,* in an envelope addressed in Kathleen's hand. Mr. and Mrs. Pendleton Tennant were announcing the engagement of their daughter, Kathleen Ayrault, to Mr. Acton Daggett.

Dan tore the paper into fragments and set himself to forget.

23

Some reluctance which she did not attempt to explain to herself impelled Laurie to withhold formal announcement of her betrothal, though her mother urged it. Mrs. Crosbie's one thought was to get her daughter safely and advantageously married. Allen Hardwick fervently supported her view.

He was deeply, pathetically, timorously in love, assiduous in all attentions, slavishly enamored, fearful of pressing unwanted devotion upon the girl. Toward him she was kind and companionable—and neutral. Naturally a sensitive soul, he felt her withdrawal and was troubled and uncertain. That Tommy Howatt had anything to do with her attitude, he did not suspect. Once or twice Mrs. Crosbie had hinted that the *P.G.* man was a rejected suitor whose advances had been so effectually squelched that he had abandoned the pursuit.

So he had, but not until after several unsuccessful attempts upon the apartment house, and even then he relinquished only his efforts to gain entry to the Valdevia. They might be able to bar him there; they couldn't keep him off the public streets, which Laurie must also use. New York wasn't so big a place but what he was sure to run into her sometime. Or, what about the parsonage? She went there to consult with Dr. Farr on the committee work. Yes, but Allen Hardwick was likely to be with her on such errands.

Not so good! When Tommy boasted to Dan Adriance that he wasn't afraid of the holy-boly, he was telling the truth but not the whole truth. Physically he had no special fear of Allen or anyone else. Look what he had done to John L.! True, there wouldn't always be a bung starter handy, but he could likely find a substitute if too hard pressed.

As Laurie's fiancé, however, Allen inspired the otherwise dauntless Tommy with a revulsion that was partly dread. He shrank from seeing the pair together. He must contrive to see the girl alone. What he would say to her, how he would make his peace, he had not determined—leave it to the spur of the moment. How to achieve the moment was the problem. He tried the Farr angle at the close of one of their games.

"Dr. Farr, doesn't Miss Crosbie ever come here any more?"

"Why, yes, Thomas. Frequently, to meetings."

"I mean alone."

The clergyman set down the glass of sarsaparilla pop beside the bottle which was the habitual house refreshment. He eyed his guest severely.

"What is your purpose in wishing to see Laura Crosbie alone?" he demanded.

"Why—why, where's the harm?" Tommy countered feebly.

"Are you not aware that she is betrothed to Allen Hardwick?"

"Yes, sir. But—"

"Has she evinced any desire to see you?"

"No, sir," Tommy admitted ruefully.

"I doubt that you are a proper companion for an innocent young girl."

Tommy was hurt. "I thought you were a friend of mine, Dominie."

"So I am. But that does not connote approval of your associations."

"Such as?"

"Notorious resorts. The Hastings woman's. The Haymarket. Clark's infamous assignation place in the guise of a restaurant. Need I go further?"

"Aw, now, Doc—excuse me, Dominie—be fair. A newspaperman has to keep in with all kinds of folks."

"I quite understand that. But the frequency and familiarity with which certain feminine names crop up in your casual and unguarded conversation rouse the suspicion—nay, the conviction that you have relationships in the Tenderloin which are more than merely friendly."

"A fella's got human feelings, Boss," Tommy mumbled.

"A sad plea, Thomas."

"I don't pretend but what I've stepped off the straight-and-narrow now and then. But not any more."

"Are you quite sure, Thomas?"

Tommy ransacked his memory for a clue to any recent errancy that might have come to the questioner's notice, and could find none.

"Yes, sir. Oh, I might have taken a drink or two with some old gal pal, but that's all. I swear to—"

"Wait! Before you perjure your soul, carefully review your actions."

(Oh, geez!—thought Tommy in dismay—Can Laurie have told on me? Second thought was reassuring; the Doc had been talking about the red-light district; Laurie couldn't have been in his mind.)

"I don't know what you mean, Dominie," he said, striving for candor with a touch of reproach.

"It is against my principles to reveal our committee's actions. But in this instance I must be open with you. I refer to a certain house on West Twenty-sixth Street."

"The Bower?"

"Precisely."

"That dirty pup Hardwick!"

"Allen Hardwick is not the source of my information."

"Who is?"

"Another of our investigators."

"What did he tell you?"

"That you were seen entering that house after midnight three days ago."

"I was."

"You admit it?"

"Sure, I admit it. Dr. Farr, I've never lied to you in my life."

"I should be glad to believe that, Thomas."

"And I ain't—I'm not going to begin now."

"Proceed."

"I went to the Bower because I had business. With Etta Holmes."

"The proprietress?"

"Yes, sir."

"Business? Newspaper business? At that hour of night?"

"Nothing to do with the *P.G.* But it was legit business just the same."

"I think you would be well advised to seek other lines of activity."

"Look, Dominie. I got a couple of commercial hookups in the district. Strictly on the level. No more to do with the girls than if I was the grocery man. Won't you believe me, Dominie?" he appealed.

Dr. Farr could recognize the accent of truth. His expression softened. "I will," he said. "And gladly."

Tommy glowed. "About the girls. I'm off that. It hasn't been easy, either. Not for a rough guy like me." He paused. "I'm kinda superstitious, I guess. I've been kinda relying on you."

"On me, Thomas?"

"You know that Kodak picture I took of you. I always carry it in my kick."

"A vain thing," the Doctor said. But he could not quite repress a smile.

"It helps," Tommy said.

No other form of flattery could have reached Dr. Farr with the same force. Yet the seemingly ingenuous statement about the photograph was guileful. True, the likeness of the clergyman was always with Tommy in his wallet. But it was not a talisman against unchastity, as its owner would have had his friend believe. It was a mascot. Never did he sit in a card game at the Tenderloin Club, be it poker, pinochle, hearts, or high-five, without invoking its occult powers. It was the agency of a ritual, adapted from a gypsy formula which he had picked up on the high road. Prefatory to any game of chance, Tommy would retire to some private spot, take out the photograph and orbit it slowly about his neck counterclockwise, while counting ten in hog-Latin.

The evening after his defense of himself against Dr. Farr's charges, he went to the club, where he found a game of poker in progress. The Tenderloin Club brand was rigidly classic. The play was for table stakes; that is, without limit other than the pile of chips in front of the bettor. Deviations were strictly taboo: no artificial jackpots; no roodles except after four of a kind; no deuces wild; nothing but straight draw poker. Such abominations and perversions as Oklahoma, spit-in-the-ocean, and one-eyed jacks were blessedly unknown. Tommy soon earned the reputation of being "shot with luck." He attributed his success to his clerical mascot. It was, in fact, due mainly to his knowing when he was beaten.

Having, this evening, ascertained that there was a place for him at the table, Tommy went downstairs to the washroom to clean up. Before washing his hands, he took from his wallet the small leather case holding the Farr photograph and laid it beside him on the marble.

He did not hear Willie Frye's approaching footsteps. It was one of Willie's several accomplishments that he could walk like a cat. Tommy was startled to hear his police pal's voice: "Who's your gal, Tommy?"

"None of your damn business. Drop that!"

But the fly-cop was already holding the photograph up to the light. "Jesus!" he ejaculated. "It ain't a gal. It's his Holy Whiskers."

Tommy pinned him in a wrestler's grip and recovered his property. Willie grunted.

"Still on the up-and-up with your parson pal?" he asked.

"Sure."

"I'd-a thought you was too smart a hombre to be sucked in by that old hypocrite."

"Lay off, Willie."

"Put a brass nickel in the plate for me Sunday. Say, didya see Etta Holmes on the towel deal?"

"Yeah."

"Is she comin' in?"

"She is in. Four dozen at twenty per doz."

"I got the French Madam and Cora Wilson. We're comin' fine, partner."

In recognition of his *Police Gazette* series, "Heroes of the Force," Tommy had been cut in on the towel concession of the high-class houses. He, Willie Frye, and two other favored ones had developed a system of buying towels at six-fifty a dozen, having them initialed in tasteful embroidery at a cost of ten cents apiece, and purveying them to the madams at from fifteen to twenty dollars a dozen. There was also a collateral emolument in the laundry collection. It was this pleasant addition to his income which enabled Tommy to take up quarters at the Windsor. He had not thought it expedient to explain the exact source of his new income to either Laurie or Dr. Farr.

Tommy turned to another and equally important subject. "Seen Nita yet?" he asked his pal.

"Yeah."

"Talk to her about the Hardwick business?" Tommy asked, first looking out the door to make sure that nobody was within earshot.

"Yeah. She don't know the guy."

"Of course not. How would she?"

"But she's all right. I've rigged it so's she'll have a chance to see him. Think he'll fall for her?"

"Sure. She'll get him. All those piety boys need is a chance."

"She thinks she ought to have fifty out of it."

"It ought to be worth that to the precinct to get rid of the holy-boly. Incidental expenses. You fix it with the pantata."

"Nah. It's too much. She'd oughta be satisfied with a twenty. Have a drink?"

"Drink is bad for my style of play. Aren't you sitting in?"

"No. Got a shootin' over in Hell's Kitchen to look into. So long."

"See you on ice," Tommy said in farewell.

24

Three months the trustees had allowed Dr. Farr to prove his charges. Two weeks short of the time, he announced that he was ready with the evidence gathered by his committee, which he would present from his pulpit on the second Sunday of November. Admission would be by card only. Advance notices went out to Newspaper Row of the event which was to make history as the Sermon of Justification.

"Like a side show," said the Old Stone Church faction hostile to the movement.

"Big day coming," Tommy Howatt said to Dan Adriance. "Off goes the lid. Out comes the stink. The Dominie had better have his stuff this time."

"I'll back him to have it," the *Star* reporter said.

Allen Hardwick was equally confident in talk with his fiancée.

"Are you sure the committee has all it needs, Allen?" Laurie asked.

"All it needs to start. Not all there is. There's no end to that."

"You're going ahead, yourself?"

"Yes. I'm trying to tie in some loose ends between now and the sermon. Corroboration stuff. Not essential, but convenient to have for background. I'm likely to have my evenings pretty well taken up for a time."

"Isn't it dangerous, Allen?"

He smiled indulgently. "Scare-talk, darling. The police have tried from the beginning to frighten us off. They arrested a couple of our boys on trumped-up charges. Dr. Farr went to court, himself, and read the riot act to the magistrate. That ended *that*. Discharged with apologies. They're a yellow lot."

At the office of the *Police Gazette,* Richard K. Fox pondered the problem of how to handle the Farr story so as to derive from it the maximum of sensation. He consulted Dan Adriance.

"You're covering the Farr sermon for the *Star,* I suppose."

"Yes."

"When you've finished that, will you do a special for us? Sort of character sketch of Farr?"

"I don't believe so, Mr. Fox."

"Why not? It wouldn't interfere with your regular job."

"Dr. Farr is a friend of mine. I don't believe the kind of story I'd write would fit into the *P.G.* policy."

The editor-proprietor smiled. "Tommy Howatt has ducked the job. He claims to be a friend of the minister's, too. Well, I guess Farr is going to need all the friends he's got. He may be a fine man—I guess he's an honest one—but he's going to shed a shoe at this jump."

"I wouldn't risk any money on that proposition if I were you," the reporter advised. "I know something of what the committee has collected. It's dynamite."

Mr. Fox leaned forward and lowered his voice. "This is confidential. I'm told that the Police Department isn't worrying a bit over Farr. They've got some dynamite of their own."

"Any idea of the nature of it?"

"Nothing definite."

"I'm betting on the Dominie," said Dan.

Three hours before church time that Sunday morning, people began to gather in Thirty-first Street and around the corner into Madison Avenue. Arriving at ten o'clock, Dan Adriance had to fight his way through the crowd and up the steps. In that part of the gallery assigned to the press, he found Tommy Howatt already settled. On its journalistic merits, the *Police Gazette* did not rate a ticket, but Tommy's was a personal favor from his friend, the pastor.

Below, Laurie sat alone in the Crosbie pew. That Mrs. Crosbie, feeling as she did about the crusade, was not present, did not surprise Dan Adriance, who was leaning out and surveying the congregation. But where was Allen Hardwick? Presently several strangers, holding cards, appeared and filled the pew. All the faces around her were excited, anticipative, but Laurie looked spiritless.

The doors were closed, not without difficulty, at ten-thirty. Every pew in the church was jammed. A sigh of curiosity and expectancy passed through the crowd as an usher bore to the rostrum a formidable packet of official-looking papers, all of a size, and placed them on a stand beside the pulpit.

Dr. Farr entered. His step was firm, his shoulders squared. He stood in the pulpit with eyes closed. His lips moved in whispered prayer. When he spoke, all the power of his personality was in the deep, quiet, even-toned voice.

"Last summer I made certain charges from this pulpit. I was relying upon common knowledge, hearsay, newspaper reports. Therein I was at fault. The Grand Jury rebuked me. The press denounced me. I was accused of being a scandalmonger and sensation-seeker who debased his high calling, compromised his church and defamed his city with accusations unsupported by evidence."

He set his hand upon the papers. "Here is the evidence," he said. "Here are more than two hundred affidavits, sworn to by men of integrity. They have gathered the data at first hand. Part I have, myself, gathered at first hand." A wave, hardly to be identified as sound, and yet mysteriously expressive of amazement, anticipation, admiration and wonder, passed through the massed people below him.

"These"—he tapped the papers with the flat of his hand—"are reports collected from brothels, gambling hells, dance halls, opium joints and some few places so indescribably foul and vicious that my soul shudders within me at the memory."

(Dan wondered whether he could have been at the Slide. He had.)

"Here are reports of police connivance so detailed as to compel belief. Money has been passed in sight of witnesses. Corrupt bargains between brothel-keepers and representatives of high officials have been overheard and noted. Law defiance so blatantly open as to be all but incredible will be shown to be a commonplace. All of this is sworn to by men of unimpeachable character and integrity.

"These documents are here for public examination. The Grand Jury is invited to inspect them. A digest has been prepared for the convenience of the press. While copies are being supplied, these services will be recessed."

Together with the other reporters, Dan Adriance descended the gallery stairs and went into the side room to get his copy. His immediate interest now was to estimate the effect of the Farr exposures upon the churchfolk who crowded the aisles in agitated groups, exchanging opinions.

"What a show!"

"A disgrace to Presbyterianism."

"Dr. Farr is a soldier of Christ. We must back him to the finish."

"Our church has been made a stench in the nostrils of decency."

"Can anybody deny that what he says is true?"

"The Mayor denies it, and the District Attorney. They are gentlemen and solid citizens. I know them personally."

"The Elders should admonish him."

"He'd tell them to go to Gehenna. That Dutch blood."

"What I say is, let him hire a hall."

"—vile women soliciting our young men under the very shadow—"

"—always has been and always will be—"

"—can't run New York like a Sunday school—"

"—touch pitch without being defiled—"

"—outlived his usefulness to the Old Stone Church—"

The babble died down as the clergyman mounted again to his pulpit. The congregation straggled back to the pews. Dr. Farr waited for the rustlings and sighings of adjustment to lapse into quiet, before resuming in tones which, at times, were hardly under his control.

"I wish to say a word about a young member of this flock without whose courage, devotion, and unflagging zeal the difficult and even dangerous work represented by these documents"—again he tapped the pile of affidavits—"could never have been accomplished. He has been the driving force, the inspiring spirit of the battle. It would be impossible to overestimate the nobility of character, the steadfastness of purpose shown by Allen Hardwick. In those dens of iniquity and moral filth whither our quest led us, he shone like a sunbeam penetrating the darkness." (The newspapers had great fun later with "Sunbeam" Hardwick, as the *Sun* dubbed him.)

Dr. Farr paused. "My dear friends in Christ," he began, and had to stop. He swallowed water from a glass. When he spoke again, his command was firm. "Allen Harwick has disappeared. I shall not conceal from you my deep, my alarmed concern for him. It is now five days since any word of or from him has come to us or to his family. It is known that threats were made against him. He ignored them. I pray to Almighty God that he may not have fallen a martyr to his efforts in a noble cause." (A suggested martyrdom over which the press subsequently made abundantly merry in sardonic editorials.) "The prayers of this congregation for his safety are requested."

A man's harsh voice from back in the rear gallery said with startling clearness: "The cops murdered him."

Something like a wave of hysteria started to sweep through the church. Brockholst Farr's mighty voice quelled it.

"I make no charges—as yet. But if harm has come to Allen Hardwick, I shall hold the Police Department of the City of New York criminally responsible. Meantime, I beg that anyone within the scope of my anxiety who may have information, however slight, about Brother Hardwick will at once communicate with me. Let us now join in the Doxology."

Before the benediction was over, Dan Adriance was making a football passage through the crowd that still filled the street, in pursuit of a passing Madison Avenue car.

What a story!

So eager was the reporter to get at his writing that he did not stop to look in his mailbox on reaching the office. With a fresh pen, a well full of purple ink, and a pile of ruled white paper he set himself to the task. Sheet after sheet he finished and set aside, working steadily and with the absorption of the trained newspaperman who can wholly sequestrate himself from outside sight and sound.

From time to time Ramsey Kelly, the city editor, walked over from his desk at the window to gather in and take with him half a dozen pages. Two or three times he asked a question and got an abstracted answer. Once he murmured approvingly, "Hot stuff!"

It was nearly four o'clock when Adriance drew three dashes below the final lines and delivered the result to Kelly.

"That's the lot?" the city editor asked.

"Yes. For the church story."

"Going to handle Hardwick's disappearance separately?"

"I thought so."

"Right. What will it run to?"

"Column."

"It's worth all of that. I've sent a man over to Brooklyn to cover the family end. You needn't bother about that. Shall I have some lunch sent in to you?"

"Thanks. A sandwich and a cup of coffee will see me through." Mr. Kelly lingered. "Mr. Adriance?"

"What?"

"Before you start, what do you think has happened to Hardwick?"

"I wish to God I knew."

"Is he a personal friend?"

"Yes."

"Do you think Farr is seeing ghosts, with his mystery talk?" Dan hesitated. "Well, you know the police," he said.

"Is Farr holding anything out on us?"

"No. I'm sure not. He's worried sick."

"All right. Go ahead with your story. I won't interrupt you again."

Dan did a specially careful job with what was soon to be called "the Hardwick mystery." It was dinner time when he put down his pen, and went for his overcoat. The day being Sunday, Katie's would be closed. He would go to the Tenderloin Club for dinner. Passing through the gate that shut off the city room, he bethought himself of his mail. He opened the box. At sight of the large, stiff envelope crumpled within, all the satisfaction of a job well done passed out of him. He knew what it was, with a sure foreboding.

He opened it. On the fashionable stationery of Bailey, Banks & Biddle, Mr. and Mrs. Pendleton Tennant bespoke the honor of his presence at the marriage of their daughter, Kathleen, to Mr. Acton Daggett on December the seventh. Above the chastely engraved legend ran two lines of unforgettable handwriting:

Don't be stupid, darling, and pretend that I'm dead. I'm not. Wait and see.

199

He ripped the stiff paper savagely.

"No, by God!" he swore.

By common consent of Park Row, the *Star*'s story on Hardwick was the best in town. Dan Adriance did not even look at his own work when it came out in the morning. It did not matter. Nothing mattered.

The reaction to the Sermon of Justification was widespread, intense, and various.

Park Row said: "This is going to hold the front page for a hell of a while."

The man on the street said: "The parson's got 'em on the run."

The Old Stone Church said: "Where is it all going to end?"

The wiseacres at Albany said: "You never can tell what'll pop up when you start one of these bloomin' committees going."

The *World* said editorially: "No prophetic powers are needed to forecast that if the Farr charges are substantiated, Tammany's misrule of the city is nearing its end."

The *Wall Street Journal*'s real estate expert said: "Owing to uncertainty as to what the pending investigation may bring forth, values in the Tenderloin District have fallen sharply. A decline from the high-water mark in local rentals is expected."

Boss Corbin said (publicly): "It is time for decent citizens to rise in protest. I have contributed one thousand dollars to Dr. Farr's committee." Boss Corbin said (privately): "This looks like the best chance yet for the Republicans to get in."

Boss Croker of Tammany Hall said (for publication): "The organization will co-operate with any honest investigation."

Citizens with a pull called up their politician friends and said: "How about a couple of seats for the hearings?"

Big Bill Nelson said, in the presence of several fellow members of the Tenderloin: "Albany had better keep its goddamned hands off. Take it from me. There ain't going to be any investigation."

Mrs. Steevens Parke expressed the sentiments of many of the Best People, who, like herself, had long owned red-light property without giving any thought to it, in saying: "New York is New York. It will always be New York. And no fanatic in a pulpit is going to change it."

Tammany Hall issued instructions to the police of the Tenderloin: "Dim the red lights."

The police passed the word along to the Tenderloin madams: "Pipe down till we give you the word."

Clark's said: "Does a girl have to go to Philadelphia to make an honest living?"

Georgiana Hastings said: "They can't pull the shutters on *me,* by God!" (But they did.)

The Reverend Dr. Brockholst Farr said to Boss Corbin: "Don't move too soon. We have only scratched the surface."

Although he was a member in good standing of the Old Stone Church, Mr. Corbin's interest in righteousness was distinctly secondary to his concern with politics. As leader of the Republican machine in the state, he was alert to extract any possible partisan advantage from the Farr crusade. Privately he was unsympathetic to it as an unwarranted infringement upon human nature and personal rights. But he appreciated its potential value as an impeachment of the ruling Democratic regime. If public indignation against Tammany Hall and its corrupt administration could be sufficiently stirred up, the Republican machine (equally corrupt, but what of that?) would have its turn at the trough. It was with this in mind that he had made his contribution.

His weapon was the State Legislature, which was strongly Republican. With the impetus of the Farr charges, he could get a Senate investigating committee appointed in Albany. It would be heavily weighted with staunch upstate Republicans, have a reliable party chairman, and be slanted in favor of Dr. Farr. The Boss was banking on Brockholst Farr, confident that his transparent integrity, his devotion to the cause, his shining purity of character, his simple dignity, and his capacity for trenchant presentation would carry all before it at the hearings.

To be sure, Allen Hardwick's inexplicable defection was disturbing. Was there some sort of skulduggery going on in that quarter? Still, at worst, Hardwick's presence at the proceedings would not be essential. Those affidavits would stand without him. It was reasonably safe to go ahead.

Word was passing along the subterranean channels of Tammany Hall that there might be trouble for a time, but everything was coming out all right in the end. Lie low and wait. The Sermon of Justification was less than a week old when this don't-worry rumor reached the news-sensitive ear of the *Star's* city editor. He summoned the reporter on the case.

"What's this about the Farr investigation, Mr. Adriance?"

"Nothing new, as far as I know."

"Do you think it's going through?"

"I don't see what can stop it."

"The big boys on East Fourteenth Street don't think so."

"You mean that crack of Big Bill Nelson's? He was just shooting off his mouth."

"That's your opinion, is it? Have you heard that the Tenderloin is going to open up quietly?"

"Yes, I've heard it, Mr. Kelly," the reporter said. "I haven't been able to verify it."

"It doesn't seem likely that the houses would open for business in the face of a legislative inquiry."

"No, it doesn't," the reporter admitted.

"You might try out Etta Holmes or Carrie Baker or some of the other wise madams," Kelly suggested. "How does the wind set at Clark's?"

Adriance duly made inquiries. Neither the brothel madams nor the independents at the all-night restaurant would talk much. However, Dan did get the feeling that there was no condition of panic over the check to operations. The Tenderloin was taking things philosophically. It'll-all-come-out-in-the-wash was the prevailing tone.

Since Dr. Farr became news, the reporter had found Harrison M. Perley a useful source of information. He was perhaps not in the inner councils of Tammany Hall, but, as an important though carefully obscure member, he might well know what was in prospect. The reporter called at his office and was pleasantly received.

"Mr. Perley, I want some information. Confidential, if you want to make it so."

"Go ahead, Adriance. I'll oblige if I can."

"Is there a movement afoot to block investigation of the Farr charges?"

"If there is, I know nothing of it."

"I understand that the Tammany leaders aren't losing any sleep."

The Honorable Harrison M. Perley smiled. "The assumption would be that there is nothing for Tammany to worry over, wouldn't it?"

"That's too much of an assumption for anyone to swallow, Mr. Perley. You've seen the evidence."

"Yes," the contractor admitted.

"You don't believe that Dr. Farr can make the affidavits stick?"

"I have expressed no such opinion."

"Then you do think that the investigation will go through?"

"Dr. Farr is no halfway man. Neither is Tom Corbin."

"No. And they're committed to this."

"Now, I'll ask you one," the contractor said. "What is your opinion of this Hardwick business?"

"I don't like it. I wish I were sure that Allen is alive."

"Alive? Alive? Why shouldn't he be alive?" Mr. Perley demanded sharply.

"Witnesses to police corruption have disappeared before now and never turned up again. Not as important people as Allen, perhaps. But, still—"

"Poppycock!" Mr. Perley cried. "Pure poppycock."

"All right," Dan retorted. "But if Allen is alive, why hasn't he sent some word to his friends? His family are as much in the dark as we are."

"Has it occurred to you that he might have run away?"

"From what?"

"Ah! That I don't know. I thought you might."

"I don't believe that Allen Hardwick ever ran away from anything in his life."

Mr. Perley's bland and florid face became somber with thought. "He's run away from Laurie Crosbie apparently."

"Yes. That's hard to figure out."

"It's equally hard to figure out why she is taking it so calmly."

"Do you think she is? She's worrying herself sick over something," Dan said.

"Not over Hardwick. Mrs. Crosbie agrees with me. The girl is concerned, of course. But she is not terrified and in anguish as any normal woman would be over the disappearance of the man she loves. She might have some private information that she is keeping to herself?"

"I'm sure she hasn't. Her bewilderment over Allen is genuine enough."

"Then there must be another explanation. By the way, she isn't really in love with him. Is she?"

"I'm afraid not."

"Is there someone else?"

"I'm afraid so."

"Is it that cub on the *Police Gazette?* That is Mrs. Crosbie's theory."

"I'm afraid Mrs. Crosbie is right."

"He's a friend of yours, isn't he?"

"In a way. But I'd hate to see Laurie involved there."

"Is she seeing him?"

"No."

"Adriance, we've got to find Allen Hardwick and bring him back."

"Don't for a moment think that the committee hasn't been doing everything it can. They've got the Pinkertons on him now."

"No clues?"

"Not a thing," Dan replied as he rose to go.

That night, at the Tenderloin Club, Tommy Howatt and Fox-face Willie Frye sat at a small table embellished with a quart of imported champagne for which the plain-clothes man had ponied up four dollars. The club was one of the few places in New York where a cop paid for what he got.

Willie said, "It's in the bag."

Tommy asked, "When are you going to spring him?"

"Hardwick? As soon as Old Hellfire tips his hand."

"You're sure you've kept him bottled up?"

"Yep. And never mind where. The less you're in on details, the better you'll be able to tell your pals that you don't know nothin' about it and not be lyin' too much."

"I guess you're right, Willie."

"You know I'm right. It's an under-cover operation. The Big Boy in Mulberry Street knows the inside, and Bernie Schmidt, and the smart cop from the precinct that worked with me, and that's all. Except Nita, of course. I've tipped Bernie just enough so you get a credit on it. Has his Whiskers been puttin' you over the jumps?"

"Every time I see him."

"Still palsy-walsy, huh? Are you carryin' around that picture of him in your kick?"

"What business is that of yours, Willie?"

"Oh, I just thought I'd like to take a slant at the old Christer's sweet mug for the good of my poor soul."

"To hell with your poor soul! Why don't you take it to the Old Stone Church some Sunday? Give it a break."

"I might, at that. With a warrant up my sleeve."

"For criminal libel, eh? I've heard all about those fake threats. Let 'em try it! Is that what you've got in mind?"

"You never can tell," said the cryptic Willie. He lifted his glass. "Here's to hell with reform."

"I'm with you there," his companion said.

They drank.

25

Unsolved mysteries fade swiftly from public interest. Allen Hardwick's disappearance was a dwindling news item which might have been dropped by the papers, had not Dr. Farr kept hammering away at the subject. The reverend-crusader was now much in demand as an after-dinner speaker.

Boss Corbin encouraged this. It contributed to the build-up for the forthcoming Senate inquiry. It focused attention upon the theme of political corruption.

"Keep it up, Dominie," the Boss said. "We'll cram those affidavits down the Tammany tiger's throat."

At his every public appearance now, the clergyman presented what he called the triple-C equation of the police-political conspiracy.

$$\text{Crime} + \text{Collusion} = \text{Corruption}$$

And then his original three-pronged spearhead of accusation.

> *Organized vice cannot exist without police complicity.*
> *Organized crime cannot exist without police connivance.*
> *Organized lawlessness cannot exist without police corruption.*

This he followed with his demand upon the Police Department to find Allen Hardwick, or, failing this, evidence as to his fate.

No effective reply came from the authorities. Mulberry Street hinted that young Hardwick had run away for reasons of his own, but produced no evidence in support. His business affairs were in order. His private life was unblemished. No reason whatsoever could be brought forward for his dropping out of all his activities. A general alarm had been sent out from Headquarters.

Relentlessly Dr. Farr pressed the question of Allen Hardwick's disappearance. More and more he identified the missing crusader with the anti-vice campaign, establishing him as the embodiment and symbol of the cause, until, three weeks after the original sermon, he brought the challenge to a head: let the police produce Allen or stand convicted of foul play in the public mind.

This is what the authorities were awaiting. They sprung the trap. On a dim and soggy December morning the irritant tinkle of his telephone roused Dan Adriance. He rolled out of bed and staggered sleepily to the outer room.

"Hello."

"Dan?"

"Yes."

"It's Tommy."

"Ahr-r-r-r! What time it it?"

"Nine-twenty. I'll be there in fifteen minutes."

"What's up?"

"Hot stuff."

"It had better be, getting me up at this ungodly hour," Dan grumbled.

He stumbled into the bathroom, cursing. Having shaved, he was worming his way into his shirt when the Howatt musical harbinger came to his ears from the hall:

> *"Missis Fowler*
> *Rush the growler.*
> *Hurroo for Casey!"*

"Door's unlocked. Come in," Dan called.

Tommy entered. "Jefferson Market Court. Ten A.M." he said.

"What's at the Jeff?" Dan asked, knotting his four-in-hand.

"Alexander J. Smith: dee and dee."

"Never heard of him. And if you think that a drunk and disorderly police court case is any excuse for—"

"Ever hear of Allen Hardwick?"

"What the hell is this?"

"Your prize Sunday-school virgin has been out on the tiles."

"You're a liar."

"I'm telling you." Tommy was unoffended. "They got him dead to rights. Witnesses and all."

"A put-up job," Dan said scornfully. "Do they expect to get away with that? He was collecting evidence, of course."

"In his underdrawers?" Tommy inquired.

"Who says so? The police?"

"He spent the night with the dame. He can't deny it. They pulled the joint at noon and he was still there."

"When is all this supposed to have happened?"

"Almost a month ago."

206

"Where has he been ever since?"

"Where the dogs won't bite him."

"That's flagrantly illegal. They can't hold him without bringing him into court."

"What the hell do the police care whether it's illegal or not?"

He had warranty for this view. The police constantly ignored the rights of citizens in the days when the brutal "Slogger" Williams, then an inspector, could boast, "There's more law in the end of a cop's night stick than in all the courts put together."

"Is this some of your dirty work, Tommy?" Dan demanded.

"Not me!" the *P.G.* man disclaimed. "The goddam softhead thought he could buck the police and got caught with his panties down. It's going to be a looloo of a story. How the holy-boly lost his sweet young virtue. It'll give you a big laugh."

Dan reflected, as they went down the stairs together, that his companion's conception of other people's sense of humor was somewhat twisted.

All the newspapers were represented in the courtroom when Tommy and Dan got there. Evidently a tip had been sent out, broadcast. But from what source? Dan asked Eugene Wood.

"Mulberry Street," the *World* man replied.

This was unusual. "Who's the complaining witness?" Dan inquired.

"Fox-face Willie Frye of the Nineteenth."

Dan whistled softly. He remembered having seen the plain-clothes man at the Tenderloin Club on several occasions with Tommy Howatt, and speculated on that association in connection with the *P.G.* man's vague threats against Allen Hardwick. Might there not be some hookup there with Allen's present plight?

Sam Williams joined the other two reporters. The *World* had considered the event important enough to put two of its top men on it.

"Why the music, brother?" he asked Dan. "Is there something phony in this setup?"

"It smells very like dead fish to me," Dan said.

"Alexander J. Smith," Wood said. "An alias, of course. Nobody's named Smith. Not until they get arrested."

"And Caroline Matson," Dan read from the other's tip-slip. "Charge, prostitution. Ever hear of her?"

"No. But I don't cover the Tenderloin. You do—or used to."

"That doesn't mean that I remember every tart who gets herself pulled. Matson? Matson? No, doesn't mean a thing."

Two pushcart cases (obstructing traffic), a shoplifting charge, and several equally minor items were disposed of before a court attendant called:

"Alexander J. Smith and Caroline Matson to the bar."

There was a hush, a murmur, and the unguarded voice of Finley Madeira of the *Recorder,* who had been up too late the night before and been roused too early in the morning, piped, "Migod! Willya look who's here!"

Half the reporters present recognized the prisoner on sight. Allen Hardwick had been newsworthy since the start of the Farr campaign. The girl with him was Nita, the Indian Princess. In his capacity as complaining witness, Willie Frye stepped forward, amplified the drunk and disorderly charge against the young man "in that the prisoner at the bar did frequent and consort with a known prostitute."

"From papers found upon the prisoner," the plain-clothes man stated, "it is established that his real name is Allen Hardwick, and," he added with vicious emphasis, "that he is a member in good standing of the Old Stone Presbyterian Church."

"Order in the court," the attendant officers shouted. It was two full minutes before the excited tumult died down.

The magistrate leaned forward and peered down at the couple. "Is this true?" he asked the young man.

"Yes, sir," Allen replied steadily.

"What have you to say to the charge?"

"Guilty," Allen said.

"And you?" turning to the girl.

"Guilty," said Nita primly.

"Ten dollars or thirty days, each," the magistrate pronounced.

He improved the occasion, with his eye on the reporters, to deliver some highly moral reflections from the bench, setting forth the destructive effect upon society of unbridled sexual license. (The following year it cost this same magistrate $10,000 in bribe money to hush up a charge of corrupting the morals of a twelve-year-old girl.)

Allen Hardwick paid his own fine and his companion's. "I'm sorry I got you into this," he said gently.

("Did I feel lousy!" Nita said later, recounting the affair to the sisterhood of Clark's. "I told you he was a perfect gentleman.")

Reporters swarmed around Willie Frye. "This complaint is dated November eighth," Martin Hutchens of the *Sun* pointed out. "Why has the case been covered up so long?"

"The prisoner has been sick," the plain-clothes man replied blandly. "Sort of amnesia, I guess."

"Didn't you make any attempt to get in touch with his family?" Steve Mather of the *Sun* demanded.

"Sure. We tried every Alexander J. Smith in the New York and Brooklyn directories. Drew nothing but blanks."

"But you announced just now who he is?" Pop Arnold of the *Press* objected.

"He only owned up to it this morning."

It was a pretty obvious lie, but the reporters had no way to confute it, unless the prisoner, himself, denied it. Allen Hardwick, stony of face, politely but stolidly refused any statement whatsoever beyond referring every questioner to the court record. This amounted to an admission of guilt.

As Allen, who had after much difficulty forced his way to the sidewalk, was putting "the co-partner of his vicious joys" (*Mail* and *Express*) into a hack, Dan Adriance set a hand on his shoulder.

"Nothing to say," Allen began mechanically.

"I don't want you to say anything, Allen," the reporter said. "I want to know what I can do to help you."

"Oh; it's you, Dan." Allen turned to his friend the face of a dead man. He spoke on the flat level of despair. "You can't do anything. Not a thing."

"Hello, Dan," Nita said from inside the hack. "Aren't you coming with me?" she asked her fellow culprit.

"No; if you will excuse me." He lifted his hat, and the hack rolled away.

Dan said to Allen, "It was a frame-up, wasn't it?"

"No."

"The police didn't frame you?"

"No. Didn't you hear the trial just now?"

"Yes."

"I pleaded guilty. Under oath. That's all, Dan. Let me get out of here." He dropped his head into his coat collar and half ran across the street.

Tommy Howatt joined Dan at the curb. "Curtains for the holy-boly," he said.

His smug satisfaction exasperated the other. "You're just licking it up, aren't you, you rat?" he growled.

"What do you expect me to do?" Tommy retorted. "Bust out crying? You wouldn't take a bet on Laurie's marrying him. What's the odds now?"

"I still think it's dirty work and that you're in on it somewhere."

"Twiggy-vous?" said Tommy with affected languor.

"I suppose you don't know the first damn thing about it."

"Sure, I know about it."

"Well, go ahead. Fill me in on it."

"Your holy-boly friend went to Clark's, looking for trouble."

"He went there looking for evidence, and you know it."

209

Tommy grinned. "Nita was all the evidence he needed."

"Go ahead."

"He picked her up."

"I don't believe it. But go on. What happened?"

"The usual thing. He fell for her. Likely she was his first. Anyway, he had the twenty and she took him to her room. Square deal, and everybody satisfied."

"Oh, sure!" Dan said ironically. "And Willie Frye's raid, in the morning? All pure chance, eh?"

Tommy's smile was blandness, itself. "Why, sure! Just police routine."

Back at the *Star* office, before starting to write, Dan Adriance called up the Valdevia Apartments. He was lucky in getting Mrs. Crosbie and not her daughter.

"It's Dan, Mrs. Crosbie. Is Laurie there?"

"Yes, Dan. I'll call her."

"No, don't. Just don't let her see the evening papers."

"Why? What's in them?"

"There's some stuff about Allen Hardwick that I don't want her to see until I've had a chance to break it to her. I'll be up as soon as I have finished here."

"What is it? Is Allen—?"

"No, no; he's not dead. He's in trouble. Can you keep Laurie from going out where she's likely to see the headlines?"

"Dan, I think Laurie must know something about it. A note came for her by messenger. She locked herself in her room and—"

"A note? From Allen?"

"I think so. What has happened to him?"

"I can't talk now, Mrs. Crosbie. I've got to finish my story."

How to present the facts least hurtfully to the girl was a problem which Dan pondered on the way uptown after having turned in his two columns of copy. Laurie was still in her room when he arrived at the apartment. She unlocked her door at his call, and came out. Her face was white and strained.

"I was going to send for you, Dan," she said.

"Then you know about Allen."

"No, I don't. Only that he has broken off our engagement."

Dan nodded. "Yes, that's what he would do."

"Do you know why? I don't."

"Didn't he tell you?"

"Only that he had been unfaithful and that he wasn't fit ever to see me again. Dan, it was a heartbreaking letter. But I'm not sure that I understand it. What has happened?"

He gave the salient facts of the court process, glossing over nothing. She listened with averted face.

"The woman? Who was she?"

"Just a girl."

"One of *those* girls?"

"Yes."

"Oh, Dan! How could he!"

Dan sought an excuse. "He probably drank more than he meant to and didn't realize what he was doing."

"Ugh! I feel so *dirtied.*"

"You'd feel worse if you had been really in love with him." Dan thought that the reminder might have a tonic effect.

"I never pretended to be."

"If you had been, perhaps this wouldn't have happened."

"Thank God I wasn't! I used to ask myself why I couldn't be."

Dan knew the answer to that one, but refrained from giving it expression. He said, "Is there anything in his letter to indicate what Allen is going to do?"

"No. Nothing. Only that he wouldn't see me again. Wouldn't that mean that he's going away?"

What Allen did was what might have been expected of him. He resigned his position with the insurance company, his office in the Old Stone Church, even membership in his clubs, the Calumet and Lotos in New York, the Crescent Athletic in Brooklyn. It was given out that he had gone on a sea voyage for his health. Laurie had no further word from him. She did not expect any.

Dr. Farr had. It was a short, remorseful note, begging the clergyman's forgiveness for having betrayed the cause. The recipient showed it to Dan; not for publication. He flatly refused to believe in Allen's guilt.

"Drunk or sober, he would never do that."

"Then why did he plead guilty in court?"

"I cannot say. But it does not change my opinion."

Dr. Farr was a very obstinate man.

"You don't think that Laurie knows more than she is letting on, Dominie?"

"No. She is taking it hard. Unexpectedly hard. I had not looked for such grief."

The Dominie's diagnosis was wrong. Disgust, not grief, was Laurie's overriding emotion. Seared and shamed by her fiancé's public disgrace, she wished only to withdraw into the shadows of a dark conviction that all men were brutes. If the one whom she had promised to marry could so befoul himself, where was there to be

211

found a decent man in the world? The less she saw of the male sex, the better for her peace of mind.

Could Tommy have known her profound disillusionment, he would have better managed their impending and unplanned encounter. Ever optimistic, he now hoped for a restoration of the old amenities. The fiancé having removed himself from competition (with an assist by Tommy, to be sure, but nobody knew that), what was to prevent the rejected suitor from re-entering the lists?

Experience, however, had taught him caution. He consulted Dan Adriance on the best method of re-establishing himself with Laurie.

"What did you do to get in wrong?" the reporter asked.

"Nothing," said Tommy with his best air of innocence. "Not a thing, Dan."

"How can I help you if you lie to me?" Dan asked. "Not that I'm sure I want to help you, at that."

"Well, I guess I—I got kinda too fresh," Tommy admitted. "I didn't mean anything, Dan. I won't try anything like that again."

Dan grunted. "You haven't done a thing, but you won't do it again," he jeered.

"Look, Dan. That was months ago. A girl ought to get over a little thing like that. Why shouldn't she see me? Her engagement to Holy-boly is off."

"This business has been a pretty bad shock to her. Better wait awhile."

Luck favored Tommy up to a point. Prepared for a session at his favorite game, he had presented himself at the parsonage, only to be told by the maid that Dr. Farr was detained upstairs by an unexpected caller, and that there was a guest in the study.

"But I guess you can go right in," the girl said.

Tommy entered and found himself facing Laurie Crosbie. She uttered a startled "Oh!"

"Hello, Laurie," he said, with a note of entreaty in his voice.

"How did you know I was here?"

"I didn't. I'm sorry. I mean, I'm glad. It's been a long time, Laurie."

"Yes," she answered and fell silent.

It would be tactful, he considered, to steer the conversation into impersonal channels. "You here on committee business?" he asked.

"Yes. I shan't be long."

"You can't get anywhere now, Laurie. You and your committee."

"Dr. Farr doesn't believe that."

"He'll come to it. Here's the straight tip; take it from me. If the Doc could ever get those affidavits of his before a Senate committee, he might put it over. Nobody, not the toughest ward heeler, can listen to that guy and not know that he's one hundred percent, twenty-four-carat pure gold. So what's the answer? Don't give him an opening. Choke off the investigation before it gets started. That's where things stand now. The public believes that all the goo-goo crusaders are just out for their fun."

"I'm not interested," she said, stiffening.

"All right. I'll try again." He was imperturbably cheery. "I see you've been visiting around socially."

"How do you know where I've been, Tommy?"

"Oh, I keep tabs on you. You're news. Just like Chauncey M. Depew or John L. Sullivan or Ward McAllister. Picked your partner for the Patriarchs Ball yet?"

"I'm not going."

"What!" Tommy almost shouted it. Here was the top event of the season and this fool girl was calmly proposing to give it the go-by. "What's the matter with you? How many tony girls wouldn't give their eyeteeth—"

"*Tony* is a horrid word."

"Look, Laurie—"

"There you go again!"

"Is it because of the Hardwick sti—mess?"

The girl's face hardened. "As far as I am concerned," she said loftily, "Allen Hardwick doesn't exist."

A bright, if somewhat erroneous, idea popped into Tommy's head. He would make capital with his lady-love by exhibiting a noble generosity toward a fallen rival.

"Aw, don't take it so hard, Laurie," he said. "Any guy is liable to have his foot slip."

Laurie regarded him with a baleful eye. She had not forgotten this man's attempt upon her innocence (she had forgotten her own instinctive response), and now he was trying to excuse the other offender.

"You would say that!" she muttered.

It then occurred to Tommy that he might better not have said it. "Who? Me?" he stammered.

"Yes, you. I know all about you." This was a shot in the dark, but it struck home.

Tommy was taken aback. "Whaddaya know about me?" he asked, his speech beginning to slip.

"Everything. The way you live. The way you act. I know how you men behave. 'Liable to have his foot slip'! Ugh! It sickens me." Gentle Laurie, stung by her sense of wrong and shame, was reckless.

213

"If Dan Adriance has been giving me away—"

"You're giving yourself away," she retorted. "You're as bad as Allen. Worse!"

"Look, Laurie—"

"I don't ever want to see you again. Ever!" Out she marched.

Her place was taken by Dr. Farr, who set up the checkerboard. In evil humor because of his misstep with the girl, Tommy was ready to take it out on his friend.

"Wouldn't take my tip, would you, Dominie! Now look where you've landed."

Dr. Farr shook a doleful head. *"Sero sapiunt Phryges,"* he murmured.

"Come again, "Tommy invited. *"I* didn't go to Hamilton."

"Excuse me, Thomas. To translate into your own idiom: 'The Phrygians get wise too late.' I fear that I have proven myself a Phrygian."

"Yeah. Once again, lay off and keep laid off."

"Take the first move, Thomas," Dr. Farr said.

26

Newspaperdom, which rejoices more over one saint besmirched than over a score of sinners reclaimed, had a heyday.

The *Globe,* catching up Dr. Farr's reference to his young aide as a sunbeam in dark places, headlined "Sunbeam Doused in the Mire."

"Snooper Caught in Sin-Bed," the *Evening World* exulted.

"Fallen Angel Admits All," whooped the *Press.*

Tommy Howatt's "Crash of a Plaster Saint" in the *Police Gazette* was quite in the spirit of the man-hunt. He indulged his poetic talent in a ballad "Where Is Our Sunbeam Shining Now?" which he showed Dan in copy, with his customary "Whaddaya think of that?" It was not bad at all of its kind.

"Go ahead and print it," Dan said.

Tommy eyed the reporter. "You got a snotty way of talking sometimes," he observed. "I don't getcha. Why shouldn't I print it?"

"Laurie Crosbie is on the *Pinky*'s free list. She'll read your little verse. How do you think she'll like it?"

"Oh, hell!" he said. He tore it up.

"Smart lad," Dan said.

"Just the same-y, Holy-boly's night with the gals sure fixed his flint with her."

"Tommy," Dan said, "there's some dirty stuff there. How much did you have to do with it?"

The accused spread his hands wide in virtuous disclaimer. *"I* didn't take him out on the tiles, did I? Say, Dan," he added after a pause. "I hear your sweetie got married. Not so good, huh?"

"Suppose you mind your own goddamned business," Dan said savagely.

"Oops! Okay-okay! I just wanted to say don't let it get you down." He was doing his best to be sympathetic.

The editorials were scathing. More or less directly, Dr. Farr was held responsible for Allen Hardwick's downfall. The *Sun* went so far as to call the pastor a corrupter of morals and a disgrace to religion.

Milder commentary suggested that he would be well advised to turn his attention to the Scriptures and eschew petty local issues.

One newspaper dissented from the chorus of recrimination. Dan Adriance, in his report of the Jefferson Market Court proceedings, laid stress upon the police mishandling of the case. There was, he pointed out in the *Star,* no satisfactory explanation for the accused man having been kept incommunicado for over three weeks. Even though Hardwick was guilty—and his plea in court seemed to leave no room for doubt on that point—there were suspicious elements in the police case against him.

Other than the *Star*'s, however, Dr. Farr's cause was without support.

Harrison M. Perley said: "You're on the wrong track, Doctor. Get back to the Bible."

Trustee Greig announced: "No more of my money goes down that sewer."

Even the Farr adherents in the Old Stone Church now urged him to abandon his crusade. The Elders duly

Resolved: that, while the evidence adduced by the Committee of Investigation is presumably authentic, this Board deplores any further activity in a field which, by its very nature, is controversial and potentially disruptive.

Dr. Farr appealed to the Honorable Thomas Cassius Corbin. He got no encouragement from the experienced politician, who merely echoed the advice already given by the others. The game was definitely up. The affidavits? Oh, yes; the affidavits were sound enough. But the disgrace of the "Saintly Sunbeam" had made a laughingstock of the whole movement. Ridicule is the deadliest of weapons against a lofty cause.

"Drop it," was the politician's advice.

"Does this mean that you will not press for an investigation, Brother Corbin?" the clergyman asked.

"We couldn't get the legislature to vote one," was the reply. Mr. Corbin refrained from expressing his own sore discomfiture over the contretemps. He was a game loser.

Dr. Farr said in depressed tones, "I shall never give up the fight for civic decency. But I suppose that I must bow to the expressed wishes of my Board. For the present, at least, I shall avoid controversial topics in my pulpit."

The Old Stone Church breathed easier. Its congregation settled comfortably back into their high-priced pews. The reporters stopped attending the services. No longer was Dr. Brockholst Farr spot news.

Having temporarily served as a shining mark for the Park Row

216

wits, Allen Hardwick dropped out of the public prints. The disgraced crusader seemed to have dropped out of the world, also. If his family knew his whereabouts, they gave no inkling. As for his ex-fiancée, she manifested no interest in the matter, and, for a time, very little in anything at all.

Christmas came and passed, and Laurie's self-imposed isolation began to bore her. She had not seen Dan for ten days when, the day after Christmas, he called up to thank her for her gift of a pearl scarf pin.

"Still sulking, Laurie?" he asked.

"I never sulk."

"I don't know what you'd call it, then. When are you coming out of your shell?"

"I'm ashamed to see people."

"Of all the unmitigated rot! You're acting like a spoiled child."

"If you're going to scold me, do it to my face."

"All right. I'll be up this evening."

"You might take me out to dinner. What's that place I've heard about? Lüchow's?"

"It's fine if you like German food. *Echt deutsch.* We'll try it."

When he arrived at the apartment, she surprised him by asking, "Dan, can you mix a cocktail?"

"Why, yes," he replied. "I suppose I could. What's the idea?"

Cocktails were not commonly of home manufacture; they were typically a bar drink; hence for men only.

"I thought I'd like to try one of the new kind. You'll find gin and vermouth in the kitchen. That's what you need, isn't it?"

"Yes. For a Lone Tree, if that's what you have in mind."

"The latest name for them is Martini. See how up-to-date I'm getting! Lüchow's might not know how to make them. Besides, Mother doesn't like me to drink in public."

Over the concoction, of which Laurie consumed delicately only half a glass, declaring that she was taking it to give her Dutch courage, she said, "Dan, you don't look happy."

"I'm all right," he returned warily.

"You're not. Dan, is it Kathie Tennant—Kathie Daggett?"

He stiffened in his chair. "What do you know about Kathie Daggett?" he asked harshly.

"I saw her on a Fifth Avenue bus. She asked about you."

"Did she?"

"She wanted to know if you were back in town."

"I haven't been away."

"I know you haven't. But she seemed to think you had."

Dan knew why. He had torn up two letters unread, and twice set the telephone receiver back on its hook when the soft "hello" had sent the hurrying blood to his heart. He did not consider it expedient to tell Laurie this.

After a pause, she said gently, "You don't want to talk about it, do you, Dan?"

"I don't. Sorry."

"*I'm* sorry." Her manner became brisk. "Let's talk business, then."

"Business? What business?"

"Didn't you once tell me that you hoped to write a play?"

"Every newspaperman hopes to write a play."

"Have you started yours?"

"I've got a drawer full of notes and outlines."

"How long will it take to finish it?"

"At my present rate of progress? Forty years."

"Oh, Dan! Do be serious. If you didn't have to do anything else, how long would it take?"

"A year, maybe."

"How much would you need to live on for a year?"

"Listen to me, my child. Your scheme for first aid to the indigent does credit to your charitable heart, but—"

"Not charity at all. It's an investment. I've got it all figured out. Plays make a lot of money. I *know* you can write a good play. I'll give you three thousand dollars for—for—well, a fifth interest in your play, in advance. Dan, are you laughing at me?"

"You're a sweetie, Laurie," he said. "And the bait is fine and fresh. But I can't do that, and you know it."

"Why not?" she pleaded. "I've got such loads of money and you haven't *anything.*"

Dan was mildly annoyed. With a weekly space bill at eight dollars a column which frequently ran above a hundred dollars, he did not like the implication of pauperism.

"I'm not so broke but what I can afford to buy you a dinner at Lüchow's," he said. "Get your hat on."

At the restaurant she tried again. "About our play, Dan dear."

"No," he said firmly. "A play is something that an author must never talk about in advance. Do you want to hoodoo me?"

Laurie said, "You won't let me talk about Kathie. You won't let me talk about your play. What do you want to talk about?"

Thinking to himself—We may as well have this out now; I want to know where she stands—he said, "Tommy Howatt."

She looked at him steadily. "I've seen him."

"When and where?"

"Sometime before Christmas. At Dr. Farr's."

Dan frowned. "I thought you were through with all that."

"It was accidental."

"Danger, Laurie. What happened?"

"Nothing. He talked about Allen. I went away."

"And you haven't seen him since?"

"No."

"He's no good for you, you know."

"You told me that long ago."

"Well, it's true."

"I know it's true. You don't have to tell me again."

"Look, Laurie," he began and checked himself in amazement. Her hands had jerked upward to her breasts. Her eyes dilated. "Oh, *no!*" she whispered through quivering lips.

"What's wrong?"

"You said that so exactly like him! He was always saying it— 'Look, Laurie'—and I was always correcting him. Oh, Dan!"

"Is it as bad as that, my dear?" he said gravely.

"Yes."

He reflected for a time, giving her opportunity to get command of herself, then asked, "Laurie, why don't you and your mother go away for a trip?"

"Where?"

"It doesn't matter. California. Europe. Anywhere."

"Do you think that would help, Dan?"

"It's worth a try. At any rate, it would get you away from the— the center of disturbance."

"What a name for poor Tommy! You're right, I expect. I'll talk to Mother."

"The change would be good for Mrs. Crosbie, too. She hasn't been looking well."

"Something is worrying her— Get the check, Dan. Let's go back." At the Valdevia, she said, "Don't tell Tommy."

"Of course not."

"Until after we've gone, I mean. Then he may as well know."

A week later the two women were aboard ship, bound for France.

Dan broke the news to Tommy over an orange-phosphate-with-rye in the back room of Perry's Park Row drug store. Tommy received it with composure.

"Did the old lady go along?"

"Of course."

"That's good. They'll both be out of the way."

"Of what?"

"Barto is opening up in *T. T.*"

"So Mrs. Crosbie was right about his threats. I'd begun to think that she was seeing ghosts."

"No ghost about this." Tommy handed a rough proof to his companion.

It was a paragraph in the familiar *Town Topics* style of half-revelation. A meteoric young beauty recently taken up by Society, it set forth, was being made the subject of titillating gossip about both her antecedents and the source of her abundant means. As to the latter, the name of an elderly millionaire, prominent in church circles, was whispered. Spicy developments were probable. Watch the pages of *Town Topics,* Society's favorite medium, for the latest sensational and authentic news.

"Where did you get this?"

"Advance proof. The *Pinky* and *T. T.* exchange 'em. You know that."

Dan read the paragraph again. "It might go over Laurie's head even if she saw it," he remarked.

"Maybe. Not Mrs. Crosbie's though."

"No. That's bad. Is he after money?"

"More likely Laurie. *And* Laurie's money."

"What do you figure his next move will be?"

A malign grin appeared upon the Howatt countenance. "I got an idea that Mr. Stannard Barto will be leaving for foreign shores soon. For his health. Like to make a social note of it for the *Star?"*

"I'll print it with pleasure when the time comes."

"Is Laurie going away for *her* health?"

"I told you, she's had a shock. She needs a rest and a chance to forget."

The grin showed again on Tommy's face, though in less diabolic form. "Forget, huh? I don't believe Laurie's so good at forgetting. Not some things."

"Meaning yourself, I suppose. Don't be too sure."

"What's that chunk of Latin that the Dominie hands out?"

Dan shook his head.

"Something about running across the ocean, but it just don't work."

"Oh!" Dan quoted: *" 'Caelum non animam mutant qui trans mare currunt.' "*

"That's it. What's the English, now?"

" 'They change their skies but not their hearts who run across the seas.' "

"I guess old Julius Cicero knew what he was talking about. You'll be writing the Crosbies, won't you?"

"Very likely."

"Give her that message from me, will you, Dan?"

"No, I don't think I will."

Tommy finished his drink.

"You shall ne'er move a lover,
Love will find out the way,"

he hummed. "I'm going back to the office. So long, Dan. See you at the coroner's inquest."

27

Although no longer an accredited member of the force, Tommy Howatt stood high in police esteem. His hero stories, enriched with imaginative detail and put out in the best *Police Gazette* style, had already established him as a friend and ally of the Department. Now it was rumored around the Tenderloin precinct that he had been a major agent in the strategy which accomplished Allen Hardwick's downfall.

This was only partly true. It was, indeed, he who laid the groundwork of the plot and suggested Nita as the temptress. But his plan included only the seduction of the church committee's emissary. He had no knowledge of a more decisive plan, set up by Willie Frye and carried out by the Haymarket bouncer. Nor had Nita.

Giving Tommy more credit than he had really earned, Captain Bernie Schmidt summoned him to the station house and offered to cut him in for a percentage of the sidewalk-soliciting assessments. Tommy expressed his appreciation but declined. Pliable though his standards were, he maintained one inviolable principle: pimp money he would not touch. As a substitute, he was let in on the graft from a group of faro joints. While less profitable than the other, it was still, in the grateful recipient's estimation, a nice piece of coin.

What with his raised salary, his literary output, and the remunerative police side line, Mr. Thomas duB. Howatt was in the money. He could now well afford to live at the Windsor. This bred in him that conviction of success which is so often its forerunner. All would be right with the world of Tommy Howatt, if only he could get a chance to re-establish himself with Laurie Crosbie. He took a resolution, dressed in his best clothes, and went to make a call.

It was the butler's day off at the Steevens Parke mansion. Mrs. Parke, returning from her Tuesday afternoon drive through Central Park, was met at the door by a flustered maid, new to her employment.

"There's a young man in the south parlor, ma'am."

"Who is he?"

"I don't know, ma'am."

"How did he get in?"

"He—he just kind of talked his way in."

"Imbecile! Tell him to get out— Never mind. I'll deal with him."

Terrible as an army with banners, the grande dame strode through the doorway to confront the intruder.

"Well, damn my eyes if it isn't the minstrel!" said Mrs. Steevens Parke.

Tommy rose with an ingratiating smile. "How d'you do, ma'am? I hope I find you well."

"You do. Sit down. Tea?"

"No, thank you."

"Whiskey?"

"Yes, thank you."

"Hell-bound," said the old lady amiably. "I'll join you. Pull that bell-cord." He did so. "You want something of me, I assume, or you wouldn't be here."

"Yes, ma'am."

"You have a hopeful gleam in your eye. Is it money?"

"No, ma'am."

"Just as well. You wouldn't have got it. I never lend money. What are you after?"

"Information, ma'am."

"Everyone likes to give information. It's flattering to one's vanity. What about?"

"Miss Crosbie."

"What's this? Why come to me?"

"I thought you might know when she's coming back."

"Did you!" Mrs. Parke said uncompromisingly.

Tommy was not easily discouraged. "Did you see her before she left?"

"Not for some time. She quite neglected me. I am not accustomed to being dropped by young chits. It wounds my pride. What ails the girl?"

"She's lost her ambition," Tommy said.

Before he could elucidate, the maid entered with the refreshments. Mrs. Parke busied herself with the details of serving, and then, as the girl withdrew, looked inquiringly at Tommy.

"You know," he said. "Getting her name in the society columns and all that."

"She never did seem to care about it," Mrs. Parke observed. "What have you to do with it, by the way?" The keen old eyes challenged him.

"Nothing much. Well, I mean—I used to kinda send around items about her."

Mrs. Parke was amused. "That is what is called being a press agent, isn't it? You seem to be a young person of wide activities. What is the name of the disreputable rag with which you are connected?"

"The *P.G.*—*Police Gazette*. It ain't—isn't a disreputable rag, ma'am."

"All newspapers are disreputable. Some less than others. Why don't you try to get employment from the *Times* or the *Herald* or the *Evening Post?*"

"I did. They wouldn't take me. Now I'd rather stay where I am. Mr. Fox treats me fine."

"Who is Mr. Fox?"

"Mr. R. K. Fox." Tommy was dismayed by her ignorance. "Mean to say you don't know Richard K. Fox?"

"Never heard of him."

"He owns the *P.G.* He's the man who gives the ten-thousand-dollar diamond heavyweight championship belt. Ever hear of that?"

Mrs. Parke voiced a Society superstition then in currency. "I have heard that Mr. Herman Oelrichs could win it if he chose to box professionally."

"Oh, my Go— I mean to say, maybe he could but I doubt it."

"Do you claim to be an expert?" she inquired.

"Look, ma'am," Tommy exclaimed. "The best sporting medium in the United States wouldn't pay me thirty a week if I didn't know something about fighting."

"Thirty dollars a week? Can one really live on that in New York?"

"I ate and slept on ten, ma'am. But thirty isn't all I make. I'm a regular contrib to the funny papers besides writing serious poetry for the mags. And since your party I've had offers to sing. Fifteen here; twenty-five there; a couple of times fifty at political picnics."

"And once one hundred from an old woman who knew no better."

He had the grace to blush. "I had to buy a dress suit that time."

"Who is your tailor?"

"Doll. Seventy-five for this outfit."

"Not quite the best." The shrewd old eyes considered the quiet, easy-fitting gray-mixture suit. "But he does you well enough. You look quite gentlemanly."

"I try to be a gentleman," Tommy replied, almost purring. "I'm glad you think I look it."

"I don't. I didn't say that you looked a gentleman; I said that you

224

looked gentlemanly. There's a distinction, though perhaps it is hardly fair to expect you to apprehend it."

"No, ma'am," said poor Tommy, bewildered.

"I am told that you are a knowing young person," she remarked.

"I got my lines," Tommy admitted with a show of modesty.

"Perhaps you can tell me whether that pigheaded imbecile of a Brockholst Farr is going on with his silly crusade."

"He's off it. They've got him stopped."

"Because of the Hardwick scandal?"

"Yes, ma'am. That gummed it."

"Hm. Was Laurie Crosbie hard hit by it? Is that why she went on this trip?"

"Laurie was never stuck on Hardwick."

"They were engaged, weren't they?"

"Well, sorta. The old lady pushed her into it."

"You mean Mrs. Crosbie, I assume. What has become of young Hardwick?"

"Waiting for the clouds to roll by, I guess. He'll be back. Wait and see."

"*Town Topics* hinted that he has vanished for good and all."

"*T.T.* don't know as much as they let on to know."

"It's nothing to me. I don't know the young man." She took a meditative sip of the whiskey. "There was another interesting paragraph in that same paltry sheet. You may have seen it."

"I guess I know the one you mean."

"What is its significance?"

"The usual thing. Blackmail."

"Does that explain the Crosbies' leaving the country?"

"Nothing to do with it. They were gone before the paragraph appeared."

"I suppose you think yourself in love with the girl, like all the other young moon-calves."

Taken aback by her abruptness, Tommy began, "We-ell—er—" when she cut him short: "Laurie Crosbie's ship docks at noon next Thursday. The *Arabia*."

"Gee! Thanks! Next Thursday? But that's only a little more than a month since they left," he cried.

"Yes. A quick voyage. They must have changed their plans. Any idea why?"

"No, ma'am," Tommy lied, hugging to himself the warm thought that he did know.

"You've got what you came for. Now sing for your supper," the old lady said and hobbled to the piano stool.

Tommy did his best, but it was a poor performance. His mind, for once, was not on the music. It was on Stannard Barto. When his disappointed hostess dismissed him with some pungent reflections, he went into action.

After the threatening bit in *Town Topics* appeared, Tommy and Dan Adriance in consultation had figured that there would be no follow-up until the Crosbies returned, and hence there was no occasion for immediate countermeasures. Now, all that was changed. There was little time to lose. Tommy called up Willie Frye at the Nineteenth Precinct station house and made an appointment for six o'clock at the Tenderloin Club.

Willie was full of his own troubles when he arrived.

"I been tryin' to get you at the *Pinky,*" he began.

"Okay. Here I am. Spit it out."

"What's the *Star* up to?"

"I don't know. What you got in mind?"

"The way they reported the Hardwick case. What have they got up their snoot? Hintin' there was something phony."

"Dan Adriance has always been leery about the way it was handled."

"That bastard! I don't like him. What's he sniffin' around the precinct for?"

"Sniffing is his business. He's a reporter, isn't he?"

"Yeah, but what's he reportin' around here? The Tenderloin ain't his beat."

"Cheese it, Willie. You're seeing things."

"Says you. He might run onto some of our little deals. How'd you like that?"

"Dan won't make any trouble for me, even if he did run onto something."

"Because he's your pal?"

Unable to restrain his natural boastfulness, Tommy replied, "Dan'll be good. I'm telling you. Don't you get in a sweat over Dan."

"Yeah?" The plain-clothes man was interested, indeed, now. "You got something on him?"

"Never you mind, Willie." Already Tommy was regretting his indiscretion. "I don't have to tell you all I know."

"Okay, if you say so." But Willie Frye was not one to forget such matters.

"Now it's my turn," Tommy said. "How's my standing with the Old Man?"

"Bernie, the pantata? Tops, I'd say."

"Do you think I could get a little quiet police action from him?"

"Why not?"

"Willie, there's a son-of-a-bitch trying to blackmail my girl's mother."

"Nita got a mother on her staff?"

"It ain't Nita."

"Well, who is it?"

Tommy hesitated.

"Come clean," the detective said impatiently. "How'm I goin' to help if I don't have the setup?"

There was nothing else for it. "Miss Crosbie," Tommy said.

"The beautiful Laurie?" said Willie, who sometimes read the society columns. "Geez! The boy is flying' high and beddin' soft."

"Nix on the bed stuff," Tommy snapped. "I'm going to marry her—if I can."

"Well, some of those Society fillies are pretty hot stuff, I hear. You say somebody's tryin' to put the bite on your gal?"

"Yes. A skate named Stannard Barto."

"Don't know him. Is he in the Gallery?"

"No, no. He's a gumshoe man for *Town Topics.*"

"Okay. I guess we can handle it. Whaddaya want done with him?"

Tommy winked. "Give him the discourager treatment. Full steam."

"Got any details to give me?"

Tommy told him as little as he could and still make clear how the case was to be handled. The fly-cop listened carefully.

"Might be some side lines to it," he observed. "Any tie-in with the Farr business?"

"You've got Dr. Farr on the brain, Willie. Barto hasn't got a thing to do with him."

The following night, Mr. Stannard Barto, emerging from his club, found himself inexplicably involved in a scuffle with an unknown who had bumped into him. Protesting vigorously, he was haled to the Tenderloin station, where Willie Frye and two station men took him down cellar and went over him with rubber hose. Two hours of this regulation police procedure reduced him to a sobbing pulp. Not only the fear but the explicit threat of death—which he could well credit—convinced him of the advisability of absolute silence in the matter of Mrs. Crosbie.

While they were working on Barto, another of Willie Frye's aids raided his apartment and got a full dossier on the Crosbie history: data which would never appear in *Town Topics* or any other print, but would be filed for future reference quite privately. *T.T.* chronicled the departure of Mr. Stannard Barto on a trip to the Continent for his health, which, in very truth, needed it. Police methods were thorough.

"Mrs. Crosbie can sleep nights now," Tommy told Dan, reporting upon the suppression of the peril.

"Good work," Dan approved.

"That punk'll never peep again," Tommy gloated.

"Do the cops know where Allen Hardwick is, Tommy?" Dan asked.

"No. And they don't care. He paid his ten dollars and Nita's, and that wipes him off the books. Just another dee and dee on the Jeff Market records."

"Do *you* know?"

"Honest-to-God and cross-my-heart, Dan, if there was ten thousand dollars' reward for that bird, I couldn't pipe a nickel. As far as I'm concerned, he's out like a glim and he can stay that way." He rubbed his chin thoughtfully. "Tell you what, though; I'll bet he comes back, and d'you know what'll fetch him?"

"No. Let's have your powerful thought."

"Nita."

"Nita?" Dan repeated. "Where does she figure?"

"If I've got the holy-boly right, he'll come back and marry her. Conscience stuff. You know. Save her from a life of shame. Ex-*pi*-ate his own sin. All that crap. He's a big enough softie."

"He won't marry Nita. Where have *you* been keeping yourself?"

"Not around Clark's, if that's what you mean. I—I'm kinda laying off the gals lately," Tommy said with the shamefaced mien of one confessing to a weakness of character. "What's about Nita?"

"Got herself a steady. Wedding ring in prospect."

"Oops! Not the sewer-pipe king?"

"No. This is a Down East Portugee."

"And she's quit Clark's?"

"Oh, she still goes there, I guess. But not for business."

"So she's retiring, huh? Oh, well, she'll come back," Tommy said with comfortable cynicism. "They always do. And Clark's will always be there waiting for her, no matter what Doc Farr and his goo-goos do."

"When did you last see Dr. Farr?" the reporter asked.

"Played checkers with him Tuesday."

"Does he know he's licked?"

"That hombre never knows he's licked."

"Well, he's still got his affidavits."

"Bum-wad. No Grand Jury would give 'em a look now. And the Albany end is dead. The Doc is back on the good ole gospel track, and I only hope he stays there. You still on the story, Dan?"

"The story is dead as Fulton Market mackerel. But there's talk going in the Tenderloin that I don't like much. Wouldn't wonder but what your friend with the foxy face was back of it."

"What kind of talk?"

"Oh, hints that the Dominie is another thrill-hunter. Like Allen."

"You mean they're fixing to pin something on the Doc?"

"I wouldn't put it past Willie Frye."

"Willie knows where I stand on that. He wouldn't dare."

"From what I hear, your friends, the cops, were cooking up something on him and waiting their chance to spring it when the Hardwick break came along and they grabbed that. Which may not mean that they've forgotten the Doctor."

Tommy stopped dead in his tracks. "Look, Dan," he said earnestly. "Any son-of-a-bitch that tries to frame the Doc—and I don't care if it was Bernie Schmidt or Superintendent Byrnes or Richard Croker, himself—he's got to put me out of the way first. I'm ag'in the Doc on his vice line. He knows that and he don't hold it against me. But if it comes to real trouble, you'll find T. Howatt in the Farr corner every time. Have another drink? No? Okay. See you on a slab."

Every minor incident of that early February evening was indelibly imprinted upon Dan Adriance's memory as by a flashback from its culminating event. He had returned from a sleeveless errand in a remote New Jersey town. It was nearly ten o'clock when he got off the Christopher Street ferry and telephoned his office. "No story. Fake tip," and got the response, "City desk says good night." He was free to go home.

Having just missed a horsecar, he decided to walk rather than wait twelve minutes for another. At the corner of South Fifth Avenue, a fight between two cabbies was in progress. It was so poor an effort that he did not take the trouble to cross the street. Outside the Black Cat, a blind beggar asked alms in a strong, manly voice. Dan gave him a dime, reflecting that it was probably mistaken charity. It was; the mendicant was later exposed as the owner of two dumbbell tenements on Goerck Street, and a villainously bad landlord, at that. Lamont of the *Evening Post* came out of the restaurant with a pretty girl on his arm and said hello. They were bound for an all-night dance at Webster Hall; would Dan come along? It gave him a shiver afterward to think how near he came to accepting.

At the corner of Sullivan Street and the Square, a drunken man stopped him to ask directions to Mouquin's. Dan pointed north up Fifth Avenue. The drunk turned south. Dan climbed the tall steps of No. 59.

Two voices, a man's and a woman's, were singing in a second-floor room the popular waltz song, "When the Girl That You Love Loves You." It is a cheery ditty and should not have added to the hearer's melancholy, but it did. By the time that he reached his landing, the riddle of the painful earth was such a weight upon his spirit that he all but turned back to get a drink at the corner.

A faint waft of perfume startled him as he set the key in the lock. Trembling, he pushed open the door. A pinpoint of light glowed in the corner where the easy chair stood. In a voice that he would hardly have recognized for his own, he croaked, "Kathie?"

Her low, contented chuckle answered him. "Were you expecting me?"

"No. How did you get in?"

"Combination of janitor's wife and a five-dollar bill." She pressed out her cigarette and rose. "Is that all the welcome I get?"

Then they were crushed together in the darkness for breathless, throbbing moments. Her voice was shaky as she leaned back from him.

"You must have known I'd come."

"No."

"Then you're stupid," she declared vehemently. "You don't understand women."

"Have I ever pretended to understand you?"

"No. No, you haven't. Turn on the light, darling." He did so. She blinked. "Why are you staring at me so? Did you think I'd be changed? I'm not; not one little bit."

"Why didn't you let me know you were coming? I might not have been here. I nearly wasn't," he said in panic.

"I was afraid you'd tell me not to come," she answered, and added, "Acton's gone away."

His heart gave a jump. "Left you?"

"No, silly; of course not. Some sportsmen's convention or something. Three days. Three whole days when I don't have to account to anyone in the world for anything I do. Well," she challenged impatiently, "aren't you going to say something? Or perhaps you're feeling high-minded and noble and moral. 'Go away, sinful woman.' Is that it? Shall I go, Dan?"

"You can try if you think you're stronger than I am."

"Then hold me closer." She gave a little purr of contentment. Then, with a sigh, "Oh, Dan! It's been so long, so long. Let's not give a damn for anything, darling, and just be foolish and wicked and happy while we have the chance."

Resentful of any separation in the brief period of their reunion, Kathie nevertheless was afraid to go with her lover on his assignments, one of which was a periodic inquiry about Allen Hardwick. Nothing had been heard of him as yet.

One night when Dan returned from following up a false rumor, Kathie asked, "What do you suppose has happened to him?"

"Allen? Just dropped out. Gone abroad or something."

"How long is it since he disappeared?"

"Nearly two months."

"And the beautiful Laurie has chucked him?"

"I'm afraid so."

"How silly! Anyone can slip once." She smiled. "Or more. She'll take him back, won't she? She would if she loved him. You took me back."

"That's different."

"It's always different when it's ourselves, isn't it, darling? . . . Aren't you *ever* going to finish that cigarette?"

Their last morning came with the swiftness of calamity. Kathie sat up and regarded him through a mist of hair. He thought that he had never known her eyes so soft, her lips so tender.

"Lie quiet," she bade him. "You're to be sultan this morning."

"I'm right in the spirit of the part," he assured her.

"Where's that darn bathrobe? Darling, your bed-slippers are e-e-normous. Now I'm going to start breakfast and you shall have it served to you in bed by your faithful slave."

He heard her splashing in the bath, then moving about by the gas stove. There was a light clatter of tinware. Her gay voice called, "Where do you keep your matches?" to which he replied, "On the shelf over the stove." "I've got 'em." It was all so domestic, he thought. If only it could last!

The curtain was pushed aside and Kathie appeared. "All set," she announced. "We've got fifteen minutes." She let the robe drop from her shoulders, kicked off the too-large footgear, and slipped in beside him. "Oh, Dan!" she whispered. "I don't *ever* want to go home!"

She was the first to hear the noise on the stairs. She raised herself on her elbow, quivering. The approaching voice sang lustily:

> *"Oh me! Oh, my!*
> *Mom-mom-momma, doncha hear the baby cry?"*

"Who is it?" Kathie breathed into her lover's ear.

"Tommy Howatt, damn his soul!"

The visitor began pounding on the door.

"Don't answer," Kathie whispered, clinging.

"Open up, Dan," the voice demanded. "I know you're there. Lemme in."

Dan gently loosed the girl's arms. "Don't worry," he muttered. "I'll get rid of him."

He went to the door and opened it. Tommy pushed his way in. He was obviously excited. "Extry-extra!" he said. "I got news."

"Make it quick," Dan said.

The invader sniffed the air and screwed his eyes into a leer. "Hope I don't intrude." He chuckled. "Okay. I won't be long. The holy-bo—" He checked himself and said soberly, "Our lost lamb has turned up."

232

"Allen Hardwick? Where?"

"At the foot of the Jersey Palisades."

"Good God!"

"Yep. Through the head. A thirty-two."

"Suicide?" He put the question mechanically.

"Sure. Left the usual note in his wallet. Disgrace and shame and all that. Couldn't bear to live with his lily-white virtue gone."

"And you think it's funny, don't you! You son-of-a-bitch."

"Aw, come off!" Tommy protested. "I feel kinda sorry for the poor sucker, myself. Got a Sweet Caporal on you, Dan?"

The other motioned him to the small stand, then, too late, noticed Kathie's hat there. It looked bigger than Madison Square Garden.

Tommy eyed it. "Madame Fogarty's latest, huh?" he commented.

"God damn you! Will you get out?"

"I'm trying to do you a turn," said the imperturbable Tommy. "This is a hot story and it's all yours. Get right over there and use my name with the Weehawken police. I got my lines there. They'll hold it for you . . . All right, all *right;* I'm going. See you in Potter's Field."

Allen Hardwick, as part of the standing assignment to Dr. Farr, was Dan's story. Even in his shock and distress he could not forget that.

He went in to Kathie. She was putting on her shoes. Her face was sultry with wrath.

"Why did you let him in?" she stormed.

Dan explained. Her mood softened. "How dreadful! Don't you think you should tell Laurie?"

"She isn't back from Europe yet. I've got to go, dearest. This story won't wait."

"You newspapermen!" she marveled.

Their parting was subdued by the tragic intrusion upon their happiness. She would not let Dan go down to the street with her.

"No," she said. "We'll say our good-byes here."

Thanks to Tommy's good offices, the *Star* beat the town on the Hardwick suicide. The Jersey authorities had been fixed; no other paper had the news of the identification in time. Dan Adriance worked all day and most of the evening on the story.

Immediately upon turning in his copy to the night city desk, he set out for the Old Stone Church parsonage. Dr. Farr, who had been forewarned by telephone, met the reporter at the door. He read the visitor's expression.

"Bad news, Daniel?"

"Yes, sir. Allen Hardwick's body has been found." Dan gave the essential facts.

"Are they certain that it was suicide?" the pastor asked in a shaken voice.

"No doubt of it, I'm afraid. There was a note."

"When did he kill himself?"

"Shortly after the police court, they think."

"The note. What was in it?"

"Remorse, mainly. It was sane enough. He had been false to every obligation, he said. There was a word for you, asking your forgiveness. Another for his family. A third to Laurie."

"Poor lad! Poor lad! And Laurie; we must get word to her."

"No chance, sir. The Crosbies are in mid-Atlantic."

"Of course. This will be a terrible shock. I had such high hopes of that match." A long pause. "And yet—and yet—she did not love him, did she, Daniel?"

"No, sir."

"It was young Howatt all the time, with her, was it not?"

"You don't miss much, do you, Dominie!"

"You favored Allen Hardwick's suit."

"Yes, sir."

"Because you mistrusted the other? You did not approve of that association?"

"Would you, if Laurie were your daughter?"

Dr. Farr thought a moment before replying. "I do not know how to appraise that young man. He insinuates himself into one's regard." He smiled. "An insidious fellow. He leads, I fear, an unseemly life."

"Laurie never trusted him. She is afraid of him."

"Or of herself?"

"The same thing, isn't it? That is the reason for her going abroad."

"And perhaps the reason for her returning so soon."

"I'm sure of it. And I don't like it."

"Daniel, do you regard Allen's suicide as a confession of guilt?"

"What other interpretation can be put on it? Aren't you convinced, sir?"

The rugged face worked. "I cannot give up my faith in Allen Hardwick. I cannot."

"Do you want to make that statement for publication?"

"Yes, yes!"

"Anything more?"

"Yes. I think so. I shall hold the funeral services in the church and deliver a memorial sermon over the body."

"Don't do that, Dr. Farr."

"Not testify to my faith in him?"

"Not in that way. You'd split your church from top to bottom.

Don't you realize that you haven't a leg to stand on? Every evidence is against Allen. At least, think it over before you commit yourself. Anyway, you would have to have the family's consent."

"Surely they would not object."

"You don't know that demoniac old Puritan, Allen's father."

"I do know him. He is a hard man, but—"

"Dominie, listen to me. I have been to the Hardwick house today. Old Hardwick said to me in so many words that his one wish now is to hide his son's shame under the earth as quickly and quietly as possible. At least, consult him before you act."

"Yes, I suppose I must. I shall go there the first thing in the morning."

"May I use your telephone?"

"You know where it is."

"You are quite sure that you want to make that statement about Allen?"

"Quite, Daniel. You know your way out. Good night, my boy."

"Good night, Dominie."

The reporter was right, as Dr. Farr found when he was confronted by Ezra Hardwick. The old man was immovable. He would listen to no argument. His son, he told Dr. Farr, had sinned as grossly against his church as against his home. He was unworthy, in death as in life, of that church's mercy. Dr. Farr left, profoundly depressed.

Allen Hardwick, fallen from grace, was buried as privately as might be from the house which held itself dishonored through him.

Dr. Farr's profession of unswerving faith in the dead man, as reported in the *Star,* caused no great stir. So long as the church was not officially involved, the members were content to pass it over. It was quite in character. "Stiff-necked old Dutchman," they commented, not without affection. But they wanted no more of his anti-vice committee and its works. The activities of that body were in abeyance.

Two days after the funeral the *Arabia* steamed up the river through the autumn mist. Dr. Farr and Dan Adriance had arranged between them to meet the Crosbies at the pier. After careful discussion it had seemed best to withhold from the women the news of Allen's death until the party was back in the haven of the Valdevia. Then the clergyman would say what was necessary.

Arriving a few minutes before the appointed hour of noon, Dan saw Tommy Howatt, seated on a packing case, swinging his legs and smoking a Sweet Caporal. His face was bright with expectancy. He waved and Dan walked over to him.

"How did you find out, damn you?" he said.

"I got my lines."

"Your lines! I admit it's a public pier—"

"It sure is."

"—and you have as much right here as anyone else. But, unless Laurie wrote and told you—"

"She didn't."

"Then you aren't doing yourself a bit of good by this foolishness."

"I'm not doing any harm, either— Dan, I've got something sticking in my crop."

"It can wait, can't it?"

The *P.G.* man shook his head. Apologies were very little in his line (except to Laurie) and he wanted to get this one off his mind. It was his first opportunity, as he had not seen Dan since his early-morning invasion of the Washington Square flat. Now he said, "Look, Dan. You ain't—aren't sore on me for busting in on you, are you?"

"I told you not to come without telephoning."

"I know, but there isn't always a telephone handy. And I was kind of excited that morning."

Dan was silent.

"Anyhow, I didn't see a damn thing," Tommy pursued, "except—"

"Oh, drop the damn thing."

"Easy on the cusswords, hombre. Look who's coming."

Dr. Farr was crossing toward them, in his long, lumbering stride. "Ah, there you are, Daniel. Good morning, Thomas."

"Same to you, Dominie."

"I did not expect to see you here. Are you meeting friends?"

"It's a public dock."

"True. True. But that does not answer my question."

"Look, Dominie," Tommy appealed. "Do I have to tell you my business?"

"No, Thomas. But, would you not be well advised to reconsider?"

The familiar formula of the checker game brought Tommy up short. To Dan's intense astonishment—for meekness was the last attribute that he would have expected in that quarter—Tommy replied, with a sheepish grin, "Want me to beat it?"

"I think it would be better."

"Okay. Here goes. Good-bye, sir. So long, Dan; see you at the embalmers."

He got down from his seat and was soon lost to view. The clergyman, somewhat surprised at the ease of his victory, remarked to Dan that there was one complication eliminated. The victory, however, was not as complete as he inferred. For Tommy had come to the pier merely to make sure that the Crosbies were, indeed, aboard the liner. At no time had he planned to greet them. Now, having caught a glimpse of them on the upper deck, he was well content to leave.

Allowing an hour for docking and customs, Tommy went back uptown and lunched, nervously, on a fifteen-cent strawberry shortcake at Thorpe's Broadway Palace. Before one he was at the Valdevia. There was a brief colloquy in the lower hallway, and Adolph was the richer by two dollars. At the Crosbie apartment a giggling Josephine, cheerfully accepting a dollar and the visitor's assurance that it was to be a jocular surprise, ushered him into the front room, where he spent the longest half hour of his life before he heard the voices in the hall. He seated himself at the piano.

Outside, Dr. Farr was saying with what heartiness he could muster, "Well, here we are. Now if you ladies will get your things off—"

He stopped short, startled into silence by the voice from the front room, singing:

> *"Some think to lose him*
> *By keeping him confined."*

It mingled with Mrs. Crosbie's querulous, "How did he get in here?"

The voice sang:

> *"Some do suppose him—poor fools!—*
> *To be blind . . ."*

Dr. Farr muttered, "He has no right."

The voice, charged with passionate conviction, sang:

> *"But if she whom Love doth honor*
> *Be conceal'd from the day,*
> *Set a thousand guards upon her—*
> *Love will find out the way."*

Dan said, "I told him to keep away. Shall I throw him out?"

Laurie said, in a voice of fury, "Don't you dare!" She whirled about and ran down the passage.

Tommy was up from the seat as she entered. She closed the door behind her and stood, waiting. He ran to her. She opened her arms. Neither spoke until she leaned back from the long kiss. Then she said brokenly, "I couldn't stand it. Not another day."

"It's what I hoped," he answered.

Her voice was hardly more than a breath when she spoke again. "What will they think?"

237

"What do we care!"

"Oh, Tommy! What a fool I've been. Ever to think I could get away from you."

"I'd never have let Hardwick have you."

"Don't speak of him," she flashed.

"Aw, now, Laurie," he remonstrated. "After all, the poor guy is dead."

She stepped back from his arms. "Dead?" she cried. "Allen dead?"

"Good God! Didn't they tell you?"

"No. Nobody told me anything. What—when—?"

"They found his body across the river in Jersey."

"Did he—was it—?"

"Yes. Shot himself. Figured he didn't have anything to live for. Guess he was right, at that."

She groped for a chair and sat down. "Don't talk to me, Tommy. I've got to think."

Desperately she tried to order her thoughts, to make sense out of this shocking revelation. Since the day of the trial, when the note from her fiancé had so revolted her, she had obscurely felt herself shamed and tainted. The male animal appeared to her in an aspect which brutally affronted her innocence. Men aroused in her soul and in her flesh not only disgust but fear. In this light, the memory of her one intimate contact with Tommy Howatt filled her with bewilderment. Laurie, at nineteen, united an unbelievable naïveté with an extreme physical sensitiveness.

She had sat silent for five minutes. Now she raised her eyes to Tommy's. "Tommy," she said. "I'm not going to pretend. Not to you. Not to anybody. I'm sorry about poor Allen. But that's all. Is that dreadful of me? I can't help it. Nothing counts now but this." She opened her arms to him again.

After a moment, she said plaintively, "Oh, Tommy, I wish I could believe that you are good."

He laughed uneasily. "I guess I'm no worse than the next guy, darling."

"Make me believe it. Kiss me again— Oh, darling, we *must* go back."

"Not me. I don't want to see them. I don't want to see anyone. Make my excuses to your mother. When do I see you again?"

"Tomorrow. And every day. Good-bye, Tommy."

She let him out and walked in upon the three people in the rear room.

"Tommy has told me," she said.

Mrs. Crosbie went to her and took her hands.

Laurie shook her head. "No," she said, refusing that gesture. "I'm sorry, of course. But it makes no difference to me. He was out of my life." Then, lower, "He was never really in it."

Dan regarded her with sympathy. Never, he thought, had her beauty been more radiant: the flushed cheek, the lips still quickened with remembrance, the eyes still heavy-lidded with passion. *Caelum non animam,* indeed!—he thought. In vain had Laurie "run across the sea"; with alien skies had come no change to the captive heart.

29

No further trouble from the reformers is expected by the sporting world. Cordial relations have been restored between the police and the night-flying ephemerae, and all is serene along Sixth Avenue and throughout the Tenderloin.

Thus wrote T. Howatt in the *Police Gazette*. The author was proud of that "ephemerae," which he had chanced upon when looking up "epidemic" in the dictionary. It had class. Tommy felt that he was developing an individual style. Mr. Fox had recognized it and now permitted him to sign his articles. Not only this, but the editor frequently consulted the youngest member of the staff on matters of policy. Tommy would not have changed jobs with Arthur Brisbane.

His estimate of the situation in the Tenderloin was accurate. The minor reign of terror brought on by Dr. Farr's disclosures was over, neutralized by the discrediting of Allen Hardwick and, through his confession and suicide, of the entire crusade. Tidings of joy had gone forth from the precinct station house to the madams: Open Up. Business resumed on the old, established basis.

A special celebration was in order. The Tenderloin Club issued invitations to a Ladies Night, in honor of the district's regulars. The leaflets, printed in scarlet on a gold-leaf paper, became a collector's item. The cover bore a design—in Archie Gunn's most flagrant nudity, two excessively female figures casting from celestial battlements, à la Lucifer, a clerical individual—above the legend: It's Farr from Heaven to Hell.

Within were the orders of the night:

No Admittance to Persons of Good Character.
Proper Behavior will not be Tolerated.
Check your Morals with the Blonde at the Door.
Costumes optional; the Fewer, the Better.
Hours, nine P.M. to Hellfreeze A.M.
Free Lunch; Free Liquor; Free Love.

On the second page was the evening's program, headed:

Hell's Bells Ring
for
The Devil's Revels

Wall cartoons, especially painted for the occasion, were in the same key but higher pitched. There was an entertainment program consisting of a four-round match between two rising young welters; a victory address by the Police Commissioner; selections by the Nineteenth Precinct Quartet, T. Howatt, still unofficially leader and soloist; and a one-act play by Bert Lee of the *Sun,* entitled: *He Went Too Farr,* or, *A Night on the Tiles with the Goo-goos.*

Having been stuck with a late assignment, Dan Adriance did not reach the club until after one o'clock. Revelry was in full swing. On the ground floor romped a Virginia Reel, led by Big Bill Nelson, the district leader, who had been opening champagne by the magnum. Someone turned the reel into leapfrog, and the floor became cluttered with rolling bodies.

In a cleared space, the French Madam and Hortense, the Empress of Fourteenth Street, the remnants of their underclothing offering little in the way of concealment, were performing the cancan with a famous after-dinner orator and a notorious horse-doper. In a side room a minor city official and a famous wine agent were stripping a young girl, whom nobody seemed to know and who did not mind in the least, to a bellowed announcement of "The hoochy-koochy, ladies and gents. No charge. Free as air. Coming up." In a corner Long Distance Lou was passionately kissing an admiral of the Spanish navy in full uniform.

There was hole-and-corner harmonizing, some of it surprisingly good. Two earnest drunks removed their coats and waistcoats, preparatory to settling a political argument. A third made book on the event.

"Pick your own odds, gents. In this corner, Thumping Theodore, mayhem champion of the Walled-off Flats—" and so on.

An architect, as famous for his amusements as for his achievements, had lined up several girls of under one hundred pounds weight, and was organizing a game of beanbags, the girls to take the part of the bags and be passed from hand to hand. Down from above floated the voices of the quartet, singing like angels.

Joy was unconfined. By any standard, it was the show of the year.

Dan was hungry. He edged his way up the stairs and into a rear room, whence issued pleasant odors. He managed, against spirited competition, to secure a plate full of assorted edibles, and was piloting it toward the exit when he was hailed.

"Hiya, Dan!"

He turned his head. "Hiya, Nita."

"Have half a chair?" She hunched aside, holding up a bottle of champagne by its neck. "Look what I got."

"Who's your rich friend?" asked the *Star* man, squeezing in beside her.

"Gammy Scarrett. He's on the Reception Committee. Busy little bird. Say, Dan, couldn't a girl get a whiskey sour here? This stuff's got no character." She waved the expensive bottle.

"I'll try," he said.

Leaving his food under her guard, he went to the supplementary bar and, by dint of some skillful open-field dodging, got the desired drink back to her, unspilled. Nita finished it in two gulps. Dan could see that it was by no means her first. It was unusual for her to show any such symptoms; she was a notoriously moderate drinker.

"Celebrating a bit?" Dan asked.

"Just a little. This is my farewell party."

"Yes. I've heard. Congratulations, Nita."

"Thanks, Dan." She gazed pensively at her empty glass. "I'm feeling pretty sick about that Hardwick business," she said.

"I can understand that, Nita."

"He was a perfect gentleman to me. If you don't believe it, look at this."

Bending over she drew from her stocking a fifty-dollar bank note, which she smoothed out caressingly upon her knee.

"My good-luck piece," she said. "Against a rainy day."

"From Allen?"

She nodded. "Said he'd made a lot of trouble and that was the least he could do, and good-bye."

While she was still gazing sentimentally at the bill, Jerry the Monkey-face came along and stopped. Jerry was just back from a joy-trip, where she had been one of a Pullman-carload of rentable femininity shipped to Baltimore for the better entertainment of a lumbermen's convention, and was sporting a memento of the occasion in the form of a resplendent bracelet. She eyed the bill.

"My-my! Where'd you get the pretty greenie?"

Nita told her with modest pride, while restoring the keepsake to its safe haven beneath her garter.

"Oh, yes. I remember. The Sunday-school lad. What's it like with a virgin? I never had the luck."

"Search me," Nita said.

"Whaddaya givin' me? Ain't it straight that you was showin' him the elephant?"

242

"Sure."

"Well, wasn't he a virgin?"

"Guess so. Still is, for all of me."

Dan Adriance sat up abruptly. "What was that, Nita?"

"Never touched me. If you ask me, I don't believe he ever meant to."

"What'd he go home with you for?" said Jerry. "To look at the wallpaper?"

"Roll your hoop, Jerry," Dan said. "I want to talk with Nita." Jerry made a face at him and left.

"Are you telling the truth, Nita?" Dan demanded. "That's all there was between you?"

"Absolutely. Why would I want to lie about it?"

"Good God Almighty!" Dan breathed. "Why didn't you say something about it?"

"Who to and what for?"

"I guess I muffed it," Dan said. "The real point is, why didn't Allen say something to clear himself, instead of letting us all think he'd gone wrong?"

Nita shrugged. "Maybe he was kinda mixed up, himself."

Dan said, "Come on, we can't talk here."

"All right. Let's get out. We could go around to Clark's."

They found the popular restaurant not half full. The party at the club had drained away much of the trade. They had no difficulty getting a table to themselves. Nita ordered the usual whiskey sour. Before touching it, she regarded Dan distrustfully.

"Look, Dan." She had caught that from Tommy Howatt. "What's all this about?"

"I'll tell you after I've had your side of it."

"I don't want to get in wrong with the cops."

"Naturally. How do they figure?" He tried to keep the eagerness out of his voice.

"Forget it. I didn't mean to say that."

"All right. Go ahead."

"I'm scared, Dan."

"You don't have to be with me."

Still she was dubious. "What's your stake in this?" she demanded.

"There's someone I'd like you to talk with."

"Who's that?"

"A friend of Allen's, Dr. Farr. You don't know him."

"But I do know him— Oh, you didn't hear about the funeral."

"No."

"I went."

243

"That was pretty decent of you, Nita."

"Allen's old man didn't think so. He blocked me off at the door. I don't know as I blame him much."

"Well, I do," Dan said hotly. "It was a rotten thing to do."

"It hurt, all right. I was crying so I didn't see where I was going after I got down the steps. The parson was just getting out of his carriage and I bumped right into him."

"Go on, Nita."

"He took me by the arm and asked me who I was and could he help me. I told him and—and, Dan, it didn't seem to make any difference to him. He said, 'Come with me.' Dan, he—he treated me just like I was anybody else," she said with a gulp.

"Did you go back with him?"

"Yes."

"And old man Hardwick?"

"I couldn't hear what Dr. Farr said to him, but it withered him up like a last year's apple. Then the parson put me in a seat and left me. Oh, Dan!"

"Look, Nita; Allen's death has hurt Dr. Farr terribly. But what hurts him even worse is his misgiving, which he won't admit to, that Allen betrayed him. You can clear that up. You can give him back his faith in Allen. You're the only one that can. Will you do it, Nita?"

"Yes, oh, yes! When?"

"Now."

"Are you loony? It's midnight. We can't—"

"We can. Dr. Farr hasn't had a night's sleep since Allen was found. He told me so, himself. We'll probably find him walking the floor. Now will you let me telephone and tell him we're coming?"

She said in a faded voice, "I guess you'd better buy me another whiskey sour first."

"All right," he reported back. "He's waiting for us. Drink up."

As he held her coat for her, a ripple of feminine comment, wondering and envious, stirred the smoky air.

"Look who's hooked who!"

"Back in the fold."

"I'd-a bet ten to one against."

"Page the Portugee."

"There don't much get past the Indian."

A few all-night hacks awaited custom at the curb. At Dan's signal, a small cabby with a hard and merry face lifted his whip and clucked his nag to wakefulness.

"Where to, Boss?"

"The Old Stone Church."

"Gettin' spliced, huh?" the jovial cabby chirped. "Congrats!"

"Mind your damned business," Dan growled.

"Oughta be worth a tip, anyway," the unrebuffed jehu said.

During the short drive, the girl was nervous. "Dan, if I get stuck, talking with him, you'll give me a boost, huh?"

"Sure. But you won't get stuck. Go ahead just as if you were talking to me. He'll make it easy for you."

Light shone from the ground-floor windows of the parsonage as the cab drew in. Dan pulled the bell.

The pastor opened the door to them. He greeted the girl with grave courtesy and led the way to his study, where he drew out a chair for his uneasy visitor, indicating another for her companion. He seated himself at the desk.

"It is kind of you to come," he said, smiling at the girl.

Reassured, she said quietly, "Thank you, Reverend, for being so good to me at the funeral."

A look of pain crossed his haggard features. "I deeply regret that there should have been any necessity," he said. "I beg of you to make allowances for a family in profound grief and confusion of soul. Had I known in advance, it would not have happened." After a pause, he added, "You have something to tell me about Allen Hardwick?"

"Yes, I guess I have," the girl said. She added anxiously, "This is just between you and I, Reverend."

"Anything that you may choose to reveal to me will be held sacredly confidential," he assured her.

Still she hesitated. "It's liable to be rough in spots," she warned.

"Do not be afraid to speak openly. Clergymen are human."

"I guess *you* are, all right, all right. Well, here goes."

Glancing from time to time at Dan for support, Nita told of picking up Allen at Clark's, going to the Haymarket with him, and taking him to her room. Here and there, a momentary hiatus in the drab narrative was noted by the quick-witted reporter. Nita might be telling the truth—he was pretty sure of that—but it was not the whole truth. What was she holding back? And why?

She ended with the arrest in the morning. When the halting recital was over, Dr. Farr, chin in hand, furrows of melancholy, concentration, and puzzlement on his brow, turned the sad inquiry of his regard upon the speaker.

"No," he murmured. "It is beyond me. I simply do not comprehend."

"The point is, Dominie," the reporter put in, "that nothing happened."

"That's right," the girl confirmed.

245

"But—but Allen spent the night in your bed," the bewildered clergyman protested.

"Dead to the world."

"I am so woefully ignorant about these matters. It would seem to me— Am I to understand—?"

"No dice," she insisted. "Don't you get it, Reverend?"

"But why, then, did he not defend himself in court?" Dr. Farr cried. "Why the note of contrition—of confession, indeed—to his fiancée? Why the flight from his home, from his church, from his honorable associations? Finally, why his suicide? How can these actions be reconciled with anything other than guilt?"

"It's what he *thought* happened," Nita tried to explain. "Only, it didn't. See?"

"He did not sin with you?"

She said solemnly, "May God strike me dead where I sit if he ever touched me."

"But you must have let him believe that he had."

"Well, sure." She was embarrassed now. "I was trying to save the poor lad's feelings. Don't you get it?"

His perplexity was painful. "No, I do not."

"Look, Reverend," she said persuasively. "Here's a husky young fella goes to bed with a girl and don't do a thing. Put yourself in his place."

"Nita!" her companion protested.

But the girl was not to be diverted from her exegesis. "Put yourself in his place," she repeated. "You'd lose all confidence in yourself, wouldn't you? Sure you would!"

The austere lips of her hearer twitched. "The *argumentum ad hominem* with a vengeance," he murmured.

"Why, you'd likely get such a setback that you'd never be any good again," Nita pursued. She turned to her companion. "Dan, you remember that Galligan boy the night he got so drunk with Marianne, the Frenchie, that he couldn't—"

"Never mind," Dan intervened. "I don't think Dr. Farr would be interested in that case. Get back to Allen."

"Okay. In the morning, when he came to, I naturally let on he'd worn me to a frazzle. Look how wrong you can go when you think you're playing it the best way," she lamented. "The poor simp takes it just the opposite from what I meant and blows the game. You get me now, don't you, Reverend?"

"At least, dear young lady," the clergyman assured her, "I am persuaded that you acted for the best as you saw it."

"I sure did," Nita said.

"Forgive me if I press you further, but I must see my way clear in this. Allen, by your account, was quite unaware in the morning of what had occurred—or failed to occur—on the previous night."

"That's right."

Dr. Farr said with a painful effort, "He was, then, so deeply befuddled with liquor that his memory was in abeyance?"

Again Dan noticed the girl's slight hesitation before she responded. "I guess he wasn't used to the stuff. It hit him hard and sudden."

"Ah, well, better intoxication than unchastity." His face brightened. "At least, this clears up the record. We have but to state the actual facts."

"Just a minute," Dan said. "How are you going to do that?"

"From my pulpit."

A little cry burst from Nita. "You promised! You promised!" Her face was a white mask of terror. "Dan, he promised."

"You can't do it, sir," the reporter said.

"Cannot clear Allen Hardwick's name?"

"Not without involving Nita."

"I have no intention of giving the source of my information."

"Do you think the police are such fools that they couldn't trace it back to her? And, though she is afraid to tell us, they're in it up to their rotten necks. What do you think her life would be worth if you give her away?"

"I do not follow you, Daniel."

"Don't you? Haven't you ever heard of the case of Shea, the poolroom witness against the Thirteenth Precinct police, who mysteriously fell out of a fifth-story window in a room where there was nobody besides himself but half a dozen officers? Don't you remember Dottie deSayles, the Seventh Avenue madam who brought the graft charges against Inspector Harrow? Has anybody ever heard of her since? No, Dominie; people who betray police operations in this town have a way of getting into fatal accidents or being washed up in poor condition on the shore of the Lower Bay, or of just quietly vanishing, and no questions asked. Are you going to expose Nita to that sort of thing, after she has trusted us?"

A deep shadow of dejection darkened Dr. Farr's face. "I fear that you are right, Daniel. Very well." He turned to the shivering girl. "You have nothing to fear, my dear," he said.

She gave one sob of relief. "If you hadn't said that, Reverend," she breathed, "it'd have been the blue bottle for me."

Dr. Farr was now well enough versed in Tenderloin mythology to be aware of the prevalent belief that every denizen kept in her room a dose of some lethal drug, commonly laudanum, as a last resort.

"Never that! Never that!" he said quickly. "Should you ever entertain so desperate an idea, I beg that you will come to me first."

She nodded her gratitude. Dan got to his feet and she followed. Their host shook hands with a slow, strong grip for each of them, before he addressed the reporter again.

"Daniel, I have to thank you for bringing this young lady to me." He turned the gaze of his deep-set eyes upon her. "As for you, Miss Nita, you have lifted the weight of a great sorrow from my soul. You have restored my faith in a young man whom I trusted and loved. For this, I humbly and reverently thank you. God bless you."

"Y-y-yes, sir," Nita responded, quite overcome. "The same to you."

Outside, Dan said to the girl, "You don't have to worry about the Dominie."

"No, I guess not," she replied.

He smiled at her. "What were you holding out on us, kid?"

"Nothing."

"Don't lie to me."

"I'm not lying," she said sullenly.

"You know damn well it was a police trick."

"No, I don't."

"Who put you up to it? Tommy Howatt?"

"Tommy had nothing to do with it."

"Willie Frye?"

"No, I tell you."

"Too scared of the cops to open up, even to me," he commented. "Maybe you'll feel different about it some day."

"Don't think it."

"If ever you do, you know where to come."

"All I want is to forget the whole thing."

His voice was gentler as he said, "Anyway, you've done a good job, Nita. Dr. Farr will sleep tonight. We've got you to thank for that."

"Okay, Dan. I hope he does. Good night."

"Good night, Nita."

30

Once more restored to his welcome in the Crosbie household, Tommy Howatt disciplined himself to a policy of rigid propriety. Laurie's social career became again a matter of importance to him; he applied himself to the cultivation of it. For himself, he looked for no such glittering success as hers; he would be content with a secondary role. Nevertheless he was constantly busy at improving himself and at fostering advantageous acquaintanceships.

His voice was a passport to many an otherwise unapproachable drawing room. It became known to Ward McAllister's Four Hundred that the jaunty little Howatt man with the seductive voice could be counted upon to perform, gratis, at any sort of charitable occasion, provided only that it was fashionable enough. He estimated his own ascent optimistically.

To Dan Adriance, he said, "Keep your eye on T. Howatt. Going up. Beginning to break into the society columns. Got two or three good friends among the social editors. One of these days you'll be walking up Fifth Avenoo—Avenue, dammit!—and who'll you see strolling down toward the Union Club, arm in arm, but three pals: on the outside, Elisha Dyer, Junior; on the inside, Stuyvesant Fish, Esquire; in the middle, Mr. Thomas duB. Howatt, the well-known man about town."

"Shall I step off into the gutter and stand with uncovered head until you have passed, Tommy?" the other asked.

"You think I'm joshing. Just save your laugh for a couple of years."

To Laurie he said, "What's the matter with you and Grandma Parke?"

"Nothing," she said.

"You haven't been to see her lately."

"She's been away."

"She's back. Look—all right; don't jump me. You aren't trying to snoot her, are you?"

"Don't be silly. I just get tired of her wanting to run my life."

"Most girls would be only too glad to have Mrs. Steevens Parke take that much interest in them. What's she pestering you about?"

"You know. About marrying this or that eligible young man. I don't believe I like eligible young men, Tommy."

"Well, you don't have to marry just to suit Grandma Parke."

"No, and I'm not going to. Not anybody."

"Look, Laurie!" (She let it pass this time.) "Nobody is good enough for a girl like you. I ain't—I'm not putting up any front for myself. I'm just a no-good fella from nowhere—"

"You're *not!*"

"Yes, I am. But give me a chance. I'm learning. It isn't easy for a guy like me with no start. You've got class and money and I've got nothing."

"What do I care!" said reckless Laurie. As always, Tommy's assumed humility disarmed her.

"What scares me is that you might fall for one of Grandma's highfliers."

"I won't. You needn't be afraid. Never. I couldn't!"

With that he had to be content and, indeed, was content in a measure. The last thing he would wish was to hamper Laurie's career. He was as ambitious for her as for himself; more so, in fact. Her social success would, he hoped, lift him to the heights to which he aspired. Nevertheless, he was clever enough to perceive the advisability of keeping in the background for the present. As yet he could not consider himself a social asset.

By careful politeness and small attentions, he courted Mrs. Crosbie's favor. He knew that she mistrusted him. But mistrust of most people seemed to be her normal condition. He understood, of course, the reason for her constant unease, and set himself to dispel it. He was dining at the Valdevia one evening with mother and daughter when Stannard Barto's name came up.

Tommy said, "There's one bird I don't have to worry about any more."

"You never did." Laurie smiled.

"Oh, didn't I! With him always underfoot. No more, though."

"Yes," Mrs. Crosbie said with something like satisfaction, "it's a long time since we've seen him."

"Since anybody's seen him," Tommy followed up. "It'll be longer, I guess, before you see him again."

"Don't be mysterious, Tommy dear," Laurie adjured him. "Where is he?"

"Where the dogs won't bite him. Not American dogs anyway. New York and neighborhood isn't going to be healthy for Mr. Stannard Barto for quite some time."

Mrs. Crosbie showed unwonted interest. "Do tell us what has happened to him. If you really know," she qualified.

"I know, all right. I've got my lines. Barto was a secret tipster for *T.T.—Town Topics.*"

"Someone told us that quite a while ago."

"They didn't tell you all of it. He's been doing some fancy black-mailing on the side. But he picked the wrong party. The police got into the game. They put the fear of God into Barto and scared him out of the country. If he ever does come back, he won't do any more damage. He won't dare."

Mrs. Crosbie listened to him with strained absorption. She sat silent for a time, then announced her intention of writing some letters. As she said good night, it seemed to Tommy that her face had lost its lines of worry. He congratulated himself on his diplomacy.

Laurie asked Tommy, "Does Mrs. Parke know about Stan Barto?"

"I don't know how much she knows. Better go light on it when you see her. Laurie, you *must* go to see her."

"All right; I will. Tomorrow."

Laurie's complaint against Mrs. Steevens Parke was well founded. To a well-tempered cynicism, the old lady added a proprietary interest in the human race. Especially did she favor young people whom she could promote and thereby control. She still would gladly have adopted Laurie had the latter been willing to cast loose from the mother with the dark past. A more cautious person would have considered the risk. Grandma Parke was not timid. She had no need to be. It took her some time to accept the fact of Laurie Crosbie's independence. It miffed her, but she got over it, perceiving, with her natural shrewdness, that she must take the girl on her own terms or not at all.

On her part, Laurie had become fond of the withered autocrat, while at the same time, wary of her. Now, calling at the grim old Fifth Avenue mansion, she was warmly received.

"You're more beautiful than ever, my dear."

Laurie smiled. She was one of those rare women who can accept a compliment without looking either embarrassed or smug. "I'm feeling fine," she said.

"In spite of that ghastly Hardwick suicide?"

Laurie changed color. "Do we have to talk about it?"

"Yes. I have plans for you and I must know where you stand. Were you engaged to young Hardwick?"

"At one time. It was broken off."

"So long as it wasn't announced, that is all right. It was never really of the heart, was it?"

"No." Laurie wondered where this strange old creature got her information; or, was it intuition?

"Then there's no reason for your going into temporary retirement or anything like that."

"Goodness, no!"

"How old are you, my dear?"

"Going on twenty. It's strange to grow up."

Mrs. Parke smiled. "It doesn't seem to have gone to your head. Not yet twenty and on your way to be the toast of the town! Ward McAllister was asking about you only yesterday."

"I like having people nice to me," the girl confessed. "But I don't suppose it will last."

"Why shouldn't it?"

"Oh, I don't know," Laurie said.

"That sounds as if you didn't care much."

"It doesn't seem quite real, Mrs. Parke."

"I know what you mean. You could make it real."

"And *I* know what *you* mean." The girl smiled. "But I don't want to."

Mrs. Parke surprised her by saying, "I don't mean marrying Stannard Barto." Her tone took on grimness. "I have been learning things about that young man, little to his credit. We shall have to find another candidate."

"Please, Mrs. Parke; I don't want another candidate."

"Oho! Perhaps you've got one of your own."

"No. I haven't."

"Then why are you turning that particularly becoming color?"

"Because I don't like to be quizzed."

"Humph! Have you seen that young ne'er-do-well with the come-hither voice recently?"

"Tommy Howatt? Yes."

"He's a bad boy. Don't fall in love with *him*."

Laurie was silent.

"Or have you already?"

"I don't know."

Grandma Parke gave her another surprise by saying, "Oh, well, that's all right, I guess."

"Do you really think so?" The girl's face was wistful.

"You're bound to be in love with somebody at your age. But don't marry him."

"No . . . Why not?"

"You can do so much better."

"What if I don't want to do better?" Laurie murmured.

"Oh! You do want to marry him?"

252

"No. I don't."

"Then what the devil! You don't seem to know what you want."

"That's just it."

"You'd better find out," Mrs. Parke snapped. "And don't make a fool of yourself."

"No, ma'am," Laurie said with suspicious meekness.

"I wouldn't trust you. There's another thing. I thought of giving one of my little parties for you in the fall."

"One of your little parties of two or three hundred guests?" the girl asked mischievously. "How sweet of you, Mrs. Parke!"

"Make it one hundred. All young people. Three or four parties. I'm feeling social. We'll plan out the dates. Come and see me soon."

Tommy was ecstatic over the news of Mrs. Parke's plans for Laurie.

"You're set for life," he exulted. "A whole string of parties. I hope I'll get invited to all of them."

"If you don't, I won't go," Laurie asserted.

A sobering second thought modified his satisfaction. "I better keep under cover as far as you're concerned."

"Why?"

"You know how it is with old gals like Grandma Parke. If she thought there was anything between us she wouldn't give you so much of a play."

Laurie's small but firm chin jutted forward. "There isn't anything between us."

Tommy said recklessly, "There came near being."

The chin quivered. Its owner said, like a child, "You frightened me so."

"And am I sore on myself! It'll never happen again."

"How do I know?" she said very low.

"I'm telling you, Laurie."

She sighed and said, "Tommy, have you seen Dan lately? He hasn't been here for days."

"Maybe he's mad. He doesn't think much of me, you know. Nose out of joint. Isn't that what they say in the plays?"

"That's all nonsense," she said calmly. "Tell him I don't like his forgetting his cousins."

Far from forgetting, Dan had Laurie very much on his mind. He laid the problem before Kathleen Daggett one happy evening in the Washington Square apartment.

"I don't see what you can do about it," she said.

"That's what I keep telling myself. And, yet—"

"It's a real infatuation, isn't it?"

"Complete."

"He's an attractive young ruffian, you know, Dan. Aunt Agatha Parke is quite moony over him. It's that devilish singing of his. How is his behavior?"

"He has learned not to eat with his knife, and he doesn't shoot his cuffs any more, if that's what you mean."

"It isn't. Is he still the darling of the Tenderloin?"

"Oh, that! No, I understand that his ancient haunts know him no more."

"Then it's the real thing with him. He hopes to marry her?"

"I'm sure of it."

"It isn't her money?"

"To be fair to him, I don't believe it is."

"And she?"

"I hope not. But I'm afraid so."

The young woman of the world ruminated. "She'll probably have a hell of a time if she marries him. But who can say she wouldn't have a worse one if she doesn't?"

"Not me. I just don't know."

"Then stop worrying about her or I shall be jealous. Keep your hands off and let nature take its course. That's my advice. Now, let's worry about ourselves. Dan, we're going to be caught at this, sooner or later."

"I don't see why," he said. "You're careful about coming."

"Oh, yes. As careful as one can be."

"Daggett doesn't suspect, does he?"

"No."

"What would he do? Divorce you?"

She shrugged. "More likely kill us both."

"Are you afraid, my sweet?"

"Not a bit. Isn't it silly!"

"Then what are you fussing about?" He set his hands on her shoulders. "You aren't leading up to telling me that you want to leave me?"

"Want to? Of course I don't want to, darling. I hate the thought of it. And I don't suppose I shall do it, ever. That's what lovers always say, isn't it, whether they believe it or not?"

"I want to believe it," he said.

Kathleen's visits to Washington Square were uncertain. Sometimes she would have no opportunity to notify Dan in advance. He would come home at night and find her there. She now had her own key. She had made a list of household utensils and sent him out to buy them. Then, when Daggett went on one of his stag trips, she would come to the apartment for an interlude of housekeeping. It was like a marriage: intimate and easy and infinitely companionable, but always clouded, for him, by the imminent parting. Of a possible divorce and marriage, she would not let him speak. She quoted Mme. Marneffe—they had been reading *Cousine Bette* together: " 'Who would change a loving mistress into a commonplace wife!' "

In Fools' Paradise there is room for many lovers. Unforeseeing, unsuspecting, Kathleen and Dan, Tommy and Laurie passed the swift days and weeks, taking with both hands such happiness as was offered to them, stilling in their hearts the lurking distrust of a world in which all happiness comes to an end.

Alone in his study, Brockholst Farr pondered darkly the evil of the city which had destroyed Allen Hardwick.

31

Peace and prosperity might well have contined to bless a Tenderloin freed from the persecutions of Dr. Farr and his vice-hunters, had not Captain Bernard Schmidt's daughter become engaged. As was proper to the circumstances, a fund was to be collected for a wedding gift from the pantata's loving friends. Willie Frye was ex officio collector.

Contributions lagged. Bernie Schmidt was not popular. Faced with an embarrassing deficit, Willie supplemented his list of regulars with several prospects who had graduated from the Tenderloin and its leading industry. To a dozen of these he sent letters of appeal, fortified with implied threat.

Therein he grossly violated a tenet of local ethics. A Tenderloin girl enjoyed few exemptions from police exactions. But this one privilege, she did have: if she quit the business to go straight she was supposed to be free of interference. She was to have her fair chance.

One of Willie's injudicious letters was forwarded to Nita, the ex-Indian Princess, now an honest married woman. It roused her to fury. Twenty-five dollars for the pantata's daughter's wedding; oh, yeah? Not from Nita! Bernie Schmidt and Willie Frye and the whole rotten blackmailing pimping Nineteenth Precinct had another guess coming if they thought they could hold *her* up. Her five-word answer to the fly-cop's solicitation, advising him what he and his superior could do with the wedding present, shocked the recipient. He had always thought Nita a nice clean girl for a hooker.

The letter to Willie did not ease her righteous wrath. She got madder and madder, the more she thought about it. Another factor was operative, the same which had impelled her to go to the funeral. After her call upon Dr. Farr she had received a letter from him which stirred both her pride and her normally torpid emotions. In it the writer had repeated his thanks for her "generosity of soul" and his assurances of secrecy, both for himself and for "Mr. Daniel Adriance, for whose honor and integrity I can vouch." And he was "Yours gratefully, Brockholst Farr."

Nita read and reread it with a glow at heart. Without analysis, of which she was incapable, she sensed the absence of moralizing, of condescension, of pious orientation. It was the letter of a gentleman to an esteemed acquaintance. It gave Nita queer feelings inside her. She could not get it out of her mind. It set in motion the machinery of thought. Particularly she brooded over one implied appeal.

"If at any time in the future," he had written, "you feel that you can, without danger to yourself" (these four words underlined) "relax the restrictions upon me, either in whole or in part, your further instructions will be carried out implicitly."

Without danger to herself. Well, suppose she did open up the whole dirty business; how could the cops get at her now? She thought of Allen Hardwick's family with pity and without rancor. Prostitutes are inured to humiliation; it is, so to speak, an occupational hazard. Nita would have liked to put Allen's mother wise. More keenly, she wished to do that good guy who was hers "gratefully," a favor.

So much for the newly stimulated spirit of human kindness. Her thought swung back to Willie Frye and his pantata, Bernie Schmidt. What a sock in the puss it would be for that pair of sons-of-bitches! Threaten her, would they! Think they could make Mrs. Manuel Cabral, with her marriage license framed on the parlor wall, come through with a lousy twenty-five dollars, just like she was back on Sixth Avenue? She reread Willie Frye's not too diplomatic hint of tracking her down. Her Manuel might have a word to say to that. She took it up with him.

"Manny, what would happen to a punk that came around here trying to make trouble?"

"Who for?" the fisherman asked.

"Me."

"What punk?"

"A fly-cop from New York."

"Come aroun' here?"

"Yes."

"Make trouble for you?"

"That's what he says."

Her husband took it under advisement. "You ever hear about that Springfield fella come here las' winter? Say Roderigo was makin' rum outa molasses? Poke his long nose here; poke his long nose there. Sniff-sniff; ask a lotta fool question. You hear about him?"

"No. What happened?"

"Body drifted all 'way 'roun' Race Point Light to wash in on Back Side by Peaked Hill Bar. Them winter tides is tricky."

It satisfied Nita. She set herself to the composition of a letter to the Reverend Brockholst Farr. In the process her feelings so far got the better of her style that she tore up the effort as unsuitable for clerical reading, and wrote instead to Dan Adriance.

After detailing her wrongs at the hands of the pantata and his henchman, she continued:

> . . . I am safe where those bastards can never touch me. So now you can tell the preacher anything you like. Tell him he can shoot the works. I'll back him to the limit. I'll make a statement and kiss the Book.
>
> You can go ahead and print it, too. It is too late to do the poor Hardwick guy any good, but it might square him with the church and his folks. I would like to have his ma know what a perfect gentleman he was to me.
>
> Nuts to that dirty bunch of crooks in the Nineteenth Precinct! All I want is the chance to show them up. What have I got to be afraid of? I am never going back to Sixth Avenue where the cops could get me, and God help any lousy son-of-a-bitch in uniform or out who came down here after me.
>
> I still got that fifty-dol greenie, Dan. It is banked for my first kid.
>
> Tell Tommy I would like to hear the "Woodpecker" once more, but am all through with that life and never miss it.
>
> Good luck, Dan. Keep your chin up and your fly buttoned.
>
> Here's Howe *and* Hummel,
>
> Nita

Dan lost no time in going to Dr. Farr, though he tactfully left Nita's communication behind.

"God be thanked!" the clergyman ejaculated. "I must go at once and break the news to the Hardwicks. Before they are subjected to the shock of seeing it in print," he added.

"No need to hurry on that account, Dominie," Dan said.

"I do not understand."

"There'll be nothing in the papers."

"Not in the *Star?* You are not going to write it up for the *Star?*"

"My city desk wouldn't touch it. No city desk would."

The clergyman stared at his visitor, aghast. "Allen Hardwick's name has been disgraced, his life destroyed. The newspapers have been the agents of his destruction. And now do you tell me, Daniel, that you will do nothing to right this monstrous wrong by revealing the facts?"

"What facts, sir?"

"Why, the statement of this poor girl, exonerating Allen, implicating the police."

"Statements aren't facts, Dominie."

"You don't believe that she is telling the truth?"

"Yes, I believe it. I know it. But I can't print it."

258

"Not print it? Why?"

"Did you ever hear of the law of libel?"

"Certainly. But, since she professes herself willing to take her oath—"

"You make me tired!" the reporter broke in. "I beg your pardon, Dominie. But I should think you could see for yourself. What have we got to go on? The unsupported word of one person, and that one a professional prostitute, charging an officer of the law with a crime. Suppose we print a statement from Nita. What happens? Why, her record—so many arrests and convictions for prostitution—is hauled out. Willie Frye swears that her charges are false, based on spite because of her arrest by him. The Haymarket bouncer testifies that Allen was helplessly drunk and had to be carried out. Finally, there is Allen's own arrest and plea of guilty. How are you going to get around all that?"

"Lies. All lies."

"All right. But try to prove it."

"I shall make the charge from my pulpit and defy the powers of evil to reply."

"No, Dominie, no," Dan urged. "You misfired once. You can't afford to do it again. Let alone that they could very likely throw you in jail for criminal libel."

"I care nothing for that. How can I, a minister of God, stand silent and let a cruel injustice go unrebuked! You say that I can do nothing?"

"Not as things stand now. If you won't take my word for it, ask anyone who knows the ropes and whom you can trust."

"I must talk with Thomas Howatt."

"Don't do that," Dan warned. "Don't let him in on this at all."

"You surprise me. He has proved himself a shrewd counselor before."

"Tommy's shrewd, all right. He's also hand in glove with the police; a kind of pseudo-cop, himself. If he hears of this, the Department will be forewarned and any chance we might have of making some use of Nita in future would be spoiled."

"But, Daniel, you have impressed upon me that there is no such chance."

"No, I didn't quite say that, Dominie. I said there is no chance as things stand now. How can we tell what may turn up? Talk it over with Boss Corbin, why don't you?"

"An excellent suggestion. I had in mind to revive the demand for a legislative inquiry, on the strength of this new evidence." (The reporter shook his head.) "No? In any case, I shall send the committee's lawyer to get a statement in legal form and duly attested."

"No harm in that."

"Meantime, I shall consult Mr. Corbin."

Summoned to the parsonage, the Honorable Thomas Cassius Corbin supported Dan Adriance's warning unreservedly.

"Don't touch it, Dr. Farr. It's dynamite."

"It could not be presented before the State Senate?"

"Positively not."

"Then you advise me to drop the whole matter?" the clergyman asked, in distress.

"Not necessarily. There might be developments. You say that Adriance of the *Star* is in communication with the woman?"

"He is."

"Adriance is a young man of judgment. Does he believe her story?"

"Implicitly."

"Hm-m-m-m. You do not, of course, know the woman personally."

"It chances that I do."

Politely concealing his surprise, Mr. Corbin asked, "Have you talked with her?"

"Not on this development. There has been no opportunity."

"It might be just as well to have a statement from the young woman. Would she be willing to make one?"

"So I understand."

"On oath?"

"I believe so."

"It can certainly do no harm to have it in legal form. Some day it might become available."

Thus it came about that, on a spring morning, Mrs. Manuel Cabral arrived in New York City and put up at the Grand Union Hotel, with all expenses paid, on the invitation of the Reverend Dr. Farr. She was at once driven to the Doctor's study, where she met an elderly and dignified gentleman who was presented as Judge Norman Cassard, the vice committee's legal adviser. There was also present, besides the host, a notary public with seal.

This is the account, with important additions, which Nita gave and which was subsequently embodied in an affidavit. The portions omitted by her were the references to the administration of the knock-out drops administered to Allen Hardwick. These were later supplied by Dr. Farr's independent investigation. They are included here in order that the full picture of that night's events may be presented as a whole.

On a Monday of the previous November, fixed by Dr. Farr as being in the week before his Sermon of Justification, Allen Hardwick was still working on loose ends and casual clues. By this time he was pretty well known for what he was throughout the Tenderloin. Every move of his was observed and reported by police spies.

The trail had taken him only twice to the Haymarket and hardly more than that to Clark's. Both of these resorts were now on his windup list. This Monday visit to the Tenderloin's most popular restaurant, he thought, would probably be his final call. Oscar, the battle-scarred waiter, spotted him at once. He signaled Nita as he went forward to meet the new arrival.

"Good evening, mister. Alone tonight?"

"Yes," Allen replied.

"This way, sir. Expecting somebody?"

"No."

"Like to meet a nice young lady?"

"No, thank you— Well, yes, I think I would."

Upon this affirmative, Oscar beckoned discreetly. Nita stepped demurely over.

"Make you acquainted with Nita, the Indian Princess, Mr. Smith," Oscar said.

"Good evening," Nita said primly.

"Good evening," the young man replied and rose to draw out a chair.

"Seeing the town?" Nita asked.

"Why, yes."

"Stranger here?"

"I'm from Omaha."

"I never was in Omaha. Is it a pretty nice place?"

"Very."

"Do they have drinks there?"

Allen apologized. "I'm afraid I'm being remiss. What may I order for you?"

"Whiskey sour, Oscar," Nita said. "Thanking you kindly," she added to her new escort.

She began to like him. He was so polite; so considerate; actually rose from his chair when she got up to go to the ladies' room, and again when she returned. Over her second whiskey sour she began to feel quite definitely uncomfortable. Taking one so guileless over the jumps seemed a shabby trick. Quite the gentleman, too. She stiffened her resolution by reminding herself that this was a spy and an informer who would put her and the other girls out of business if he had his way. She would go through with it all right. So she suggested the Haymarket. He agreed.

"Mr. Smith" proved an expert dancer. But that was all. He failed to respond when she pressed her body close to his. It seemed to embarrass him. Experienced Nita reflected that a man couldn't be expected to get worked up on beer. When they sat down, she had another whiskey sour and suggested for him a razzle-dazzle.

"What's that?"

"A specialty of the house. Very mild. You'll like it."

In reality, a razzle-dazzle consisted of ginger ale and brandy liberally laced with absinthe, and was one degree milder than dynamite. Mr. Smith blinked over the first taste, but swallowed most of the concoction. Inspired by it, he plied his companion with questions about the place and its denizens.

"I'll bet you're a newspaperman, writing the joint up," she said. He only half denied it, looking pleased.

"Don't you think it's awful noisy here?" she suggested.

"It is rather."

"Then how about us going around the corner to my nice, quiet room?"

He fidgeted. "I can't exactly do that," he mumbled. "Some other evening."

"Going to ditch poor Nita?" She looked sad.

"I hate to have to leave. But, you see, I've got this engagement."

"Wifie waiting?"

"No, no. It's a—a classmate. He's at my club."

Nita was experienced enough to recognize a ground-floor Johnnie when she saw him. "If you gotta, you gotta," she said philosophically.

"Of course, I know I've no right to—to take up your time without —well, I mean I expect to pay for it just the same as if—you understand, I'm sure."

"Couldn't be fairer," she admitted. "But I kinda liked you," she added.

The *ci-devant* Mr. Smith looked about for a waiter, meaning to call for his check. Watching for this possible development, Willie Frye, who was standing near the exit in conversation with Corry Moore, the Haymarket bouncer, said under his breath, "The stiff's goin' to walk out on her."

Corry lounged over toward the box. He and Nita were old friends. She waved a greeting. Choosing to interpret the gesture as an invitation, the bouncer entered the box.

"Haven't seen you in a dog's age, Corry," the girl said. "Meet my gentleman friend, Mr. Smith. Join us in a drink?"

"Don't care if I do," Corry replied, shaking hands.

As a fresh round was served, Nita's attention was distracted by a cheerful hail from behind. She slewed her chair around to exchange words with a young male acquaintance. Thus she missed seeing a swift pass by the bouncer which deposited a few drops of a colorless liquid from a small vial into her escort's drink. A short time afterward Allen quietly slumped to the floor.

The suddenness of it all surprised her. She laid it to the potency of the razzle-dazzle. Corry heaved up the young man's inanimate form, and Willie Frye hurried to the spot to help him carry out the burden. Not only this, but the fly-cop carried his helpfulness so far as to whistle up a cab, hustle Nita and Allen into it, give the cabby Nita's number, and, when they arrived, aid her to get her charge upstairs.

He said to her, "He'd oughta come out of it in a couple of hours."

"Out of what?" the girl asked.

Willie winked. "Outa the drops." He looked at her narrowly. "Meanta say you didn't see Corry do the slipover act?"

"No, I didn't see anything. I was talking with young Spud in the box behind us."

"Oh, hell! I thought you was onto it or I'd have kept my trap shut. You forget it. Savvy?"

"Okay, Willie."

Still he was not satisfied. "You'll never say a word; so God strike you dead," he prescribed.

Nita shivered, but repeated the formula. "May God strike me dead."

Thus it was the fear of divine vengeance that impelled her to suppress from her affidavit all mention of the drugging.

It was late morning when Allen awoke in unfamiliar surroundings. A figure beside him rolled over in bed, sat up, clasped arms around its slender knees. He stared and rubbed his eyes.

"Hello, pal!" Nita said brightly.

He groaned.

"Not feeling so good?"

"My head. My mouth!"

"Take a bite of apple."

She reached for a bedside plate upon which she always kept a morning freshener for the customers. Allen blinked miserably at the proffered fruit and swung his feet out upon the floor. The chill of his nakedness struck him to the marrow. He grabbed at the coverlet to swathe himself. Nita smiled comfortably upon him.

"Take it easy, boy."

"Where am I?"

"Right here in Nita's room. All okay."

"What time is it?"

"Noon or so."

"I can't remember. I can't remember anything."

"Don't let it worry you."

"Have I been here all night?"

"Surest thing you know."

"W-with you?"

"Neck and neck."

("He looked at me like he'd never seen a girl before," was Nita's report. "And I guess he hadn't. Not that close.")

"Aren't you coming back to bed?" she invited.

If he heard her, he made no sign. Hastily drawing on his underwear, he made his way to the washstand, dragging his bare feet a little, filled the bowl with water from the pitcher, and soused his head. The treatment failed to restore clarity.

"I can't remember," he groaned, again.

"What do you want to remember?"

"Did I—? Did we—? I mean—" He broke off, staring at her in wretched uncertainty.

"Sure we did," she said encouragingly. "You got your twenty dollars' worth."

"Then I'm a fornicator," he half-whispered.

"I'll say you are!" the girl returned cheerily. ("Thought I might as well give the poor guy a good opinion of himself," she explained.)

"I've got to go," he muttered.

She rolled out of bed, crossed the floor, and closed the window. It was the police signal. Willie Frye and his partner climbed the stairs and burst in the door.

Four weeks passed before Nita saw Allen Hardwick again. Their meeting was in Jefferson Market Court, where, after his plea of guilty, he paid not only his fine, but his companion's as well, "like the perfect gentleman he was."

During the recital, Dr. Farr's expression steadily darkened. At the close, he asked the girl, "Who devised this infamous plot to get Allen drunk?"

"Willie Frye, I guess. The pantata was in on it, too."

"You became their accomplice."

"I had to, Reverend."

"Were you paid to perform this wicked act?"

"Aw, now, Reverend!" Nita became tearful. "I didn't want to. I had to."

"By what compulsion did you have to?"

"It was that or quit the business. The cops would have run me out of town if I hadn't done what they told me to. A girl's got to make a living. There wasn't a thing I could do but play in with them. Won't you believe me, Reverend?"

Dr. Farr's tone was gentler as he said, "That may well be. You say that Allen succumbed suddenly?"

"Like he was shot. That razzle-dazzle hit him like knockout drops."

The lawyer said, "Mrs. Cabral, would you be willing, if necessary, to go on the witness stand in support of the statement which you have made?"

"Here in New York?"

"Yes, if necessary."

The girl's face became rigid. "I'd never get out of town alive."

"We could guarantee you protection."

"No. No. No. No. *NO!*" Her voice rose to a shriek.

The judge gave it up. "Very well. I shall not insist. We owe you a debt of gratitude, as it is."

Having been put into form and duly sworn to and signed before witnesses, Nita's affidavit was subsequently deposited in the vice committee's safe. To Dr. Farr's hopeful suggestion that salient portions of the material be prepared for publication, Judge Cassard interposed cold, legal objections, pointing out the same difficulties which Dan Adriance had already cited.

"At least," the clergyman said, "I can clear Allen's reputation with his family."

"Not yet," the lawyer said. "This is a committee matter. Mrs. Cabral is here at the committee's expense. I can permit no invasion of the committee's rights until the matter has been passed upon in full meeting."

"Then let us call an emergency meeting at once," Dr. Farr urged.

"Several members are away. One is ill. This can well rest for ten days, until the next stated meeting."

With this the impatient pastor had to be content.

He gave much thought to how he could best revive the tragedy with the least pain to the family. But, before the ten days were up, the matter had been taken out of his hands.

32

The *Pinky* had been put to bed. The hastily recruited week-end aux-
iliary staff, having consumed their pint rations of whiskey and pocketed their ten-dollar honorariums, had scattered in the night. With the
final run of proofs duly endorsed "O.K. R.K.F.," Mr. Fox had de-
parted behind his span of sleek blacks. Tommy Howatt remained at
his table, studying a checkers problem.

Yesterday's game with Dr. Farr had been called off. Important
business, the clergyman had apologetically explained. (The business,
as he did not explain, was meeting Nita Cabral at the Grand Central Depot.) If Tommy would find it convenient to drop in Tuesday morning, Dr. Farr would be glad to, etc., etc., etc.

Tommy's late-night research into the strategy of his favorite game
was punctuated by Deacon Waldo's characteristic and batrachian
whuck-whuck-glug of appreciation as he bent over an item rejected
as a bit too salacious for publication.

"Oh, naughty, naughty!" the Deacon chirped.

"What's so juicy?" Tommy growled.

"The boarding-house lady and the star boarder at three A.M.
wanta read?"

"No. Too sleepy." He yawned. "Guess I'll hold up a Broadway
car."

Deacon Waldo said, "I read that memo you left for the chief,
Tommy."

"Which one was that?"

"New angle on the Hardwick story. Nix, say I."

"Why?"

"Nothing in it. Sunbeam Hardwick is dead. Boss Corbin's slick
scheme for a Senate investigation is dead. Dr. Farr's vice-snooping committee is as good as dead. Nothing left. Where did you pick
up this bit, anyway?"

"Ever hear of a girl called Jerry the Monkey-face?"

"Don't remember the name. Who is she?"

"One of the Clark's ten-dollar-a-shot gallery."

The Deacon leered at him. "Naughty-naughty! I thought you were off the gay girlies."

"Don't be so damn funny, Deacon. Jerry picked up some stuff about Hardwick at the club party."

"Was she the girl that was arrested with him?"

"No. That was Nita, the Indian. Nita talked too much before Jerry. The other night at Clark's Jerry passed it along to me."

"Well, what is this big sensation?"

"Remember my story, 'Crash of a Plaster Saint'?"

"Yes. Good story."

"That's what I thought. I was nothing but wrong. He didn't crash. He kept his Sunday-school purity lily-white and shiny."

"Any details?" the old man asked languidly.

"Nope."

"And you think that's *P.G.* stuff?"

"Not top-of-column news," Tommy conceded. "But I could spice up a snappy paragraph, *Town Topics* style, maybe without names but plain enough so that Carrie Baker's pet parrot could read between the lines."

"You don't have to tell me the kind of fluff. 'Chastity Miraculously Saved'; 'Sunbeam's Light Undimmed,' " the Deacon improvised in imaginary headlines. "Something along those lines, huh, with a certificate of virginity from Old Dr. Gringle. Sell it to *T.T.*"

Loath to give up his project, Tommy laid it before the proprietor next day. R. K. Fox gave it due consideration.

"Not up to *Gazette* standards," he decided.

"The Farr angle makes it worth printing," Tommy argued. "Anything about Dr. Farr and his doings still has news value."

His editor examined him with an amused and suspicious eye. "Why are you so sweaty to get it into type?" he demanded.

Abashed lest he convict himself of sentiment, the employe stammered out, "Why, I kinda thought—I sorta figured out— Well, Boss, Dr. Farr says Hardwick's folks—I mean, his people—they're taking this awful hard, and the worst of it is, in their book, that he stayed with a girl and has sure gone to hell. So, I just thought if we could kinda clean up the record in the *Pin*— the *P.G.*, it would—ah, nuts! Don't you get it, Chief?"

Mr. Fox bestowed his most genial smile upon his underling. "All right, tough boy. Put on your hat," he said.

"What for?"

"There's a better way than printing it in the *Gazette*. Just hop over to Brooklyn and give it to the Hardwicks straight."

"Who? Me? Oh, gee, Boss! Have a heart. Face that old dame and the old geezer and give 'em that song-and-dance about Allen taking

Nita home and not—and nothing doing? How'd I make 'em savvy? What do they know about things like that?" he cried wildly. His alarm produced an inspiration. "I'll tell you, Boss. Let me get Dr. Farr to do it. He'll make 'em believe it. It's right in his line."

Mr. Fox's regard became chilly. "Dr. Farr is not working for the *Gazette*. You are. Get going."

A woebegone young man dragged his shadow after him up Oak Street and around the turn into Brooklyn Bridge. Rather than take the three-cent bridge car, he elected to walk, as giving him more time to plan his difficult course. Emerging into Brooklyn, he stopped in at Val Schmidt's for a fortifying drink, but changed his mind and his order to sarsaparilla at the last moment. A tainted breath, he foresaw, would be no passport to the Hardwick household.

By the time he reached the mansion on Joralemon Street, he had a fine and frank line of lies worked out. Tommy had a pretty good conceit of himself as a born actor. This was to be a test of his histrionic capacity. Here was a job to do and he wasn't going to let any inconvenient considerations of veracity interfere with it.

Luck met him at the door in the person of Stacey Hardwick, Allen's younger brother. It might have been the old man. Tommy opened up with Lie No. 1.

"I come from Dr. Farr," he said. "My name's Howatt. Tommy Howatt."

"Oh, yes; I know about you," the young fellow said.

(And I know about you, and plenty!—Tommy thought—You're the lad that got burnt in Georgiana Hastings' house. You're the one that started Allen and Dr. Farr on this whole screwy razzmatazz.) Aloud he said, "I'd like to see Mr. Hardwick."

"My father is a sick man. He doesn't see anyone."

"Well, I guess you'll do. It's about your brother."

"Then you certainly can't see Father. He would refuse—" He broke off. "You knew Allen, didn't you?"

"Sure thing. We were pals from the word Go." He delivered Lie No. 2 with admirable aplomb.

"My mother would like to see you, I'm sure. Or—is it something that it wouldn't do for her to hear?"

"No, it's something she ought to hear."

Stacey led him upstairs to a small library where a small and beautiful old lady sat, reading the esteemed William Dean Howells' recent work, *The Quality of Mercy*. She lifted her eyes and smiled on the two young men. Tommy read that expression and began to feel sorry for himself. He had his story pat, every lie, large and small, ready for production. But how was he to lead this angel-face through the purlieus of Clark's and the Haymarket and up the stairs that led

268

to Nita's twenty-dollar-a-week bedroom in West Twenty-sixth Street? Stacey was speaking now.

"This is Mr. Howatt, Mother; a friend of Allen's."

"You are very welcome," she said. "Where did you know my son?"

"At Dr. Farr's, ma'am, and the Old Stone Church. We used to sing together a lot," Tommy answered glibly.

"Ah, yes," Mrs. Hardwick said. "My boy had a fine baritone." She looked more closely at the caller. "Oh," she exclaimed. "You're the young man with the extraordinary tenor voice. I heard you once in church. A true gift."

"Yes'm," answered Tommy modestly. "I sing tenor."

Her face became eager. "There is a piano in the front room. Perhaps you would sing some of Allen's favorite songs for us."

"Yes'm; I'd be glad to. First, though, I've got a—a kind of a message to give you."

She paled. "A message? From whom?"

"Well, it's not exactly from—I mean, it's to square up something that you all got wrong."

An exclamation from Stacey Hardwick checked him. Outside an intermittent tapping sounded along the hallway. Mrs. Hardwick's lips formed a frightened whisper, "Don't let him in."

It was too late. Before Stacey could reach the door to bar it, it was pushed open.

Tommy got a quick impression of the wreckage of a once powerful personality. A soiled and wrinkled dressing gown hung loosely on the great frame. The man's face was haunted, the eyes burning. Long fingers gripped the head of a heavy cane to support the wasted body.

"What is this?" the apparition croaked. The cane was lifted to point at Tommy.

"Mr. Howatt," Stacey began, and in the same breath his mother said, "He comes from Dr. Farr."

The old man's glare was uncompromising upon the stranger. "What is your errand?" he demanded.

"I'm a friend of Allen's," Tommy said in a tone intended to be propitiatory. It was not successful.

"Do not speak that name in my presence." The command was almost insane in its violence. "He who bore it has been dead to this family since he shamefully consorted with a harlot."

"He didn't," Tommy blurted.

"It is useless to lie. You only participate in his sin."

Tommy had seen Brockholst Farr in righteous indignation. This was different. Here he was confronted by the implacable rigor of a monstrously egoistic piety, outraged to its depths. How to meet it?

"I'm not lying," he declared.

The grim lips before him hardly moved, but their utterance was as clear as it was savage. "A lecher. A whoremonger. A soul lost to decency and honor."

Mrs. Hardwick gave a little cry. Tommy was outraged. He had cast himself in the role of defender of the innocent dead, and his reward was unmerited abuse. Okay; okay. He'd play it to a finish anyway. Noble sentiments seethed within him, though the words wherein he clothed them were less than noble.

"Liar, yourself!" he shouted. "He wasn't. And I can prove it."

He jumped to his feet. Mr. Hardwick drew back, groped for a chair, sank into it. "Speak then," he said tonelessly.

Tommy spoke, eloquently, angrily, with passionate conviction. Before he had gone far, the old man had covered his eyes with his forearms and bowed his head. Mrs. Hardwick ran to her husband and put her arms around him. Something told Tommy that this had not happened for a long time.

"And that is God's own truth," he concluded, and wiped his moist forehead.

Two hours later, he left the house, wrung and limp. It was not sarsaparilla at Val Schmidt's popular bar, this time, but straight rye. He returned to New York and reported at Mr. Fox's office.

The editor eyed him. "How did you make out?" he inquired.

"Oh, Jesus!" Tommy said lamentably.

Mr. Fox disapproved of profanity on general principles. But he was not at all sure that this was profanity. "You look like you'd been pulled through a knothole," he commented.

"Oh, Jesus!" Tommy repeated, and swabbed at his sweating neck with the back of his hand.

His employer became solicitous. "Have a drink." He reached toward his desk.

"I've had a drink. It didn't do any good."

"All right," Mr. Fox soothed him. "Take your time."

Tommy steadied himself. "What a day! I'm a wet rag." Pride of achievement asserted itself. "But I put it over, by God! I made 'em believe it."

"Well, it was true, wasn't it?"

"Sure, it's true. But I'd have made 'em believe it, even if it wasn't. I was *good,* I'm telling you."

"Then what are you so jumpy about?"

"Reaction, you might call it. I was okay so long as I was up against the old man. Howe and Hummel together before a jury couldn't have done a better job. Then the old lady made me talk about Allen. Did I pass out the sticky stuff! For a solid hour I lied like a pushcart peddler up against Judge Duffy. Allen was my closest pal. I loved him like a brother. To hear me tell it, we were the Siamese twins. They ate it alive. Nothing would do the old lady but I must sing her Allen's favorite songs; me that don't know whether he liked the 'Pilgrim's Chorus' or 'Johnny Get Your Gun.' Oh, holy Moses!"

"I wouldn't have thought it would hurt your feelings to stretch the truth a little," the boss observed.

Tommy gulped. "Yeah. It was tough, but I got away with it. Then, at the end, she came over and God-blessed-me and asked could she kiss me because I had been such a friend to her dear boy and had restored their faith in him and all that, and how the *hell* I ever got out of the house I don't know."

"Now you'd better have that drink," Mr. Fox said, reaching out again. "That's an assignment, too."

The brandy was something special. Tommy swallowed it gratefully. In the subdued voice of introspection he said, "At that, I guess the holy-boly wasn't such a bad guy, after all."

Tuesday morning he presented himself at the parsonage for the inevitable defeat at the hands of the best checkers player in the Presbyterian synod. He still doggedly declined to accept odds, in the optimistic faith that he was improving to the point where he would one day be able to hold his own.

As he settled himself in place, Dr. Farr said, "You were at the Hardwicks' last Friday, Thomas."

(Tommy thought—Here's where I catch hell for using his name to bust in.) "Yes, sir," he replied.

"You did not mention to me that you had such a visit in mind."

"I didn't have, last time I saw you," the young man answered truthfully.

Dr. Farr's smile was both kindly and quizzical. "I take it that you consider that call private."

"Kinda," said Tommy, on his guard now.

"I think that I should tell you that I have received a letter from Mrs. Hardwick."

He patted his pocket. Tommy's hand jerked forward, but the clergyman shook his head.

"No," he said. "You have a sufficiently high opinion of yourself already." His lips twitched. "I was not previously aware of any great intimacy between you and Allen Hardwick," he remarked.

Tommy made an uncomfortable noise in his throat.

"Where did you obtain your data?"

Tommy told him about Jerry the Monkey-face.

"How much did the young woman know, I wonder," the clergyman mused.

271

"All she told was about their bedding down and nothing doing. That was a big laugh in her book. Why? What more was there to know?"

"That I cannot tell you at present, Thomas."

"Anything in my line?"

"Quite possibly."

"Important?"

"Potentially very important."

"When'll you open up, Dominie?"

"Possibly in a week. After the meeting of our committee."

"Committee stuff, huh? Can't you give me a lead?"

"No, Thomas. Continue with your account of the visit to the Hardwicks."

There was reminiscent sweat on the young man's brow as he finished. His host's smile was restrained but benign.

"Though you did permit yourself certain liberties with the strict truth, my boy," he said, "it was, I am sure, with the best of intentions. And your message was a blessed one."

"You won't give me away, will you, Dominie?"

"No, I shall not divulge your well-meant mendacity. Some day I may show you the letter. In the meantime—but never mind that. Your first move."

The morning mail brought to Laurie Crosbie an envelope with the imprint of the Old Stone Church parsonage. Within was Mrs. Hardwick's letter to the pastor and, clipped to it, a memo sheet with Dr. Farr's writing.

May I be forgiven for my misjudgment of a kind and gentle heart! Read the accompanying letter, and you will see him in his true colors. You estimated him more justly than I did, my dear. Forget my well-meant warnings and follow the dictates of your heart.

B.F.

Self-controlled Laurie was tearful before she finished reading the letter. Tearful and humble and grateful. It was then that she let her mind assent to her desires. Since Dr. Farr was convinced, surely she could put her fears away from her. She so passionately longed to be convinced that Tommy was essentially good.

33

Normally Dr. Farr read only such criminal news as might pertain
to his special line of investigation. It must have been the finger of
God, he maintained, that directed his eye to the headline in the
Times, as he sat at breakfast, a week after the signing of Nita's affidavit. The item reported the death of a deep-sea mate from the after-
effects of a drug administered in the notorious Bowery dive known as
Suicide Hall. One sentence sharply recalled to his mind the girl's
"hit him like knockout drops."

In several respects the circumstances of the seaman's misfortune
paralleled Allen Hardwick's case. What specially struck Dr. Farr was
that the victim, after emerging from his first narcotic sleep, was unable
to recall, under police questioning, any detail of what had befallen
him. He had died in a hospital thirty-six hours later. This was the
same blurred state of mind which had led Allen Hardwick, in the
complete lapse of his own memory, to accept Nita's version of what
had taken place between them and believe himself guilty. Dr. Farr
left his coffee unfinished to go down to his study and call up Dan
Adriance.

A sleepy and resentful voice demanded to know who the hell was
waking its owner up practically before daylight.

"This is Brockholst Farr, Daniel."

"Oh! Sorry, sir. What's on your mind?"

"Allen Hardwick's case."

"Still rattling those dead bones, Dominie?"

"Not so dead, perhaps."

"Eh? What's that? What's turned up now?" The reporter's voice
was no longer somnolent.

"Can you tell me what the narcotic in knockout drops is?"

"Chloral hydrate usually."

"Where can I obtain data upon its effects?"

"Academy of Medicine Library, I should think."

"Thank you, Daniel."

"Here! Wait! Don't cut off. I'm coming up as soon as I can get dressed, Dominie."

"Don't do that. I am just going out. If you care to meet me here about twelve o'clock—"

"I'll be there, sir."

Adriance was waiting, with a mind busy in the formulation of pertinent questions, when Dr. Farr entered the parsonage. It was not the reporter, however, but the clergyman who started the interrogation.

"Have you read the *Times* this morning, Daniel?"

"Not yet."

"Look at this." He pointed to the item which he had cut out.

Dan ran through it rapidly.

"Is the police court procedure in the Hardwick case clear in your memory?" Dr. Farr pursued.

"I think so."

"Was no suspicion aroused in your mind at the time that Allen might have been drugged?"

"It did cross my mind. But there was absolutely nothing to support it."

"Now there is. Mrs. Cabral has made an affidavit."

"Who? Oh, Nita. Go ahead, Dominie."

"This is not for publication until released, Daniel. Understood?"

The reporter nodded. "Does her affidavit admit that Allen was drugged?" he asked.

"No. There is no mention of any such matter."

"She may have pulled the trick, herself."

"I do not think so. If she were *particeps criminis,* would she have been likely to make any statement?"

"That's a point. Did she mention anyone else?"

"Yes. A Haymarket employe named Corry Moore."

"I know him. A bad actor. Police record."

"There was also Willie Frye, Captain Schmidt's confidential man."

"A sweet pair. There's no trick that they aren't up to."

"Do you recall whether the testimony in court covered the time when Allen and the girl left the Haymarket?"

"About midnight. Before rather than after."

"And he became unconscious at once?"

"The testimony is that they had to carry him out, drunk."

"It was noon, I believe, when he came to in Miss Nita's apartment."

"There or thereabouts."

Dr. Farr leaned forward. "Daniel, what do you understand his condition to have been then?"

274

"He must have been all right. He had that talk with Nita, you know."

"Exactly. Were there any symptoms of relapse?"

"Not so far as I— Wait a minute, though. There was something about the cops having to help their prisoner down the stairs at Nita's after the arrest. Hang-over, they said."

"Precisely!" There was triumph in Dr. Farr's manner. "That hang-over was the secondary effect of the chloral hydrate. Just as in the *Times* report. Furthermore, in both cases we have the obliteration of memory which is typical of the narcotic."

"You seem to be well up on it, sir."

"I followed your direction and consulted the case histories in the Academy of Medicine Library. Now, Daniel, according to Mrs. Cabral's affidavit, she was taken to the West Thirtieth Street station house and—I believe the police term is—booked."

"She and Allen both."

"Not Allen."

"What! He was not booked?"

"No."

"How do you know?"

"I have been to the station house and consulted the record."

"Well, I'm da— You'd have made a bird of a reporter, Dominie. Didn't they make any fuss about letting you see the books?"

"I went direct to Captain Schmidt. He is in no position to evade inquiry by me," Dr. Farr pointed out.

"If they didn't take Allen to the station, what did they do with him?"

"That is what I must find out."

"Well, of course, Willie Frye and his side-kick may have put him on ice somewhere. Though I don't see just why."

"My theory is that he was in such condition from the secondary effects of the drug that they feared for his life and rushed him to a hospital."

"That's an idea, too," the reporter said.

"It is a logical assumption. The question is, which hospital?"

"Might be Bellevue. More likely St. Vincent's, though."

"Does the hospital keep records?"

"Of entries? Oh, yes."

"Then it would be a matter of looking up their register for the day of Allen's arrest."

"Would you like me to do that for you, sir? They know me there."

"I should be grateful, indeed."

"I'll stop in on my way to the office."

"Telephone me what you find."

275

There was unprofessional excitement in the reporter's voice over the telephone, two hours later.

"Hello. . . . That you, Dominie? . . . You win."

"Allen's name is there?"

"Not his name. But the entry is. Narcotic poisoning and alcoholism. They always throw in alcoholism on general principles."

"What else?"

"Not very much. Name, Blank Smith; address unknown; discharged two days later in the custody of the police."

"Daniel, I cannot thank you enough."

"Okay, Dominie. You've done a job that I ought to have done, myself, and done it better, but I won't hold it against you. What's your next move?"

"I think that I must have another talk with Mrs.—with the lady in the case." He was learning the advisability of caution in talking over the wire.

"Good luck, Dominie. Let me know if I can help."

The hospital entry was a distinct step forward. The investigator, however, was far from satisfied. Experience had impressed upon him the unwisdom of overestimating evidence. The sage counsel of Tommy Howatt came to mind.

"Don't bet your kings as if there weren't any aces in the pack."

Reckoning up his assets, he now had support for the assumption that Allen Hardwick had been drugged. Convincing though it might be to him, to prove that the Blank Smith of the hospital book was the Alexander J. Smith (that is, Allen Hardwick) of the Jefferson Market Court conviction three weeks later, was a different and difficult matter. If challenged, the police were quite capable of producing another Smith, identifiable as the narcotic patient, to fill the bill.

What was needed, and sorely, was direct testimony to the events at the Haymarket. Dr. Farr had to admit to himself that it was a long chance. But, what chance there was, lay with the young wife. Might not she have left out something from her narrative, unimportant in her mind, but actually vital? Dr. Farr took train for Boston.

There was comment in the little Cape Cod town of Truro over young Mrs. Cabral's arrival at the railroad station, dressed in her sober Sunday best, to meet a stranger. The comment was curious rather than critical, due not only to the lady's unimpeachable record as a wife, but also to the visitor's obvious respectability of demeanor and to his clerical garb. Even when she took him to her cottage, in the absence of Manuel, who was at sea, and was observed by casual passers-by along Portugee Walk absorbedly conferring with him over a helping of tea and crullers in the parlor, there was no scandal.

276

There was, however, considerable excitement, permanently unassuaged.

Forewarned by letter of the visit, Nita came to the point at once. "Anything I got, it's yours, Reverend."

"Thank you, Miss Nita. I beg your pardon, Mrs. Cabral."

"Just Nita'll do." She smiled.

He bowed, as in acknowledgment of a gracious favor. "I would like to go back to that night at the Haymarket," he said.

"You ask 'em and I'll answer 'em," she said.

"Were there many people present?"

"Pretty good for an off-night crowd. Hundred and twenty-five, fifty, maybe."

"Did you chance to recognize any there present?"

"Recognize 'em?" she repeated in surprise. "Why, I knew half of 'em like they lived on the old block at home."

"Could you recall some of the names for me?"

A pucker of anxiety appeared upon the small and vivid face. "This isn't going to get 'em in wrong with the cops, is it, Doctor?"

"No. I will take no action without your approval."

"Fair enough. We—ell; let's see now. We had a floor box, so all the dancers passed right before us. There was a couple of girls from Myrtle Bergen's place—I could get you their names—with their pickups. Dora Day was doing the York with that necktie salesman of hers. Then there was the wall-eyed tart from Seventh Avenue, Polly Something, with the Harlem Coffee Cooler. He's a prize fighter, you know. And, of course, the usual lot from Clark's: Gwen, and Tessie, and Jersey Jenny, and Lou, and Annabel, and— What's the matter, Reverend. Isn't that what you wanted?"

"Not precisely. I had hoped that you might recall the presence of some potential witness, not closely identified with—er—the world of the Tenderloin, who might be helpful."

"Helpful how? I don't getcha. Put her over the plate, mister."

"Of course. You must pardon my ineptitude. I had hoped that there might be some person, not of Tenderloin associations, who could conceivably have overseen the drugging of Allen Hardwick."

Nita stiffened in her chair. "Who says he was doped?"

"I do. There can be no doubt of it. We have the hospital record."

"What else do you know?" she asked fearfully.

"We do not as yet know who administered the drug. Do you?"

"So help me God, Reverend, I didn't see a thing."

He sighed patiently. "Very well. I will not press you further. Let us retrace our steps. Think. Was there no one in the adjacent boxes whom you know?"

"The boxes on both sides of ours were full. I don't know as I can remember who was there, except for that half-witted hooker from the panel-house down on Christopher Street, and she don't know enough to tell whether pants open up the front or down the back. Oh, gee! I didn't mean to say that. Lemme think." She closed her eyes and lost herself in effortful thought.

Her hand shot across the table and gripped his wrist. "I got it! I got it! The young fella in the box behind that gave me a nice hello."

"Did you know him?"

"Sure I knew him. That is—well—you know—"

"Never mind that. His name."

"Spud," she answered with triumphant promptitude.

"Spud what? The last name?"

"Now, Dr. Farr!" she protested. "How would I know his real name? It isn't as if he was one of my regulars."

"Where can I get in touch with him? Does he come to the Haymarket? Have you seen him since? Does he live in New York? How can I get his address? Is he a regular patron of the place?" The eager, anxious queries came like rattle of hail.

Nita threw up her hands. "Help! If they did know at the Hay, they wouldn't let on."

The inquisitor strove to control his impatience. "Let us start again. You can give me no clue to this Spud's address?"

"No, sir."

"A description, then?"

Here the girl was specific. Spud was young, not more than twenty-one—tall, broad and powerfully built, red-haired, blue-eyed, pleasant-spoken, nose looked like it had been broken sometime.

"A prize fighter?" the clergyman suggested.

Nita didn't think so. She knew most of the fighters in town. This boy wasn't a pro.

"What does he do?"

"Nothing, I guess. Just goes to his classes."

"Classes?" Dr. Farr's eyes became intent. "Do you mean college?"

"Sure."

"Which one?"

"Yale, I guess. Maybe Harvard. Oh, I dunno. What are some of 'em?"

The visitor ran through a list, pausing hopefully after each name for the girl's response, which was a repeatedly shaken head. Hope dimmed.

Patiently Dr. Farr asked, "Did he wear anything that would be an indication? Some insigne; some badge? A hatband, perhaps? An emblem of some kind? Think!"

278

Again those silent and melancholy negations. Suddenly she brightened. "What's siss-boom-ah?"

"Princeton!" he exclaimed. "I said Princeton before."

"Well, that's it, sure. He and some other boys got a little tanked one night and did a singsong like that."

Here, at last, was a lead. Reverting in his shrewd mind to the athletic build and the broken nose, Dr. Farr followed up. "Was he perhaps a football player?"

"I'll bet he was! Some sort of game, anyway. He told me he had his picture in the papers once."

With this for foundation, the clergyman returned to New York and, at the first opportunity, ran down to Princeton to lay the case before a friend on the faculty of the theological seminary.

"Spud?" said the theologue. "Certainly. Spud Harstrom, our center rush. Would you like to see him?"

"I should. Oh, I should!"

Spud Harstrom presented himself, a cheerful young giant, respectful to the two clerics and with a rather precise memory of the evening at the Haymarket.

"Yes, sir," he replied to the opening question. "I knew Nita. I was just about speaking to her when the thing happened."

"Exactly what did you see?"

"This thug in the box with Nita spilled something into her young man's drink."

"And then?"

"He passed out. It was dirty work. I was for doing something about it, but my cousin, who was with me, held me back. He said we'd both get shot, likely as not."

"Your cousin was right. Yours was a foolhardy idea, however commendable. May I have your cousin's name?"

"Oh, I couldn't do that, sir."

"Why not?"

"He couldn't afford to be mixed up in it."

"And you?"

"No, sir. I wouldn't want to either."

"Were you there for a purpose of which you are ashamed?"

"No, sir; not that time." He grinned sheepishly as he realized the implication. "But—well—you know, sir, the Haymarket. The family wouldn't like it. Nor the faculty, either."

"I will look after the faculty end," the seminarian interposed.

Dr. Farr's eloquence was known throughout New York. Never had he spoken more movingly than in his plea to the young athlete to help him clear Allen Hardwick's name and punish those who had driven him to suicide. Spud listened and was persuaded.

"Okay, sir," he said. "You win. You want an affidavit. I guess I've got to do it, only I look to you to square me with my people." (Dr. Farr nodded.) "And if you'll go to my cousin and talk to him like you've done to me, I think he'll come through." He gave the name of Stanford Haynes and his address.

Brockholst Farr left the campus, treading on air. He tried not to feel vainglorious, but he could not divest himself of the conviction that, to a perfectly adjusted mind, detective work was really quite simple. Certainly it had its high satisfactions.

Such time as could be spared from his church work in the next few weeks, he put in following up clues which might produce other Haymarket witnesses. All proved futile. On the other hand, Spud's cousin, a youngish and respected Wall Street man, reluctantly promised his testimony if it should be needed.

Of that brief but exciting phase of the ministerial career, Mrs. Steevens Parke observed, "Brockholst Farr must be up to some special kind of hellment those days. For weeks he has been exhibiting the habits, the manners, and the appearance of a preoccupied hound in rabbit season."

Having reduced his findings to a concise report, the pastor of the Old Stone Church presented them to the Honorable Thomas Cassius Corbin. That astute politician devoted an evening to an analysis of the new evidence in its bearing upon New York's deteriorating conditions. It resolved any doubts in his mind. The time was ripe for a new offensive.

The police had been making themselves widely unpopular. Having successfully defeated the Farr crusade, they had resumed their established attitude of tyranny. They had maltreated inoffensive citizens; the papers were full of police brutality. Lawful businesses were blackmailed, right and left. Not only were prostitution, gambling, and illegal liquor-selling winked at, but police inspectors and captains were now selling protection at stated rates to extortioners, counterfeiters, and thieves. The Department was honeycombed with drunkenness, profligacy, and corruption. No citizen was safe from its criminal impositions. A helpless public was waiting only the chance to express its resentment.

The Farr report was, in Boss Corbin's expert opinion, solid enough to warrant action. He returned it to its author with the endorsement:

"Good work, Dominie. Go ahead. Albany will back you to the limit."

Once again the Old Stone Church was front-page news. The Farr sermon of June third began with a simple and moving tribute to Allen Hardwick, "a modern Galahad, a pure and spotless soul, a martyr, foully destroyed by his enemies and cruelly misjudged by those who should have been his friends." Without mincing words, the preacher laid before his electrified congregation the full events of Allen's night with Nita, backed up by affidavits and the hospital record.

"Drugged, disgraced, and defamed, believing himself to have sinned mortally, Allen Hardwick sought refuge in self-destruction. Let us not too harshly judge that deed. The guilt is not so much the suicide's as that of the criminal organization which conducts and controls the affairs of New York City."

Coming out from behind the pulpit, the speaker advanced to the very edge of the platform, his great arms hanging loose, his eyes fixed and burning. He spoke now with a deadly quiet.

"The city's police force has been dubbed the 'Finest' by the unscrupulous time-server who heads it, and a servile and fawning press adopts and perpetuates the sorry fraud. I have shown you these 'Finest' in action. From this pulpit I have repeatedly charged them with minor crimes. I now add to that indictment the charge of murder. The death of Allen Hardwick lies at the door of the Police Department of New York City."

A thrilled congregation poured forth at the close of the service to cluster on the sidewalks in absorbed discussion. There was an awed sense that history had been made that day. The Honorable Thomas C. Corbin said as much to Adriance of the *Star,* who had stopped him at the exit.

"This will turn the town inside out," the Republican Boss asserted.

"Will Albany take it up?" the reporter asked.

"Certainly. Nothing can stop a full-dress investigation next session. You may quote me to that effect."

281

Indignation swept the city. From having been a discredited busybody and troublemaker, Dr. Farr was now established as the representative of an outraged citizenry.

Something like panic beset the Tenderloin precinct. It gained impetus from the visit of one of the Big Boys from Mulberry Street, who found Captain Schmidt and his confidential man glooming in the back room of the station house.

"How straight has this damned parson got his facts?" Police Commissioner Brophy demanded.

"Only about one hundred percent," Willie Frye made melancholy answer. He was too dispirited to try to lie out of it.

"Who's the hooker that gave him the tip-off?"

"One of the Clark's bunch. If I could get my hands on that Indian bitch's gozzle—"

"Yeah," Captain Schmidt put in bitterly. "Your pal, young Howatt, guaranteed her."

"How could he know she was going to turn respectable?" the flycop whined.

Commissioner Brophy shook an ominous head. "Bad stuff. Corbin's going after us with his gang of upstate hayseeds. They don't like the looks of it at the Hall. Not a little bit."

"Nor me," the pantata said morosely.

"Well, *do* something."

"What can we do?"

"Clamp down on everything, for Christ's sake! You'd ought to have done it before."

Raids. They were the logical defense against criticism, in the police book of strategy. The houses must be closed; temporarily, anyway. Gambling joints, too. Everything. It must be done in spectacular fashion to convince the public that the police were acting in good faith. Saturday night was set for the majesty of the law to assert itself.

There was hell to pay in the district.

"Tenderloin's Night of Terror" was the caption which Deacon Waldo put on Tommy Howatt's article in the *P.G.* This was something of an exaggeration, since most of the madams had received private hints in advance. There was, however, a good deal of disturbance, and some lively resentment developed as the raiding forces descended upon the dives.

The patrol wagon would pull in at the curb. Uniformed cops piled out. They carried bars and axes.

"Bust in the door, boys."

Loud wails from within: "The cops. We're pulled."

A battering on inner doors: "Open up. The police."

Feminine shrieks rent the air. Windows flew open. Figures dropped out. Back alleys teemed with respectable citizens from Des Moines, Kansas City, and Louisville, Kentucky, fleeing in their underwear for dear life and reputation.

Impassioned protests from the madams met the raiders.

"Haven't I paid my assessments regular?"

"Shuddup! Get in the wagon."

"I'll go to the inspector. I'll have you broke for this."

"D'ya want a clout on the jor, ya bitch?"

The wagon filled up, delivered its scantily clad passengers to the station, and went to the next street for another load.

Plain-clothes men attended to the street-cruisers, the dance halls, and minor gambling joints. The air was rent with the plaints of the persecuted. Several cops were bitten. The shock was so severe to a Sixth Avenue policy shop proprietor that he suffered a heart attack and died in the patrol wagon. A quiet second-floor bookmaker, who had paid his weekly ten dollars to the ward man for three years without a break, cut his throat in his chagrin. The West Thirtieth Street Station was so crowded with prisoners that all the passageways and even the captain's room were filled. Never had the Tenderloin seen such a turnout.

Jefferson Market Police Court was swamped the next morning. Professional bondsmen and shyster lawyers enjoyed a bonanza. All day long the judge droned out, "Ten dollars or thirty days." The ward men whispered to the madams: "The captain'll send you word when to open." The pimps said to their cruisers: "Lay off for a few days; the weather'll clear." A raiding cop said, behind a splayed hand, to the girl he had just arraigned: "Don't blame us. It's the doin's of that preacher-bastard." Cops, prostitutes, and pimps all joined in cursing Dr. Brockholst Farr.

Throughout the city the topic of discussion was the clergyman's attack and the police action following it. The raids were, of course, a tacit admission that the charge of corruption and connivance was well founded, but the police were too stupid to perceive this.

The girls at Clark's discussed the crisis in an atmosphere of gloom. Word passed from rouged lip to rouged lip:

"They're closing up the town."

Proof was at hand. The sale of liquor in the place stopped at the legal hour of one A.M. Clark's forced to submit to a dead-letter blue law! The memory of the oldest regular ran not to any parallel. Each hour brought fresh and dismaying rumor.

"Nellie Somers has been raided."

"The cops cleaned out the Cremorne and barred the doors."

"The shutters are up at the Buckingham."

"Corry Moore has skipped town."

"They say Baldy Jones is pulled."

"That's right. And the French Madam's."

"Christ! They'll be closing Georgiana Hastings next."

"They have. I was by there an hour ago. Tight as the skin on a seven-month belly."

"I hear the House of Nations is sending notices to the customers."

"How you ever going to know where you stand in this business?" Flo Durant of the Green Shutters cried, voicing the wrongs of her sister madams. "You think all the fuss and trouble is over and you can get back to a nice, quiet, respectable trade. You send out the all-safe notice to your regulars and, bam! the rattler's at the door and the joint is pinched."

"The old town is sure going to hell," was the general view.

The Tenderloin Club took cynical cognizance of the upheaval in local mores.

"This is a hell of a note."

"Politics! Dirty politics!"

"It's going to ruin the goddam city: that's what it's going to do."

"What's the out-of-town businessman goin' to think if he can't have a little fun, nights, in New York?"

"He won't come any more. He'll go to Philadelphia."

"Bernie Schmidt must be crazy."

"Nah-h-h! He can't help himself. Orders from downtown."

"Why, a man ain't safe running a legitimate business any more. They grabbed Tony Bibb's faro layout."

"And you can't get a drink at a bar after one o'clock. Hell!"

"Keep your shirt on. It'll all blow over. It always has."

It did not blow over for the unfortunate ruler of the precinct and his henchman. Seeing Willie Frye in the act of swallowing a rye-and-bitters at the club bar, Tommy Howatt joined him.

"Hey, Willie. What's the good word?"

"Good-bye's the good word with me," the fly-cop answered sourly.

"Huh? What's the idea?"

"The sticks."

"Transfer?"

"At the toe of the Commish's boot. Me and the boss both."

"Geez! Tough luck. Where to?"

"Morrisania. Where the little birdies sing in the woods."

"You must have seen it coming. If you ask me, you're lucky to be out of jail."

Willie's laugh was more like a bark. "How long since you seen a cop in jail? And how about you? Just because your preacher pal didn't bring in your name, that don't let you out."

Tommy was fairly comfortable on that point. "Don't you worry about me," he said carelessly.

"You think this'll fetch down a committee of hicks from Albany, Tommy?" There was an anxious ring to the question.

"Surest thing you know. Nothing can stop Doc Farr now."

"Don't you be too goddam sure," the policeman snarled. "He ain't bulletproof, is he?"

Tommy reached out and gripped the other by the wrist. "Look, you son-of-a-bitch! If anything like that happens to the Doc, they'll be hanging cops to the lampposts in this town. And you'll be the first up."

Willie gave him a sullen glance. "Okay. I guess I didn't mean it. There's other ways of fixin' him."

"Oh, go chase the squirrels off your beat," Tommy said cheerfully.

The fly-cop got out his notebook and the pair went over the last month's takings from the towel concession.

"Not so good," Tommy commented.

"That's your pal, the parson," Willie retorted. "Didn't I tell you he's a business-killer?"

Tommy was philosophical about it. "We're bound to get busted out of the concession anyway, as soon as the new pantata gets the precinct organized," he pointed out.

That was the rule of the game: a new captain meant a new deal in all the petty graft of the precinct. Oh, well! Tommy had made a neat little pile out of it already. He couldn't complain if it was somebody else's turn now. He possessed a nicely growing account in the Corn Exchange Bank. And he was doing nicely with his singing engagements and frequent sales of doggerel at improved prices.

He bade his partner good-bye, promising to come and see him soon in his far northern exile.

The Thirty-second Police Precinct offered thin pickings for a young cop who was trying to get on in the world. Not an assessable brothel was to be found in the district. The small and cheap poolrooms were a monopoly controlled by the Tammany district leader, hence untouchable. Barrooms closed at the legal hour of one A.M. because there was no trade after that hour. Gambling? Penny pinochle in back rooms. Willie Frye faced the desperate prospect of having to live on his salary.

Hardly had he and his pantata settled in to their new duties when the pencil-printed envelope was delivered at the station house. Anonymous letters are commonplaces in police practice. This one, tossed across the desk by Captain Schmidt to his confidential man, promised little.

Some kind of funny business going on in old house E. side Webster Ave. between 163 & 164 Streets. Girls. Daytimes. Watch out for Amsterdam Jake. I do not want nothing for this. Just get the Son of a Bitsch.

A friend

"Grudge stuff," said Willie Frye.

"Ever hear of this Amsterdam Jake?" his chief asked.

"Nope. But you never can tell. The *Pinky*'ll have his record if he cuts any ice. I'll call up Tommy Howatt."

The *Police Gazette* did have the record, which Tommy obligingly read off to his friend. Jacob Amster, alias Amsterdam Jake, was a high-grade counterfeiter, producer of the finest twenty-dollar note in the trade. As such he was of more interest to the federal authorities than to the local police. Still, Willie reflected, there might be something to horn in on. But girls: where would girls figure in shoving the queer? Unlikely combination.

Ever mindful of his magazine's interests, Tommy asked over the wire, "Any story in it for us, Willie?"

"Might be, later. I'll let you know."

"Sound out this Amster about doing one of our 'Con' series."

" 'Confessions of an ex-Green-Goods Man,' huh? Okay. I'll speak to him."

The fly-cop set about some preliminary snooping.

The suspect house looked respectable. It was an old-fashioned frame dwelling of four stories; its white paint faintly tarnished; the high railed steps leading up to the stormhouse slightly decrepit. Shades were drawn on all the windows. One would have thought the place untenanted. The plain-clothes man climbed the steps and applied himself to the bell-pull, without result.

Opposite was a neighborhood German saloon. Willie was already on friendly terms with the barkeep.

"Sure, there's somebody living there," that functionary said. "Name's Johnston, so he claims. Been there a couple of months."

"Customer of yours?"

"Rushes the growler now and again. Once in a while a pint of rum."

"What's he like?"

"Tall, bony, thin-faced. Quiet-spoken. Might be forty; might be fifty. Game leg on the left side."

Willie nodded. "That's him. That's Jake."

"There's a couple of others works with him."

"What kind of work?"

"You got me there. Then there's the girls."

"Yeah. What about 'em? Hookers?"

The bartender didn't think so. There were four of them who were pretty regular. All of a kind. Youngish; none over thirty. Swell dressers. Seemed to know their way around. Businesslike. Came. Climbed the steps, very brisk. Pulled the bell. Went in. Stayed an hour, two hours, maybe three. Usually one at a time. No; there were never any men with them.

"Not a meet-up joint, then," Willie said, disappointed.

The barkeep was sure not. "One of 'em is in there now," he added.

"That so?" Willie said. "Guess I'll stick around."

As it was darkening, the door at which Willie had vainly sought admittance opened from within and a young woman descended the steps. She was trim and well dressed. She turned south. The fly-cop cut across to intercept her.

"Hi, sister," he hailed.

"Pull your freight," said "sister."

"Aw, be nice," he said. "How about a little drink?"

"I'll call a cop."

"You've got one." He shifted his overcoat to show his badge.

"You got nothing on me. I'm here on business."

"Okay. All I want is a little information. What's the business?"

"Posing for the camera," she replied promptly. She took a card from her bag. It read: AVIS TAYLOR. MODEL FOR STYLES AND FIGURE.

"Professional, huh? Well, that's all right with me. Pose in the raw?"

The girl said uneasily, "You wouldn't think anything of it if it was a painter's studio."

"That's right, too. You got nothing to worry about, sister. Who works the camera?"

"I don't know his name. The girls call him the Professor."

"What does he do with the photos?"

"How would I know? I get my two dollars an hour and no questions asked."

"Okay. I ain't buttin' in on your deal. On your way and be good."

Willie went back to the saloon for a quiet one. "Did you find out what the game is?" the barkeep asked.

"Looks like the tickler trade."

"What's that?"

"Peddlin' noods."

"What do they fetch?"

Willie shrugged. "I wouldn't know. Ten, fifteen, maybe twenty for a real hot one."

287

"Good money," the barkeep said admiringly.

The fly-cop shook his head. "Peanuts for a high-class operator like Amster. I think I better pay a little visit to Brother Jake when he ain't there."

Among other relics of a varied past, Officer Frye had preserved a choice collection of skeleton keys. Armed with these, several evenings later, he lay in wait at the saloon until he saw the Professor, carrying a large briefcase, emerge from the white house, lock the door carefully after him, and limp down the steps into the darkness. After a safe lapse of time Willie crossed the street, mounted the steps, and let himself in at the door without too much difficulty.

With his bull's-eye dark lantern he guided himself through the hall, peered into a bare back parlor, went on to a shabbily furnished dining room, and thence to a disordered kitchen. Nothing of interest on this floor. Retracing his steps, he climbed the broad stairs to the second story. In the front room, north, he came upon a clue.

The room was a working studio. Two cameras of professional type, one large, the other medium, were mounted on tripods. Accessories stood near at hand: plates, plate-holders, and other apparatus. There were several chairs of quality and comfort, a luxurious divan with cushions, some ornamental screens and hangings. Nowhere did the intruder see any photographs.

At the end of the room a heavy door gave upon what Willie took to be a closet. With this lock he had some difficulty before it yielded to his patience and skill. He gave a grunt of satisfaction as the opened door revealed shelves stocked with cardboard mounts. Gathering an armful, he carried them across the room and dumped them upon a marble-topped table that stood handy.

They were what he had expected. Six different models had been used; there were some forty pictures. All were nude except half a dozen in the filmiest kind of nightwear. Some were seated, smiling faintly or gazing pensively out. Others had been posed lying full-length on the sofa. There were three dancing groups. Nothing in any of them suggested indecency. Willie Frye doubted that they were even illegal. They could probably be defended as high art. The workmanship was excellent. Amsterdam Jake knew his business.

So far nothing useful. Willie Frye dumped the lot upon the divan, and went back for another load. Here he got his first surprise as he noted a heap of discards on the closet floor. Upon scrutiny they proved to bear the imprint of leading Fifth Avenue studios: Pach, Sarony and the like. All the subjects were dressed in fashionable masculine garb, mostly of the Prince Albert type. All were headless.

With popping eyes the investigator went back for further specimens. This time the exhibits were more sensational. The male and female elements, about equal in the matter of nudity or near-nudity, had been juxtaposed in a series of striking duos.

Willie recognized several of the male subjects. One was a corporation executive who would have found it difficult to explain to his board of directors his intimate proximity to a nymph in a scanty nightgown. A well-known lecturer at afternoon teas was exhibited in the midst of a bevy of admirers whose costumes were conspicuously lacking, and a benevolent banker's household would have been surprised to note the location of his hands with respect to a languorous charmer perched upon his knee.

Willie Frye walked waveringly to a chair, sat down, and took his chin into his hands for meditation. When he painfully forced it to think, his brain churned up an unholy potpourri of distinguished citizens, nude female models, and decapitated unknowns with hardly a handkerchief-worth of apparel among them. What did it mean? What the *hell* did it mean?

Arranging the exhibits on the table he wheeled the chair around to face the door. He got out his police revolver and satisfied himself that it was in working order. His Department badge he pinned to the lapel of his coat. He doused his lantern and waited.

Shortly after a church clock struck eight he heard the front door open. He cocked his ear to listen for talk. There was none. Footsteps moved along the lower floor. Peg-and-dot went the footsteps. Jake Amster was alone. That was good. As the man mounted the stairs, Willie, weapon in hand, crept across the room and huddled into the closet, leaving the door narrowly open. By the time he was effectively disposed, the new arrival had reached the second floor. The gas chandelier there guttered slowly into full illumination. The man limped forward into the studio. He caught sight of the littered divan. The briefcase which he held in his left hand fell to the floor. His swiftly indrawn breath hissed.

Willie Frye said quietly, "I've got you covered, friend."

The newcomer said, breathing hard, "What is this? A holdup?"

"Police."

"You got the wrong man."

"Okay. But keep 'em up."

"I ain't heeled."

Emerging, the policeman satisfied himself, by sundry pats and prods, of the truth of this statement.

"I'm Officer Frye, special detail, of the Thirty-second."

The man bent to recover his briefcase. Willie, too quick for him, kicked it out of reach. Jake tried bravado.

"Where's your search warrant? My name's Johnston and I carry on a straight business—"

"Your name's Amsterdam Jake Amster and I don't need no warrant for the likes of you. What's in that briefcase?"

"Nothing."

"Open it up and hand it here." As the other hesitated, Willie made a threatening gesture with the butt of his revolver.

The opened case was put into his hands. He drew from it an imperial-size photograph which he held up to the light. The Frye sensibilities were toughened by long years of police experience. He would have said that he was shockproof. But the posture and companionship in which his scandalized eyes beheld one of the most respected bankers of the metropolis, upset his equanimity.

"Sweet Jesus," he breathed.

The fly-cop was not devoid of crude reasoning powers. Given, a number of headless photos in compromising postures: given, other and standard pictures of prominent citizens: given, the clever imposition of one such citizen's head upon a male figure whose intentions were quite unmistakable—the operation stood forth starkly. Blackmail. By some expert new process a composite portrait was evolved: the face of an unsuspecting innocent transferred to the body of a writhing lecher.

Into the mind's eye of Willie Frye flashed the ascetic visage of the Reverend Dr. Brockholst Farr. His vengeful fancy fitted it neatly upon one of the headless male trunks, so grossly coupled with a companion female nude. Willie was no scholar, but the phrase *in flagrante delicto* had become familiar to him through police court procedure. He joined it, with venomous delight, to the name of Brockholst Farr. Taken *in flagrante delicto*—and Willie knew where a photograph of the proposed victim was to be had.

So pleased was he that he modulated his tone to amiability in his next words to his captive, as he held the exhibit up to the light.

"I know this guy. How much?"

"How much what?"

"How much hush money is this going to cost Mr. Mayberry J. Porson?"

"I want to see my lawyer," Amster said sullenly.

"Now! Now!" Willie said in appeasing tones. "You don't need no lawyer with me. I'm a reasonable fella."

Amsterdam Jake's strained expression eased. "I don't want any trouble with the police," he said.

"Sure! That's good sense. You'll need protection in your line of trade. We can work together, I wouldn't wonder. What was you goin' to ask for this little piccy? Ten thou? Fifteen?"

"Hell, no. Nothing like that."

"Made any sales yet?"

As his victim hesitated, the fly-cop explored further the recesses of the briefcase. "Yoops!" he said in triumph and drew out a package of greenbacks, which he counted.

"Five thou," he said. "Good business! Did you invent this picture-doctorin' game?"

"I haven't heard of anybody else working it," Jake answered with some pride.

"It's a slick layout. All you need is a partner."

The other looked pained. "There's a lot of expense," he began.

"And ten years in stir if you get caught," the other reminded him. "You need a partner that knows the ropes. That's me."

Jake had had dealings with the police before. "What's the bite?" he asked.

"Fifty-fifty."

Jake raised a lamentable wail. The business wouldn't stand it. He'd rather shut up shop and get out.

"And leave this evidence with me?" the fly-cop said significantly.

Jake's resistance crumbled. "You'll have to cover me."

"Sure thing. We gotta let the pantata in on this. Don't squawk, now. It's his precinct you're doin' business in, ain't it? I'll take care of him. How about a cash-down now to bind the bargain?"

Money passed in solemn silence. His promise to Tommy Howatt came to Willie's mind.

"D'you read the *Pinky,* Jake?"

"Sure. Everybody reads the *Pinky.*"

"I gotta pal on the staff you might do a little business with some-time." He set forth Tommy's suggestion for a "Confessions" series. "You could pick up a coupla hundred, easy."

"I could sure use some side money," the ex-counterfeiter said. "Now that I'm not making my own any more," he added with a twinkle. "What's your friend's name?" He drew out a notebook and carefully noted Tommy's name and business address.

"Now, how about doin' a little job for me?" the plain-clothes man asked.

"What kind?"

"Darkroom. Doctorin' up a photo."

Jake stared. "Going into the business for yourself?"

"No. This is something else. Private. You'd have to handle it your-self."

"Where's the picture?"

"I haven't got it with me."

"Depends on how strong the print is, whether I could do a good job."

"It's a Kodak."

"Not so good. Amateur work don' reproduce right."

"This one's good and clear."

"Well, I'll do my best."

"There'll be a little piece of money in it for you."

"Okay, Mr. Frye."

"Willie to you. This is all on the q.t. Nobody to see it but you."

"Okay, Willie. When will I have the photo?"

"As soon as I can get it. A week or so."

"I'll be waiting. Meanwhile I'll go on with the lomacks."

"The what?"

"Lomacks." He tapped his briefcase. "That's what we call 'em in the trade."

"Oh. Lomacks, huh? Sure. Go ahead. Just be careful."

Afire with his great idea, Willie hurried around to the police station, where he was lucky enough to find Captain Bernie Schmidt, alone and disconsolate. Willie began:

"I got the lowdown on Amsterdam Jake, Boss."

"Yeah? What's his lay?"

"Darkroom stuff."

"What's that?"

"Camera stiffs. Photo gang."

"Speak English," growled his superior.

"It's a new racket. There's three in the gang. Jake is the head brains. The others are just operators. Jake gets on the track of some rich and important guy that's maybe a bit of a sport on the side, though he don't have to be. The gang comb the town till they turn up a picture of him. Generally they can find a professional job in one of the showcases of some swell photo gallery. Those bigwigs are always gettin' their mugs taken for their friends or their families or their clubs. Once Jake's runners find the piccy, the rest is easy. They turn it in to Jake and he doctors it up. And is he some doctor!"

"What's he want to doctor up a professional—?"

"You'll see in a minute, Boss. After Jake has done his fine work on Mr. Respectable's piccy, one of his staff calls at Mr. Respectable's house. A very polite and slick young fella. Wouldn't Mr. Respectable like to buy a very fine photo of himself? Mr. Respectable would not. Maybe, says the young fella, Mr. Respectable might change his mind after he's had a glim at the article. Out comes the piccy from the caller's briefcase. Mr. Respectable takes one look. And does he change his mind! Oh, momma!"

"You're tellin' me nothing," Captain Bernie said wearily. "Put up or shut up."

"I'd oughta have one of 'em to show you," the fly-cop said. "Anyway, the photo shows the old geezer, sprawled on a sofa with a chippy in her chemise or maybe not. 'How'd the wifie like that?' the smooth young fella says. 'The negative is cheap at a thousand.' Mr. Respectable may beef, but he comes through. What else can he do?"

"A thousand, huh?" the captain commented. "That's doin' business." (Wouldn't his soft-boiled eyes have popped out if I'd given him the solid Muldoon about the real price—Willie said to himself.) Avarice wrinkled the heavy German face. "There'll be ground-rent to pay," said the precinct commander.

"So I told Jake," said Willie, exhuming a roll of bills from his pocket and counting them into his chief's receptive hand. "Two hundred. Hunky-dory?"

"Maybe this Morrisania ain't goin' to be so bad after all." The exile smiled.

The plain-clothes man hunched his chair forward a pace. "That ain't all of it, Boss. That ain't the best of it."

"Well? I'm a-listenin'."

"I know where I can put my hand on a Kodak of the Reverend Brockholst Farr." The lowered tone was for expressiveness, rather than secrecy. The captain was not impressed.

"Yeah? And where does that get us?"

"I already put you wise to Amsterdam Jake's setup," Willie said with exemplary patience.

Willie's pantata was also being patient, in his way. "What about it?" he demanded.

It was too much. Willie waved his arms in the air. "Where does that get us! What about it! Holy mud! Dr. Farr! Jake Amster and Jake Amster's lomack kit; that's what about it!"

"Don't you yell at me, goddam you," Captain Bernie protested. "What're you gettin' at with your Jake Amster-lomack crap?"

Willie recovered his shaken composure. "Lissen, Boss. Lissen and try to get this," he implored. "I toldja I know where there's a Kodak of old Farr. Okay? Well, I take it to Jake and he does a lomack job on it. Doctors it up like I been tellin' you." His voice strained to a throaty caw of exultation. "Where does that leave the Reverend Doc? What'll the Old Stone Church folks say when they see an au-thentic photograph of their bee-loved pastor dandlin' a nekkid whore on his Presbyterian knees?"

For a long moment Captain Bernie sat silent. Then he rose and thrust forth the hand of congratulation to his underling.

"Willie—you're a great man and a great cop," he declared. "This had oughta put us back into the Tenderloin."

35

"Undoubting Thomas," Dr. Brockholst Farr was wont to call Tommy Howatt in gentle deprecation of his cocksureness. It was, in the main, a just characterization. Tommy was constitutionally overconfident of himself and his destiny. Only in his relationship with Laurie Crosbie did his self-assurance wane. He was honestly and deeply in love with the girl, and the very novelty of such emotion involved uncertainty, timidity, and even humility.

Tommy was now sufficiently *persona grata* with Mrs. Steevens Parke to call on her for personal advice. This he did one afternoon at the tea hour, having arrayed himself choicely in a black-ribbed cutaway coat, a low-cut, broad-lapel white piqué waistcoat, an ash-hued ascot set with a modest gold pin, gray silvery-striped trousers, and "gaiters" of dove-colored suede above correct patent-leather buttoned shoes. His hostess regarded him with approval.

"Any new songs, Tommy?" she inquired.

"No, ma'am. I've got something on my mind."

"Get it off."

"What do you think of me as a marriage prospect?"

"Why, Thomas! This is so sudden!" The old lady chuckled.

"Huh? What?—Oh!" He grinned in appreciation. "I'm serious, though."

"Laurie Crosbie, of course."

"Yes, ma'am."

"Where is the minx?"

"Gone to the Old Sweet with the Mannerings."

"Had a tiff with her?"

"No, ma'am. Everything's fine."

"And you want to marry her?"

"Oh, Lord! Do I!"

"But she doesn't want to marry you?"

"Well, that's the trouble. She doesn't exactly know."

"And you want my advice as to what to do?"

"Yes, ma'am."

"Well—don't."

"Not ask her?"

"Not for a time, anyway."

Tommy looked disconsolate. "I thought you'd be on my side."

"Be logical, then. Don't destroy your own handiwork."

"I don't getch— I don't believe I understand you."

"Have you forgotten your gloatings over her newspaper clippings?"

"Well, sure. I always did get a kick out of seeing her name in the society columns," he admitted.

"Yes. You are her unpaid press agent, by your own admission."

"But it was you that put her over. I used to wonder why."

"Did you? I'll tell you. Vanity; sheer vanity. The sense of the power to take a girl whom nobody knew and maneuver her into the inner circles."

"Is that all?" His disappointment sounded in his voice. "I thought it was because you liked her."

"Don't be a damned fool. I love Laurie. I would adopt her tomorrow if she would consent. She could have her pick of the young bachelors of the town."

"And where would that leave me?"

She said implacably, "Do you consider yourself justified in standing in her way?"

"Yes."

Mrs. Parke was pleased. "I like straight talk."

"Give me some, then. If Laurie marries me, she loses out. Is that it?"

"You cannot regard yourself as any great catch," she pointed out.

"Not yet."

"Or think that you could further Laurie's ambitions."

"She hasn't got any, Mrs. Parke. Not in that line. She doesn't give a merry hoot."

"That is unfortunately true. I fail to understand it. Instinctively and naturally she is a lady."

"And I'm not a gentleman." He spoke without rancor.

The time-worn eyes twinkled at him. "You are an apt learner."

"I could be with you for a schoolma'am. Not but what you've done a lot for me already," he added.

"You haven't done badly for yourself." She appraised him. "You wear your clothes like a gentleman. You are no longer cocky, though you think no small pease of yourself, I suspect. That air of quiet self-assurance—carefully cultivated, I doubt not—is effective. You are an easy talker; a little too intelligent for the average drawing room. You must be careful about that. You have no distinction, it is true. But you have charm, and you are not too conscious of it. Then, of course, there is that voice. By the way, you'd better stop singing for hire."

"Yoops!" said Tommy. "There goes money, rolling."

"You do not want to be a performing bear all your life. You are getting beyond that. Sing for charity as much as you like. Any cause; I don't care what it is. On that basis I can get you into all the best houses on Fifth Avenue, and as guest, not hired voice. You have the foundation to build on. You are a natural snob; that is a good start. I shouldn't be surprised but what you could worm your way into the Patriarchs in time."

"That would be something," he murmured.

"To come back to Laurie— She did try to break with you."

"Yes. With Allen Hardwick. It didn't work."

"No. It wouldn't have worked, even without the tragic turn that it took. I know why. I know that virginal one-man-or-none type. I have watched you two together and perhaps seen more than you realize; certainly more than she realizes. Be careful, Thomas Howatt." She bent fierce brows toward him. "If anything happens to that girl—"

"It won't, Mrs. Parke," he interrupted. "Don't you ever think it. I never would—well, you don't have to worry."

It was a lame conclusion, but it satisfied the hearer. "I suppose in the end she will marry you," she said. "Not that you're worth it."

"Give me time."

"Time. Ah! Now you put your finger on the spot. Give yourself time—and her. If you are content to wait, say three or four years—"

"Three or four *years!*" It was an ill-modulated squawk.

She laughed at him. "Lover's impatience. Well, I think none the worse of you for that. But have you considered the practical side? Laurie is a rich girl."

"Don't I know it! I can't live up to her scale. But I'm not going to live on her money, either."

"You're both young. You can afford to wait."

"As long as you're on my side," he began, but again she was laughing at him.

"Don't jump to conclusions. At least, I'm not against you. But Laurie comes first." She limped over to the piano and struck random chords. "Come; you have to pay for advice in this house."

When the private songfest was over, the old lady said, "I'll have a talk with the child."

"Yes, ma'am," said Tommy. "And thank you."

"Don't thank me until we see how it comes out."

"Give me as good a break as you can," he pleaded, lifting his gloves out of his hat.

Conspicuous in the pile of mail which awaited Laurie Crosbie on her return, was a note in the bold Parke handwriting, of which the purport was: Come at once— Important. Laurie was not overimpressed. Anything which might pop into the old lady's head became immediately if flittingly Important. After telephoning, Laurie presented herself at the Fifth Avenue mansion.

"You're prettier than ever," was the hostess' greeting. "How do you do it?"

"I guess because I'm happy."

"Have you seen that young scapegrace yet?"

"No. He's coming this evening."

"I want to have a plain talk with you, child. Have you been to bed with him?"

The girl's face flamed. "Mrs. Parke!"

"I gathered from him that you haven't."

"You asked Tommy *that?* How awful of you!" Laurie gasped.

"I didn't exactly ask him. I warned him not to. Now I'm warning you."

"I want to go home," said poor Laurie.

"Don't be a ninny. You'd like to go to bed with him, wouldn't you?"

"Oh-h-h-h!" It was protest and resentment and plea for mercy all in one.

"Perfectly natural," pursued the implacable questioner. "Nothing wrong in it, so long as you don't do it."

"I don't want to talk about it. I'm not going to do anything."

"That's what you think. And you may be right. How near have you come to it?"

Laurie was on her feet now, a picture of maidenly dignity, offended. "I won't stay here to—"

"Sit down, my dear." The deep voice was suddenly gentle. "Let me ask one more question and then I'll promise to harass you no longer. Have you ever felt toward any other man any part of what you feel for Tommy?"

"No. Oh, no!"

Mrs. Parke sighed. "You could do *so* much better. But, I expect it'll come to your marrying him. Hold out as long as you can, though. Now let's have some tea."

"Please, Mrs. Parke," the girl entreated, "don't talk to Tommy about me again."

"No need," was the brisk answer.

It was a struggle for Laurie not to be self-conscious with Tommy when he called that evening. There was restraint in her kiss of welcome, but she spoke with satisfying warmth.

297

"I've hated being away from you, Tommy," she murmured. "Have you missed me, too?"

"Have I!" he returned. "Just try to get away again."

"You could have come along, you know. The Mannerings wanted you."

"Yes. I'm looking up in the world. But don't forget I'm a working-man."

"Moneygrub!" she jeered.

"Money is right! I'm going to need it."

"Are you? What for?"

"To keep my end up. I'm thinking of marrying a rich girl."

"Congratulations."

"Glad you approve. So does Grandma Parke."

"Did you have to have her permission?"

"No. Only yours."

She freed her hand, which had been contentedly curled within his, and set it on his shoulder. "Tommy, you haven't been honest with me."

"Haven't I? What about?"

"Why didn't you ever tell me of going to the Hardwicks?"

"Good Lordy! How did you find out about that?"

"Dr. Farr. Why didn't you tell me, yourself?"

"Well, I thought you wouldn't like to be reminded of Al—well, of that whole business."

"Tommy, you're an awful fool about some things, and I love you for it."

"Enough to marry me?"

"I—I guess so. Sometime."

"I'm not trying to rush you. Just so I know where I stand."

"Let's wait till I'm twenty-one. Then I can do as I please with my money."

"As if you didn't now! People will say that I'm marrying you for your bankroll."

"Well, aren't you?" she asked mischievously.

"I'll show you! Give me a little time and I'll be making enough for us both," he boasted. "I'm not so far from it right now."

"That's wonderful, Tommy. Have they given you another raise at the *Pinky?*"

"Yes. And I'm getting a rake-off on any new advertising I bring in. That isn't all, either. Did you ever hear of graft?"

"Graft? No. Is it a new word? What does it mean?"

"There's honest graft and dishonest graft," he set forth. "Dishonest graft is knocking down money like barkeeps, or blackmailing people like *Town Topics,* or putting up dirty deals like Bill Howe and Abe Hummel make their living on."

"And what's honest graft?" Laurie obligingly asked.

"Getting inside info from your political lines. A district leader I did a favor for in the *P.G.* let me in on a real-estate deal last week, and I got eighteen hundred nice, round smackers out of it."

"Eighteen hundred dollars? Tommy, you're marvelous!"

"That's all on the q.t." he warned. "We don't talk about those things. There's something doing in the Department, too, that may pan out."

"The Police Department? I thought you were through with all that."

"Officially I am. But they come to me now and then for inside stuff on the Tenderloin." He displayed the edge of an envelope in his pocket. "From the Commish," he said with an offhand effect. "Wants me to talk over some special business with him tomorrow."

"Is that important?"

"The *Commish,*" he repeated. "The Police Commissioner. Larry Brophy, himself. Important!"

"What's it about?"

"I expect he wants some pointers." Tommy tried for an offhand manner, not too successfully.

"Would it be about Dr. Farr?"

"Well, it might."

"He probably wants your horrid old *P.G.* to write some more of its lies about him. You ought to be ashamed of yourself."

"Don't blame me, sweetness. I don't make the policy of the magazine. Talk to R. K. Fox."

"I'd like to. But he'd only want to put my picture on the cover of his pink monstrosity."

"Oh, come off it, Laurie," he protested. "Be fair. At that, I'd like to have a showdown with the Big Boy—the Commish—about Dr. Farr," he continued thoughtfully. "I think he'd take it from me; he's a pretty good guy. I'd just like to warn him. 'The Dominie's politics may be cockeyed,' I could say to him, 'but he's a straight-shooter and I'm not going to stand by and see any fouls pulled on him.' Oh, speaking of the Doc, that reminds me of something."

"What?"

"I'm out of luck. That is, I thought I was."

"Why?"

"I lost my mascot."

"You never told me you had one."

He had nearly given away the secret of the Kodak, but remembered in time Dr. Farr's prohibition.

"Something the Dominie gave me."

"Oh! A pocket piece?"

"Well, yes; sorta."

"What happened to it?"

"Don't I wish I knew! A week ago I first missed it. Somebody must have lifted it. New York is full of dips."

"Are you specially superstitious about it?"

"I was. I guess I don't need it any more. You're the best luck I ever had."

He drew her into his arms and turned her face up to his. She sighed happily. Her breathing became uneven. "I—I don't think we ought to kiss each other that way," she whispered and pressed closer to him.

His laughter was very tender. He was moved by her innocence, not alone to passion but to protectiveness as well. "What a woolly lamb!" he said. "Where's the harm? We're engaged, aren't we?"

"I s-s-suppose so. But we're not married."

"I love you," he said.

"It's taken you a long, long time to say it," she accused him.

"I never have said it before," he replied on a note of surprised self-discovery. "Not any time to anybody. That's the first."

"Yes," she murmured. "I've wondered about that. I've waited."

"I'm dumb, I guess. It's hard for me to put things into words." She laughed a little at that. Her voluble Tommy, dumbstruck!

"Well, I mean things like that. Things that I feel a lot."

"I shall have to train you. Kiss me for good night."

"I love you," he said, finding it astonishingly easy to say.

"Oh, yes! You must tell me that now. You must tell me always."

"I'll say it to you every day of my life all my life."

"You'd better go now, darling. I've got to steady myself to face Mother. Good-bye until tomorrow."

Waking that night in the small hours, Tommy brought to mind lines from *Much Ado about Nothing,* a play that had never seemed to him to make much sense. He had copied the passage with a view to improving it sometime to the point of salability, by turning it into rhymed verse. Now, getting out of bed to refresh his memory, he came to the modest conclusion that perhaps he could not better it and that it said what he wanted to say just as it was.

> *The idea of her life shall sweetly creep*
> *Into his study of imagination;*
> *And every lovely organ of her life*
> *Shall come, apparelled in more precious habit,*
> *More moving-delicate and full of life,*
> *Into the eye and prospect of his soul . . .*

Making a fresh copy for the morning, he rose early and left it at the Valdevia. Laurie read it on awakening.

"My Tommy is growing romantic," she said, and laughed and kissed the paper.

36

The loss of Tommy Howatt's mascot, of which he had complained to Laurie, had taken place farther back than he supposed.

While she was away, having nothing better to occupy his evenings, he had resumed his place at the Tenderloin Club late-evening poker table. For him the game had become a source of steady, though not invariable, profit; nobody can win all the time in an honestly run game. Tommy was a shrewd, cool, cautious player, possessed of the prime virtue of knowing when to drop a losing hand.

He was comfortably ahead of the game and playing them close, a fortnight before Laurie's return, when a whiff of cigar smoke back of him made him aware of a new arrival. He threw in an unprofitable two pairs and turned his head.

"Hello, Willie," he said. "What brings you out of the forest primeval?"

Willie Frye had come there for a specific purpose, which was not expressed in his response to the greeting.

"Night off," he said. "Thought I'd take a glim at the old joint."

"Want in?"

"Might take a small lot." He laid down a ten-dillar bill and received three assorted stacks from the banker. "Any time limit?"

"I've declared an out for one o'clock," Tommy answered.

Consulting his watch, the plain-clothes man found that this would give him nearly two hours. "Same for me," he said.

Both quit, moderate winners. Willie proposed a drink. Tommy assented.

"How's things in the precinct?" the exile asked.

"Tight," the *P.G.* man replied.

"Old Hellfire still got 'em bluffed?"

"The new pantata is eating out of his hand. They say he goes to the Old Stone Church for his orders." Tommy chuckled.

He proceeded to give his companion a précis of the situation in the Nineteenth. Captain Mark Carpenter, promoted from the Tenth, was making a record for himself as a law-enforcing officer. He raided here; he raided there: nobody knew where he was going to strike next. It was bad for business. What had been the richest police graft in the city, was unproductive. No tribute was coming in. Nor could any be expected so long as the night trade was in constant fear of the police and the police in constant fear of what might next belch forth from that ecclesiastical volcano, the pulpit of the Old Stone Church.

As Willie expounded, an effusive drunk, from Boyle's Billiard Parlors around the corner, reeled up to Tommy and grasped him affectionately by the coat lapels. He had been reading the signed articles in the *Pinky,* and he was there to tell the world that Thomas Howatt was the best dam' writer in the whole dam' city of New York, and it would be a pleasure and a privilege to buy him a drink. Tommy tried to elude him and found himself engaged in a good-humored scuffle, in the course of which his coat was wrenched open, exposing the small leather photograph case. Willie expertly lifted it. He then pried Tommy's alcoholic admirer loose.

"Let's all have a little drink," he invited.

Tommy did not discover his loss for several days.

In the camera room of the Morrisania mansion the morning after the club episode, Amsterdam Jake inspected the Kodak brought to him by the fly-cop.

"Amateur work," he said.

"Will it do?" Willie asked anxiously.

"I can make a job of it. It'll take time. What do you want for scenery?"

"Scenery? Oh!" Willie caught the idea. "The hottest you got. Let's see them female samples."

He selected one which, in nudity and posture, left nothing to the prurient imagination.

"This'll do," he said.

Urged on by the impatient Willie, the technician completed his difficult task of reconstruction in ten days. The finished work of art commanded the plain-clothes man's ungrudging approval. Wrapping it delicately in tissue paper and stowing it in a borrowed briefcase, Willie took the long trip downtown to Mulberry Street and asked to see Police Commissioner Brophy.

"What the hell is he doing here?" the great man asked angrily of his attendant. Since the Hardwick debacle, Willie and his pantata had been pariahs in the Department. "Tell him to chase back to the goats."

The messenger, having delivered this rebuff, came back with a sealed envelope in his hand, which the Commissioner ripped open. Within was a sheet of paper with a single word written on it. Mr. Brophy read it.

"Fetch him in," he ordered.

The fly-cop entered and greeted his superior respectfully. Commissioner Brophy opened the door of the inner office, directed his visitor inside with a jerk of the head, followed and locked the door. He held up the sheet of paper bearing the lone word and tore it into small fragments, which he dropped into the wastebasket.

"Farr," he barked. "What about it?"

"How'd you like to put the kibosh on the Reverend Dr. Bastard?"

"He's more likely to put it on us," the official said gloomily. "God help us if he ever gets before an Albany committee. Thanks to you dumb cops in the Tenderloin."

"There ain't goin' to be any Albany committee," Willie Frye asserted.

"Whaddaya mean, there ain't going to be any?" the official snapped. "Whatcha got in that briefcase?"

Silently Willie Frye opened it, unwrapped the contents, and laid the display on the Commissioner's desk. Brophy's protrusive eyes stared, blinked, and stared again.

"Holy hell!" he exclaimed. "You could be pinched for even havin' this stuff in your possession."

"Hot tamale, huh?" Willie said complacently.

"Who's his Whiskers on the bed?"

"Don't you reckanize him?"

The Commissioner looked more closely. "It ain't— It couldn't be— By God, it *is!*"

"Hellfire Farr, himself." Willie sniggered.

"Who's the naked girl?"

"Does that matter?"

"You're right; it don't. Where's the place?"

"The Bower. The pink and white room."

"Etta Holmes's joint."

"Right."

The official brain set itself to work. Brophy was a knowledgeable policeman. "That's where the leapfrog party was put on for Farr and his snoopers," he said.

"Nothing wrong with your memory, Chief."

"And this? The finish of the party, huh?"

"Yeah."

The Commissioner thought further. A frown creased his brow. "Hold up, there! That party was a night show. You can't work a camera at night."

"This was next morning."

"You're tellin' me that Farr spent the night there? I thought he left with young Hardwick."

"So he did."

"Well, then, what the hell—"

"Sposen he came back."

"Back to Etta's?" the Commissioner said stupidly.

"Why not? What's to stop him? After he'd shook young Hardwick."

"Is *that* what he done?"

"I'm layin' it out for you, Commissioner."

"Yeah. But how you goin' to prove it?"

"Sposen we produce two-three witnesses to identify old Farr as the man they seen comin' outa Etta Holmes's place at nine o'clock next morning?"

"Witnesses? What kind of witnesses?"

Willie winked. "Citizens that happened to be walkin' across Twenty-sixth Street at that time. I couldn't name 'em yet. But they'll be good."

"They'd better be!" The official thought uncomfortably of some of the regular police narks and perjurers and the poor showing that they might make on the stand. "None o' your professional five-dollar book-kissers for this job."

"Don't worry. Abe Hummel's got the best stable of witnesses in the trade."

The Commissioner nodded. "Okay. I'll leave that part of it to you. Say, though; that show at the Bower was a hell of a long time ago. Where's this picture been ever since?"

The plain-clothes man's face took on an expression of cunning. "It turned up in a raid."

"Some madam's private art gallery?"

"We don't have to prove possession on her. She might have been holdin' it for a price."

"It'd be worth it, whatever it is." The Commissioner regarded the photograph with admiration. "Who'd have thought it? The horny old bastard! Who took it?"

Willie looked pleased with himself. "I can get him."

"We'll sure need him. He'll testify to this, huh?"

"Well, not exackly."

"Huh?" The Commissioner scowled. "Why not?"

"Because he wasn't there."

"Then what the hell— Are you riggin' a fake on me, Frye?"

"Don't get mad, Commissioner. I wanted to see how the trick would work on a smart man like you. You took it all in, didn't you?" he ended triumphantly.

"You better not get too flip," Brophy warned in a growl.

"If it was good enough to fool you, what would it do with the public?" the fly-cop said, unperturbed. "The camera don't lie. That's what folks believe. There's what the camera tells 'em; and there's the Reverend Farr in indelicate flagrancy. Is that good? I ask you!"

"Come through! And make it straight, too."

Willie laid before him with all necessary detail the account of Amsterdam Jake's highly skilled operations upon Tommy Howatt's original. It was a truthful narration in all respects but one: he represented himself as having paid $250 for the exhibit. (Why not make a piece of change out of it?—he thought. When Commissioner Brophy promptly wrote out a check, he cursed himself for not having made it five hundred.)

"You know what, young fella?" the official said with heavy geniality. "You're liable to come out of this a detective sergeant. We need brains like yours down here."

"Thanks, Commissioner. When do we spring this on the newspapers?"

"We don't. I got a better use for it." He bore the photograph over to a safe standing in the corner, spun the dial, opened up, and closed the door again upon the treasure. "It stays right there until I've had a private talk with the boys on Fourteenth Street."

"That ain't the way I figured it," Willie said, not troubling to conceal his disappointment. "I figured we'd give the story to the papers: how Farr made a sneak with one of Etta's girls and got caught at it. Etta'll swear to it. I got a bird lined up for the photographer—he is one, too—that'll go on the stand for us. Why, we'll run that old bum out of the church and right off Manhattan Island. We might even get him indicted for—I dunno—immoral conduct unbefittin' the clergy or something. What's the matter with that, Commissioner?"

"It ain't bad," the official allowed. "But we can do better. Just leave it lay till I give you the word. You're right on one point, though," he added with profound satisfaction. "Tom Corbin can hang his hayseed committee out to dry. Who knows about this picture?"

"Jake Amster, of course. He fixed it up."

"And a hell of a fine job. Anyone else?"

"Tommy Howatt."

"Where does he come in?"

"This lomack"—he tapped the concocted photograph—"is taken from a Kodak of Farr that Howatt snapped."

"What of it?"

"He's liable to spot the face in the lomack as the same as his original."

"Yeah. But why should he squeal even if he does spot it?"

"He's pals with his Whiskers. They play checkers together. Checkers, for Chrissake!" said the fly-cop with an expression of extreme distaste.

"So, if we spring the lomack, he could ditch us, huh?"

"He could, but he won't."

"You got something on him?"

"Not on him. On his girl. The little Crosbie." He took from the briefcase an envelope bulky with newspaper clippings, documents, and notes, the latter in the careful writing of Stannard Barto. The Commissioner went through them, nodding his head from time to time.

"Gone respectable, huh?"

"Gone High Society, Commissioner. Look at the clippings."

"Ain't that something!" Brophy said admiringly. "Sutter Street Kate and her kid in the Four Hundred. Well-well-well! And young Howatt is stuck on the little chippy?"

"Wants to marry her."

"He can have her!" Brophy said with a grin. "Quite a record for a youngun. This ought to sew up young Howatt's lip. Need any help, handling him?"

"I might. He's tough."

"Not in this office, he won't be," the official said confidently. "I'll have him here Tuesday morning for a quiet little talk. You be here with those exhibits A and B. Ten o'clock Tuesday morning."

"Right-o, Commissioner. G'bye."

This was the basis of the Commissioner's invitation to Tommy, which the recipient had so boastfully interpreted to Laurie Crosbie.

With Commissioner Brophy's friendly summons in his pocket ("Drop in Tuesday morning about ten. Got something to show you"), Tommy presented himself at Mulberry Street. He was ushered at once to the Commissioner's office. The Big Boy greeted him pleasantly.

"Morning, Tommy."

"Morning, Commissioner."

"How's the *P.G.?*"

"Fine. R.K. sent you his best."

"I'll have a red-hot story for him one of these days."

"Is that what I'm here for?"

"Partly. How's Mark Carpenter doin' in the Nineteenth?"

"Same like any other new pantata. Mopping up. When is he going to ease off?"

"When your friend, Dr. Farr, lets up."

"He's got quite a ways to go, then."

"Oh, I don't know. Willie Frye's got a different slant. Here's Willie now."

The fly-cop entered, exchanged greetings with his superior, and nodded silently in response to Tommy's cheerful "Hi-ya, Willie?" The Commissioner produced a box of cigars. Tommy declined, brought out his packet of Sweet Caporals and lighted one. The two policemen also lighted up.

Willie Frye addressed Tommy. "Remember that Kodak camera picture you showed me of Dr. Farr?"

"Yes."

"Show it to the Commissioner."

"Say! Who's giving orders 'round here?" Tommy said, annoyed.

"That's right. Easy does it," the Commissioner put in pleasantly. "I'd like to see that picture just the same."

"I haven't got it. Somebody pinched it on me."

The Commissioner performed a sleight-of-hand motion. "Is this it?" he asked, and displayed the photograph.

Tommy cursed vividly. "What's my snapshot doing here?" he demanded.

"For the Rogues Gallery," the fly-cop said with his evil grin.

"That's funny, I guess," Tommy said, stony-faced. "Ha-ha!"

"The Commissioner's got something even funnier to show you." Willie chuckled.

Brophy crossed the room to the office safe, manipulated the combination, and came back with Jake Amster's "lomack." Tommy stared at it in stupefaction.

"What the hell is this?" he demanded.

"Reckanize the face, doncha?" Willie Frye asked.

"Where did you get it?" Tommy said stupidly.

"Doncha know? Use ya brains."

Light burst in upon Tommy, albeit not full comprehension. "My snapshot. It was you that pinched it, you son-of-a-bitch."

"Tut-tut!" said the Commissioner. "Be nice."

"But how you fixed it up that way— I don't get it."

"Doncha spot the setup?"

"No."

"You'd oughta. It's the Bower. And that's one of Etta Holmes's special gals your reverend pal is havin' himself such a swell time with. Don't he look it?"

"It's a goddamned fake."

"Who says so?"

"I say so."

"Don't say it in the wrong place; that's all," the plain-clothes man warned ominously.

"Who's going to stop me?"

The official interposed. "We'll come to that later. Right now, Tommy, you may as well get it into your head what we're goin' to do with this little work of art."

"I'm listening."

"Dr. Farr has been yelpin' for an investigation. Well, if he insists, he'll get his investigation. It won't be exactly the one he and Tom Corbin have planned, but it will do. And Exhibit A will be this photograph of the Bower."

"And what'll I be doing?" Tommy challenged him. "Standing by and letting you put this over on the Dominie? I'll see you both in hell first."

The Commissioner was patient. "There will be witnesses—"

"Cathouse witnesses. What's their testimony worth?"

"Police and citizen witnesses, too."

"Yeah!" Tommy snarled. "And there'll be a witness named Howatt. Ever hear of him? Tommy Howatt of the *P.G.* Wait till I tell R.K. about this stinkin' deal—"

"Keep your shirt on, young fella. What will this Howatt witness testify to?"

"I've got the negative of that Kodak. Any fool can see that the fake picture is the same as the snapshot. I don't know how the hell it was done. But just let the committee compare the two pictures, side by side, and there goes your case against Dr. Farr all to hell."

Commissioner Brophy sighed. He eyed the recalcitrant young upstart with something akin to compassion. Reopening the desk drawer he brought out a neatly taped envelope, holding it up so that the visitor could read the legend on it: "Stannard Barto Documents on Mrs. Theodore Crosbie and Miss Laura Crosbie."

"Take a thought for the girl," he said.

"What girl?" Tommy asked weakly.

"Your girl. Maybe you can guess what's inside." Brophy dropped the envelope on the table with a *planck*.

Tommy rallied. "I know all about that San Francisco case. Old stuff. You got nothing on Laurie Crosbie."

"You poor sucker!" Willie Frye's voice was bitter with contempt. "Tenderloin Tommy, the Mister Know-it-all of the *Pinky*. Ain't even wise that his girl was the star boarder in her mother's whorehouse. Fourteen-year-old kid come-on for the burnt-out trade at Sutter Street Kate's."

"You're a goddamned liar," Tommy shouted.

"Quiet!" the Commissioner warned. "Do you want me to throw you into the jug?"

"I don't give a goddam what you do to me. You lay off my girl."

"*Your* girl!" the plain-clothes man jeered. "*You're* puttin' up the dough for that swell flat on Madison Avenue, I suppose. On the lousy salary the *P.G.* pays you."

"Never you mind what the *P.G.*—"

"Where do the Crosbies get all that money?" the Commissioner interrupted.

"Oil wells." Tommy was trying to make his voice confident.

"Yeah! Oil wells. Where?" Willie was doing the talking again.

"Empery, N.Y. Down near the Pennsylvania border."

"Ever been there?" Brophy asked.

"No."

"Read this."

The official took from the envelope two documents and handed them to the visitor. One was from the State Geological Bureau. The last oil well in the Empery region had stopped flowing nine years before, it stated. The other was a letter from a county official, certifying that the name Crosbie appeared nowhere as a property holder in or near Empery.

Still Tommy was not beaten. "I've seen the checks at the bank."

"Yayah? Who signed 'em?" the fly-cop demanded.

"Harrison Perley, her guardian."

"Oh, you poor sucker!" Willie Frye said again. "Guardian! Jesus! That's a hot one!" He hooted with derisive laughter.

Tommy turned to the Commissioner, and spoke through lips that were pinched and gray. "What are you going to do with that stuff?"

"That depends on you." Mr. Brophy's manner was bland to the verge of kindliness.

"What do you want of me?"

"Not much. Just to keep your mouth shut."

"While you put that rotten stuff over on the Dominie. Dragging me in on it."

"We ain't askin' you to do anything," the Big Boy said persuasively. "Just not to butt in on our plans. That ain't so much, is it?"

"Oh, no! Only to cut his throat, the best friend I got in the world."

"It don't have to come to that. We'll give the Doc a break, if he'll act reasonable. Lissen, now; you pull quite a stroke with him, I hear."

"That's right. And I'm not—"

"Okay. You're the lad to handle this. Put it up to him straight that we got the goods on him, but we don't necessarily have to use what we got. He's tried to do us dirt, but we got no hard feelin's." (A low growl from Willie Frye indicated dissent.) "Will he play ball or not?"

"What kind of ball?"

"He turns over those stinkin' affidavits to us and resigns—and may he go in peace," concluded Mr. Brophy piously.

"Can you see a man like the Dominie listening to that kind a proposition?"

"It's ruin and disgrace for him if he don't. Let him agree to quit this exposure bunk right away, and we'll give him a couple of months to get out of town. We don't want to rush him. Let him agree to that, and we'll drop the whole business. Fourteenth Street will back it; you know you can trust Tammany on a deal like this. Farr can give his own reasons: bad health, wants to travel and write a book; anything. What's more, we'll turn over this lomack, here—ain't it a dandy!—to you together with all the Crosbie data, and that'll be the end of it. Least said, soonest mended. No further trouble for anybody."

"I'd sooner cut my throat before I'd go to him with that."

"Then you'd better cut his, too," Willie Frye snarled. "It'd save him from worse."

Tommy had another thought. "Even if I went along with your dirty deal, it'd be no good."

"Why not?"

"You're figuring to produce that photo at the investigation, you say."

"Correct."

"Dan Adriance will be covering it for his paper. He'll see the picture."

"Adriance of the *Star?* What if he does?"

"He's seen my snapshot of Dr. Farr. D'you think for a second he won't remember and guess what's going on?"

The Commissioner's face darkened. "How many other people have you shown it to?"

"Nobody."

"Oh, well; that's not so bad. We'll have to find a way to stop Adriance; that's all. You know him, Frye?"

"Yes. Don't like him."

The Commissioner asked the typical police question. "Got anything on him?"

"I haven't. But Tommy, here, he claims he's got plenty."

Tommy glared at him. That silly braggadocio! Boasting to Willie of his hold on Dan Adriance. Why hadn't he kept his goddam fool tongue between his teeth! Now he *was* in it— Brophy was speaking again.

"Think you can handle him for us, Tommy?"

"Oh, look, now, Commissioner!" Tommy began in desperation. "What d'you expect me to—"

"Sure, he can, Boss," the fly-cop broke in. "He told me, himself, he had Adriance by the short hairs. Some woman scrape, I guess."

Brophy looked searchingly at the *P.G.* man. "I'll make you responsible for Adriance," he said. "Make him savvy that he's got to shut his yap and keep it shut." Tommy tried to protest, but the official raised a hamlike hand. "You don't even have to do that, if you can get Farr to quit. It's up to you. Just as sure as he keeps makin' trouble, we'll put the picture up to him. And just as sure as you or Adriance or any other son-of-a-bitch spills on us about the picture, it's good night for your girl and her mother. His girl, too, if he's got one. Get it?"

Mute with misery, Tommy fumbled for his hat, found it, and made for the exit. At that moment Willie Frye's evil genius impelled him to one further jab.

"Another slick story spoiled for the *Pinky,*" he said. "Society's darling an ex-inmate and an old man's flossie."

312

Tommy made a choked sound in his gullet. Willie addressed his superior across Tommy's shoulder.

"You'd almost feel sorry for the poor simp, wouldn't you, Commissioner? A real looker, too, the gal. I wouldn't wonder but what I might take a crack—"

Tommy's fist, crashing into the speaker's mouth, sent him reeling against the wall. His assailant was upon him instantly, throttling him with murderous intent. The Commissioner grabbed a blackjack, hanging beneath his desk, and applied it scientifically back of Tommy's ear. Tommy slumped to the floor, down and out.

When he came to he was in a basement cell of Headquarters. A police surgeon was bending over him.

"Careless of you to trip on those stairs," the medico said.

"What stairs?" Tommy asked dully.

"Never mind. There's no fracture. Only a little concussion. How do you feel?"

"Kind of wuzzy."

"Better go home and stay in bed the rest of the day."

"Got something to do," the patient mumbled.

The doctor peered into his eyes. They flickered. "Put it off until tomorrow," he advised. "Give that brain of yours a chance to get over the jar."

The physician's advice was sound. It was a less than sane mind that guided Tommy back to the Windsor to get his police forty-four. Ugly and disorganized thoughts boiled and seethed within the aching brain. To outward appearance this was a normal young man as he asked for his key at the hotel desk. Actually he was a monomaniac. Disruption of a loved ideal plus the rage of mortally wounded vanity, fused in his still jumbled thoughts to burn out the processes of reason.

What an easy mark he had been! A softie, a come-on, a pushover. How they must have been laughing up their sleeves all these months of his devotion, the madam-mother and the kept daughter. Harrison M. Perley, too: that mealy-mouthed bastard.

Okay-okay! He'd settle with them.

The innocent young girl whose purity he had respected!

The reformed, pious, retiring Mrs. Crosbie!

The old goat, Perley!

The "cousin," Dan Adriance: probably getting his on the side!

He, Tommy Howatt, the lad who knew it all: a simp, a laughing-stock, a sucker!

Jesus Christ Almighty!

And what was he doing, protecting those two women? Why hadn't

313

he told Commissioner Brophy to go ahead and show them up and be damned to them? What was it to him if the name of Crosbie was scandalously headlined all over Park Row? What did he care if mother and daughter were run out of town, hauled into court, thrown into jail? Sacrifice Dr. Farr to that precious pair! What had he been thinking of? Well, he'd figure that out later. Now there was but one preponderant idea in his mind, to square accounts. Perley first.

In his room he drew out his watch. Twelve-forty. He was about to restore it to his pocket when a thought struck him: it had been a birthday present from Laurie Crosbie. With a whirl of his arm he sent it hurtling against the nearest wall. It burst like a golden bomb. That was some relief to the pressure.

Making an effort to hold his voice steady, he called up Harrison M. Perley's office. Could Thomas Howatt of the *Police Gazette* see Mr. Perley on a matter of importance? The reply came back: two-thirty. From his closet shelf he took down the cardboard box in which lay the police revolver, which he had not turned in as regulations stipulated. Satisfying himself that it was loaded, he settled it in his breast pocket, adjusting the well-fitted coat so that there might be no suspicious bulge.

It was after lunch time, but Tommy felt no hunger. He went down to the bar and had a sherry flip with plenty of nutmeg on the creamy yellow surface. The bartender eyed him with solicitude.

"You feeling all right, Mr. Howatt?" he asked.

"Yes, I'm okay, Jim. Guess I'll have a whiskey sour for chaser."

"You don't look too good," said the white-coated one, reaching for the rye bottle. He liked Tommy, as did all the hotel staff, and was surprised at this midday indulgence on the part of one who was usually moderate in his drinking.

"Nix on the worry about me, Jim. Don't drink any embalming fluid," Tommy said with a hollow attempt at jauntiness.

Returning to his room, he left a call for two o'clock, having now no means of knowing the hour. He threw himself on the bed and, with no conception of what he was reading, ran through the *Sun,* the *World, Life,* and *Scribner's.* When the call came, he washed up, set his hair in order, and went down to the lobby.

Outside, the air was bright and crisp, the right kind of day for walking, Tommy thought. There was plenty of time and the exercise would help his head, which felt light and empty. That was all right, too; he did not specially wish to think.

At the contractor's offices he was kept waiting a few moments before being admitted to the inner room. Seated at a glass-topped table, Elder Perley greeted his caller pleasantly. A thin and withered stenographer rose and went out. No sooner had the door closed softly behind her than the visitor stepped over and bolted it. Elder Perley's eyes narrowed.

"You make yourself at home, young man," he observed.

"I want to talk to you."

"Talk, then, and be quick about it."

"About Laurie Crosbie."

"This interview is ended."

A silver punch-bell stood at the contractor's elbow. Mr. Perley stretched his hand toward it. Tommy whipped out his revolver and leveled it across the table top. Mr. Perley said, "Put that thing down, you crazy young fool!"

"I'll put it down after you answer my questions. What's Laurie to you?"

"What concern is that of yours?"

"You know damned well what concern it is."

"I suppose you think you're going to marry her."

"Me, marry your kept woman?"

"Keep your voice down."

"Are you going to answer me or not?"

"You've answered yourself." There was contempt in Mr. Perley's manner, but no fear. Tommy did not understand that. He had expected him to cringe. There was a pause. Then, "Yes, I'll answer you." He took a bunch of keys from his pocket, selected one, and made to open a side drawer of the table.

"Drop it," Tommy threatened. "You think I was born yesterday?"

"Unlock it yourself, then," the other returned wearily. He placed the keys on the table top. "Second drawer, right-hand rear corner. You'll find a small leather case." He rose and walked away.

Still holding his weapon at the ready, Tommy fumbled amidst odds and ends until his fingers closed on the sought-for object.

"The spring is at the back," the calm voice instructed him.

The cover lifted under the pressure of Tommy's finger. There was revealed to him a miniature of two figures, beautifully and tenderly painted. The girl was leaning back against the knee of the seated man. The man was a younger Harrison M. Perley. The girl was as unmistakably Laurie Crosbie at the age of six or seven years. The likeness of daughter to father sprang to the eye.

"Oh, my God!" Tommy whispered. The pistol dropped with a clatter on the glass.

"Does that answer your question?"

Tommy stared at the miniature with distraught eyes. "Christ! What a fool I've been." The words were wrenched out of him in anguish. He closed the case and restored it to the drawer. "Who—who else knows?" he asked.

"Nobody. Her mother, of course."

"Mrs. Crosbie?"

"Yes."

"Not Laurie, herself?"

"No."

"Why not?"

"We thought it best for Laurie, her mother and I, that she should be shielded from that knowledge."

"You took a hell of a risk."

"Advisedly."

"What about Laurie's fath—Mr. Crosbie?"

"A figment. No such person."

"And Laurie's money? The oil wells?"

"Another figment. Are you through?"

"I—I guess so."

"Very well. Now, what is all this about?" Mr. Perley pointed to the revolver, still lying on the desk top. Tommy picked it up and thrust it back into his pocket. He took a deep breath.

"I guess I better tell you the whole thing," he said.

"I think so indeed!"

Beginning with the ill-starred Kodak, Tommy set forth the plot as developed by the police conspirators. His hearer's face grew stiffer and paler as the details were unfolded. At the end he said, "And so, as a solution, you proposed to shoot me—and then what?"

"Laurie and myself." The words were barely audible. "I was crazy when I came in here."

"Are you sane now?"

"Yes."

"Then let us see if we can find any way out of this. You say that you are sure your Kodak is the basis for this police picture?"

"Must be. Dr. Farr never had any other photo taken."

"Have you any idea how it was done?"

"No. Something new."

"And the police are prepared to make public this vile concoction against Dr. Farr?"

"Unless he gives in."

"And to shut your mouth by the threat of exposing Laurie and her mother?"

"That's what the dirty bastards have got framed up. Just as sure as Dr. Farr goes on and the committee of snoops comes down from Albany, they'll spring the fake picture, and if you or I or anybody tries to show it up, they'll pull the stuff on the Crosbies."

"Howatt, Brockholst Farr is the man I most respect and revere and love of any person living."

316

"That goes for me, too."

"But Laurie Crosbie is my daughter. She is the dearest thing in the world to me."

"That goes for me, too," Tommy repeated.

"Yes, we're in the same boat. We must work together on this."

"Yeah. But what's the answer?" Tommy propounded miserably.

"If Dr. Farr could be induced to resign, could we trust Commissioner Brophy to live up to his bargain?"

"Yes. That part of it is okay."

"Then he must be brought to resign."

"The Doc? Fat chance!"

"Not even when it is pointed out to him that if he doesn't, he is finished forever?"

"Who's going to do that little job of pointing out?"

"You are. You have all the data."

"Me? I'd as soon take my gun and put a bullet through his head."

Mr. Perley rose, went to the window, and stared out unseeingly across the stir of Union Square. His face was somber but decided when he turned back.

"Very well," he said. "I will go to him, myself."

"And tell him about the lomack—the picture?"

"If necessary."

"Whee-ew! Well, good luck to you," Tommy said. He considered. "There's the Albany angle."

"Tom Corbin's investigating committee?"

"Yes. He ought to be tipped off on what's coming."

"Do you think it would be safe to let him in on this?"

"Yeah. He's a cagey old bird. He'll get the point. Like as not, he could help you out with the Dominie."

"That's an idea, too. I know him pretty well, though we're on opposite sides of the fence politically. I'll go to see him."

Tommy's face was heavy with thought. "Mr. Perley," he began.

"Yes, Howatt?"

"It's Laurie or the Dominie, isn't it?"

"I'm afraid it boils down to that."

"What a mess! What a *hell* of a mess!"

"One point in our favor: we've got a little time to work it out. If only he will listen to reason."

"If he don't," Tommy said, "God help him."

"God help us all," said Harrison M. Perley.

38

Hardly knowing whither he was heading after the talk with Perley, Tommy walked up Broadway. Back to the Windsor? No, that wasn't where he wanted to go. He stopped at Madison Square and sat down on a bench, waiting for his head to settle. It still felt muddled. One thought came into the clear. He must see Laurie Crosbie and clear his conscience of the guilt of having believed her a kept woman. Crazy! He must have been crazy. How could he have committed so deep a treachery of soul! He felt as if he had wantonly soiled the image which he carried in his heart.

He got up and set out toward the Valdevia. One block short of it he stopped. What was he going to say to Laurie? His burning instinct was to confess how he had wronged her in his thoughts. If he saw her now, that was what he would do. His emotions would drive him to it. And then—?

No, he didn't dare risk it. He didn't dare see her. Time. He needed time to let the emotional turmoil within him abate. He went to the hotel and wrote her a note. An out-of-town assignment had called him away. He would be gone several days, perhaps a week or more. To back up the lie, he packed a suitcase and took it down to the *Gazette* office. There he would settle, in one of the *P.G.*'s emergency rooms for week-end substitutes.

The third day's mail brought in several exchange clippings. One of them made Tommy blink. It was an advance proof from *Town Topics*.

A little chippy bird, who roosts high in the tall trees of the Tender-loin, whispers in our off ear that if the vice-snooping committee ever comes down from Albany—and that's a big, big if—the star witness will be in for a mud bath.

Tommy took it in to R. K. Fox, who ran through it and handed it back. The editor-proprietor said with his quizzical air, "Is it news to you, Tommy?"

This was Tommy's clue to play dumb. He said, "I don't know where they get that kind of stuff."

"Old Colonel Mann has pretty good lines."

"Yes. But what's this 'big if' of his?"

"The talent thinks there won't be any Senate investigation."

"The Amen Corner says there will. Corbin's on record."

"Tammany might take the play away from Corbin and his hand-picked dummies from Albany."

"How do they figure that one?"

"Pull an investigation of their own and pull it first."

"I don't get it. Investigate what?"

"Farr and his charges. Your mind doesn't seem to be quite up to *P.G.* standards today, Tommy. Look at it this way: a Corbin-Republican committee would be slanted for Farr and his vice-snoopers, wouldn't it?"

"Why sure, but—"

"So why let it get to Albany?"

"How are they going to stop it, Chief?"

"By sicking the Board of Aldermen onto Farr first. They'll form a committee of their own and cite him before it on charges of defaming the city."

"That's no crime," Tommy objected. "The Dominie don't have to answer that."

"It's no crime. But it's a challenge. Can you see Brockholst Farr ducking a fight in a good cause?"

"No."

"Dirty fighting, too, it'll be. No holds barred. Abe Hummel for counsel. You know what that means. With a Tammany committee and Abe slinging the mud, it's likely to be rough going for your parson pal."

"Where do you get all this, Chief?" Tommy's tone was flattering.

The editor chuckled. "Didn't you ever notice how my ears stick out from my head? What do you think they were made that way for?"

His employe adopted a casual manner. "Any idea what the line of attack will be?"

Mr. Fox made no direct response. "Somebody in the Commissioner's office is trying to sell me an advance story, on the quiet. Hot stuff."

"About the leapfrog show at Etta Holmes's Bower? That old chestnut?"

"What he has is new. Or so he claims."

"I wouldn't touch it, Chief."

"Not even if he has proof?"

"What kind of proof?"

"Go and take a look. The Deacon's got it under lock and key. It's office-confidential, remember."

Tommy sought out the Deacon. "Did R.K. say you were to see this?" the old man asked.

"Yes."

"It's a looloo. Whuck-whuck-whuck!" the Deacon guggled. "This'll make 'em sit up in their barber chairs."

Tommy ran rapidly through the two pages. "Libelous crap, I call it," he said. "Don't tell me you believe it?"

"Why not? Most parsons are all right. But when one does cut loose— Oh, naughty, naughty! Whuck-whuck-whuck!"

"Don't we give Dr. Farr a chance to deny it?"

"Sure. You know the office rule. Would you like the assignment of putting it up to the reverend gent, whether he was in bed with the gal or not?"

"Not by a goddam sight!" Tommy exploded.

"Keep your shirt on, boy," the Deacon advised. "There's a loose end to the story. We ought to find out what Tom Corbin is going to do."

"I'll cover that," Tommy offered eagerly. He very much wished to find out from the Republican Boss whether he and Mr. Perley had been to see Dr. Farr, and, if so, with what result.

Confident of finding his man at the Amen Corner, he called at the Fifth Avenue Hotel. Mr. Corbin was not at his usual place in the lobby; had not been seen there for two days; was not expected until the following week. The caller left a message with a political lieutenant of the Boss and called up Harrison M. Perley's office. There he had no better luck. Mr. Perley was down with an attack of la grippe and would be abed for a week at least.

Normal sources of information were thus closed to Tommy, who had no way of ascertaining whether or not the question of resignation had been laid before Dr. Farr. Enlightenment came to him when, on the following Tuesday, he was summoned to see the Honorable Thomas Cassius Corbin, not at the Amen Corner, but at the Boss's house in West Seventy-second Street.

"I got your message," the quiet-voiced politician began. "Whatever it is that you wished to ask me about can wait. I have another matter to take up with you."

"Shoot," Tommy said.

"It is the threat to Dr. Farr. Mr. Perley tells me that you are familiar with the circumstances."

"Yes. Everything." Tommy wondered how far Mr. Perley had confided in this man. Surely not to the extent of letting him know about the Crosbies and their involvement. He, himself, must be careful to give no hint of that.

"About this incriminating photograph," Mr. Corbin resumed. "Do you believe it to be authentic?"

"It's Dr. Farr, all right." Tommy was being cautious.

"But, the surroundings? The woman? The—the posture?"

"A damn dirty fake."

"Can you prove that?"

"No."

"Have you any theory as to how that photography was managed?"

"No."

"You say it is a fake. Dr. Farr was never in that brothel?"

"The Bower? Sure, he was. He and Allen Hardwick were there, getting evidence. It's all in the affidavits."

"But he was not in the position represented in the photograph?"

"Hell, no!"

"You are convinced of his innocence?"

"Of course."

"Yet you agree with Mr. Perley that he should resign his pastorate."

"Look, Mr. Corbin. They've got him. The cops have got him. They'll swear his soul into hell and back it up with the photo. He hasn't got a Chinaman's chance."

"Have you considered that if he resigns under fire, it will be presumed to be a confession of guilt?"

"It wouldn't be under fire. The cops will keep mum if he gets out."

"How can he abandon his campaign in full course without some explanation?"

"Yeah, there's that. Couldn't he be taken sick, or something? Or have a call to go to Africa as a missionary? Can't you church people figure out some sort of excuse that'll let him out?"

"You are forgetting Dr. Farr, himself."

"I guess I was," said Tommy heavily. "Has it been put up to him?"

"Harrison Perley and I tried to point out to him a reasonable course of action."

"What'd he say?"

"As to resigning, he would not listen to us. He had offered to resign earlier, when it was a question of church policy. Now that it was a question of his character as a minister of Christ, he would fight to the end."

Tommy nodded. "That's the Dominie."

"Even though the trustees requested his resignation, he told us, flatly, he would refuse. Let them bring specific charges against him before the Presbytery, if they wished."

"Oh, God!" Tommy groaned. "How is he ever going to get out of this?"

Boss Corbin pondered. "You talked with Commissioner Brophy, Howatt?"

"Yes, sir."

"What is the most lenient settlement that he would accept?"

"They're after the Dominie's hide. It's drop everything, the affidavits and all, resign and leave town, or they'll make a holy hash of him."

"As a last chance, Howatt, don't you think you could talk some sense into him?"

"Don't ask me! I couldn't face him."

"I could not, myself, again," the Boss admitted. "It was an ordeal." He fetched a long sigh. "And now, what was your errand with me?" he asked.

"About the Board of Aldermen."

"What about the Board?"

"We got a tip at the office that they're going to appoint a committee of their own to investigate the Farr charges."

"That is within their authority."

"Wouldn't that block the Albany investigation?"

"Speaking for publication, the answer is no. But you know as well as I that if Dr. Farr's reputation is destroyed, anything that our committee might attempt would be discredited in advance. I assume that Dr. Farr will be confronted with the photograph at the hearing."

"Sure thing. That's the object."

"Well, at least, we've done our best to warn him. I will talk with Mr. Perley as soon as he is well enough. But I see no other solution but that Dr. Farr should abandon his crusade."

"Same here," Tommy said. And upon that note of gloom the interview ended.

The *Police Gazette* was not the only office to be stirred by rumors of developments in the Farr case. The talk reached the news-sensitive ear of Ramsey Kelly, city editor of the *Star*. He called his crack reporter to the desk.

"What's this grapevine about Brockholst Farr, Mr. Adriance?"

"You mean the political angle?"

"Yes. Does the Board of Aldermen really intend to subpoena him?"

"They could never make a subpoena stick."

"No. But would Dr. Farr fight it?"

"I think he'd welcome it."

"There are pretty nasty whispers going about, though."

"Yes, I know."

"Is it that leapfrog party at Etta Holmes's Bower?"

"So they say."

"That has all been covered before."

"This is supposed to be new stuff."

"Have you taken it up with Dr. Farr?"

"No. I thought it better to wait until there was something definite to go on."

"Well, I don't know. You're sure it won't come out before the hearing? We don't want to be beaten on the story."

Dan hesitated. "The *Pinky* has some inside stuff readying up."

"The *Police Gazette?* Is there anything to it?"

"I can ask R. K. Fox."

"You couldn't get to see it, I suppose."

"I'll try. But I doubt it."

"See if you can confirm the alderman angle," the city editor said.

"All right. I'll tackle Bart McGovern. He's acting president."

Before looking up the alderman, however, Dan went around the corner to the *P.G.* office. Mr. Fox was out at lunch. Dan bethought himself that Tommy Howatt, being in the owner's confidence, might be able to throw some light on the subject. To the reporter's discreet questions Tommy entered a blanket denial. There was no such article on the hook. Wouldn't he know it if there was? He pooh-poohed the whole thing.

"Fishy as a smelt, Dan," he said. "And, say—" he added as if an afterthought.

"Well?"

"Are you liable to see Laurie?"

"Yes. Tomorrow, probably."

"Don't let on that you've seen me, will you?"

"What's the idea?"

"I'm out of town."

"Laying low, eh? Okay, I won't give you away."

Tommy nodded and went out.

Dan was not satisfied. Tommy's nonchalance had been overdone. The *Star* man hung about the *P.G.* office until R. K. Fox came back from lunch. The editor was not inclined to be overcommunicative.

"Is this for your paper, Dan?" he inquired.

"Yes, sir."

"I'll tell you this much. But there's nothing in it definite enough for you to print. We've got a pretty nasty story on Dr. Farr."

(So Tommy had been lying to him—Dan thought. Well, it wasn't the first time.)

To the editor-owner he said, "What does Dr. Farr, himself, say to it?"

"He won't even see a *Gazette* man."

"Not Tommy Howatt?"

"Tommy won't take the assignment. Says he'll quit first."

"Yes, I can understand that. Why don't you go, yourself, Chief?"

"Me? To see Dr. Farr?" Mr. Fox blinked.

"Why not? You're an expert judge of character." Dan glanced upward at the bookshelf above the desk, where, in sober incongruousness amidst surroundings of pugilism and equine biography, appeared the title:

Phrenology Proved
by
Orson & Lorenzo Fowler

"I should like to have your judgment as to whether Dr. Farr exhibits the marks of depravity."

"Hmmm! I wish I had more carefully observed his cranial phenomena on my previous visit," Mr. Fox said. "A second opportunity might— You think that Dr. Farr would receive me now?"

"I'm sure I can fix it."

The editor gave the matter a minute's thought. "Okay. So do," he said.

Dan got on the telephone, announced to his chief an appointment for the morrow, and then went up to Tammany Hall, where Alderman McGovern was attending a district leaders' meeting. Dan waited. His patience was rewarded by a semi-confidential statement from McGovern which enabled him, without citing his authority, to file a story for the next day's paper. It was headed:

VICE-HUNTER TO BE CITED
CITY FATHERS WILL CALL DR. FARR
NEW PROBE OF CHARGES

The date of the hearing, the article stated, was not definitely set, but it would be within six or eight weeks.

Dr. Farr took cognizance of the *Star*'s article on the Sunday following its appearance. Dan Adriance, covering the Old Stone Church on his regular assignment, took down the preacher's words:

"It is reported on reliable authority that the Board of Aldermen of the City of New York will formally inquire into my accusations against the city administration and its police, and will summon me before it to defend my position. I am advised by counsel that they lack authority to compel my attendance. It is immaterial. As a loyal citizen of New York, I shall hold myself at the Board's disposal."

324

Reading the Monday newspapers in his business office, Commissioner Brophy scowled and swore.

"He's askin' for it," he said to his mistress-secretary. "Now, by God, he's goin' to get it."

39

That week of self-enforced separation had almost wrecked Tommy. He would not have believed that his world could be so stale and flavorless as it was without Laurie. He lay awake nights trying to frame a pattern of lies plausible enough to stand up against her questioning when the showdown should come. It would have to be good, for, though Laurie was naturally trustful where she loved, she had a shrewd mind. There would be questions about his attitude toward Dr. Farr, to which he could find no sufficient answers.

Soon or later he must face her. He could not endure the present status much longer. In one desperate access of loneliness and apprehension, he all but decided to make a full disclosure of the agonizing truth, beg her to marry him at once and go away with him somewhere out of reach. He found that he could not do it, could not bear to blight her happiness with the revelation that her mother had been a madam, and that she, herself, was a reputed prostitute. While he was still wretchedly mulling over the insoluble problem, a message came from Police Headquarters. Commissioner Brophy wished to see him.

Presenting himself at Mulberry Street, he was shown at once to the Commissioner's office.

"Sorry I had to sock you, Tommy," the official said genially. "No harm done, I hope."

"No. I'm all right."

"What about your parson pal?"

"He won't quit."

"That's as I get it. You tried, huh?"

"Everybody tried," Tommy said sullenly.

"You can't say but what we've given him a fair chance. Last Sunday's sermon just about clinched it. Oh, I don't say but what, even now if he'd pull out—eh?"

Tommy made a gesture of hopelessness.

"No dice? Okay. The hangin's set for the twenty-seventh."

326

"That quick?" said Tommy, startled. "I thought it was set for next month."

"We've pushed it forward a little. Your parson pal is rarin' to get in his licks, they tell me."

"Mmph," was Tommy's noncommittal response.

"He'll get his innings all right. How about that little parlyvoo with Adriance of the *Star?*"

"I haven't got hold of him yet."

"The time's gettin' short."

"Look, Commissioner; the chances are he might not even—"

"Chances, hell! We're takin' no chances on this. If you want to take a chance on what'll happen to the two Crosbie dames, that's your lookout."

"Lay off, Commissioner," Tommy groaned. "I can't take any more."

"Then quit stallin' and get busy."

"Okay. I'll put it up to him."

"Now you're talkin' turkey. Beat it, and good luck."

Uneventful days passed. Routine work occupied Tommy's office hours. Several attempts on his part to get a look at the complete article on Dr. Farr's supposed erotic exploits were unavailing. He knew that Ralph Enders, the most brilliant and least reliable of the *P.G.*'s casuals, had been set to work putting the material into final form, in a guarded room with a carefully rationed allowance of rye to keep him going. Tommy guessed that Deacon Waldo might be having reporter trouble, his usually amiable disposition having turned sour.

Less than a week remained before the advanced date of the aldermanic hearing. It was almost time for the article to be getting into galley proof, if it was to be run before the hearing, and Tommy's journalistic instinct told him that, as a sensation, it would lose force by being held later. Yet Enders' activities seemed to have ceased. The cubicle set aside for his labors stood empty for two days. Off on a drunk, Tommy surmised. Who, then, would take over the job? Tommy asked the Deacon.

A morose grunt, followed by an uninformative whuck-whuck, was the response.

The inquirer was not to be so easily rebuffed. "Come on, Deacon," he urged. "What's cookin'? Tella fella."

"I'm not the make-up man," growled the old man.

"You're in charge. When are we going to run it?"

"Ask R.K. if you want to know."

"Has he got it?"

"Yep."

"It's finished, then."

"Yep."

"And on the hook?"

"No."

"Held over?"

"You can call it that."

"What date?"

"No date. Further orders. You ask *me*, I say it's killed."

"Killed?! Why? R.K.?"

"Who else but the chief would have the authority to kill the juiciest story that's come into the shop for a year!"

"Killed!" Tommy marveled. "What in hell do you reckon happened?"

"All I know is that R.K. had a palaver with that highty-tighty pal of yours on the *Star,* and next morning came the order."

"Dan Adriance?" Tommy asked. A chill crept along his chest. Why was Dan mixing into this. What could he have found out?

"That's him," said the Deacon. "They were sweating over Enders' piece for two-three hours."

"Well, I'll be double-damned!"

"You ask me," the disgruntled Deacon said, "this shop is going plumb to hell."

"Is the chief in his office?"

"Not back from his lunch yet."

"Get me in to see him as soon as you can, will you, Deacon?"

The old man nodded. Two appointments were waiting to see the editor, after which Tommy had his turn. He came to the point at once.

"I hear the Farr story is killed, Chief."

"Yes."

"That's slick! I thought if you had a talk with him he'd bring you around."

"Then you're wrong. It wasn't his talk."

"What was it, then?"

"His head."

"His he—" Tommy remembered. "Oh! You mean you examined Dr. Farr's head?"

"Not as thoroughly as I might have wished. I had trouble persuading him. He began by saying that phrenology was heathenish nonsense. Phrenology! The greatest advance of the century in the science of humanity! Then I got him to admit that he had never read the Fowler classic. He's a reasonable man, your Dr. Farr. He apologized handsomely for hurting my feelings and ended by permitting me to make a superficial cranial survey. It was convincing. I tell you, Tommy, his bump of amativeness is almost indiscernible. No sane man could believe him a lecher. The *Gazette* has been saved from a grave injustice to a fine character."

"Boss," said Tommy, "you're a wonder!" After a pause, he asked, "Did Dan Adriance get you to go to Dr. Farr?"

"He engineered the interview, yes."

"I wonder why. Did he tell you?"

"A sense of justice, I suppose. You might ask him."

"Thanks, Chief. I'll do that thing."

It was high time, anyway, Tommy felt, that he went through with the dreaded talk with the *Star* man. Who could know what course Dan might take that would disastrously complicate matters? There was danger in delay. For that matter, there was danger in the alternative. Dan was a prickly one to handle. Tommy nerved himself to the encounter and set out.

Mulling over in his troubled mind the problem of approach, he had a helpful idea. For he knew that he had a coadjutor at call, bitterly reluctant though she might be to assume that role. He must be sure that Kathleen Daggett was in town. He called up, found that she was at home, and caught an uptown car. Two hours later he made connection with Dan Adriance at the *Star* office.

"Hello. . . . That you, Dan? . . . Got something I want to talk with you about."

"All right, Tommy. Go ahead and talk."

"Not over the phone. How about Andy Horne's?"

"I've got a two-stick piece to finish. Make it twenty minutes."

"Okay. I'll be in the back room."

On his friend's arrival, Tommy ordered beer. Two tall, thick glass steins were deposited on the table before them. They had the place to themselves.

"Hello, Dan," Tommy began. "What did you tell R. K. Fox about the Farr article?"

"What do you know about the Farr article?" Dan demanded.

"I've seen the outline."

"That's all you ever will see. You or anyone else."

"Yeah. So you advised the chief to kill it."

"What I advised the chief is his business. What's all this about, Tommy?"

"You're covering the hearings, aren't you?"

"Of course."

"What line are you taking in the *Star?*"

"It's a dirty, rotten, stinking police frame-up. You know that as well as I. That whorehouse picture is a fake, but I can't prove it and so I can't print it. Not yet, anyway. If I can find a way I'll blow the whole damned investigation right out of the water."

Tommy leaned across the table. "Lay off, Dan."

"What do you mean, lay off?"

"Keep out of it entirely. You can't do the Dominie any good. They've got him dead to rights."

"Just like Allen Hardwick, eh?" the *Star* man said sardonically.

"No. This is sewed up. Airtight. And, Dan, if you've got the brains God gave a louse, you'll keep your trap shut."

Adriance stared at him. "Are you for Brockholst Farr or are you playing in with the crooked cops?"

"Never mind me. I'm telling you, the Doc is through, and if you butt in, there'll be worse hell to pay than you ever dreamed of in your life."

"Hell to pay for who?"

Tommy answered slowly, "For the last person in the world that you'd want to see in trouble."

"If you drag her into this, I'll kill you."

Unmoved, Tommy said, "If she gets into it, it will be your doing. All I'm asking you to do is keep your clam shut."

"You treacherous son-of-a-bitch!"

"Okay, okay. Call me anything you like, but just sit tight when the evidence comes up. All I'm asking you now is that, whatever turns up, you don't shoot your mouth off. How about it?"

"I'll see you in hell first."

Tommy stood up. "Well, that's that. I'll have to play it the best way I can. You'll be out of this mess in spite of yourself. Only, don't blame me for the way it turns out. So long. See you in Potter's Field."

Seething with anger and apprehension, Dan went back to his office and was at once sent down to the far end of Staten Island on a promising murder, which failed to live up to its sensational prospect. Back at his desk, he was busy with the half-column which was all that the story was worth, when the head office boy summoned him to the telephone. Kathleen Daggett's voice came to him over the wire, low and strained.

"Dan, I've got to see you."

"Anything wrong, Kathleen?"

"Yes. Can you get away?"

"Not for half an hour. Where is—?" He left the name unpronounced.

"Out of town."

"Can you come to the apartment?" Dan's voice was quick and eager.

"Oh, no, no! Meet me somewhere where nobody that knows us could possibly be."

He considered. "Pabst's Harlem Casino. Go up to One Hundred and Twenty-fifth Street and take a cross-town car west. It's on the downtown side of the street. You can't miss it. Nine o'clock all right?"

"Nine o'clock," she confirmed.

For once she was ahead of time. The great restaurant was almost empty. She drew away when he tried to kiss her. They found a table. Dan ordered haphazard from a portly Teutonic waiter.

"Now tell me, darling," he said.

"That dreadful Howatt creature!" she said.

"Have you seen him? When?"

"This afternoon. He came to the house."

"Why did you let him in?"

"I didn't dare not. Oh, Dan! He knows."

"Damn his soul to hell!"

"It's awful, Dan. He's had spies on us right along. The night watchman at the Square has got the dates when I was at the apartment; the time I came, the time I left. The janitor's wife knows about the extra key. Other tenants have seen me on the stairs; they could identify me. Dan! Dan! What fools we've been!"

"I know, darling. I wouldn't have had this happen for anything in the world," he said weakly.

"Well, it has happened. And now you've got to get me out of it."

"What exactly did he want of you?"

"It all works in with Dr. Farr's trial. Something he wants you not to tell. You must know what it is."

"Well, I don't exactly. I've got a general idea, that's all."

"Whatever it is, you must do it. You *must,* Dan."

"Kathie, they're out to crucify Dr. Farr."

"I can't help it."

"And, if I have this right, there is something coming up where I can save him."

"I don't care! I don't care!" she cried.

"It means the ruin of a good man's life."

"What about my life?" she demanded vehemently. "Are you going to let that be ruined?"

His voice was heavy and spiritless when, after a pause, he spoke again. "No. No. I can't do that. I love you."

She drew a painful breath of relief. "Oh, Dan! I knew I could trust you. But the Howatt creature: will he play fair?"

"If he doesn't, I'll kill him. I mean it, Kathie. And he knows it. But what I can't see is why in God's name he has turned on Dr.

Farr. Time and again I've heard him say that the Dominie is the best friend he's ever had. What has changed him?"

"I can help you there. It has something to do with Laurie Crosbie."

"With Laurie!"

"Yes. I've always felt that there was something mysterious about her and her mother."

"I'm beginning to see. What a fool I was not to suspect it!"

"What is it, Dan? Has somebody got a hold on Laurie, and is Howatt try—?"

"I don't think I can tell you right now, darling."

"It doesn't matter. Not so long as I can be sure that you can stop that poison snake from talking. But, oh! Oh! How can I ever feel safe again?"

It was a miserable meal, with long silences, futile self-reproaches, vain regrets. In the hansom cab, driving back, she pressed close to him.

"It's been a happy time, Dan. I've loved it. But I've always told you it couldn't last."

He said, "The apartment is out, of course. You can never come there again. There are other places."

"Not if I get out of this awful mess. I'm through, Dan, through. I've had my lesson. I'm going to be a model wife— And go to church— And do good works— And darn his socks— And have six babies." She went on, her voice deepening and softening. "It's been so sweet, darling, so wonderful. Miss me always, but not too much. Now kiss me and let me out."

He drove to Washington Square in desolation of spirit. This, he knew, was final. He accepted it.

The telephone was ringing when he entered the apartment. It was Kathleen.

"Oh, Dan! I had to call. I had to know that you're all right."

"I'm as all right as I ever shall be without you," he said.

Four more times that night she called, the last time at half past one. Then he said, "Kathie, you're torturing me. Do you get some sort of pleasure out of making me suffer?"

"*Dan!* What a cruel thing to say to me."

"Once and for all, Kathie. Will you come back to me?" He knew the answer before it came across the distance.

"No, darling, never. I can't."

And that was all.

Through an all but sleepless night Dan sought to allay his misery by trying to figure out his course as regarded Tommy. The mere thought of seeing him was sickening. Yet it seemed necessary to have a further talk before the hearing began. While he was still considering, chance made the decision for him.

With an early-evening assignment, Dan went to Katie's for dinner. He had settled himself at a small corner table of the restaurant on the upper level, and had ordered, when the outer door opened, revealing Tommy Howatt and a fellow *P.G.* man named Strong. They stopped at the bar for a cocktail. Tommy's roving eye sighted the lone diner. He left his companion and came up at once.

"Hello, Dan. Can I sit down?"

"No."

"You hate my guts, don't you?"

"Yes."

"You wouldn't if you knew the whole thing."

"You threatened Kathleen Daggett," the *Star* man said under his breath.

"I had to."

"In order to blackmail me."

"What else could I have done?"

"Jumped off Brooklyn Bridge. That's the best thing you could do now."

"You wouldn't listen to reason—"

"Reason! Good God!"

"Will you give me a chance, Dan?"

Dan looked at the face, hunched a little on its neck as if in expectation of a blow. The typical jauntiness was gone. The features were white and strained. Rancor ebbed out of Dan's heart and was supplanted by a sort of hopeless weariness.

"All right," he said. "Sit down if you want to."

"Just a second, till I square it with Strong." He rejoined his fellow staff man at the bar, made his excuses over a Manhattan, and came back. "Mind if I order?" he asked hesitantly.

"Go ahead."

Ernst, the waiter, was summoned and recommended lamb chops. Tommy merely nodded, then sat, drumming on the table.

"This is tough," he muttered.

Dan offered no help.

"We're both in the same fix," Tommy stumbled on.

Still no comment from his companion.

"It's Laurie with me. It's Kathie with you."

"Leave them out of it."

"Wish to God I could!" Tommy groped in his mind for a starting point. "You know that rat, Barto," he said at length.

"Stannard Barto? Yes."

"Remember that more-to-come paragraph of his in *T.T.?*"

333

"The *Town Topics* threat? Of course I remember."

"Okay. Listen. He did have more—a whole envelope full—and the cops have got it. Everything."

"Good God Almighty! How did they get their hands on it?"

"They must've pinched his papers when they gave him the treatment and ran him out of the country."

Dan stared at him in dismay.

"So, now you see how they're putting the squeeze on me. If I go to the front for the Dominie—" He spread his hands in a gesture of despair and surrender.

"Have you got evidence—?"

"I could shoot their case full of holes, and they know it."

"What on? The photograph?"

"Yeah. The photograph."

"Does Dr. Farr know that you can ditch them with your evidence?"

"If he doesn't, he will as soon as they show him the lomack—the rigged photograph."

"I begin to get it. It is faked from that snapshot of the Doctor that you had? You think they doctored it up from that?"

"Yeah. Willie Frye pinched it. Now they're putting it square up to me. The Commissioner, himself, had me on the grid. Either I play ball with them or they spring the Crosbie stuff."

"So you're going to stand by and see the Dominie smeared."

"What else can I do? Look, Dan, if you think that I like being a treacherous son-of-a-bitch like you called me," Tommy cried lamentably, "you got another guess coming."

"I'll take that back," the *Star* man said. "But, for God's sake, where do Kathleen and I come in on this?"

"That's the rottenest part of it. The Commish put it up to me to keep you quiet. If I let you spill the beans they'd cut loose on the Crosbies. I had to blackmail you just like they're blackmailing me. I told you we were both in the same fix."

"And so an innocent man has to be sacrificed. Do you believe for a minute that Laurie Crosbie would let him be ruined to save herself? Have you thought of that?"

"I know damn well she wouldn't. Not to save herself. But what about her mother? Not the stink alone. Maybe jail. I wouldn't put it past those skunks. Where would that leave Laurie? Have *you* thought of *that?*"

Dan shook his head. "A few minutes ago, when I saw you coming through that door, I wanted to kill you, Tommy. Now, I guess I'm sorry for you. Myself, too. We've broken the rules, both of us, and who has to pay for it? Brockholst Farr. If that's God's eternal justice, I want no part of it."

"I know, I know," Tommy agreed. "We're a lousy pair. But what else can we do? I ask you, Dan. What else can we do?"

"Nothing," the other replied.

"Nothing can save him," Tommy said bitterly.

After a long pause, Dan said, "I only wish I didn't have to go to the damned slaughter."

Tommy made a gallant try for his habitual show of light spirits. "Among those present," he said, "will *not* be Mr. Thomas Howatt of the *P.G.* So long, Dan. See you in the mortuary chapel."

40

Back at his office, Tommy found a letter from Laurie, marked "Please Forward." It was both plaintive and indignant. Where was he? Why had he not sent her so much as a line since he went away? What kind of love was that? How would he like it if she went away and never so much as wasted a two-cent stamp on him? And-so-forth-and-so-on.

Tommy took stock of impending events. Nothing could keep from Laurie knowledge of the aldermanic investigation of Dr. Farr, now less than a week away. It would be just like her to attend the sessions, if she could manage it. Not through him! In any event, she would be a passionate partisan of the accused clergyman.

For a time he mulled over the wild project of trying to persuade her that the imminent charges against Dr. Farr were true, that he was a hypocrite, a renegade, a lecher. He dismissed the notion. Laurie's loyalty would revolt at the mere suggestion. She would refuse to listen. As an alternative, he might reveal the whole plot to her, plead with her that it was for her sake that he was being forced to betray his best friend. Again, he knew her too well to believe that she would accept the sacrifice of an innocent man, especially when that man was Brockholst Farr. She was quite capable of exposing the whole miserable scheme.

Yet, if he, Tommy, refused to support the clergyman when the test came, what would Laurie do? He well knew the answer to that. She would go straight to the accused man and learn the truth from him. And that would be the end of Tommy's hopes. For on one point he was quite clear: Laurie might love him, but it was Brockholst Farr whom she would trust and believe. Against the minister's word, his own would count for nothing. To Laurie he would appear as the coward and traitor that he, indeed, was committed to become. He would lose her.

No, by God! There was another way. Marry her at once, before the trial. As his wife, she would side with him, even against her pastor. She would have to! What else could she do?

Restless, unhappy, and in turmoil of mind he pocketed Laurie's letter and ambled over to the window to look out upon the bleak façade of Brooklyn Bridge.

He was too unquiet to work. Anyway, it was a slack time. He went to Deacon Waldo.

"Got anything for me, Deacon?"

"How about those rewrites?"

"Finished and on the hook."

"You look flummoxed. Not feeling good?"

"Not too good."

"Take the rest of the day off," said the benevolent Deacon. "Go and blow yourself to a couple of drinks."

Drink was not what Tommy needed. He was fortunate in that he had never been able to find relief from his troubles in alcohol. He went to the telephone and called the Valdevia. Laurie answered the phone.

"Hello, Laurie."

"Oh, Tommy!" Her voice was excited. "You're back!"

"Can I come up?"

"Yes, of course. Right away?"

"I'll be there as quick as a pair of spavined Fourth Avenue car horses can get me there."

"Wonderful! I'm all alone and it's such a horrid day."

She answered his ring, herself, drew him inside with arms clasped about his neck, and kissed him with reassuring warmth.

"Not that you deserve it," she scolded. "Don't they have any two-cent stamps where you were, wherever it is?"

"Baltimore," he said. He glibly improvised a woman-scandal in the politics of the city, which, after all his work, had come to nothing printable. "Libelous though true," he explained. "Had a hard week."

"You look it. Is anything the matter, Tommy?"

"Not a thing. Not a thing in the world."

"There is! Is it Dr. Farr?"

"Where do you get that notion?"

"You haven't been to see him. Tommy, his feelings are hurt."

"Oh, Lordy!"

"How long is it since you've played your checker game?"

"I don't know— Well, I've been away. You know that."

"Yes, but does he? Did you send him any word?"

"I meant to. I guess it slipped my mind."

"Such a slippery mind, lately!"

337

"Aw, cheese it, Laurie. Let's talk about us."

"What about us?"

"This is the first time we've been alone together since God-knows-when."

"I know. I haven't liked it, either."

He took her hand and examined it critically. "What size wedding ring do you wear?"

"How should I know?" She laughed. "I've never been measured for one."

"Then it's time you were."

"Is this a proposal?" she asked gaily.

"Yes. Let's get married, Laurie."

"I thought that was all settled."

"I mean now. Right away. Tomorrow."

Then she heard the strain in his voice; saw the anxiety in his expression. "Why, Tommy! Why, darling!" she said. "Anyone would think you were afraid of losing me."

"I wake up at night with the fear of it on me."

"Silly Tommy!"

"Do you blame me for wanting to be sure of you? How do we know what might happen?"

She gazed at him wonderingly. "What could happen?"

"You never can tell. Look, Laurie. I've got a friend that's an alderman. He'd marry us any time. On the dead q.t. if you want it that way. You could sneak out tomorrow and meet me, and we'd go to Frankel's office—he's Alderman Frankel—and you'd be Mrs. Thomas duB. Howatt before you know it."

"Be married by an alderman?"

"Why not? It's legal."

"I wouldn't think of being married by anybody in the world but Dr. Farr."

(I knew it!—said Tommy to himself.)

"Suppose he wouldn't?"

"How ridiculous! Of course he would."

"He's never been for me, Laurie. He wanted you to marry Allen Hardwick."

"And you're holding that up against him? That's petty."

"He tried to stop us once. And I don't believe he's really for me now."

"Then why did he send me that wonderful letter of Mrs. Hardwick's? And the message he wrote across it?"

"Message? You didn't tell me about that."

"He said that he had misjudged you and—and—well, a sort of bless-you-my-children effect."

"Then there's all the more reason for hurrying if you want the Dominie to marry us."

"Whatever do you mean?"

"Laurie, I hate to tell you this, but you know there's an investigation coming."

"Yes. I don't see how they dare."

"Oh, don't you! Well, when that's over, the Dominie won't be marrying anybody because he won't have any church to marry 'em in."

"Oh, Tommy! You do exasperate me with your mysterious croakings. What are you holding back?"

"I don't want to tell you, Laurie."

"And you're afraid to tell him," she charged with a flash of enlightenment. "That's the reason you've been keeping away from him."

"Yes."

"I don't think much of you as a friend," she said scornfully.

She was leaning back in the corner of the low, broad couch, her hands clasped back of her head. Now he dropped beside her, took her hands, and drew them over his shoulders. The hands clung.

"Laurie," he said hoarsely, "we gotta be married."

Half breathless with the harsh pressure of his body against her breasts, she said dully, "Got to? Why?"

His mouth closed down upon hers with a long, clinging insistence. "That's why," he whispered, drawing back for a moment.

"Oh, darling," she gasped. "That isn't fair."

"You can't pretend you don't want me," he said fiercely, triumphantly.

"Oh, I do; I do! But—oh, please! Let me up, Tommy."

"Not till you promise—" He broke off, raising his face from hers. There was a gentle rattling of a door, a soft gush and pressure of air as the elevator made its ascent.

"It's Mother," the girl whispered, wrenching herself free and struggling to her feet.

He turned his head. "No. It isn't stopping. It's going on." He caught her to him again. "Will you go with me to Dr. Farr tomorrow morning?" he demanded. "Will you, Laurie? Will you?"

She put both hands to her head. "I think I'm crazy, darling. But— oh, I suppose so."

At once he became businesslike. He consulted the ormolu clock. It marked ten minutes past five.

"Ought to catch the Dominie at home now," he said.

"Hadn't you better telephone him to make sure?" she suggested, patting her hair into place.

"Good idea," he returned. He started for the dining room.

"Do you really think he'll do it, Tommy?" she said. "What reason can we give?"

"Leave that to me," he replied with an assumption of confidence which he did not feel.

Wild projects were already teeming in his mind. He would make some kind of deal with the clergyman. Something based on the coming hearings, on his, Tommy's, inside knowledge and ability to help. What or how, he did not know; but surely they could figure out something between them. No, that wouldn't work; that would mean the exposure of the Crosbies— Well, he could make Dr. Farr believe that this was a marriage of necessity; that he and Laurie were already lover and mistress; even, if it came to a final resource, that the girl was pregnant. How could the minister refuse an appeal based not only upon friendship, but also upon morality? Or, some other expedient might suggest itself when he came face to face with Dr. Farr. Tommy had faith in his powers of persuasion.

He cranked the telephone handle briskly. The parsonage maid responded. Yes, Dr. Farr was in. But he was engaged— Couldn't he be interrupted for a moment? This was Tommy Howatt— The maid was doubtful. It was an important caller. She would see— Then the Dominie's deep, deliberate voice sounded on the wire, with friendly warmth.

"Thomas! You have been neglecting me shamefully of late."

Feeling like a delinquent schoolboy, Tommy mumbled something about having been awful busy—had to go away on a job—lot of work on his hands—meant to come around but—"you know how it is, sir."

"Then I have not unwittingly done something to offend you, my boy?"

"Who? Me? You? Oh, gosh, no, Dominie," Tommy gulped.

"This is a fortunate circumstance. I have a caller who is anxious to get in touch with you. Just a moment."

Tommy had a sinking sensation, as he stood waiting.

A calm voice came over the wire. "Mr. Howatt?"

"Yes."

"This is Judge Cassard. Could you come to Dr. Farr's house at once? It is quite important."

A chill struck to Tommy's heart. Judge Cassard, the counsel to the vice committee; prospective counsel to the clergyman in the coming proceedings. Only too clearly Tommy forecast what was in store. He tried to steady himself.

"Yes, Judge," he said. "What was it you wanted—?"

"I prefer not to discuss it over a public telephone."

340

"I getcha, Judge. But, you see, well, gee! I gotta lot a things to do right now." Under stress of anxiety Tommy's carefully guarded speech was losing its hard-won refinements. "I don't see how I could come right now. I'm due at the office. Couldncha kinda gimme a line on what you want with me?"

After a longish pause, the Judge said, "Dr. Farr thinks that an object now in your possession might be germane to his case. You will recall a Kodak picture—"

Tommy heard no more. At the word Kodak, he very quietly hung the bulbous receiver on its prong. He stood, gnawing his lip for a moment before striding purposefully back to the front room. Laurie ran to him.

"Tommy! What is it?" There was a note of alarm in her tone.

"He won't marry us."

"Did you ask him?"

"Yes," Tommy lied.

"I knew he wouldn't approve of a—a—well, a clandestine sort of wedding like that. But, oh, darling, don't look so—so crushed. We'll just have to wait."

"He'll never marry us."

"Did he say so?"

Suddenly life and vigor came back to Tommy. He gripped Laurie by the shoulders. "Go and pack a bag, Laurie. Quick! Quick!"

"What for?" she said, a bit dazed by the violence of his demand.

"We've got to get out of here. Before your mother gets back."

"What for?" she repeated.

"We're going to a hotel."

"A hotel?"

"Just for tonight. Tomorrow we'll be married. Get your things. You won't need much. What are you standing there for? We've got to hustle, I tell you."

She said with a strange, withdrawn gentleness, "Tommy, I couldn't."

"You won't go with me?"

She read the desperation in his face. "What happened on the telephone, Tommy? Tell me."

"You won't go with me, Laurie?" he insisted.

"Don't ask me to do that. Please, darling, please!"

"It's our last chance."

"It isn't! Why should it be?"

His face took on a sort of calm recklessness. "Okay," he said. "Leave it to Lady Luck."

Taking a dollar from his pocket, he hefted it in his palm. Laurie stared at the bright silver.

"What are you going to do?" she asked.

"Heads, the Dominie; tails, your mother," he answered. He spun the coin high in air. It fell, rolled a short distance, and toppled, falling with the eagle upward. Tommy laughed shortly. "I guess it's easiest that way," he said as he pocketed the dollar. "When'll she be back?"

"Mother? Any minute now."

He sat down. "I'll wait."

After a silence she said timidly, "Sing to me, Tommy."

He shook his head. "Not now."

"Are you angry with me because I won't go with you? Don't be. I want to go. I do want to. But I just can't. Please understand, darling."

"It's all right, Laurie," he said vaguely.

They sat in strained silence until they heard the elevator stop. Laurie rose.

"Do you want to be left alone with Mother?"

"Yes."

She went out, brushing her hand caressingly across his neck as she passed him. He heard the voices of the two women in the hall. The words were indistinguishable until Laurie's came clear, "I don't know, Mother." Then Mrs. Crosbie entered the room. Her eyes were questioning and frightened.

"Has something happened?"

"Yes. Sit down."

"To Laurie?"

He shook his head. "Mrs. Crosbie, there was something about that Barto business I didn't know."

She took a step toward him. "What?"

"He kept records. Documents."

"Oh, God! Where are they?"

"They're at Police Headquarters."

Her left hand went to her throat, the fingers scrabbling at the wrinkled skin. "Oh, God!" she breathed. "The police. What are they going to do?"

"They're using the stuff to blackmail me."

"You? *You?* Why, you?"

"It's part of a put-up game on Dr. Farr. They're set to railroad him."

"Yes. Harry told—Mr. Perley told me."

"I don't believe he told you the whole thing."

"Give me a minute's time." He pushed a chair toward her. She groped for the back of it and sat down. "All right," she said after a moment. "What didn't he tell me?"

"About the photograph?"

"He did say something about there being one. I didn't pay much attention. I was thinking of Laurie."

"Yes. So am I. I'm going to tell you the whole story."

He explained in swift but sufficient detail the use to which the lomack was to be put.

She interrupted him to say indignantly, "Nobody would believe that of Dr. Farr."

"Oh, wouldn't they! You don't know the kind of case the cops can make."

"But you do. Can't you do something about it?"

"Yes. I can blow their case to hell-and-gone."

"You're going to, aren't you?"

With slow and painful utterance, he said, "What would you think of me if I don't?"

She was bewildered. "You've got proof of Dr. Farr's innocence?"

"Not positive proof, but good enough."

"And you're hesitating to use it?"

"I asked you what you'd think of me if I don't."

"Think of you?" she burst out. "I'd think you were a snake, a toad; I'd think that Benedict Arnold was a decent and honorable man compared to you."

"Laurie would think that way, too, wouldn't she?"

"Of course. Who wouldn't."

"Mrs. Crosbie, I can't do it."

She stared at him in disbelief. "You're not going to defend Dr. Farr?"

"No."

She stood up. "Leave this place. I won't stay in the same room—"

His hand fell on her shoulder. "Because, if I do, the police will open up the Calloway case. Sutter Street Kate will be headlined in every newspaper in New York."

He had to catch at her quickly with his other hand to save her from crumpling to the floor.

When she could speak, she said, "Th-th-th-that's what you meant wh-when you said they were blackmailing you."

"Yes."

She began to sob dryly. "What shall I do? What shall I do?"

"Get this right. If I keep my mouth shut, the cops will keep theirs. I even think I could get 'em to turn over the Barto stuff to me. Then you and Laurie would be in the clear."

She clutched at him. "You'll do it, won't you, Tommy? You must! Not for me. I don't matter. For Laurie."

"And what about the Dominie?"

"I know. It's awful. But you can't bring this disgrace on Laurie. You can't; not if you love her."

"If I ditch him, what will Laurie think of me? She'll never speak to me again."

"She needn't know."

"Nuts! She's bound to know. She suspects something already. She'd never forgive me, and you damn well know it."

"She might, if she understood why. She would. I'm sure she would," the mother said desperately.

"Now, we're coming down to cases," Tommy said with an effect of practicality. "You make her understand that it's all for her; that I'd rather cut my throat than do the Dominie dirt, but that as between him and her I'm slipping him the double-cross."

Mrs. Crosbie held him under a contemptuous scrutiny. "Do you know Laurie as little as that?"

"Why—what—?"

"Let alone your asking me to tell my own daughter what I've been. Don't you know that she'd sacrifice herself without a second thought to save Dr. Farr?"

"No. I don't believe—"

"Then you're a fool," the mother cried. "I know her. I know what she would do. It would be utter ruin for us both. And you'd be worse off than before. And don't you dare go to her with your whimpering, puling plea that you're doing it all for her sweet sake. If you do, I swear to God Almighty, you'll never set eyes on her again," she concluded with a murderous glare.

The angrier she became, the cooler Tommy grew. "Will you listen to me for a moment, Mrs. Crosbie?"

"Go on."

"I'm going to marry Laurie, come hell or high water."

"I hear you say it."

"Will you help me?"

"Why should I?"

"Why shouldn't you? You know she wants to marry me."

"She did want to. But when this comes out—"

"You know she'll never marry anybody else, don't you? Don't you?"

"I suppose so, God help her!"

"Okay. Now you say that she would give the whole show away, and to hell with the consequences, rather than see the Dominie get it in the neck."

"I'm certain of it."

344

"As things stand now. But what if I can get her to marry me? Before the hearings. Right away. Tomorrow."

"What's that got to do with it?"

"I'll be her husband then. It'll be a question of her husband that will be ruined if she spills the beans. Don't you get it? She might sacrifice herself for Dr. Farr, but would she get up in court and show up her husband as a liar and maybe a perjurer? Just let me get her safely married, and I'll guarantee to handle it."

"Oh, I don't know what to say. I'm frightened."

"Don't be. All I'm asking is that you help me save Laurie and yourself."

She put both hands to her head. "What do you want me to do?" she whispered distractedly.

"Stand by me when I put it up to Laurie to get married right away. She wants to. I had her going. She was ready to, and then— never mind that. Let's get her in here now and settle it."

"It's all wrong. I know it's all wrong," she wailed softly. "But I don't see any other way."

"Just leave it to me," he told her, and went out to call Laurie.

She came back with him and stood, looking anxiously from his face to her mother's. "Have you two been quarreling?" she asked.

It was the mother who answered. "No," she said. "Laurie, do you want to marry him?"

"Yes."

"Are you sure?"

"Oh, yes. Absolutely."

"He wants to be married right away."

The girl gave Tommy a long look of trust and longing. "Are you going to try to stop us, Mother? Please don't."

"I'm not going to. I—I want you to marry Tommy."

The girl ran to her. "Mother! That's wonderful. What changed you?"

"I want to see you settled down."

It was a lame answer, but, for the moment, it satisfied Laurie. Tommy moved toward the door.

"I'll telephone," he said.

"To Dr. Farr?"

"No. To Sol Frankel." He added, for Mrs. Crosbie's information, "He's my alderman friend."

"Wait, Tommy. Don't do that. Please, darling," Laurie said sweetly.

"Why not?"

"I want us to be married by Dr. Farr. I thought you understood that."

345

"But Dr. Farr won't marry us, I tell you," Tommy barked.

She looked at him in surprise, but her own tone was still gentle as she replied, "He will, now that Mother is willing. I'm sure he will. I'm going to explain to him, myself."

Tommy caught at her arm. "Laurie! Laurie! It's no use. Don't do it. Please don't. If you do, we're both going to be sorry for it all our lives."

With all her gentleness, Laurie Crosbie could be a very obstinate person on occasion. "I'm going to telephone Dr. Farr," she said, "and nothing can stop me. So don't try," she warned Tommy.

She left the room. They heard the tinkle of the box-bell as she cranked it. Then the door closed on her voice. A moment later she was back, pale but steady. She said, "Tommy, you never asked him if he would marry us."

"No."

"Why not?"

"Because I knew what he'd say."

"What do you think he'd have said?"

"Just what he's said to you just now," Tommy said desperately.

"But he didn't."

"What?!!"

"He said that he would marry us after the hearings, if I still felt the same way about you. What did he mean, Tommy? What did he mean?"

Tommy reached for his hat. "I told you we'd both be sorry all our lives," he said in a dulled and deadened voice, and went out of the room without farewell.

The Farr investigation was in its fourth day. Every nook and corner of the stately and dingy aldermanic chamber was jammed with humanity. The air was electric with anticipation of sensational developments, long delayed, and fetid with a blend of alien perfume and indigenous tobacco reek. A low platform, down front, held five comfortable chairs for the accommodation of the committee who were sitting in judgment.

Bribery, intimidation, cajolery, blackmail, and assorted influences, political, social and financial, had been invoked to secure the precious privilege of admittance to the spectacle. Opening night at the Metropolitan Opera with the de Reszkes and Calvé was as nothing to it.

"You couldn't get a seat for prayer or price," said Mrs. Steevens Parke in characteristic phrase.

By which she meant that less fortunate persons could not. With her unparalleled and sometimes unprincipled contrivance for obtaining what she wanted, she had possessed herself of two places in the front row, contiguous to the reporters' table. Her companion was Laurie Crosbie, whom she had brought at the girl's urgent plea and against her own better judgment, and who, as she confided to Dan Adriance in a clearly audible undertone, had "no more business here than a hummingbird in a privy." With a quarter of an hour before the call to order, Dan briefed Laurie on what had taken place at the previous sessions.

Most of the time had been taken up with recapitulation of the old and familiar affidavits gathered on the vice committee's rounds. Each had to be read at length and sworn to by Dr. Farr. Only once, thus far, had the clergyman been questioned as to his own part, by Abe Hummel, acting as counsel to the committee. Dan read from his notes.

Q. All these visits were for the purpose of collecting evidence, Dr. Farr?
A. Yes, sir.
Q. They had no other purpose or motive?

A. None.

Q. And your conduct and actions went no further than was essential to procure the evidence which you and your companions sought?

A. No, sir.

Q. You state this upon oath?

A. I do.

Laurie was just asking the reporter whether it was some kind of trap, when Dr. Farr entered the room with his counsel, Judge Cassard. Places below one end of the platform had been assigned to them. Laurie fixed her eyes upon the clergyman and murmured to Dan, "He looks dreadful."

Mrs. Parke asked, "Is he alarmed, do you think, Mr. Adriance?"

"No. He's ill," the reporter said.

"Then why do they make him come here?" Laurie cried. "I think it's outrageous."

"He wouldn't allow an adjournment. Anyway, it isn't serious. He had a tooth out this morning before coming here."

"Could I go and speak to him, Dan?"

"No, I wouldn't, Laurie."

"They can't really do anything to him, can they?"

The reporter's expression was unhappy. "Don't get your hopes too high. They're a tough lot. There's nothing too crooked for them to do. And Abe Hummel is a dirty fighter."

"Looks like an overdressed scorpion," was Grandma Parke's commentary.

"Of course, the committee is packed," Dan went on. "Four Tammany men and one lone Republican, put in for show. Bowen, the chairman, is a decent enough fellow, but he's got his orders from Fourteenth Street."

"Do you know what is coming on, Mr. Adriance?" Mrs. Parke asked.

"They've been holding back Etta Holmes. I think she'll be called first."

"She's the woman who kept the place they call the Bower, isn't she?" The Parke memory was good.

"Yes. She's the star performer. Next to Dr. Farr, of course. You're lucky to be in on the Big Show."

A burly, bright-eyed man with an air of importance crowded into a seat back of them. "That's Police Commissioner Brophy," the reporter whispered. "One of the Big Boys."

As the press table filled up, Laurie kept watch on the side entrance where the reporters were admitted. She leaned forward to Adriance again.

"Dan, where's Tommy?"

"I don't know."

"Isn't he going to be here?"

"No."

"Are you sure?"

"He told me he wasn't."

"Dr. Farr expects him."

"Are *you* sure?"

"He wants him, anyway. I'm sure of that much, because he telephoned me several times in the hope of locating him."

"Could you help?"

"No. I haven't seen him for a week. He's been acting strangely. Do you think——?"

Dan shushed her as the chairman entered and the call for order silenced the buzzing crowd. At a summons from the Chair, Judge Cassard and Lawyer Hummel advanced. There was a brief huddle. Chairman Bowen announced:

"Owing to the official duties of the next witness, the planned order of procedure will be altered. Will Perry Kent take the stand?"

A florid man of thirty-five, wearing graceful clothes and an outsize turquoise ring, stepped up to be sworn. In a musical voice he indentified himself as a mail carrier on Route Sixteen at the time of the since famous leapfrog party at Etta Holmes's place. He confirmed the date on the affidavit of the Farr vice committee recounting that event. The examination proceeded:

Q. You carried Route Sixteen?

A. Yes, sir.

Q. That comprises West Twenty-sixth Street between Sixth and Seventh Avenues?

A. That's correct.

Q. Are you familiar with the premises at No. 146?

A. I am. Etta Holmes's joint. The Bower.

Q. Did you on October seventeen deliver mail to that address?

A. Yes, sir. A registered parcel for Anne——

Q. You need not specify. Did you, as you mounted the steps to the doorway, meet anyone?

A. Yes, sir. A man coming out.

Q. Did you address him?

A. Yes, sir. I said, "How'd it go, old sport?" and he yawned and said "Whee-ew!"

Q. You addressed him as old sport?

A. Well, that's how he looked.

Q. Could you identify him if you saw him now?

A. For a ten-spot!

Q. Will Dr. Farr kindly stand up?

The clergyman got slowly to his feet. His face was deep-lined and grayish. It was a palpable effort for him to straighten to his full height. He wavered.

Chairman Bowen bent forward toward him. "Dr. Farr, are you sick, sir?"

The answer came, low but steady, "A momentary weakness only."

The official was not satisfied. "If you would like an adjournment, the committee would meet your wishes."

"I thank you for your consideration, sir, but I am quite capable of proceeding."

"At least, sit down." Dr. Farr did so. The Chair addressed the witness.

Q. You have seen this gentleman?

A. Yes. That's the one, all right.

Q. (By Mr. Hummel): Do you identify him as the individual whom you encountered as he was coming out of the Bower on the morning of October seventeen?

A. Pos-a-lootly. He's dressed soberer, but I'd swear to him across the Bowery.

Q. This encounter was on your regular morning delivery?

A. Yes, sir.

Q. And the hour?

A. Nine-fifteen, or nine-twenty, A.M.

JUDGE CASSARD (rising): Mr. Chairman, we have had the uncontroverted testimony of the affidavit, supported by the cabman who drove them, that Dr. Farr and Mr. Allen Hardwick left the Bower at approximately two A.M. Now we are confronted with a surprise witness, with the obvious intention of contradicting this. I ask for a recess, that I may consult my client.

LAWYER HUMMEL: I shall not, of course, oppose the request of my learned friend. But, in the interest of time-saving, may I suggest that I have supporting witnesses in this vital matter of the hour. Would not Judge Cassard prefer to hear this collateral evidence now?

This being agreed to, a succession of witnesses identified Dr. Farr as having been on the front steps or adjacent sidewalk of the Holmes place at the specified date and time: a street cleaner, a hotel clerk, a newsstand woman, and the assistant treasurer of a railroad. Judge Cassard declined to cross-examine. After consultation with the chairman, Mr. Hummel called:

"Will Mrs. Holmes please come forward?"

The new witness revealed herself as a quietly dressed woman of fifty, with a hoarse voice and a resentful manner. As she faced the committee, Alderman Duryea, the sole Republican member and a henchman of Boss Corbin, who had been sprawled lethargically in his padded chair thus far in the proceedings, straightened to attention. Lawyer Hummel was putting Etta Holmes through the formula of identification.

Q. Your occupation?
A. I keep a house of entertainment on West Twenty-sixth Street.
Q. (*By Alderman Duryea*): A disorderly house?
A. There's no quieter-run place in New York.
Q. By disorderly I mean a place run for the purpose of prostitution.
A. If you want to put it nasty, Alderman.
ALDERMAN DURYEA (*to the Chairman*): Mr. Chairman, I wish the record to show the character of the witness as bearing upon credibility.
MR. HUMMEL: There is no conflict on that, Alderman. May I proceed?
ALDERMAN DURYEA: Proceed.
Q. Now, Mrs. Holmes, I wish you to tell this committee the circumstances of the midnight call of two strangers on that October sixteenth.
A. There was a young feller and this older gent. They said they was in town for a good time. They bought the house.
Q. (*By Judge Cassard*): Bought the house? Is the committee to understand—
A. Took the place for the night. Shut to customers. They paid extra.
Q. Who paid?
A. The old gent with the mothy whiskers. (*Laughter.*)
THE CHAIRMAN: Kindly refrain from characterizations, Mrs. Holmes.
THE WITNESS: Well, I didn't know him from Adam. He had on a sassy shirt and floorwalker's pants and he had a sparkler in his tie like a headlight on the Erie, and when he said he was a businessman from Akron, Ohio, I believed him.
Q. Have you seen either of the visitors since?
A. That's the old cock over there. (*Pointing to Dr. Farr.*)
Q. Where were the callers after—er—buying the house?
A. In the red parlor.
Q. What occurred there?
A. Well, Minnie the Creole went over and sat on the old boy's knees and made a play for him. You know.
Q. Did he reciprocate?
A. Recip— Gee, no, Counselor! Not right there in public. (*Loud laughter in the chamber and cries of "Order! Order!"*)
Q. What did he do?
A. He drew away and looked dignified, but there was a gleam in his eyes like he was—
Q. No, no, Mrs. Holmes. You are not here to interpret ocular gleams.
A. Well, I ought to have suspicioned then. But I only spotted 'em for a couple of Ground-floor Johnnies.
Q. Perhaps you had better explain that term.
A. Ground-floor Johnny? Why, that's a guy that buys the wine but won't go upstairs.
Q. The visitors did not go upstairs?

A. Oh, sure! Later. When we put on the show.
Q. What was the nature of this show?
A. Leapfrog. Like it says in the affidavit.
Q. The visitors did not participate in the pastime?
A. No, they sat it out.
Q. What time did they leave?
A. Somewhere around two o'clock.
Q. (*By Judge Cassard*): As testified to by Dr. Farr and Allen Hardwick?
A. I guess so.
JUDGE CASSARD (*to the committee*): Then, there is no conflict here.
LAWYER HUMMEL: Just a moment, my friend. (*To the witness*): Did you have any conversation with either of them as they were leaving?
A. Yes, sir, with the old sport.
Q. Kindly refrain from using that term. If you mean Dr. Farr, you may repeat what he said.
A. He got me aside and said, "Don't close up. Tell Minnie I'll be back." (*Sensation in the chamber.*)
Q. And you replied?
A. I whispered in his ear, "Okay, old buck. Minnie'll be waiting." (*Murmurs of excitement, breaking out here and there into laughter and exclamations. A voice in a rear row: "Wait till the clouds roll by, Minnie; wait till the clouds roll by." Expulsion of the singer and fantasia by the Chairman's gavel.*)
Q. And did he, in fact, come back?
A. Yes, sir. Under an hour. (*Renewed outbreak. Threat of Chairman to clear the room.*) You see, he had to shake young Hardwick—
Q. No conclusions, Mrs. Holmes. Tell us only what you know.
A. I know he came back. I know Minnie was waiting up. I gave 'em the pink room. No extra charge.
Q. Do you know how long they remained there?
A. Until morning. Nine o'clock, like Sally says.
Q. Sally?
A. Yeah. The mailman. Sally in Our Alley. That's what the girls called him.
Q. Do you know the present whereabouts of Minnie the Creole?
A. Don't I wisht I did! She owes the house fifty dollars for a gown she got on tick.
Q. That is all. You may examine, Judge Cassard.
Q. (*By Judge Cassard*): How long have you been in the business of prostitution, Mrs. Holmes?
A. I didn't come here to be insulted.
THE CHAIR: Answer the question, Witness.
A. I don't even know as I'm in the business any more.
Q. When did you retire?
A. Retire, my foot! The cops would let us operate while this committee is sitting? Yeah, like hell!

Amidst roars of appreciative mirth from the floor and angry rebukes and threats from the committee, the witness haughtily withdrew. The chairman, consulting his watch, announced an hour's adjournment for luncheon.

So lively was the interest that even the sensation-hardened reporters lingered around the table for exchange of opinions. Laurie Crosbie, hoping for expert information, kept her seat and excused herself to Mrs. Parke, who had an invitation for both of them to lunch at India House, down in the Swamp only a short walk from City Hall, and famous as having the finest cuisine of any club in the city.

"Dan will take me somewhere," she said.

From what she could overhear, the general trend among the newspapermen was favorable to Dr. Farr. Lyman of the *Tribune,* temporarily detached from his editorial functions to report the *cause célèbre,* expressed an almost unanimous opinion.

"They've staged it like a criminal trial, with Dr. Farr as the accused, and what kind of case have they made? No jury would convict on it."

"They might recommend action by the Grand Jury, at that," Slaght of the *Herald* said.

"I can't imagine what the charge would be."

"Corrupting the morals of a hooker." Willy Willis of the *Sun* chuckled.

"The whole case rests on whorehouse testimony," Eugene Wood of the *World* pointed out. "Who's going to take the evidence of a prostitute against the reputation and character of a man like Dr. Farr?"

"There's those nine-o'clock witnesses, though," said Arthur Greaves of the *Times.*

"A sleazy lot," the *World* man said. "I'd like to run down their records."

"No time," Willis said. He turned to Adriance. "What do you think, Dan?"

The *Star* man hesitated. His face was drawn. "This show isn't over yet," he said.

"Think Abe has something up his sleeve?" Williams asked.

Dan said, "I'm not betting either way."

He got up and joined the waiting Laurie.

"There isn't too much time," he said. "We might walk around to Mouquin's in Fulton Street. That's near and good."

As they went out together, the girl said, "I can't understand it. All those witnesses. They can't all be mistaken."

"No, but they can all lie," Dan replied. "Abe Hummel's perjury bureau is in good working order."

"You mean they're bribed?" she said incredulously. "Surely not the railroad man. Or the mail carrier."

"More likely Little Abe has some hold over them. Maybe the rail-road treasurer has had his hand in the till and been dumb enough to confide his case to Howe and Hummel. That would make it hard for him to decline a pressing invitation to testify. As for the gent with the turquoise ring, he'd be vulnerable for reasons that are plain enough, though you wouldn't understand them."

They lunched lightly, hurried back, and were walking through a corridor toward the aldermanic chambers when a door opened and two men, emerging from an office, almost ran into them.

One was Tommy Howatt. He stopped dead. The other, a minor official of the Board, in whose office Tommy had been, said, "So long," and passed on.

Laurie cried, "Oh, Tommy, I'm so glad!"

"Hello, Laurie," he returned heavily. "I expected this."

Dan said, "I thought you were going to be among those absent."

Tommy muttered, "Brophy's men got me. Come inside. We can't talk here." He led the way back into the office.

"Been hiding out?" the *Star* man asked.

"I tried to. They had me tailed."

"Are they putting you on the stand?"

"Whaddaya think they brought me here for?" Tommy retorted bitterly. "To sing 'The Star-Spangled Banner'?"

"Does Dr. Farr know you're here?" the girl asked.

"No."

"Oh, Tommy! He'll be so relieved. He's been so anxious."

"Don't you think he ought to be told?" Dan put in.

"Hell, no!" His expression changed to one of weary assent. "Yeah. Go ahead and tell him. It makes no odds now." Laurie looked at him in wonder.

As the door closed behind Dan, the girl went to Tommy and lifted both hands to his shoulders.

"I've been so worried about you, darling." Her voice became confident, happy. "You are going to testify, aren't you?"

"Yeah. I'm going to testify."

"Dr. Farr is relying on you."

"How much do you know about this, Laurie?"

"Only that there is something you can tell that will clear up everything. When do you go on?"

"Next witness but one."

Under her hands he was stiff as a wooden Indian. His eyes did not meet hers. She relaxed her hold. Her arms fell to her sides.

"I've kept telling Dr. Farr that you'd be here," she said, animation ebbing from her voice. "It's all right, isn't it, Tommy?"

"Laurie, will you do something for me?"

"What is it, Tommy?"

"Go home."

"Go home?" She faltered.

"Yeah. Get outa here."

She said wonderingly, "You don't want me to be here when you are called?"

"No, I want you to go home."

"You're not going to testify for Dr. Farr?" Now the words were drawn out, slowly, agonizingly.

"Look—Laurie!"

"You—you're not going to testify against him!"

"It ain't that I want to," he groaned.

Her face was drained of life, of color, even of beauty. She breathed out, "You are! And he trusted you. He thought you were his friend."

"Laurie. For Chrissake!"

Still in that dead, even tone she went on, "You would have married me. You would have got Dr. Farr to marry us and next day you would have come into court and lied and betrayed and ruined him."

"Laurie, for Chrissake, go home."

"No. I'll not go home. I'll be there to see it, or I'll never be able to believe it. I'll be there where you can't help but see me. I'll be there, willing you not to do it, praying that you won't do it. I'm going back now."

"Okay, sister. If that's the way you wanta play it. So long. See you in the morgue."

She was only a minute late in regaining her place. Through all her wrath and bewilderment and misery she felt still a fearful curiosity as to what malign threat was building up against Dr. Farr: that threat which Tommy could avert. Could, but incomprehensibly would not. Why? Why? Why?—she asked herself in anguish.

With the resumption of the session, a new witness was in evidence, a dark, handsome young fellow who, with a confident smile, identified himself as Dominick Casera, a free-lance photographer who had been present at the Bower on the specified night of October 16-17. Mr. Hummel proceeded with the examination.

Q. You were there in your professional capacity?

A. That's right. With my camera.

Q. You took a photograph?

A. Yes, sir.

Q. (*Handing him an imperial-size cardboard*): Is this it?

A. That's the article. (*It is offered in evidence.*)

JUDGE CASSARD: I should like to see it.

THE CHAIRMAN: In a moment. (*Passes the exhibit around the committee, whose faces, as they consider it, evince varying phases of astonishment and shock.*) For the information of the full Board, I will state that this photograph shows Dr. Farr and a woman—

JUDGE CASSARD (*sharply*): I object, Mr. Chairman. There is no evidence that the photograph represents Dr. Farr.

THE CHAIRMAN: Your point is well taken, sir. The chair apologizes. The photograph shows a man and a woman in a state of nudity, seated side by side on the edge of a bed.

A VOICE FROM THE FLOOR: Mr. Chairman, is not this Board to be allowed to view the exhibit?

THE CHAIRMAN: Alderman Dillard, the character of the photograph is such that it is not proper for public exhibition. (*Murmurs of discontent and resentment.*)

JUDGE CASSARD: I request again that I be permitted to examine it.

THE CHAIRMAN: Certainly. (*Hands the imperial to the lawyer, who, with his client, bends over it in study.*) Barring objection, it will be received and marked in evidence.

Q. (*By Mr. Hummel*): Mr. Casera, can you state who the woman is?

A. Minnie the Creole.

Q. Could you identify her companion?

A. Yes, sir.

Q. Will Dr. Farr kindly rise? Is that the man represented in the photograph?

A. It sure is. (*Sensation.*)

Q. You are quite certain?

A. If it ain't, I'm the Statue of Liberty. (*Laughter.*)

Q. (*By Judge Cassard*): You are a free-lance?

A. Yes, sir.

Q. Do you practice your art mainly in brothels?

A. I do business wherever I can.

Q. And you sell these pictures?

A. Sure. They're for sale. I'm a businessman.

Q. For sale under pressure of blackmail?

A. Nah. Nothing like that.

Q. For what purpose are they sold—or, rather, bought?

A. Well, souvenirs. After a night on the loose, a guy likes to have something to show his friends privately what a hell of a fella he is. (*Laughter.*)

Q. I see. And did you attempt to sell this exhibit to its subject?

A. No.

Q. Why not?

A. He didn't look like a good prospect. Besides, he didn't even know it was being taken.

Q. Ah! The camera was concealed?

A. Yes, sir. I was shooting through a panel. He couldn't see me.

Q. What disposition was made of the photograph?

A. I gave it to Etta—Mrs. Holmes.

Q. For a price?

A. No, sir. For a favor.
Q. Do you know why she wished to have it?
A. No; I didn't ask her.

After the examination was concluded, there was a pause while Judge Cassard and his client engaged in a conversation which presently took on the aspect of a spirited debate. It ended with a declaration by Dr. Farr so emphatic in tone that it was audible to the entire committee.

"No, sir. No adjournment. I wish this matter settled here and now. I have no fear as to the outcome."

Looking deeply troubled, Judge Cassard addressed the chairman.

"Mr. Chairman, we are informed of the presence of a prospective witness whose testimony may be vital to our case. I was about to request an adjournment for consultation, but my client refuses to consider it. He is confident that the evidence adduced by this witness regarding the photograph, Exhibit A, will clear him beyond the shadow of a doubt. May I ask my learned opponent whether he intends to call Mr. Thomas Howatt of the *Police Gazette?*"

"Such was my intention," the little lawyer returned blandly. "But in view of Dr. Farr's apparent foreknowledge and declared confidence, you may call Mr. Howatt as your witness if you so desire."

Wood of the *World* said in his neighbor's ear, "Did I hear the sound of a steel trap being set?"

Judge Cassard called, "Will Thomas Howatt take the stand?"

Tommy pushed himself up from his chair and moved forward. His eyes were set in a stare, straight before him. His face was rigid.

Mrs. Parke whispered to Laurie, "If ever I saw a damned soul!"

After the ritual of name, age, and occupation, the judge got down to essentials.

Q. Mr. Howatt, have you ever taken a photograph of Dr. Brockholst Farr?
A. Yes, sir.
Q. Please state the occasion.
A. A Sunday-school picnic on the Herrenden estate.
Q. What was the date?
A. June a year ago.
Q. What kind of camera did you use?
A. An Eastman Kodak.
Q. The picture so taken was a snapshot, so-called?
A. Yes, sir.
Q. Can you produce the original?
A. No, sir. It has been lost.
Q. That is most unfortunate. Can you produce the film?
A. No, sir, I destroyed it.

Q. Why did you do that?

A. I thought the Dominie—I mean Dr. Farr—would want me to. He's got a down on pictures of himself. Told me he never had any taken since he was in college.

Q. I see. Have you a clear recollection, an accurate mental picture of the Kodak photograph taken by you?

A. Yes, sir.

Q. Mr. Howatt, we have reason to believe that your snapshot has been made the basis of a vicious photographic forgery, mysterious in method—

MR. HUMMEL (*shouting*): No! No! I object, Mr. Chairman, I object. This is sheer, unwarranted, outrageous assumption.

JUDGE CASSARD: Very well. Withdrawn. Mr. Howatt, you have testified to having a clear recollection of the snapshot taken at the picnic two years ago. I now show you Exhibit A. (*Covering with a square of paper the lower part of the imperial, thus exposing only the head and the shoulders of the figures.*) In part, only, if there is no objection.

MR. HUMMEL (*after a slight hesitation*): None.

Q. I ask you, Mr. Howatt, do you recognize the face of the man in this exhibit?

A. I do.

Q. Is it that of Dr. Brockholst Farr?

A. It is.

Q. Have you, to the best of your knowledge and belief, ever seen that photograph—that representation of Dr. Farr—or its reasonable and recognizable facsimile, and, if so, when and where?

A. I have never seen it before. (*A swelling murmur of excitement through the audience. Rap of the Chairman's gavel. "Order! Order!"*)

Q. Mr. Howatt, you are here under your solemn oath. Do you state to this committee that this exhibit is not—

MR. HUMMEL: Is my learned friend attempting to impugn or to intimidate his witness?

Q. Do you deny that you recognize the photograph of Dr. Farr in this infamous picture as identical with the snapshot which you, yourself, took?

A. I told you already, I never seen—never saw that picture before.

A feminine voice from the first row: "Oh! Oh! How wicked!"

THE CHAIRMAN: Officer, remove that young lady. (*Laughter, jeers, and protests as the offender is led out.*)

JUDGE CASSARD (*after a moment's consultation with his client*): Your witness, Mr. Hummel.

Q. (*By Mr. Hummel*): Mr. Howatt, I wish to make this important point unmistakably clear to the committee. Examining the exhibit in your hands, tell us: does that picture of Dr. Farr resemble in any identifiable way the snapshot which you took?

A. No, sir, it does not.

Q. So that the Kodak could not possibly have been used as the basis for the photograph?

A. No, sir.

The witness stirred restlessly in his seat. Plainly, he wished nothing so much as to be finished with this inquisition. The audience was hushed, waiting for any further question, while the little lawyer seemed uncertain as to whether to push the examination any further. As he glanced at the notes before him, a deep and quiet voice, raised in the cadence of prayer, said:

"May God forgive him!"

Tommy said hoarsely, "Lemme outa here!" and seemed to be striving for further utterance, but was drowned out by the angry protests of the committee, through which the Chairman could be dimly heard, ejaculating, "Gross impropriety! Gross impropriety!" The lawyer charged toward Dr. Farr like a small and infuriate billy goat, his face alight with triumph, his eyes slitted with malice. He shouted:

"If the defendant—if Dr. Farr is so anxious to shoot off his mouth, Mr. Chairman, let him take the stand again. Step down, Howatt. Don't leave the court. Step up, Farr—I beg your pardon, Reverend Doctor Farr. You know where the stand is, I believe. You've been there before. You're still under oath. Don't forget that. Step up and speak up, Reverend Farr, D.D."

The clergyman staggered a little as he started forward, but shook off his counsel's hand. His face was sad and peaceful and unafraid as he sat down, turning to the little lawyer and awaiting the attack. Mr. Hummel had snatched the imperial away from the retiring witness, and now thrust it with quick, little jabs, like dagger feints, toward the tall figure in the chair, vociferating:

"Look at this again! Look at it and deny it if you can. You, the pillar of piety, who, to sate his own base lusts, organized a vice-investigating committee for the suppression of the very corruptions in which you, yourself, wallow. A hirer of women's bodies. A patron of nude and licentious revels, a frequenter of resorts so degraded that I refrain from soiling the records with evidence about them. Out of your own mouth I convict you. You sought to invoke the friendship and affection of this incorruptible and upright young man, the last witness, and persuade him to deny the truth of the camera, the camera that never lies, that cannot lie. What have you to say in the light of your own witness's testimony that exposes your absurd and trumped-up hints of a forged photograph? Come, Reverend Doctor, sir! There must be some explanation, some further trickery at your command. What is it?"

As the tirade went on, Tommy had slumped deep into his chair, and sat, quivering at every thrust directed by the little lawyer at his helpless victim. Dr. Farr's suffering look, turned now here, now there, as if seeking support where there was only enmity and derision, came to rest upon his betrayer. He raised his arm and pointed.

"I think my young friend can answer that better than I," he said.

"You are not satisfied with the answer he has already given?" the lawyer taunted.

"No. Nor, I think, is he." The minister leaned forward to address directly the huddled form below him. His tone was gentle as he said, "Would you not be well advised, Thomas, to reconsider?"

The phrase, made lovingly familiar to memory by many an unforgotten crisis of the checkerboard, now uttered with a touch of the old friendly raillery, was too much for Tommy's resolution. He uttered one gasping sob, then sprang from his chair, flinging his clenched fists above his head in an insensate fury of defiance.

"I lied! I lied! God damn my soul, I lied!" he yelled. "Lemme back there. Lemme on the stand. I'll tell the truth now, and hell, itself, won't stop me."

Abe Hummel, beside himself with wrath, rushed at him. "I saw him signal you," he yelped. "I saw your minister-friend give you the high sign. Collusion! Perjury! You admit it!"

"Sure, I admit it. And who got me to do it?"

Bedlam had broken loose. People left their seats and jammed forward. The chairman's frantic gavel hammered, unheeded. Police Commissioner Brophy bulled through the intervening mass and grabbed Tommy by the shoulder.

"You're under arrest," he growled, and directed two officers, who had followed in his wake, "Throw him in the can."

Tommy had time for one Parthian shot as he was hustled away. Thrusting his face up under the big official's, he snarled, "I got plenty more to tell. Don't you make any false moves."

It was a shot in the dark, but Tommy noted with satisfaction the shadow of doubt on the beefy face before him.

Something like order having been restored, Lawyer Hummel returned to the attack.

"Don't think I didn't see you," he said savagely to the witness. "Contempt of this committee, that's what it is. You made a sign to Howatt, a private sign."

"That is not true, sir."

"It is true—true—true! What hold have you over that unfortunate young man? What unholy and corrupt pact exists between you, enabling you to bend him to your will?"

The witness made no reply. He seemed to be gazing far into space above his questioner's head.

"No reply?" the lawyer pressed. "No apology for so blatant a disregard—" The question died. The speaker called shrilly, "Is there a doctor here? Quick!"

The little man made a valiant attempt to bolster the massive form from toppling. It was too much for his powers. Both plunged to the floor as a physician burst through the encircling crowd.

42

The back room of the *Star* office, ten days after the aldermanic session on Dr. Brockholst Farr had come to so abrupt and dramatic an end. Ramsey Kelly and his top reporter were in private consultation.

"Is it official?" the city editor asked. "Will Dr. Farr recover from the stroke?"

"Yes," Dan Adriance replied. "But it wasn't a stroke."

"What was it, then?"

"Nervous collapse plus the concussion from his fall."

"He'll be able to preach again?"

"Not in the Old Stone Church," Dan said significantly.

"I wouldn't have thought that the trustees would fire him."

"They didn't. They couldn't. Haven't got the authority. They regretfully announced his resignation, due to ill health."

"Forced resignation, eh? What were his friends doing?"

"I doubt if he actually resigned. I doubt if he even knows of it. A handful of the faithful did stand by him, led by Harrison M. Perley, who got up from a sickbed to go to the meeting, and I guess it finished him. He's dying of pneumonia, I understand."

"I'll put a man on him. Why didn't they just fire Farr instead of this beating about the bush?"

"You don't understand the Presbyterian setup. The only way of getting rid of an undesirable legally is to cite him before the Presbytery and prefer charges."

"I see. Will he put up a fight?"

"I doubt it. He knows that it would split the church. He's hopelessly discredited, and his fight with him."

"In spite of young Howatt's disclaimer?"

"They've pretty well squelched that. What is going to stick in the public mind is that damnable photograph. People believe what they see rather than what they hear. That wretched fake has been privately circulated all around town. Privately! My God!"

"You're satisfied it *is* a fake?"

362

"Of course it's a fake. But nobody can prove it. It's too damn expert."

"There are points about that Howatt business that I don't get. Where is he?"

"In jail."

"Could you get to him?"

"Nobody can. The police are holding him incommunicado."

"They can't hold him long, can they? What's the charge? Perjury, I suppose."

"That's where Brophy has been smart. It's perjury, but that isn't all. They're holding him for investigation into his mental condition. Get it? You can guess what a police surgeon will find upon due examination."

"Why, that's outrageous. How long can they hold him on that?"

"Indefinitely. But maybe they'll make a deal with him. We're running into a mayoralty campaign next year, remember, and the Good Government lot are pretty active. If Tommy Howatt should tell all he knows, Brophy and Company might face some pretty nasty questions."

"He's got something on Brophy, then?"

"Well, I think so. But I don't know what. Whether he has or not, Brophy is afraid he has, which might be just as useful."

"Then why hasn't he used it?"

"Because Brophy has a hold on *him*. So it's likely to figure out to a deadlock. If one man keeps mum, the other does likewise."

There was a silence. Mr. Kelly drummed idly on the wooden arm of his chair. Presently he said with apparent irrelevance, "Mrs. Crosbie and her daughter have sailed for Europe, I believe."

"So I have heard," returned the reporter in a tone which suggested that pursuit of the topic would be unprofitable.

"Do you look for any immediate developments in the Farr case?"

"No."

"Well, watch it."

It was an October evening the following year in the *Police Gazette* office. The forms were closed. Several of the staff, regular and emergency, still sober, were sitting about waiting for their ten-dollar bills. From Richard K. Fox's private office could be heard a desultory dialogue, the other party to which was a club-footed stranger of furtively prosperous aspect who had called late in the afternoon, asking for Tommy Howatt. Informed that Tommy was unavailable, he said that he had something to offer the *Police Gazette,* and could he see Mr. Fox?

He could. The two were closeted for a half hour, when the sanctum door was flung open and the editor's florid and handsome face appeared. It was alight with excitement.

"Where's the Deacon?"

"Right here, Chief," responded Deacon Waldo, scurrying out from behind a cabinet.

"What have we got in the morgue on Brockholst Farr?"

"Plenty."

"Fetch it in."

"All of it?"

"Every blessed word."

"It'll take time to get it in order."

"Never mind the order. Bring it in as is. And, Deacon—"

"Yes, Chief?"

"Hold the boys. All of 'em. Savvy?"

"Okay, Chief."

The old man bustled off to the record room.

Enders, of the staff, gazed after him, yawned, stretched, and said lazily, "Hellfire Farr? Thought he was dead."

"Might as well be," said Bill Strong. "Haven't seen him in a headline since the Old Stone Church kicked him out. That's over a year ago now."

"Maybe he's staging a comeback," Doug Morris suggested. "The Good Government folks could use him in this mayoralty campaign."

"Damaged goods," Spunk Wood said. "He cuts no ice now."

"The goo-goos haven't got a look-in," Terhune declared. "Tammany Hall will sweep the city."

"Good thing, too," Enders grunted. "To hell with reform." He shifted his coat lapel to exhibit a campaign button inscribed with this edifying sentiment.

"What ever did happen to old Farr anyway?" Stenny White asked.

"Ask Saqui."

A pudgy, sore-eyed little man looked up from his doodling. Saqui Smith, a recruit from the flimsies, was a walking library of information on local matters.

"Farr?" he said. "Brockholst Farr? Missionary. North woods. Lumber camps."

"Huh! I can't see the ex-minister of the swell Old Stone Church making a hit with a bunch of tough lumberjacks," Enders sneered.

"There you're wrong," Saqui replied. "They think the more of him, because they take him for a guy that knows the ropes. 'Been through it, himself, the old sport,' they say, and they open up to him as a fellow sinner."

"And that's where he's been all this time?" White asked.

"Ever since he got well."

Deacon Waldo, with a box full of clippings, passed the group and vanished into Mr. Fox's office. When he reappeared they held him up for information.

"Who's the bozo with the boss?" Morris asked.

"Name of Amster. Never saw him before."

"Jake Amster?" Saqui Smith asked. The Deacon nodded. "Top-line green-goods operator," Saqui said.

Half an hour passed. Again the Deacon was summoned inside. He emerged on the jump. Breathlessly he asked, "Saqui, where can we reach Dr. Farr?"

"Blue Mountain Lake post office, last I heard."

"Could you find him?"

"Guess so. What for?"

"Get going. Here's fifty. Wire for more if you need it. Only, get Farr and fetch him back if you have to chloroform him."

"Okay. But what's the big idea?"

"The boss'll brief you. Bill"—turning to Strong—"call up Good Government headquarters."

"Pretty late. The goo-goos are too discouraged to work long hours on a lost cause."

"Ring up some of the leaders, then. Hatfield. Wright. Stevens. Anybody."

"If you'll tell me what the hell—"

"Enders, ring up the *Star* office. Get Dan Adriance around here on the double. R.K. wants him for the lead story."

"Story? What story, for Chrissake? What's stirrin' up all the mystery? Spill it, you old craphead."

"Here's the chief. He'll give it to you. All you need to know."

Mr. Fox appeared, ushering out the stranger with a hand on his shoulder. "Be here at nine tomorrow morning. The money will be ready," the employes heard their boss say. He turned to them and spoke.

"That's Jake Amster. He's in bad trouble. Got to skip the country. Came in to sell me a 'con' piece: 'Confessions of a Crack Counterfeiter.' Wanted a thousand. Not worth more than two hundred, I told him. That wouldn't do; had to have the thousand. There was another article, but it was dynamite. Brockholst Farr's name came out. Then he spilled it. That famous photograph was a fake, a lomack, and he was the expert who doctored it."

He paused. Someone said, "Wow!" in awestruck accents.

"Was that worth a thousand, he wanted to know," the editor continued. "I almost kissed him. So we're ripping the mag wide open. And we're ripping the town wide open. All that you boys have to do is pitch in and do the darndest, quickest remake on record. There'll be a midnight feed and an extra ten-spot all around. Not a man leaves the building until the rag is put to bed. I'm taking no chances of a leak. That's all."

He returned to the inner room. Deacon Waldo followed him with a face of trouble. "Have you thought what this is going to do, Boss?" he asked.

"Show up every newspaper in New York."

"Yeah. But politically?"

"Earthquake."

"That's what I figure. But won't it be playing right into the goo-goos' hands?"

"What's that got to do with it?"

The Deacon stared. "We're Tammany, aren't we?"

"We're the *National Police Gazette* and we've got the biggest story of the year."

The old man shook a bewildered head. "I don't get you, R.K. It's only ten days to election, and—"

"That's what is going to give the story its whoopdelawhoop."

"You think it might turn the election?"

"It will if Dr. Farr gets back into it."

"Yes; but will he?"

"The letter I've given Saqui Smith for delivery to him ought to fetch him. You know the kind of show he can put on."

"I don't believe he could make it stick."

"Then you're a fool. Dr. Farr is coming back as a martyr, much more so than young Hardwick—and look what a play they made with that. Here's the Doctor, turned out of his church, abandoned by his friends, all but a few, ditched by Boss Corbin, shamed and disgraced—and we're showing it up as the dirtiest plot in history. Why, Deacon, he'll be wearing a halo a rod wide. And we're the lads that hung it on him."

"If it isn't too late."

"Hundred to one on it. Ten days isn't much time, but it'll do. This'll put new life into the Good Government people. You'll see things whiz, Deacon."

"It's a queer turn, though, Chief, the *P.G.* showing up Tammany."

The rubicund face darkened. "I warned those fools they were on the wrong track. A man with the head-shape of Dr. Farr *couldn't* be what they claimed. But would they any of 'em listen to me? Crocker? Byrnes? Brophy? No. They had Farr where they wanted him, and the whole movement with him. To Hell with Reform, huh? It's a hot slogan. They'll be tooting it out of the other side of their mouths, come next week Wednesday. Sit tight. We'll see what we'll see. Let's get to work."

Clark's restaurant at four-fifteen A.M. of Election Night. An all-night session had been arranged, in anticipation of a joyous celebration by the Tenderloin elite. The patronage was disappointing. Only a handful of patrons were at the tables, and their visages were far from festive.

The feminine regulars were grouped at the rear long table. Several were fuddled if not absolutely drunk. All were buying their own sours. Above their heads spread a banner inscribed in scarlet letters:

TO HELL WITH REFORM

The same sentiment appeared variously upon dress fronts, brassards, and bone buttons, sported by the flower of the district. In rebuttal, a special edition of the *World,* rumpled upon the table, indicated a startling reversal of hopes. The Tammany Mayor, running for re-election, was lagging dismally far behind in the early returns. Long Distance Lou crumpled the sheet in her two white hands and hurled it to the floor.

"It's a lie," she snarled. "I wouldn't believe that rag on oath."

"I'd hate to," Little Sue said. "Think of New York with a goo-goo mayor. Clamtown-on-the-Pike."

"Prayer meetings on the Broadway corners," Ollie the Sophomore added.

Oscar, the scarred waiter, was appealed to. "It don't look too good," he said. "But it's early yet. Mr. Adriance will have the low-down when he gets here."

"Is Handsome Dan coming in?" Lou asked.

"Just phoned from the Tenderloin Club to order a T-bone steak," the waiter answered. "I'll have to hold the cook." He went out.

Blonde Annabel was still concerned with the political crisis. "It's all that bastard of a parson," she said in her refined accents. "Shooting his gab all over town."

"I heard him Saturday night," Little Sue said. "Madison Square. Whoopsie! Does he sock it to 'em!"

"Pity that bullet missed him," Gwendolyn remarked.

"Was that Willie Frye took the pot shot at him?" Lou asked.

"Nah; Willie was already in jail."

"And Bernie Schmidt has flew the coop."

"So has Big Boy Brophy. Read the *Pinky* and bought a railroad ticket."

"They say Abie Hummel is going to be indicted."

"Don't you believe it. Little Abie is too slick for 'em."

"I hear Etta Holmes hit the blue bottle."

"So they say. She's in St. Vincent's."

"There'll be plenty others. Better that than panhandling."

"Yeah. How's a sportin' lady to make her living with things the way they are now?"

"Streetwalking on Brooklyn Bridge," Ollie suggested bitterly.

"Or turn honest woikin' goil," Little Sue snorted.

"Three dollars a week, pay rent on your sewing machine, and try to find air to breathe in an Avenue A loft," Gwendolyn contributed. "*I* should turn respectable!"

Jenny gave expression to the general gloom. "Line for Potter's Field forms on this side."

"Aw, rats!" said Annabel, who was prone to look at the brighter side. "They've closed the Tenderloin before. It didn't stick."

"That was Hellfire Farr's doings, too," Lou recalled.

"Yeah. And how long did it last?"

"But this time he'll have the goddam reform bunch in the City Hall to back him," Ollie pointed out.

"Thumbs up; thumbs down," Gwendolyn said. "They won't last. . . . Well, look who's here. Welcome back to the mainland, Jerry."

The cordial greeting was a delicate reference to the Island, where Jerry the Monkey-face had just completed a six-month term in the matter of a diamond stud, which a Cincinnati grain-and-feed merchant claimed (and proved in court) had been extracted from his shirt while he slumbered in the girl's hospitable bed. The company now clustered around to celebrate the exile's restoration to freedom. She was hungry for news.

"Not much of a bunch here tonight," she observed. "Where's Cora?"

"Croaked," Sue answered with a realistically hollow cough.

"Oh, gee! Well, Bella? I had a coupla postals from her in stir. Foreign stamps."

"Yep. She lit out with a Mex."

"Did Nita stick it? I'll bet she's back."

"You lose. She's got a kid. Doctor Farr Cabral is the name."

"After Old Hellfire? I hear he's back in circulation. How come?"

There were a dozen contributions to the symposium of information elicited by the question.

"The *Pinky* did it, you say?" Jerry marveled. "Ain't that something! Tommy Howatt, huh?"

"Not so as you could notice it! Tommy got the boot as soon as he got sprung."

"From the *Pinky?* Whatcha givin' us?"

"It was all mixed in with the Farr business," Sue said. "I never did get the straight of it. They say R. K. Fox gave him a hell of a going-over."

"What's he doing now?"

"Turn at the Imperial. Had a contract waiting for him. Tenderloin Tommy in his Songfest of Grave, Gay, and Giddy."

The returned exile searched her memory. "What about that millionaire Society bud he was going to marry?"

"Got the boot there, too," Gwendolyn said.

"Yep," Little Sue confirmed. "The lovely Laurie told him to go chalk the sidewalk and play potsy."

"Ah-h-h-h, he was only after her bankroll, anyway," the cynical Annabel drawled.

"That's what he tried to put over," Jenny said. "Couldn't let on that any girl on earth would ditch *him.* Tommy has his pride, he has."

"I heard him pull that bluff about its being her money he was after," Gwendolyn put in. "And then what does he do? Busts right out cryin' into his beer."

"Must have been spiffed."

"He did hit it up pretty heavy for a while. Didn't help any, I guess. Tommy never was a natural boozer, anyway."

"What did the Society beauty do? Marry somebody else?" Jerry asked.

"Living in Europe, they say," Ollie said. "Here's Handsome Dan, now. He'll know. But somebody else can have the job of asking him."

The *Star* reporter was hailed by a feminine chorus summoning him to the communal table, local etiquette having been relaxed for this special occasion. He found a place between Jerry and Lou, and ordered drinks around.

"The game is up, girls," he announced. "Tammany is licked. I win a few dollars," he added, with a grin.

"You don't need 'em, you lucky bum." Lou chuckled. "How's the show going?"

"We won't run *Ben Hur* off the boards, but the S.R.O. sign is still up."

Ollie obligingly explained to Jerry that Dan Adriance's farce, *Both Ends Against the Middle,* was filling Wallack's. To the playwright she said, "Jerry, here, was asking about Tommy Howatt. Why is he out of the *Pinky?*"

"R. K. Fox fired him. Personal reasons."

"How about his swell sweetie?" Gwendolyn was half drunk or she would never have ventured the question. Respectable women were not regarded as proper subjects for public mention at Clark's.

"Clam up, Gwen," Ollie warned under her breath.

Dan's expression became aloof. "I don't know what you are talking about," he said.

The girl was not thus easily to be diverted. "Sure you do. The one he was all set to marry. I hear she's living in Europe. Is that right?"

"Address it to the Question and Answer column," Dan growled.

With intent to direct the conversation into safer channels, Ollie asked, "How much do you think Old Hellfire had to do with the upset, Dan?"

"He was ninety-nine percent of it. You never saw anything like his meetings. The crowds were ready to march on the City Hall if he had let 'em."

"Will his church take him back?"

"In a minute, they would! He'll never go back."

Newsboys appeared with early editions: *Sun, Times, Press, Star,* and others. All confirmed the bad news. The waiter bustled about suggestively.

"Any more orders, ladies and gents?"

No response. Oscar cleared his throat and delivered a historic announcement: "Starting tomorrow, no drinks served in this place after one A.M."

Clark's closed with a groan.

Letter of November tenth, from Daniel Adriance to Miss Laura Crosbie, The Berkeley, London, N.W., England:

You ask my advice, Laurie. Here it is. Come back. That is what you want me to say, isn't it? That is what you intend to do, with or without my advice, because you cannot help yourself.

Do I think that you will be happy with Tommy? No; probably not. Not for long, at least. But you will never be happy without him. That is a certainty. Where there is only one chance, take it. You might win. The other way is a sure loss.

You say you know now why Tommy had to testify against Dr. Farr. You know, too, how he tried to make amends. His attempt was too late to undo all the harm. But, when it came to the showdown, he did his best. The Dominie gives him credit for that. The Dominie has forgiven him; believes him to be a regenerate character. The Dominie is an incorrigible optimist. Yet, he might be right. There is always the possibility of change. Tommy might go straight.

If anyone could bring about that metamorphosis, it would be you. You have the courage and the character. It is worth the trial. There is not so much happiness lying around loose in this mischance of a world of ours that any of us can afford to pass up even the longest odds.

And so, my dear, I say—come back.

Note in *Town Topics:*

The Old Stone Church on the Sunday morning after the election. Never, not even in the days when any utterance of Brockholst Farr's was a front-page "must" for the metropolitan newspapers, had there been such a pressure for places. From his gallery press seat Dan Adriance marveled at the uncanny hush that held the vast congregation in a rigor of attention.

In the body of the church one vacant pew was marked by a wreath of white lilies. It was a memorial to Harrison M. Perley, the trustee who, unable to save his friend and pastor from the crowning disgrace of desertion by his church, had died in the desperate and gallant defense.

The sermon was over. The gaunt, knob-jointed frame of the guest-clergyman had moved forth from behind the pulpit to shamble to the front of the rostrum. The face, haggard and sorrowful and peaceful, brooded over the hushed and grief-stricken gathering for a long moment before the deep-toned music of the spoken word filled the spaces.

"So, this is farewell to the church that I have loved. I go back to my simple duties with simple-hearted men. It is my farewell to this great and ruthless city, this mighty juggernaut which has destroyed so much that is dear to me.

"I have seen the hope and happiness of young lives blighted. I have watched brave and true spirits break under the stress. Because of what I have been forced to do by my duty as I saw it, households have been disrupted, family bonds sundered. For my part in all this, I humbly ask your forgiveness. In the words of a far greater man of God, I could not do otherwise.

"Yet there have been times when I have fathomed the blackest depths of despair, contemplating what has seemed the waste and anguish wrought in a lost cause. We know now that the cause was not lost; that the travail was not for nothing. Yet the sorrow remains.

"Men die. Lives are ruined. The city endures. Out of those tragic sacrifices has risen the spirit of victory. The powers of darkness are in retreat. But they are not destroyed. Let none who hear me be tempted to believe that our triumph is more than temporary and unsure. The enemy will gather their forces for attack time and time again.

"Righteousness, my dear ones, is never a straight path upward. It is an eternal spiral, now rising, now descending. But this much we can cherish to our souls with firm confidence, that never again will this mighty and terrible city of ours be as evil as it has been. Thus and thus only are the sufferings, the tragedy, the wreckage of lives and hopes justified to God and man.

"You are the guardians of the city's future. This is the task, the test, the trust that I impose upon you. May God, in his infinite mercy, bless and uphold you."

ABOUT THE AUTHOR

SAMUEL HOPKINS ADAMS began writing books in the early 1900's and wrote so many, of such variety, that an exact count is difficult. It is known, however, that TENDERLOIN is at least his fifty-fifth book. Soon after his graduation from Hamilton College in 1891, he went to New York City and became a reporter on the *New York Sun,* where he acquired much of the first-hand knowledge he used to such happy advantage in writing TENDERLOIN more than fifty years later. After nine years on the *Sun,* he joined the staff of *McClure's Magazine.* He became interested in medical science and public health, out of which grew his famous series of articles in *Collier's Weekly* exposing patent medicine quackery, a series that is credited with furthering the passage of the first Pure Food and Drug Act. At the same time, he was writing short stories for many magazines. Many years later, a story of his became one of the most popular motion pictures ever made, *It Happened One Night.*

His first novel was published in 1905. The roster of his works includes such well-known books as *Grandfather Stories, A. Woollcott: His Life and His World, The Harvey Girls, Canal Town* and *Sunrise to Sunset.* Several books in the Random House Landmark historical series have been written by him, including *The Pony Express, The Santa Fe Trail,* and *The Erie Canal.*

On November 16, 1958, Samuel Hopkins Adams died at the age of eighty-seven, just as TENDERLOIN was going on press.